GW01605698

This volume is Number 98 of the First Edition and is dedicated to Vivian Cowle with kind regards.

MATSON BOY

MATSON BOY

JOHN RYDE

Published by
Centenary Arts Limited.
125 The Promenade.
Cheltenham.
Glos. GL50 1NW.

British Library Cataloguing in Publication Data

A catalogue record for this book is available
from the British Library.

ISBN 1 85421 196 X

Designed & Produced by Images Design & Print Ltd, Hanley Swan, Worcs.
Printed & Bound in Great Britain by Hartnolls Ltd, Bodmin, Cornwall.

Introduction

It was on his eighteenth birthday that my Great Great Great Great Great Grandfather began to keep his Journal.

A note from Strawberry Hill bade him attend on Horace Walpole for tea. Mr Selwyn sat quietly in the corner of the Library whilst Horace rested his gout by the window. He was watching Mie Mie play with Miss Tuthill, down the long daffodilled banks to the Thames.

Not yet old enough to be at ease in such enlightened company, my ancestor took support in the shape of Jack and Harry. He knew they would be welcome.

"Such beauty," cooed Horace. The three friends were washed and scrubbed and swanked in their best brocade.

"Sir, may I have the honour to introduce Mister John Bannister and Mister Henry Angelo." The three bowed low and Horace, limp of hand and leg, fluttered his acknowledgement.

"Draw near, Joseph. I wish you to benefit singularly from my counsel." Was that satire that flickered in the rheumy eye, or just benevolence?

"I am sensible of having more follies and weaknesses than most men, but I have been favoured with the powers of observation and perception. These powers will go with me to the grave, for I have recorded nothing save a few worthless letters and a volume or two, a deficiency that will be deplored by future generations." He sipped black tea from a wide china cup.

"Mister Selwyn tells me that nature has furnished you modestly with diligence; and has directed you towards profligacy and caprice. I can suggest no more congenial way of passing a life."

A great brown volume, leather bound and sporting a brass lock, lay on the table by Horace's chair. It bore a coat of arms and the initials R W inlaid in gold. Underneath H W had been added, and now J P shone brightest of all.

"My Father was Prime Minister when he presented me with this diary. I have written not a word therein. I pass it to you in the hope that you will use it to speak with your descendants."

About fifty years later my Great Great Great Great Great Grandfather wrote this note:

My Dear Descendants,

In the dusk of age I am no longer able to record much of interest to you. These journals contain my life which I now hand to my Son with my love. My earnest hope is that he will add his own life, whatever it holds, and then pass it to one who will continue the story.

Let six generations pass before my writings are revealed, for they are my intimate thoughts and I have no wish to cause pain to the kin of those I dismiss. I send my warmest greetings to you all.

Through my writings

I hope forever to remain

Your kinsman

Joseph Paget.

Editor's Note – I have tried to remain faithful to the original text but I have had to interpret obscure and incomplete passages and modernize, as unobtrusively as possible, some of the more exhuberant English. At the end of the book I have added explanatory notes. A book mark may make reference to them easier.

John Ryde

Cheltenham, November 1992.

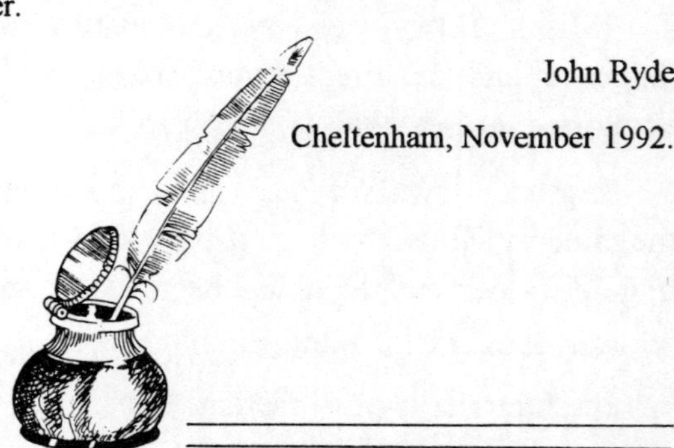

Chapter One

My first journey from Bristol to Gloucester was completed in two days – one in the womb and one out. I had been expected later in the month, and Father and Mother were walking the turnpike when I gave notice of my intention to vacate. I must have learned a lesson, for I have never since arrived early.

Mother sought the shelter of the Frome Bridge that crosses Mr Kemmet's new Navigation Canal[1], and my debut was greeted by the raucous cheers of fifty navvies digging the Cut. I doubt that even John Small[2] has ever had such an enthusiastic welcome onto the field of play.

Father cut the cord with his shears and tied the knot as neat as an acorn. I was wrapped in a shawl, clamped to Mother's lovingly remembered breast and we were on our way within the hour.

My father was a journeyman tailor[3], and work was not plentiful in the fifties. In the eyes of most masters, his inclination to alcohol and argument outweighed his skill. There were wage disputes in most towns, and violence over rising prices. The system of travelling brothers provided a turn house in each town, where the journeyman could find a bed and a meal. But there was little help to find work. Now that I was lustily demanding my rights, Father needed all the help he could get.

However cloudy their sky most people have one star that shines. Father's was Mother. She was Celtic but I know not from where. I can recall so little of my parents that the clear picture I have retained of her is more precious to me than gold. Hair as black as jet, curling and tumbling over her shoulders, big laughing eyes that mocked the hardships of her life; and a lilting voice that sang away my tears. She will be forever young and comely to me and, although prurience has lately overtaken Latin in my scale of priorities, I doubt that I shall ever encounter a more desirable female.

There was a lot of sympathy for us in Gloucester but little else. The local masters were sacking and the journeymen trudging on. My parents were given supper and ale in the Club, but told that there would be no entertainment. One of the brothers, no doubt enamoured with the infant and even more so with its mother, said the great house at Matson wanted a couple for gardening and cleaning. That fragment of information contained my destiny.

About four miles south of Gloucester, above the Upton road, Matson House stands square and smug, gloating over its landscape. We were at the tradesmen's entrance the following morning, where the affability of our reception bode well for Mother's comfort but ill for Father's temper. The Estate Manager, Mr George Holyoake, was a large voluptuous figure of middle years, thick lipped and arrogant eyed, who spoke to Father but looked at Mother.

"A pound a week and a cottage. You'll work on the improvements and she'll clean".

The foregoing was told to me by my Father one afternoon in the autumn of 1765, as I rode with him back to Matson high on the forehead of the Oxford wagon[4]. I sat in his lap holding reins that hung loosely down the flanks of Arthur the shire[5], who knew the way home better than Father and had no need of guidance. Father's plump fingers encircled my wrists, and his huge biceps were the arms of my chair. My head rested on the top of his generous belly.

I remember most vividly his smell and his sound on that day. He had been tending his brushwood fires since first light and woodsmoke clung to his every pore. It was in his waistcoat, in his breeches, in the bright red cotton kerchief tied at his neck. And his chuckle, deep and resonant, it bubbled and flowed from his bristled face like warm molasses, as he told me of the mite that emerged to the roared approval of Mr Kemmet's navvies.

I was a sturdy eight year old and had spent the day on Robinswood Hill helping to cut and stack fuel. In truth, much of my day had passed on the upper reaches of the hill, where the beech wood gives way to a grassy summit. Here the climber can command an aspect as fair as any in England: West, where the silver Severn writhes its way across the valley to Bristol; South and the green cliff of the Cotswold escarpment, brooding and mysterious in the morning shadows, then soft in the afternoon sun; East where the new resort of Cheltenham is sheltered by the head of the valley; North, and the ramparts of the Malverns, like a row of naked buttocks warming the wind, embracing the great Abbey of Tewkesbury.

At the foot of the hill, close enough to touch, the city of Gloucester clusters around its Cathedral, a beacon to the coasters and barges and trows that have fought the river tides from Bristol. Closer still, the old gables of Matson House are framed by two grassy knolls of such symmetry, the beholder is tempted to the thought that Capability Brown was responsible for the entire valley.

I was King Charles directing the seige of Gloucester[6], and all day messengers sweated up the long slopes of the hill, to bring me news of my Army encamped at the City Walls. I had 30,000 men under arms and had already taken Exeter and Bristol. Gloucester, under the dog Massey, was as obstinate as ever. Word was that Cromwell had dispatched Essex from London to relieve the City. My pale and tragic hero reached the zenith of his performance, the guns of Essex firing from the hills beyond Cheltenham, when Father's booming voice announced our imminent departure.

Father had fixed the locking chains of the laden wagon and we began the painstaking return journey, slithering down the track to Larkham Farm. We were still high above Matson House but I saw, far down the Valley, a chaise and pair pass through the gates on the Upton road and disappear into the trees to climb the drive. As it reached the front of the house, uniformed figures emerged from the porch bowing and curtseying as if to music. The door of the chaise was opened and a becloaked figure, languid even at this distance, stepped down. Mr George Augustus Selwyn, owner of the Estate, two Farms, Robinswood Hill and a goodly portion of Gloucestershire had returned home. The measured rhythm of rural life was about to be dislocated.

We left the loaded wagon in Larkham Barn and released Arthur into the meadow. Father swung me easily onto his shoulders and as we marched across the Park, skirting the formal gardens, he sang his journeyman songs:

I have tramped all day in the cold and the rain,
and I've nowhere to rest my head.
My belly has nothing and my feet have pain,
it's away to the turnpike bed.
I shall lay my baggage in the deepest ditch,
and dream of Queen Betty's law,[7]
and I'll pray for the idle and I'll pray for the rich.
Dear God make the leeches poor.

He roared the last two lines across the valley as if he wanted Mr Selwyn to hear. From my vantage point I could see three or four sleek black carriages in the Courtyard, and through the trees I glimpsed the bright colours of ladies and gentlemen gathered around the bowling green steps. The local quality had lost no time in paying their respects to Mr Selwyn. There was no sign that Father's irreverence had caused any discomfort.

Mother greeted us with hugs and laughter at the door of the cottage on the Painswick road, and we tumbled into the kitchen where the smell of rabbit stew made me dribble. Father drank deep from the cyder jug while Mother brought steaming bowls of rich brown gravy to the table. She sat with us and long before my bowl was empty, I had curled myself into her softness and fallen fast asleep.

Jud Holyoake was not the prettiest thing on the Estate, but he was the best. Mother used to say that he had been behind the door when God had given out the faces. His was squashed with a crossed eye and hair the texture of a hog's. Mother said he must have been given a double helping of kindness. I never saw him kill anything. Not a rat, not a slug, nor even a wasp. He was my friend. My unfailing, unswerving, unutterable friend.

His parents, George and Hannah Holyoake, were entirely responsible for the administration of the Estate. They lived in the new wing of the House above the kitchens and stores. Their front door opened into the Courtyard and it was to here that all tradesmen, workmen and casual visitors reported.

George was a man of stature and appetite. No maiden in clutching distance was safe, and there was an unspoken understanding at Matson, that favours bestowed by him on female workers were returned in kind. Whether or not Mother made the occasional contribution to his wellbeing I shall never know, but he was always kindly and affable to me. His belly testified to the four square meals he consumed each day, and he carried with him the odour of ale and pickled onions.

Hannah evidently found these attributes agreeable for she had borne him seventeen children, of whom eight survived to endlessly persecute her. There were two little ones, Jud, Sarah who was ten, and four youths who worked on the Farms. Hannah Holyoake was unfailingly jolly and to her were brought all the ills, all the pains and all the troubles of the Estate. She could deal with a girl's broken dreams, an old man's ague, a youth's nocturnal emissions and injuries to whatever part of whatever person they occurred. She dispensed common sense, sympathy and bandages. She believed in scrupulous cleanliness and applied gin to anything that shed blood. She had no answer to the occasional epidemics of fever that culled the working families of the

Estate, but as a general rule if it was not infectious, she had a remedy.

She even found time to give Jud and me the rudiments of an education. In a corner of the Kitchen we would sit on high stools frowning at pictures under which were unintelligible signs, and giggling or shin kicking whenever Hannah's attention was elsewhere.

Jud had pets all over the Estate and each morning would take a bag of stale bread and visit them all. I used to go with him when I could get out of bed. There was a fox with three legs in Robins Wood that used to wait for him by an elm tree and greet him like any farm dog; and I have lain in the undergrowth, still as a gravestone, watching him tickle a badger's chin as if it were the stable tortoiseshell.

If Jud had a favourite it was a barn owl that haunted the derelict gables of Moat House just down the hill. Hannah said we must never go near the old Manor, with its ivy smothered chimneys, sightless windows and gaping doors. She said that death stalked its passageways and Nick himself had been heard there at night. Young Elizabeth Robbins had been there alone one evening while her parents were at the theatre in Gloucester. A gang of footpads had broken in to what they thought was an empty house and on finding Elizabeth, had violated her and then hung her with whipcord from the gallery. Her parents had found her on their return and no-one had slept in the house since. A colony of pipistrelles lived in the rafters, and Hannah said that if one got caught in your hair the rest would attack and suck every last drop of blood from your body.

Mr Selwyn had lately bought Moat House and word was that he intended to demolish it. Hannah was all for ridding us of the Devil's abode; but Nick had not yet finished his business.

Jud and I would go there in the falling light and watch bats swoop in and out of bare timbers. Sitting amidst the fallen masonry Jud would call his friend with hisses and snores, and by and by a wraith on the softest of wingbeats would circle us in the gloom. It landed once when I was there, but as soon as the great amber eyes spotted me hiding in the shadows, it was off in a whisper.

Mr Selwyn was a lavish entertainer, and the parties he gave for his London friends used to last for days. Some evenings Jud and I would hide in the shrubbery at the edge of the bowling lawn, to watch our betters at play. Even at that age I was not entirely convinced that they were better than Mother and Father; but I was bound to admit that at play, Mr Selwyn's guests were nonpareils.

As the orchestra played, wigs and gowns, frock coats and lace, ruffles and bows bobbed and curtseyed in extravagant charades of formality. The French wine augmented the laughter, until the whole ensemble were braying to such effect that a pair of jackasses could have danced the quadrille without being noticed.

On fine evenings, couples often left the assembly to entwine themselves in the shadows of the garden. I can see the bouncing form, white in the moonlight, of a lady wearing only a corset being chased across the lawn by a gentleman without trousers. His thing was not soft and swinging like Father's, but like a cudgel raised to punish a victim. He caught her about two feet from our hiding place and ripped the corset from her. Her objections were surprisingly muted. They fell to the ground where they writhed and puffed and began to steam. He seemed intent on pushing his thing into her every crevice; her mouth, the cleave of her breast, her thighs and even her arse. She moaned like Hannah Holyoake giving birth and rolled her head from side to side.

"My God, my God," he bellowed, and with that was still. When he got to his feet I could see that his thing had come off. I concluded that he had left it inside her. It was to be years before I gained the joyous knowledge that it was only resting and, upon recovery, could be used again and again and again.

On a March morning in 1766 Mother ruffled my hair and with a damp cloth wiped the sleep from my eyes.

"There'll be some excitement today," she said, "they're pulling down the chimneys of the old house. If they ask for a littl'un to climb the ivy with the rope, you're to say nothing, d'ye hear?"

"Yes'm." No-one would have to ask me. If Father just looked at me, I would be half way up the chimney.

Most of the Estate workers had turned out to see the show and when Mother and I arrived, Arthur was being harnessed. The main chimney stack had been built of sterner stuff than the roof and it stood, gaunt and unbowed, a tower of ivy fifty feet high. I stared unblinkingly at Father, willing him to look for me, but Mother had a tight grip on my scruff. It was Jud who was picked from the crowd. He took the thick rope which was already attached to Arthur and began to climb through the leaves. Father joined us and swung me to his shoulders. We walked closer to the house for a better view.

At about thirty feet Jud stopped. He threaded the rope through the ivy, around the chimney, and proudly tied a bowline the way his father had taught him. As he started to climb down, Arthur reared as though peppered with musket shot. He must have been bitten by a horse fly and with eyes wild red and ears flat he tried to run from his tormentor. The chimney swayed and began to topple towards the throng. Jud scrambled and tumbled the rest of the way as the ivy bent and burst from the brickwork. Father flung me from him and grabbed Mother's arm. She seemed to twist as she turned and fell to one knee. The chimney exploded into the front wall of the house which in turn collapsed with a deathly thud onto two people below.

I remember little of what followed. I know I screamed until my throat was raw. I know I scratched and bit and ripped everything and everyone who tried to help me. I know I threw myself into the mountain of rubble and masonry and timbers that was my Parent's grave. I know I clung to Hannah Holyoake and sobbed for the rest of the day and through the whole of the night. I know I spent a week in Hannah's big warm bed and at night George was sentenced to a blanket on the floor.

I did not attend my parent's funeral. They were laid side by side in the graveyard of the little Church that serves the Estate, and were covered in wildflowers gathered by the children. By the time I was well enough to visit them, the colours were fading and April winds were tidying the fallen petals. Already their warmth was chilling, their laughter growing faint, their embrace slipping into memory.

I had plenty of visitors during my tenancy of the big bed. Jud and Sarah spent long afternoons trying to raise my spirits and Hannah read Goody Two Shoes to me over and over again. The small Holyoakes came and stared at me and even George brought me some bread and honey every day.

On the morning of the third day Hannah bustled into the room with a bowl of water and a cloth. She wiped my face and slicked my hair. She straightened the bed clothes and dusted the tables. She swept the floor and threw the crusts and cores out of the window.

"Mister Selwyn himself is coming to see you," she fussed. "You must sit up straight and under no circumstances will you sniff."

I sat to attention for at least fifteen minutes and without the hindrance of a regular sniff, my snot had reached my upper lip, when a gentleman of middle years and quite wondrous beauty appeared at the foot of the bed. He wore a powdered tie wig which framed a soft pink face, kind eyes, pretty pursed lips and a large fleshy nose. His frock coat was of deep blue satin trimmed with lace and sporting silver buttons. He wore a dazzling waistcoat of embroidered silk. His knee breeches were fastened with silver buckles, his stockings embroidered with clocks of stitchery. Even his buckled shoès had crimson heels.

"This morning I resolved to call upon the bravest man on my Estate." He took a scarlet handkerchief from his coat and held it to my nose. "I am told by Holyoake that you have borne your grievous loss with great fortitude. You honour your Parents and you honour me." He gravely bowed low, a gesture that unnerved me to such effect that I sniffed. He took no offence.

"I have discussed the future with the Holyoakes, and they have agreed to act as your guardians. You will live under their roof and be brought up as one of their family. You will sleep with their male children. Survival in that maelstrom of evil will serve you well when the rigours of life have to be faced. You will receive an education at my expense and from time to time, when I am in Matson, I will endeavour to instruct you in the ways of the World. This will be an intellectual exercise as the World has yet to reach Matson." He strolled from the room but his perfume lingered for hours.

From that moment the gentle tempo of my life, the security of being an only child in a loving home, was rudely and wantonly dissipated. I was cast headlong into the rivalries and tumult, the competition and sport, the emotional summits and troughs, of a large family. No one had time for my finer feelings which, within weeks, had been bruised beyond recall.

I slept in a dormitory of six beds, with Jud and his brothers: James, the eldest, was already a man of eighteen, broad, dark eyed and smouldering; George, christened after his Father when the first George died, gaunt and handsome, a magnet for every maid in the village, Job, quiet and thoughtful; and Tom, his antithesis, noisy and thoughtless.

There was a natural chain of command in the dormitory, and I took my place beneath Jud. Strength decided all disputes, manners were those of the farmyard and language that of the garrison. My meagre frame was only too evident when we stripped before bed, and I think I should have sunk without trace in the storms that raged around the room, had Jud not watched over me.

He taught me to prosper in a world of larger beings and to use adversity to garnish sympathy. He taught me to play symphonies of plenty on the strings of Hannah's heart and to enact honest toil whenever George hove into view. Above all he taught me to compete, to protect what was mine and to take punishment only when it was deserved. At play he was ruthless, at work useless. But he was my friend and I loved him.

My waking thoughts were so entirely occupied by family intrigues that I hardly noticed my parents fading into the mist of memory. There was no time for reflection or remorse. As the year brightened into Summer, my tears dried and then Harvest took the energy and attention of the Estate. There was none to spare for the infirm.

The corn had to be cut and from first light to dark, everyone with an able body sweated in the wide gold fields that sloped down to Upton. We worked in gangs of five. The scytheman, sweeping his blade through the stalks for them to fall into rows of regimental precision, a gatherer and a binder to sheave, a stooker to stand the sheaves in bundles of eight, so that a cut field would seem to be covered in small thatched huts; and a raker, which was my lowly station.

The work was exhausting and I grew blisters like shillings; but meals under the hedge, of cheese and bread and cool green cyder from a stone jar, sitting with the men and being part of their rough laughter, were worth the pain and much more.

Autumn ripened and Jud and I lived in the orchards that groaned with fruit. Pippins and pearmain, damson and greengage, we climbed long rickety ladders to the tops of trees, to find prizes missed by the gatherers. Leaves yellowed and fell, swirling on the October winds, and rain dark clouds hurried up the Severn.

November spread its chill over us and the damp air crept into every corner of the house. We slept in our clothes under heavy rough blankets and sniffed and coughed and sneezed as winter ills began their relentless assault. Anyone that Hannah could not cure was taken to the Wise Woman who lived in a tumbled shelter of sacking and sticks at Upton. Jud used to say that if she was any good she would live in a house. Children would stand for ages, puzzling over the letters scratched on her rickety old door.

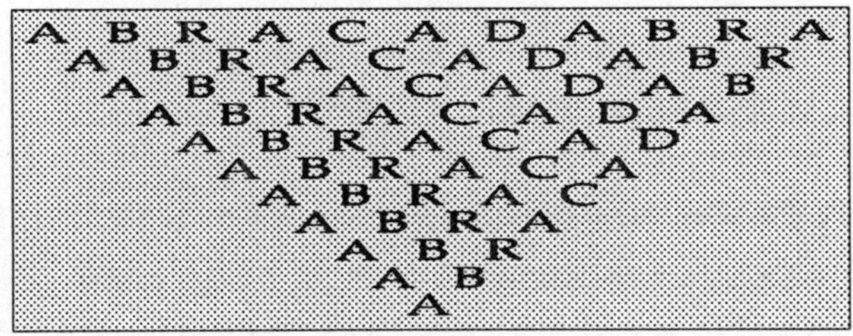

She was disappointingly ordinary, plump and pippin cheeked with a large grey bun of hair, and she dispensed her remedies with a sympathetic twinkle. Dung tea, crab's eyes, viper's flesh and, worst of all to Jud, stewed owl. He had lost his friend after the demolition of Moat House and was sure the Wise Woman knew its fate. She had specific cures for some ailments. Pike eye was for toothache, snail tea for a sore chest and patients with ague were advised to "drink their own warm yourin". Although ague was unknown to us, we tried the cure one day behind Larkham Barn. Jud's tasted better than mine.

As soon as a girl began to bleed, her mind would close to any subject but the identity of her future lover. Jud and I were indifferent to such things, thus we did without their company. They seemed rooted in the magic and spells of their grandmothers. They sought their men in coffee grounds and at the bottom of teacups. They got up early on May mornings to hear the cuckoo, who told them of him. They made dunch cakes, two by two, in order to dream of him. They sewed hempseed at midnight, saying "Hempseed I sow, hempseed I hoe, and he that is my true love, come after me and mow."

They used to walk backwards into the garden on Midsummer Eve and gather a rose to put away in clean sheets until Christmas, when, if it was still fresh, they put it to their bosom for a sweetheart to take out. They put bridecake on their pillow, threw apple peel over their shoulder, put two nut kernels on their forehead, bay leaves on their pillow; and ate boiled eggs, shell and all, filled up with salt, without speaking or drinking. This was meant to make them dream of their lover. It would have made me fart.

I am glad that I am not a girl, for they seem to have such little latitude. They may be clever, or funny, or artistic, or adventurous, but woe betide them if they cannot attract a man, and woe betide them even more, if they fail to learn the workings of the household. They must make pickles and wine, cordials and puddings, cakes and dresses. Above all, they must learn from the manuscript household book, all the recipes, culinary and sexual, for keeping a husband content. I will allow that Latin is every bit as painful, but at least it provides an escape route for those with wider horizons.

The austerity of Winter was sometimes tempered by a festival. Guy Fawkes was burned, although George often said he should have been crowned; Christmas, when the little Church was filled with light; and Twelfth Night, when fires burned like stars across the valley floor, were times of eating and wassailing. Valentine's Day was for blushing and giggling and trysts in the Beech Wood, observed from the high branches by Jud and me; and on Shrove Tuesday we filled our bellies for Lent with pancakes and jam.

Grey winter landscape was washed and swept by the wind and rains of March, and yellow Spring flowers were scattered across the greening meadows. My birthday, on the nineteenth, was a time of shy gifts, soft kisses and a glorious tea party in the stables, to which I invited the noisiest, dirtiest, hungriest children that Hannah had ever known. She plied us, in defiance of Lent, with cakes and buns and sweets and jellies; and the Wise Woman was kept busy for a week.

In the kitchen Jud and I were stripped, plunged into a bath of steam and scrubbed, to our considerable embarrassment, by Hannah. She was assisted by Sarah, who gained singular amusement from tweaking my private appendage and asking, with mock innocence, what purpose it served. Rigged in our Sunday best, bemused by instructions in humility, we were marched along the Servant's Passage to the main Hall. There we stood, two timorous mites in a grand panelled silence, broken only by the sonorous tock of a very large clock.

George Holyoake, liveried and bewigged, led us to a door upon which he knocked. On a muffled command, he opened the door and in a voice that was not his, announced, "Master Joseph Paget and Master Jude Holyoake." He pushed us into the room where Mr Selwyn stood with his arse to a log fire.

"Come here and let us see you. I would like you to meet some very dear friends of mine".

I realised that two of the high backed fireside chairs were occupied. We edged towards the fire and were inspected by two torpid gentlemen.

"Allow me to introduce Mister George Pitt",[8] a handsome man, dark and severe, nodded and smiled, but only with his mouth. "And the Reverend John Chester",[9] this one was thin, with a grey face and worried eyes. "Will they do for you, Jesus?"

The Reverend Chester frowned at this heresy. His mouth opened soundlessly, and for a moment I thought he was in pain. "P..please Bosky use my p..p..proper name," and then, looking gravely at us, "I th..th..think they'll d..d..do v..v..v..very well." His words came in spurts, like milk from an udder.

"Joseph," I tore my eyes away from Mr Jesus. "I believe it is time for your education to begin. The Reverend Chester is the Headmaster of Cheltenham Grammar School and has kindly consented to accept both you and Jude as pupils. He is as yet unaware of the risk to his person such a sacrifice entails." George entered and filled their glasses with rich red wine. "I have made arrangements with Holyoake for you to receive a miniscule allowance to subsidise your frivolity, and I shall accompany you to Cheltenham tomorrow to acquire suitable clothing." This announcement afflicted me with a similar complaint to that suffered by Mr Jesus.

"Th..th..th..thank you sir."

Before we were dismissed, Mr Selwyn gave me a small doeskin purse as a birthday present.There were five shining shillings inside which increased my cash reserves tenfold.

On the twentieth of March, seventeen sixty seven, I left the Estate for the first time since being carried there from Gloucester. The new berline had been brought from the Coach House. It was lustrously black with ivory handles, brass lamps and four spoked wheels. I sat inside with Mr Selwyn on red Morocco leather, and Jud sat up on the box with James, splendid in the olive green livery of a coachman. Mr Selwyn was in a jovial mood. He hummed a bright tune as we bowled down the lane towards Gloucester and then crossed Ermin Street[10] for the Cheltenham turnpike. I looked around at the soft rural scene and tried to copy his cultured tones.

"It is a most agreeable aspect, Sir."

"Aye, it is young fella, but nothing a hundred villas an'a theatre or two wouldn't improve."

"But do you not love the landscape in Spring, Sir?"

"It's the same shape as the landscape in Autumn, just a different colour. I'm sure I should love it more, if there were not quite so much of it."

"I love the flowers. The fields are painted yellow now, with buttercups, but in a month or two they will be red with poppies."

"I would sooner leave the painting to my good friend Josh Reynolds. His colours are more various and more lasting. When I display them in my drawing room, they do not wither and need no water. But harken not to me, young Joseph, for I have long forgotten the joys of infancy, the freshness of discovery. My morning dew evaporated a thousand dawns ago, and more distilled pleasures are now necessary to awaken this ancient frame."

Cheltenham was a rum sort of village. One long street along the course of a stream. A mixture of poor buildings with here and there, a new edifice looking out of place and pretentious, and an avenue of young elms leading from an overlarge Church up the slope to what appeared to be a temple. Mr Selwyn directed James to drive down the street where a few trade establishments looked in need of custom. We passed the Church on our left, and stopped beside an old grey building of crumbling stone that stood between an inn and a boarding house.

"Your education will begin here, Joseph. Maudlin College Cheltenham. Not Oxford, I'll allow, but Jesus has more need of you than Oxford."

We alighted from the berline and looked up at the stained walls of our gaol. The inscription "Schola Grammatica" had been carved above the door, and Mr Selwyn explained that this was the Latin tongue I had to learn. My confusion was complete when he added that Greek too would need to be mastered. The door, which had been hung upon an inadequate hinge, was opened in a series of hops to reveal the worried countenance of the Reverend Chester.

"Here they are, Jesus. Two prodigals to swell your army of swots." The worried countenance frowned at this new adversity.

"I th..th..th..think it w..would b..be more appro..pro..pro..fitting if you w..were t..t..to use my m..more f..f..f..f..formal address."

The paradox of learning an alien tongue, from a source that was nigh unintelligible in English, was not lost on me.

"My dear Reverend Chester," Mr Selwyn executed a sweeping bow. "Please forgive the indiscretion. Joviality overcame my manners. You are not yet ready for deification."

"N..now you m..mock me, George. It is m..m..m..more than a p..p..poor p..p..parson deserves." He ushered Jud and I into a long dim schoolroom across which was hung a brown curtain. From behind the curtain disembodied voices chanted foreign sounds.

"Ah, the exquisite pain of Cicero," said Mr Selwyn.

"Not p..p..painful enough, it would sseem, for that is E..E..E..Erasmus." He lifted a corner of the curtain around which we peered. My spirits had already reached their nadir, but had it been possible for them to descend further, they would have done.

Seventeen unhappy boys sat along a bench, with elbows on a long oak table, eyeing a formidable lady who wielded a stick at the far end of the room. Beyond her was a board, upon which were chalked meaningless symbols. She pointed the stick at each symbol in turn and conducted the chant with her free hand.

"This is the j..j..junior c..class who receive their tu..tu..tu lessons from Mistress Gale. I teach the senior b..boys."

"Where are they?"

"Only f..four arrived this m..m..morning so I gave them L..L..Latin syn..syn..syntax to st..st..study, and sent them home."

"Capital news. You can join us for refreshments at the Plough. My two young friends will report to Mistress Gale on Monday week, ready to wrestle with Cato."

"The Elder or the Y..Y..Y..Y..Y..Y..Younger?"

We walked along the river bed that masqueraded as a street, to the Plough. A notice in a ground floor window boldly described the premises as the premier coaching inn of this celebrated resort. A smaller sign recorded that one stagecoach, the Old Hereford, called each day.

Opposite the Plough were the rooms of Signor Pirelli, tailor to the Royalty of Europe. I wondered that he had time for the meagre patronage of Jud and me, but when Mr Selwyn pushed us through the door and informed the Signor that these were the fittings of whom he had written, our reception was voluble, even effusive. Signor Pirelli was fat. Quite the fattest person I had ever seen. I concluded that he had somehow been impregnated and was about to give birth. When he laughed his breath smelt of Jack by the Hedge. He measured our limbs and our heads, our waists and our chests, even the extent of our arses was carefully recorded.

We returned to the Plough where our patron and the Son of God waited in the Tap Room. We ate apple tart and I drank claret wine for the first time. Although I cared little for it I resolved to try again. Later we visited the Temple on the slopes above the village. It was a pump room where a jolly lady relieved visitors of three pence and a wordy sign described the efficacity of the renowned waters. I sipped from a cup and I think I shall never experience a more distressing flavour. It was as if a spoonful of clay had been dissolved in a pint of Jud's yourin. Unlike claret wine, I anticipate that any further contact with Cheltenham waters will be strictly external.

The following day Mr Selwyn left for London. Jud and I enjoyed a precious week; bitter sweet days of condemned felons awaiting the gallows.

Hannah took us back to Signor Pirelli where we were decked in breeches and tail coats and stockings and buckle shoes, two pairs of everything, and powdered wigs and tricorn hats which we pledged never to wear, even should death be the only alternative.

At least we brought style to that awful academy, stepping down from the berline on the appointed morning, flawless in our bespokes, dismissing James with imperious waves and strolling into the dungeon with noses high. Even Charles would have approved our majestic progress to the scaffold, upon which Mistress Gale waited, axe in hand. But once the curtain was drawn behind us and we sat in that forsaken place, the pageant of our arrival became an illusion, and the realities of enslavement were thrust upon us.

The short period of my life spent under the piercing gaze of Mistress Gale is an episode, the memory of which still awakens me on black nights, muttering the catechism or shivering from the horror of declining nouns. I sat, with the other inmates, in damp misery, as images of Erasmus and Cato the Elder, and Ascham and Cato the Younger, floated across our recalcitrant minds, leaving not the semblance of an imprint. I learned to loathe Latin grammar and syntax with equal intensity; and the seeds of a nature that rejects authority discipline and the established order, were sown deep in my fertile soul. Poor Mistress Gale cannot have known that in the eyes of her young flock, she was evil incarnate.

I have one legacy of value from Cheltenham Grammar School: the ability to fight. I am equally at home in a ring, at ten paces, or on the floor of a bawdy house. I can succeed within the rules of pugilism, or when the occasion demands, bite and kick and scratch with the best of them. My education in the art of physical domination began with sorties against the Charity School pupils, a collection of underfed scoundrels that the incumbent of the Parish Church was attempting to civilize. His efforts had so far gone unrewarded, for I do not think that even James Cook[11] can have encountered a more evil bunch of savages.

They wore a kind of uniform of long coat and yellow stockings and caps with dark stripes. When they were allowed out to play among the gravestones, they resembled a swarm of giant hornets and were about as amicable. On the irregular occasions that a full complement of Grammar School pupils reported for tuition, a noon raid on the Graveyard offered welcome relief from Cicero.

We would muster behind the Church wall armed with stones and other missiles of war. When the enemy emerged from their schoolroom a cannonade sent them running for cover to be decimated by the swift advance of our cavalry. They sometimes adopted the tactics of the revolutionary, hunting amongst the gravestones in groups of three or four for any of us that had become detached from the main force. I was cornered once and experienced their revenge, which was uncompromising and bloody. My coat was ripped, breeches lost and nose disfigured. It took three weeks for my face to revert to shape and even longer for my poor foreskin, which had been inked inside and out and abused with sealing wax.

The ignomy of my return to School, and the later abuse I suffered from Hannah was such that I determined forthwith to acquire the skills of the pugilist; and Jack Goss knew more about pugilism than any man I have since met.

Jack was the Village butcher, a laughing giant, with fingers like the pork sausages he made, in the dark and bloody shed behind his cottage. His ill used face bore testament to the prize fights he had lost: veined eyes, scarred and puffed into slits, ears turned inside out and a wide nose punched boneless by a thousand knuckles. There was a rope square in his field where he gave lessons in the art to local youths. James Holyoake was his nonpareil.

He was often visited by his lifelong friend Jack Broughton.[12] The two Jacks had grown up together in Cirencester. Both big and strong, they used to tour the village fairs and challenge all comers to fight for a guinea, to a knockdown or fall. If the challenger looked frail, JG would handle him, but local heroes were looked after by JB who, in twenty years, was never beaten. While the pupils grunted and sweated and occasionally wept, the two old warriors would sit by the shed exchanging gory reminiscences.

I enlisted in this academy, and before long any Charity School urchin crossing my path suffered profound remorse.

I wasted a year with Jesus and was released on my eleventh birthday. I suspect that I shall never receive a more welcome present. The only clear recollection I retain, from twelve unrelenting months, is of the visit, on a boisterous March day, of John Wesley.[13] Holy Jo must have been a friend of Jesus, because the two men, arms linked, conducted our morning prayers with a zeal sufficient to frighten the bestiality out of the French.

He was a wisp of grey, with flowing white hair and the face of a man trying to shit; but the voice that came from this forlorn frame was rich and melodic, and his message one of joy and hope and humour. He spoke to us in language we could understand; common words about common topics. He knew about country life, about hardship, about mischief. He sympathised with the insuperable problems of Latin syntax. He understood our fighting, our tears, our energies, the voiceless rage that was within us.

Thus far in my life, I have avoided the joyless bonds of religion, but if ever I weary of fleshy sins, I shall become a Methodist. John Wesley's faith belongs to the people. It belongs to the journeymen, to the tinkers, to the whores; it belongs to the ale house keepers and the milkmaids and the hangmen. It is not the private preserve of a bunch of overfed clerics hoarding overfilled coffers, and threatening the rest of us with eternal damnation.

At nine o clock we were allowed out to hear him preach. He was not welcome in the Parish Church, which served to reinforce my perfidious view of the Incumbent, so he stood on the steps of an old cross in the graveyard and harangued his meagre audience. His words were poisoned darts aimed at the Church door.

> *"I would consider first, who is a Christian? What does the term properly imply? It has been so long abused, I fear, not only to mean nothing at all, but what is far worse than nothing, to be a cloak for the vilest hypocrisy, for the grossest abominations and immoralities of every kind, that it is high time to rescue it out of the hands of wretches that are a reproach to human nature."*

I now know that much of it was evangelistic extravagance, echoed from town to town. But I also heard Whitefield,[14] who lived in Gloucester, and I can remember nothing of him other than that he was bigger, louder and more eloquent. There is a light within Wesley that compels attention and I suspect the World will be a poorer place when it is doused.

A Tutor was employed by Mr Selwyn, to attend upon our thirst for knowledge. Rooms were provided for him at Matson to ensure that our waking hours were entirely at his disposal. We viewed this arrangement with alarm, fearing even more disruption to our pleasure than that caused by Jesus. Our fears were unjustified.

Pierce Creagh Esq. of Abbeyleix, was neither a man of letters or the cloth. He was a gentle young Irish romantic, full of poetry and slow smiles, who wanted nothing more than to walk on the hills and sing songs and teach us to draw. He was an innocent abroad in the chaotic world of the family Holyoake, but he won us with stories of the Slieve Bloom Mountains and Kilkenny and Tipperary, and the banks of the Shannon flowing down to Lough Derg.

Each morning we reported to a little attic room where Pierce struggled to explain arithmetic. As the day brightened he was drawn to gazing from the window in long wistful silences. Before we had finished a page of the hated sums, he would turn to us, push back his wayward hair and smile. *"At distance I gaze and am awed by my fears."* He usually declared his fatigue in verse, and we soon learned that Thomas Parnell was the harbinger of a sketching expedition.

With pads and boxes of pencils and a bag of food from Hannah, our lessons would be continued under a chestnut tree in the meadow, or high on Robinswood Hill, or strolling in Pierce's wake around the Village. Arithmetic was forgotten and Latin consigned to history; but he taught us about poetry and proportion and perspective and reflection. He taught us how to draw a circle and an ellipse, light and shade, still life and human, landscape and building, animal and plant. When the weather was set fair, we would harness the grey cob to a dog cart and trot around the orchards and hamlets of the Valley, trying to match the rustic scenes with lines from Parnell or Pope, Shakespeare or Swift.

We took pretty, dish faced Welsh ponies from the stately block of stables, newly built by Mr Selwyn from the ruins that had killed my Parents, and raced them bareback, up and down the slopes until we could ride like Americans. On fine evenings we would climb to the top of Robins Wood to watch the sky, blood red in the setting sun and chase fireflies until we could chase no more; and Pierce would read to us by the light of a flickering lantern, Shakespeare, Defoe and sometimes the Bible, though never as a catechist, always a poet.

A woman cloth'ed with the sun, and the moon under her feet,

And upon her head a crown of twelve stars.

Pierce Creagh's only qualification for the task of educating Jud and I was an acquaintance with George Selwyn. But I commend his methods no less than if he had been a graduate with honours. In the short years of his guidance I learned more of the essence of life than I would have in as many decades with Jesus.

Chapter Two

For weeks before Whitsun the Estate was in turmoil. Costumes to be made, the haycart decorated, outrages planned, competitors practiced, players rehearsed. Children made hobby horses out of elder sticks tied with rope tails, cotton bag heads stuffed with paper and painted with eyes and teeth. We rode as King's men around the Estate, accosting all who crossed our path and demanding tithes of halfpennies or cakes.

The Holyoake family had provided the Whitsun King of Coopers Hill for more than two hundred years. George had inherited the job from his father and was grooming James to carry on the tradition.

Early in the afternoon, Arthur, decked in brasses, tinkling with bells, winking with rosettes, was harnessed to the haycart. Beribboned harvest ladders were fitted, and the wagon packed with dressed children. Some were dressed as never before, for there were Will-o'-the-wisps, Tom Pokers, Old Shocks and a gaggle of Green Men, all chattering and screaming and laughing and climbing. Jud and I sat high on the foreladder as George clicked and Arthur plodded.

Through Sneedham Green and Upton we waved at the village folk, and some threw us cakes and sweets for which we fought with anarchial glee, along narrow lanes between hedgerows bright with wild flowers, and then climbing, by honeystone walls sharp against the dun of distant fields, higher, into dark woods of beech and ash, where travellers joy lines the road. And all the way the throng of folk in our wake grew ever more numerous and vociferous. Beside George, on the forehead of the cart, stood a barrel of sweets into which he would dip from time to time, and throw manna to the multitude.

George was dressed in a linen smock that reached below his knees, with white stockings and buckled shoes. He wore a large black tricorn hat entwined with red white and blue ribbons; and he brandished a handbell when not dispensing sweets. Arthur did not share a love of bellringing and performed his task with flat ears and a sour face. When Arthur could climb no more we left the cart, and George strode to the top, his troops following in his wake, bearing the covetted barrel.

The East face of Coopers Hill is a steep grass bank which only the young or foolhardy can ascend. The lower slopes are gentle, but it rises at an ever more fearful gradient until almost vertical. The summit is a plateau of common grazing land from where the Severn Vale is laid, like a dish of orchids and fruit, at the feet of the beholder.

At the highest point, a Maypole, in the shape of a pine trunk from Whitcombe Wood, had been erected, and all around traders and pedlars were hawking their wares. Coloured tents and booths vied for space with disgruntled sheep, a discordant band played two tunes to one rhythm, and large men with purple faces roared for money. It seemed to me that every person from Cirencester to Tewkesbury was on the Hill, and the colours and the smells and the noise transcended any experience I had ever known. I was like a ram in a field of ewes on heat, bewildered by the profusion of wonders before me.

The hubbub became a scramble, as the Master of Ceremonies arrived midst a fountain of sweets. In a voice that would have been covetted by George Whitefield, he bellowed the programme of events: skittles and running races, cudgels and high jumps, apples in a bucket and grinning through the collar. There were prizes to be won all over the Common, but cheese rolling[15] was the sport we had all come to see.

The first race was to be for the main trophy: a 20lb Double Gloucester Cheese tightly packed in sackcloth. It was wheeled to the crest of the bank whilst George dared the young bloods to stake their manhood. James Holyoake and two or three labourers stepped forward. Some girls surrounded Young George and tried to drag him to the Maypole, but he lay on the ground smothered in their petticoats. Two thin sallow men, unshaven and dressed in rags, joined the line. Half of the face of the shorter one was covered by a maroon weal, livid and weeping. When ten contestants had gathered, George mounted a rostrum and rang his bell.

"My lords, ladies and gentlemen, I have the honour to introduce the main event of the day. Gather ye round to witness the pagan ceremony of cheese rolling." The crowd at the back pressed forward while those at the front, in fear of falling down the precipitous slope, pressed back. From top to bottom spectators clung to the bushes at each side of the bank.

"Take your seats, gentlemen."

The ten young men sat on the lip of the hill and hung their legs down the bank. A fat man wearing a chain of office sat in their midst holding the cheese.

"One to be ready," roared George, every eye was on the cheese. "Two to be steady," the young men tensed, cats waiting to spring. "Three to prepare," the fat man released the cheese. "And four to be off."

As one man the ten heroes hurled themselves down the bank in a tumbling tangle of limbs, all trying to gain the lead, all trying to stop the others. The crowd cheered and the young men fought. Like a runaway cartwheel the cheese gathered pace until it was bouncing higher than a man.

Where the slope eases into the meadow the pursuers began to catch the prey, and I could see that James was in the vanguard. Even from my vantage point at the top of the bank I could discern that the mood of the fighting had changed. The kicking and punching was now in earnest. Heads were being broken. Blood was being spilt. I saw James roll away from the bodies and get to his feet. He kicked savagely as one of the others grabbed for him. He lunged a few yards further down the slope and claimed the cheese, which he raised above his head in jubilant salute to the crowd.

James and the cheese were borne aloft, like sporting champions, on the shoulders of the laughing crowd. A river of humanity flowed up the winding path through the woods, to the Maypole where King James of the Wake was crowned by his own Father.

The boy's race was next, for a ten pound cheese. Tom Holyoake entered but could not emulate his brother. There was a great scramble for vantage points when George announced the girl's race. I doubted that many were concerned with the result; it was the tableau of whirling petticoats, bright knickers and soft pink thighs that captured their attention.

A big orange sun sank behind the Welsh Mountains and fires were lit all around the Common. Woodsmoke drifted on still air out across the deepening mauve of the valley. Some of the crowd began journeys home, and others sat around the fires talking and singing and supping cyder from stone flagons. Children laughed in inexhaustible play, running and tumbling and chasing in and out of the coppices. Courting couples strolled around the edge of the Common and some, with more serious intent, sought the privacy and quiet of the black woods.

Jud and I raced until we could no longer stand; and then we fell upon the ground and rolled; and then we crept behind bushes to leap upon unsuspecting prey; and then we raced again; and then I was alone.

Alone in a sea of unknown, flickering, firelit faces. No Jud, no George, no Hannah, no friendly voices. I ran from fire to fire calling for my Father and my Mother. Some looked at me with concerned eyes and called for me to come, but I ran on with flooding tears. Then I saw James fleetingly, with the cheese under one arm and the prettiest of the Larkham milkmaids on the other, walking away down the steep path as though bound for Matson.

I screamed his name but he paid no heed. I hurried across the Common in his direction, colliding with people and animals and stumbling through the day's debris. When I reached the path I could see nothing, and my calls were answered only by the grey stillness of the rising moon.

I plunged down the path and within a few yards fell. I bounced and rolled and slithered, gathering momentum, until crashing head first into a beech trunk. How long I lay at the foot of the tree I know not, but when my senses returned, I could hear voices.

"I told 'un twere badger."

"B'aint no badger in this wood you."

"Fox then, or sheep. Larst 'is foot'n on the bank."

"If twere one 'o them kids an' we were seen, we're gallows meat". The voices grew louder and I held my breath. My heart thumped; hammer blows that had to be heard.

"Oi can 'ardly see you Ben. If oi can 'ardly see you, doan see 'ow any kids can." I moved my head and squinted around the trunk. What I saw turned me to stone.

The two ragged competitors for the cheese stood by the tree. The taller one held a broadsword, its edge stained dark in the moonlight, and the other held the cheese. They were still and taut, hunting dogs sniffing the breeze. A vixen cried from further down the valley and that seemed to satisfy the shorter man.

"C'mon then you, we've ten leagues to walk." They climbed away from the moon on a diagonal path that skirted the Common.

I stayed anchored to the beech long after their sounds had faded. I shook as though chilled, although the night was warm. When finally I felt brave enough and the Moon was high enough to silver the clearings, I carefully edged my way down the path. When I found the milkmaid's body, ripped and slashed, an abandoned rag doll, I was not surprised. Her bare legs were spread wide and her breast, full and white, had been chewed, as if by dogs. James's savaged corpse lay close by.

All feeling drained from me. There was no shock, no terror, no tears, just a numbness, a void in which I hung, incapable of decision, an animal with only base instincts to guide it. I ran, away from the horror, away from the crowds, away from the unspeakable evil that I had seen. Down and down. Sometimes running, sometimes falling, sometimes crawling. Through bramble and thicket, ripping at my clothes, my hands, my face. Falling into ditches, crashing into trees. No pain, no feeling, just the all consuming instinct to be a world away from that place.

Staggering now, lurching through undergrowth from trunk to trunk, lungs in spasm, blood thudding in my ears, then a snap of pain in my leg and at last, the blessed softness and warmth and darkness of my Mother's breast. No more terror, no more running, just a gentle hand ruffling my hair and the balm of her voice healing my wounds.

I knew nothing of the upheaval my absence was causing at Matson. George and Hannah were accustomed to nocturnal excursions by their elder boys, and the apparent defection of the milkmaid reinforced their view that wild oats were being sown. The Haycart had left Coopers Hill laden not only with children, but with a goodly proportion of Matson's population. George had seen Jud in the crowd and assumed I was with him; Jud had seen George and reached the opposite conclusion. When they arrived home and gave Hannah the news that I was mislaid, they were subjected to a gale of abuse sufficient to blow the Frogs out of Paris[16].

By dawn most of the Estate workers had been conscripted, horsed and dispatched, with orders to only return with my person. As early light stole over the valley, the woods echoed to the shouts of searchers, one to another, as they moved line abreast through the trees. The sun had barely climbed above the rim of Cleeve when a call, stricken with frenzy, brought them running. George, hurrying in fear of Hannah's tongue, fell over his son's cold, hard, white body. He cursed at the log and then, as he rose, saw with a terrible grief the thing that lay at his feet.

In the tears and the torment that filled that day, my fate was forgotten. I lay in the brambles, scratched and bloodied, one leg folded under my body, unaware if my future lay in the here or the hereafter. Unconscious of time and with only an occasional impression of light or dark, I floated on the deep river of destiny. The Angel that came to me had a porcelain face and chestnut curls. Her voice tinkled as a brook over pebbles, bubbling and capricious as she called her companions to inspect her find.

"Hurry, Mama, hurry. And you, Humphreys. Come and look, I think it's dead."

"Maria my dear, we have discovered more than sufficient fauna for one day. We are late for tea."

"But Mama, this is a dead person."

"Child, if you continue to disregard me, Mister Smythe will be informed. Bring her to me, Humphreys." Presumably Humphreys was despatched in my direction, because my next recollection is of a piercing shriek uncomfortably close to my left ear.

"Humphreys, you must run for help." A calmer voice, full of motherly sense and authority. "Find two men at the Farm and bring them here with a hurdle. Maria, empty your lemonade bottle and fill it from the stream."

"But, Mama, I am still thir . . ."

"Immediately, child." The tone brooked no further argument and presently my face was being cooled with damp, perfumed silk. I was later to discover that the stream is named Salcombe Brook, and is the head of the River Frome. I was being restored with the same water that had cleaned away my afterbirth.

I was washed by tides of reality, flooding with barbs of pain and ebbing into blessed unconsciousness. I had no sense of time, but I saw the sun lowering towards the far horizon as Humphreys returned with two labourers. One of the men carefully raised the upper part of my body while the other inched the hurdle under me. The wattle was hard and the sharpened larch poles scratched my arms. When I was safe aboard, big dung smelling hands lifted my head and pillowed it on a jerkin. Thus arranged, the cortege wound its way across the wide meadows of Prinknash Park[17].

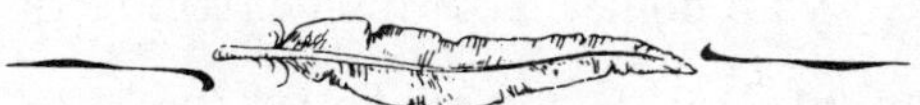

I know little more of my first days as a guest of the Howells, for I must have fallen into a fever. There are glimpses in my mind of worried eyes, of cooling hands, of whispered pity. A Surgeon attended to my leg so that when I began to revive, I found it strapped and immovable in tight stays. It had not been broken but my knee was hugely swollen and lacerated.

My bed seemed an acre of snow white softness with fat pillows that were plumped by every visitor. My porcelain angel spent hours sitting by my side, chattering brightly about herself, not an enthralling topic, but sufficient to keep me from thoughts of James and his sweetheart. She was Maria Smythe from Hampshire, visiting her Mama's good friends Captain and Mistress John Howell, who had lately acquired Prinknash as their home.

Mama had cool determined eyes and an empty voice. She was calm and kind but was as if a fire within her had been doused; her quiet smile a barrier behind which her true self was imprisoned. Her friend, Elizabeth Howell, seemed opposite to every facet of her character, colourful and irreverent, a plump young mother who chortled and winked and slapped my bare arse with unbridled enthusiasm.

"He'll make a few maidens squeak before long," she said, as the two ladies watched me being bathed by Humphreys. "He should be ripe in seven years," she nudged her friend, "and we'll still have not seen forty summers." Humphreys blushed prettily and it was at that moment I felt the first tremor of a most agreeable sensation, deep within me, at the base of my stomach. As she washed my legs all of my strength seemed to become concentrated in my loins. The ladies attention was directed at my lower abdomen. Mistress Howell winked lewdly and said, "The harvest could be earlier than I thought."

"Elizabeth, you are wicked and shameless. You are embarrassing the boy."

"He does not look embarrassed to me." Another wink. "Indeed he looks uncommonly proud."

"Cover the boy." said Mistress Smythe. "Cannot you see that this scurrilous talk is painful to him?"

"I suspect that he will inflict more pain than he suffers."

The two ladies sat on either side of the tepee that had been formed when Humphrey arranged a sheet over my swelling. Mistress Smythe held my wrist in elegant fingers and watched the mantel clock.

"I think you are mending, boy. We must get word to your parents. What is your name? Where is your home? Your mother will be distraught."

"My Mother is dead, Ma'am, and my Father too."

Mistress Howell leant over me, her eyes brimming. "My poor boy!" she whispered and lightly kissed my brow, her plumpness surrounding me. "Do not trouble yourself, you are welcome here. Rest until you are strong and we will then decide on your future. Come, Betty, we have disturbed him enough."

"But, Ma'am."

"Hush."

"But, Ma'am."

"Later."

They closed the door quietly and I was left to my thoughts, my pain; and my thrilling new attribute.

The room in which I was so splendidly accommodated had a ceiling of the most elaborate decoration. Cornices and mouldings and whorls and fans and pendants swam above my head, ever changing in the restless light. A bas relief of the Red Rose encircling the White Rose, with a gilded falcon at its centre, watched me with unblinking malevolence. This ceiling and my porcelain angel were the only entertainments in the days that followed, but I continued to heal, and soon could lean upon Maria and hop to the closet. I considered this a major advancement of my circumstances, for the indignity of having to shit in a pan under Humphreys scrutiny was hard to bear.

On a day that I judged to be Sunday, because I could hear bells calling across the valley, the door of my room burst open and a huge man entered. His hugeness was not of stature – although wide, he was not fat, and he was less than two yards high – it was of presence. He filled the room. His voice boomed and his beard jutted and a wicked grin lit his face.

"Well here's a bit o' flotsam we don't need. Over the side with him Jimmy," he said.

A shadow darkened the doorway and then a giant, black as pitch, ducked under the lintel. He wore breeches and boots, but above the waist nothing save a leather jerkin. He was hairless and glistened as if oiled; and his face gave no intimation of his thoughts. His soul smouldered deep in hooded eyes. This great Nubian advanced, and I am ashamed to admit that I stained the snow white sheet.

The bearded one roared with laughter and slapped his leg. "Thats no way for one o' my crew to behave. Out o' your hammock, sir and let's see your bollocks."

The power of speech had died within me and just as I thought my end was come, Mistress Howell hurried into the room. "Get out, you baboon, and take your freak exhibition with you."

"My love, you are at your most glorious when the tempest is in your eye." He put his hand on her hip and with the other, tweaked her breast. She feigned anger and pushed him to the door.

"Out, I say, or I'll take the shears to bed and the morrow will find you as carnal as this gelded ape." She glared at the mountainous Jimmy, and her husband skipped around her with childish glee to execute an exaggerated formal bow at the foot of my bed.

"Captain John Howell at your service, sir. And to whom do we have the inestimable pleasure of giving succour"?

As Jimmy retreated to the door, I recovered sufficiently to stammer my name.

"And do you have quarters, Master Paget, or were you washed up on the Severn Bore[18]?"

I raised my nose to an angle I judged sufficient to communicate disdain. "My guardian is the Member of Parliament for the City of Gloucester, Mister George Augustus Selwyn[19] of Matson House."

"Well bugger me to starboard, your poor little arse". He turned to his wife. "We've got old Bosky's latest catamite here. He'll be stealing them from the crib before long". I knew not what a catamite was but I suspected the knowledge would not amuse me.

Later, Jimmy carried me, a sparrow perched on Arthur's flanks, down polished oak stairs to the Hall, where a wheeled basket chair had been placed. Seated therein, Jimmy as propellant, I was conveyed in magisterial pomp to the garden. With Maria as my guide, we chattered around lawns where peacocks strutted, we chattered through shrubberies full of exotic greenery and we chattered along gravelled paths under bloom laden arbours.

We walked all around the old stone mansion, an assemblage of turrets and towers, of gables and chimneys, without form or symmetry. It is as if a collection of architectural whims and follies from the outposts of the Kingdom has been thrown together and, by extraordinary fortune, has made exquisite harmonies – dark mossy eaves under stone tiles, colonized by flocks of sleek swallows that dart and swoop in endless ballet.

In early summer, when the weather is fine, I can still recall with absolute clarity the perfumes of that day, the birdsongs, the colours, even the murmuring insects. But clearest of all is the vivacity, the effervescence that Maria brought to every object and subject that attracted her attention. She was like a waterfall throwing bejewelled spray in every direction, overflowing with the excitement of new discoveries.

She was a year older than me, already budding, and I fell deeply in love with her. Perhaps love implies too sexual a motive for the canine devotion I felt, for I would have happily followed her around that garden, on a chain if necessary, for the remainder of my life. Nothing but Pope was adequate:

Where'er you walk, cool gales shall fan the glade,
Trees where you sit shall crowd into a shade,
Where'er you tread, the blushing flowers shall rise,
And all things flourish where you turn your eyes.

I had clean forgotten my friends, but word must have been sent to Matson, for my adorations were curtailed by the arrival, in much dust and lather, of the dog cart bearing Pierce and Jud. Their jubilation could be heard all down the long drive, as they shouted and cheered at the sight of me; and when they had raced across the lawn, their embraces were enough to cause me further injury.

Tea and cakes and lemonade were brought to the garden, and Captain and Mistress Howell and Mistress Smythe heard, for the first time, a coherent report of my oft punctuated early life. I had great difficulty in recounting the events that led to my flight through the woods, and Pierce and Jud too were much troubled by the memory.

When Captain Howell heard of the fate of James and his maid, he was taken with a terrible anger.

"What has been done to apprehend these fiends?" His face had darkened and, without a grin, he looked an evil man. "They must be caught and butchered."

"Until we heard that Jo was safe, we had no testimony," said Pierce. "George Holyoake thought the men might have come from Stroud and we rode there on the following morning. But no-one speaks to strangers in that forsaken hole[20]. The famine has made felons of them all." Pierce had red rimmed eyes, whether from weeping or exhaustion, I knew not. "An ale house keeper outside the Town told us that two men carrying a cheese had drunk with him that day, and had said they were Bristol men. They had blood on their coats and he presumed they were poachers."

"Well now we have testimony and we must have revenge. I am owed many favours by the burghers of Bristol, and I have contacts in the foulest corners of that great city. We shall raise a mounted force and pursue these creatures to the grave." His voice dropped, cold, hard, full of cruelty and venom. "I have hunted many a man, and only Jimmy lived. It is time I had some more sport."

We rode in the dog cart back to Matson, with Captain Howell and Jimmy as outriders. They were an improbable pair, a cavalier with flowing hair and pointed beard; and a silent black pirate, graceful as a dancer, menacing as the darkest night. Down the steep Port Way, where ancient hill tribes had tramped to Wales, then around the hay meadows, rippling green in soft westerly breezes, we galloped at break neck pace until the cob was white with sweat and dust.

Hannah hugged me to her breast and sobbed in great orgasms. Not tears of joy, but grief for her dark fiery son. George had shrunk, his face pale and troubled, with shadowed eyes that would not meet mine. He went out to the Courtyard.

"Is your Master at home?" asked Captain Howell, who had not dismounted.

"No, sir. He returns from London tomorrow."

"Are you the Father of the murdered youth?"

"Yes, sir."

"Sleep well tonight Mister Holyoake, for I shall bring the murderers to justice, you may rely upon that. Give my compliments to your Master and beg him to call upon me in the morning. Tell the best men of Matson that I am raising a force and there will be bounty on the heads of our prey." He roared for Jimmy to follow and they clattered out of the Courtyard, leaving echoes around the walls.

My return brought purpose back to the Holyoakes. They were not yet able to smile, but the need for preparation and the prospect of revenge gave them a goal, a target upon which they could focus their despair. Hannah bustled around the House, preparing and provisioning for our journey, and George hurried about the Estate, picking men, horses and muskets. He hired a fly wagon and team from Ballards and sent word to Bristol for fresh horses. Mr Selwyn returned the following day and rode over to Prinknash to meet with Captain Howell.

Early next morning there were assembled in the courtyard at Matson, twelve mounted brigands, mean eyed and threatening, one black giant with a bandoleer slung over his vast torso, one packed fly wagon, its fretting team of four hackneys champing and jingling on their bits, and a Cavalier Commander, gleaming with the light of battle, astride a prancing Arab stallion. King Charles had returned to the fray.

I sat in blanketed luxury behind the wagon driver and, despite the sombre mood, could not dent my excitement. As we moved away from Matson, Hannah and her younger children waving at the gate until we rounded a bend in the lane, I knew that games and play would never again suffice; for I was a real soldier, in the company of real men, riding to war.

We took the lane through Sneedham Green and across Whaddon Fields to the turnpike road. There we lit out for Bristol as though our lives depended on haste. We must have crossed Frome Bridge, under which I screamed my first, but nothing could divert the exhilaration of speed that filled me – wind whistling through the hoops and tugging at the canvas, the bumping, swaying, jumbling wagon, the crack of the whip on four straining rumps that heaved us, ever faster, down the rutted highway.

For five hours we raced down the valley, the hills to our left. Occasionally, when our road breasted an incline, we could see the river, ever widening as it neared the sea. And then we could see Bristol, first a few distant spires among the cornfields, then larger lower buildings taking shape one after another, then houses, and as we descended into their midst, people hurrying on horseback and carriage and foot.

We rode down the twisting narrow streets, a small invading army, stared at by all that passed. I struck a disdainful pose, which I hoped would lend notoriety to my appearance. Houses and taverns and inns and bagnios* crowded in upon us. My senses were assailed by a thousand new sounds and smells, and then by the all pervasive smell of the sea – of tar and timber and salt mud flats, of fishing nets and cork floats and clean chilled breeze. It is a smell more evocative than any other. It bears flavours, exotic and exciting, of unknown lands and strange beings. It carries bewitching unborn music to any that care to hear.

My first sight of Broad Quay is another indelible print upon the pages of my memory: a devil's kitchen of seething humanity, worker bees in endless industry, loading, unloading, victualling, mooring, building and repairing an armada of ships, waiting in line along the dock. A forest of masts and rigging that dips and sways and frets as though impatient to be off. Mountains of coal and Mendip lead, competing for space with stacks of boxes and crates from potteries and glass blowers and bottle makers and soap boilers and distillers. Out of the bowels of the merchantmen come foreign treasures, tobacco leaf, tea chests, cocoa and rum; and pouring into this cauldron, a river of seamen,

---

* A house for bathing and sweating.

women, children, pack horses, asses and sledges.

At the far end of the quay, the privateers; dark, elite brigantines and barques, that hunt the oceans for plunder and take no prisoners. We made our way to the largest of them, black hulled with a golden carved figurehead, and the name Jamaica Sun in bright new paint along her leeboards. Captain Howell dismounted and climbed the gangplank. I saw a ruffian stand to attention and heard the Captain bark an order. So this was the spring, from which flowed the wealth, of the Master of Prinknash.

The Captain soon waved for us to come aboard, and when the horses had been tethered and fed, Jimmy gathered me up and we climbed the gangplank. I slept that night in a coarse canvas hammock, swaying gently on the tide, lying athwart off Amboina[21], waiting for a Dutch East Indiaman.

Others spent the time seeking information. Morning brought the news that our quarry were Kingswood[22] colliers. Jimmy was sent on an errand and returned in a while with an evil eyed villain. There was a conversation between the Captain and this man, after which money was exchanged. The horses were prepared and the man swung up onto the wagon to sit beside the driver.

We travelled east from Bristol, along the London road, past a stone cross that marks the way to Bath, and into a wilderness of shanties and mine workings. The road was busy with coal laden carts and drivers grimed with soot, and the air was heavy with smoke from woodmen's fires. What must have once been a verdant forest was being cleared so that in parts, not a tree nor bush survived. About a mile further on, a track crossed the way and our guide directed us left. Here the forest was thick, with oak and ash and the occasional cedar, and the path meandered around the great trunks. We came to a meere stone* where we were told to wait. The villain slipped away into the depths of the forest. The Captain ordered his men to dismount and take up firing positions in the trees.

We waited, still and watchful, straining to hear discordant sounds in the music of the forest. But only an occasional snort from our own steeds made us jump. How long we sat I know not, but as I stretched my cramped leg, three men, moving as one, materialized from a tree and leapt upon the wagon.

---

* Boundary mark

My arm was twisted sharply behind my back and the driver was cudgelled to the ground.

"Any move an' the boy's dead."

The Captain stood motionless beside the meere stone and no sound came from the watching men.

"Now, one at a time put yer guns by the stone. All on yer." A rasping voice , menacing, leaving no doubt.

The men began to emerge and lay down their muskets. When they had finished there was silence; and then a growl.

"Thers one more on yer. Three an 'is throats cut." He put the sharp cold of a blade under my chin. "One, two." Another of our men crashed out of the undergrowth and the pressure on my throat was eased. He whistled, long and low, and we heard movement from where our captors had appeared. A short, squat man with curling eyebrows stepped out of the shadows, followed by a troupe of armed bodyguards who took positions around the clearing. Then two men, chained with iron collars and manacles, were led to the stone and pushed to the ground.

"Curse you John Howell, I thought never to see you again", growled the eyebrows. "You're bad luck to me. The last time we did business we lost the bounty on a whole cargo of blacks. Now you want two of my best men".

"If they're your best men, Jacob[23], you've not long to live," said the Captain.

"You forget, I've not become a gentlemen. I can't take snuff and wear perfume and don powdered wigs, and sniff after female arses, like a poodle. If I want a fuck I send for a wench and if I want money I send my butchers to the London road. So if you want them, you'll pay for them. Are these your men?"

The Captain called to me. "Joseph, come down here." The calloused fingers that encircled my wrist slackened and, considerably relieved, I alighted from the cart.

The two lay on the ground, their faces wild and terrorized. As I drew near I recognised the mark on the face of the shorter man. I could go no further. "They're the ones," I whispered, and ran to George Holyoake to bury my face. The two privateers began to haggle, farmers trading beef cattle.

"How much for their necks then, John? They're worth good money to me. If I sent them hunting for a plump old squire, they'd as like come back with a hundred crowns."

"They'd as like come back with the military, and you'd be up on the gibbet with'em. They're rotten meat, Jacob, and sooner or later they'll poison you."

"I've a strong stomach, John, but for old times I will take five hundred guineas for the pair."

"I will allow that your stomach is stronger than your head. They're not worth a pinch of dogshit." He tossed a pouch to the ground. "There's a hundred in there."

"Two hundred and fifty, and there's nothing more to say." Captain Howell threw down another pouch and called his men to prepare to leave. The prisoner's chains were fastened to the back of the wagon and, as we began to move, they stumbled in our wake. We travelled north through the forest and then up Staple Hill to Mangotsfield, where we paraded our prizes. When we reached the Gloucester road they were lashed to the tailboard like two sides of mutton, and we headed for home.

I have heard many a discourse on the evils of strong liquor and have happily heeded none, but if you seek evidence to support a life of abstinence, then search no more.

Our triumphant army reached Whitminster in high spirits, and a visit to the Swan was believed justified. Captain Howell was reckless enough to charge the glasses of the entire troupe, most of whom felt obliged to return the compliment. After an hour, the first strains of George Ridler's Oven shook the windows:

The stwons that built George Ridler's Oven,

And thauy quem from the Bleakeney Quaar;

And George he wur a jolly old man,

And his yead it graw'd above his yars.

The air was thick with the smell of ale and pipe smoke and sweat from bright red beaming faces. I drank half a quart of flat dark porter and then swayed outside to where the horses were tethered, and rubbed the nose of a sorrel mare.

Taking care to keep my distance, I looked around the back of the wagon.

The shorter man lay with his head to the side. His eyes stared unfocused and unblinking and his tongue protruded from an open mouth. The other lay on his back, still, eyes closed, arms crossed on his chest. In a more sensible condition, I would have recalled that his wrists had been manacled behind his back. I hesitated, but the goad of bravado had been sharpened with ale. Eyes wide open, faculties intact, I sprung that most unsophicated of traps. As the hands closed like a vice over my mouth, the fables of George Ridler burgeoned:

Mine hostess's moid (and her neaum 'twur Nell)
A pretty wench, and I loved her well,
I loved her well, good reauson why,
Because zshe loved my dog and I.

I was trussed tight and my mouth stuffed with an evil rag. With a noose around my neck, I was made to stand on the tailboard as a hostage to pursuit. As the cart moved I clung to the hoops like a starved leech on a bloodboil. We pulled away from the Swan yard but the noise we made was as nothing to the saga within:

My dog has gotten zitch a trick,
To visit moids when thauy be zick,
When thauy be zick and like to die,
O thether gwoes my dog and I.

Although aggrieved by the lack of concern about my fate, I was relieved that my captors had no immediate need to launch me.

We drove west at great speed – happily the term break neck was not to be appropriate – past the park of Frampton Court, and Rosamund's Green, a sward of elegant landscape in the heart of the village, then right to Saul and on through a daisy chain of villages that fish the Severn[24]. The smell of the river hung in the air as we crossed the flat meadows of Longney to the narrows at Waterend. The horses were reined in before we reached the elver fishers cottage, and I was taken down in silence from my scaffold.

We hastened to the cottage where I was tied to a post. The tall man carried a cudgel with which he rapped on the door. The old man that answered was overpowered, and the blows to his head were such that I feared for his life. I heard crashing sounds as the cottage was ransacked.

They emerged cramming food into their mouths. I was untied and pushed down the hard to the water's edge where a wherry bobbed in the shallows. We clambered in and I was made fast to the transom. From our rocking, splashing, swearing progress, I deduced that each of us was afloat for the first time. There was little wind but the current was strong, and we had only struggled to mid stream, when the tall one began to complain.

"Time you 'ad a go Ben."

"I'm not movin'. I carn't swim."

"No more can I. I carn't row neither."

"Well thisn boats too 'eavy you. Throw the sprat in."

"We need'm as bait. We'll catch some big fish with 'im, you."

We hit a patch of rough water and spray cleared the bow. The wind had not changed, but here and there the surface was broken by an eddy. Then all around us the water began to churn and the wherry lurched violently, throwing me against the transom. The men's shouts were drowned by roaring tossing foaming waves, swamping us and hurling the boat into the air, as flotsam on the ocean, a stick in a waterfall. I saw an oar smash into the face of the tall man, and my last impression of the other is of flailing screaming terror as he was plucked from the bow. We were engulfed by a white wall of tumbling water and I must have perished, had the wherry not been swept to the bank with my right arm securely fastened to it.

I lay, not for the first time in recent days, in a battered half conscious state, somewhere between the here and the after, lungs full of muddy water, choking and puking on the sand, a bedraggled, jettisoned wretch. At such times the mind can be unfathomable. Mine had only a single thought: but for the accursed George Ridler and his vile oven, I would not be in such pitiful circumstances.

I was rescued later by a trader from Newnham who thumped my back without mercy until I was emptied. He then took me to Mr Clutterbuck's[25] mansion at Frampton. After being cleansed and revived with hot cocoa, I made a second triumphant return to Matson.

Chapter Three

Upon reading again the first chapters of these inadequate scribblings, I find that I have not yet properly described Matson House and the Estate.

Mr Selwyn's residence was built by his forebears in the reign of Good Queen Betty. It is a square house of two main storeys, with a much gabled roof in which there is a warren of attic rooms. The outside is solidly handsome but unadorned, save for a large sundial mounted on the south wall. Punctuality is a creed to George Holyoake, and the workers have to employ liberal invention when justifying lateness, the time of day being so clearly published.

The eaves around the main entrance are castellated, otherwise the house is unpretentious and has the air of an inflated rectory.

Mr Selwyn has caused many improvements since his incumbency began, not least the addition of a commodious north wing. I am told that its fashionable appearance, with bare red brick and gothic windows, is a tribute to my patron's admiration for Mr Walpole[26], not his architectural prowess. It is within this wing that the business of the Estate is conducted, all victuals stored, all meals prepared, and the Holyoakes and servants billetted.

There is a courtyard, enclosed by the wing and the handsome new stable block. Here are housed the coaches, the grooms and fourteen horses. It is these stables that have been built with the stones that took my Mother and Father. Hannah says that my Parents will never sleep until they have been avenged by fire. She says she has seen them in the Courtyard, hand in hand, just standing and watching, waiting. She says the block will burn in a great inferno and many will perish. She wags a fat finger at me and tells me to mark her words. I have hidden on dark nights, behind their gravestones, waiting for them to walk, longing to hear his laugh, feel her warmth. But my vigils have been rewarded with nothing but cold stillness.

The formal gardens have been transformed, even in my short tenure, to such effect, that Mr Selwyn's mother, the delicate Mistress Mary[27], was found wandering about the drive one morning, quite lost. There is a long avenue of elms to the elegant gates, a small lake on the lower slopes and walled kitchen gardens. A bowling lawn under the sun dial is enclosed by an arboretum of planes and tulip trees and larches and cypress. Below, lilies float on a still green canal. On summer days, Pierce would read to us while we watched fat carp, languid in the viscid water, and flashing blue dragon flies.

There are two farms. Larkham runs the sheep and timber on the hill, and Robins, the crops and cattle in the meadows, seven hundred acres of best Gloucestershire. Stockmen and ploughmen, woodmen and dairymen, I knew all of their names. I once estimated that upwards of two hundred mouths were fed by Matson.

This was our domain, Jud's and mine. This was the bosom to which we clung, as our childhood slipped away. It might have belonged to Mr Selwyn, and been run by George Holyoake, and been home to the workers and their families. But nobody else had the key to every corner. We roamed free as the fox, and it was only when honoured guests were present that Mr Selwyn expected us to remain out of sight, although even this restriction was removed when the Marchioness Donna Costanza Fagnani[28] came to stay.

The new year was born in a white blanket. Between Christmas and Twelfth

Night the days were thick with fat lazy flakes, drifting down from a dead sky, blurring and softening the contours of our world. When the sky eventually cleared, an icing of sugared frost spread across the beechwood and down into the valley – stilled silent days of apple cheeks and wet noses and steaming breath.

Each morning, Jud and I, warmed with soup and wrapped in skins, took sledges up the hill and raced down again, bumping and shouting and rolling into drifts; and then we frayed our tempers in rancorous snowball fights. Jud could throw further and more accurately than I, and the anger was usually mine.

One afternoon, after more than sufficient iced explosions on my face, I sulked my way alone, back to Matson. Once in the safety of the Courtyard, I determined to lay in a store of balls and exact revenge upon my former ally. I lurked behind the wall until there was movement in the yard, then leapt to my feet, hurled two missiles and took cover. Sinking below the wall I perceived that my target had been larger than Jud, my aim had been unusually accurate and the victim was now making a great deal of noise.

I recognised the tone of the noise – for there can be no mistaking fury in a female voice – and its intended recipient. But the content was unintelligible: a torrent of strange sounds, uttered without pause for breath, reverberating around the Courtyard. And then I heard Pierce's worried call from an upper window.

"My darling, what has happened?"

The reply, in operatic English, "I am under attack," belonged to one of Mr Handel's oratorios.

"Joseph!" I had never heard such authority in those soft Irish vowels and I looked up. To my dismay our eyes met, for he was leaning from the window of an attic room and could see clearly over the wall. "Come out with your hands up. You're under arrest."

I stood, and shuffled around the end of the wall into the Courtyard. I was faced with a proud, dark lady in red velvet habit, black hair in ringlets around her shoulders. I withered in the full force of her glare. I removed my cap and nervously executed a small bow, so nervous that it was more a nodding curtsey than a bow. For a moment we faced each other, as if about to commence a grossly unfair duel. Then she laughed, an earthy chuckle that would not have been out of place in a bawdy house.

"It ees the dread Meester Turpin," she cried, "I am ondone." She swept her hand to her brow. "Take amy possessions signore, budda leave amy honour I beg of you." Pierce ran into the yard and the concern on his face melted when he saw her smile. It was a smile that would have melted the Arctic: liquid eyes full of mischief and a wide scarlet mouth.

"Your honour is safe with me, madam," said Pierce. "I shall defend it even unto death. This brigand shall not have his way. On guard, sir." The pair advanced towards me, Pierce holding a stick as though it were a rapier. "Defend yourself, you blackguard!"

As the two lunged at me, I slipped on the ice and fell on my arse. They in turn tumbled over me, and the sight that greeted Mr Selwyn, as he opened the drawing room window, was of an uproarious tangle of arms and legs, two clad in unseemly drawers, rolling across his Courtyard.

He waited until we had subsided and then called, "My dear Marchioness, it is customary in England for rape and pillage to be carried out in a more decorous manner. The raper may grunt a little and the pillager has been known to gloat, but the victim must at all times make a virtue of necessity. The display of anything but pained forbearance is not considered de rigueur. You are displaying more than a heated strumpet."

We got up and brushed the ice and snow from each other, Pierce paying particular attention to the red velvet rump. "And whadda does sweet old Bosky know abou' rape, huh?"

"More, madam, than you appear to know about propriety." She tossed her black curls and snorted.

"I know all abou' the Eenglish steefa leep. Italian man 'e go steefa somewhere else."

"Irish man 'e go steef all over, if we are much longer in this yard." In the rush to rescue his distressed maiden, Pierce had donned no topcoat and was shivering.

"Come to me, poor Caro Mio, I 'old you." She clasped him to her ampleness. He pressed a cheek to her breasts and assumed the countenance of a devoted spaniel. "An' my leetle bambino, I 'old you too." I was gathered into the folds and we giggled our way to the kitchen and a slice of Hannah's spiced almond cake.

During the weeks that followed I transferred all of my filial devotion to the Marchioness. She came with us on our poetry trips, swathed in silky furs and enthroned upon the horse drawn sledge. Chuckling and cuddling Pierce, she would sing Italian songs and warm those January days with tales of her home in Milano, and of lazy Mediterranean islands.

I remember the cathedral stillness of the woods, young snow bowed beeches, arching far above, spectral mist threading through the high branches. I remember the virgin snow, broken here and there by a fox's lonely track. I remember stark solitary elms, frosted to windward, black against a yellowing sky. I remember the white and grey valley, smudged in the half light. She sharpens all of those pictures with her overflowing beauty.

Her rampant carnality was the asset that Pierce panted over, but for me, her exhuberence and love of life and her dark laughing eyes were mirrors from which my Mother smiled. When she left, the thaw had begun and the first whispers of Spring were quickening the blood, but Pierce and I were deaf without her. The miracles of nature went unnoticed. The colours that ebbed back into the landscape, greening meadows and early yellow flowers, remained grey to us. Until Captain Howell came to visit on the morning of my fourteenth birthday.

Breakfast was wild and noisy, an endless supply of salt pork and eggs, ladled by sweating maids into troughs from which the Holyoakes gobbled with ravenous slurps. Joseph Paget sat back, awaiting his turn which never seemed to come, a pearl amidst the swine. Small wonder I was growing thin. It was like feeding with a pack of hounds. No mention of my birthday, no gifts, only the arrival of the Captain, clattering into the Courtyard like a troop of cavalry, and hallooing my name around the walls, revived my injured pride. For in his wake trotted my present. Not just a present, but a pony.

And not just a pony, for Bewitched was a Welsh palomino filly by Merlin[29], with a pretty dish face, gentle eyes and fair flowing mane. She was to become the friend of my puberty, the amiable companion with whom I could share the fears and resentments that burgeoned in me. An anchor in my fast changing world.

I rode upon her delicious dancing grace that day, flying down the broad slopes to Upton and along the lane to Sneedham Green. We leapt over streams swollen with Spring rain and chased hares across the Whaddon meadows, then, as the day began to die, hell for leather through Robins Wood, climbing and climbing and climbing to the summit, sweating, heaving flanks, nostrils flared red. She would have run until death. Then the sweetness of the Spring evening, rooks coming home across the valley, the smell of woodsmoke and the creak of the Oxford wagon, and my Father's voice calling me.

The Captain had also bought darker news. Only one body had been recovered from the wreck of the wherry, but he had received word from Bristol that Ben Hurst had been taken and would be in Gloucester Castle on the morrow. It would be necessary for me to attend an identification parade and swear a statement for the Court.

Mr Selwyn took me to Gloucester to identify Ben Hurst. We were both dressed in sombre clothes and sat, unsmiling in the berline, reapers about their grim business. It must have been market day, for the city was thronged with country folk and we made slow progress down Eastgate Street to the Cross. We had to wait ten minutes while a river of sheep, tight packed between the tall houses, drovers and dogs whistling and shouting and barking and jumping, crossed our path on their way to the Beast Market. The inns and ale houses were full of noise, and street vendors threw their voices into the hubbub.

Along wide Westgate Street, where the great Cathedral tower soars above the City, we passed the serried timber galleries of Booth Hall. A fire eater, advertising the evening performance, seemed in danger of incinerating the entire building. And beyond, a winding lane took us to what is left of Gloucester Castle.

The site of the Castle has a most pleasing aspect, out across the river to Sudd Meadow, and its immediate surroundings are ordered and cultivated. But the building is a gaunt, half derelict fort, buttressed with brick piers and damp with river mist. It is an unhappy place, grey and forbidding and shunned by the city. I shivered as we approached, as if a prisoner about to be dragged through its gates.

We were met by the Governor, clearly in awe of his Member of Parliament, who included me in his deference. As we passed through the gates into the prison yard, I aped my patron by taking a perfumed kerchief from my top pocket and dabbing it to my nose.

The squalor that awaited me was beyond all nightmares: starving men, and some women too, chained like dogs to the wall, bony limbs trembling through thin tattered rags, some naked altogether, with yellowing open sores and grey skin. One man lay dead, his upper lip rolled back on rotting teeth; I suspected he was envied by many of his fellows. Their soil lay where it fell and the cologne was no match for the stench. One of the women was heavy with child, and several urchins played in the dirt. They were the only free spirits in that malevolent hole.

"The prisoners har only confined for your conwenience, Your Worship," announced the Governor for all to hear. "It was feared your presence may hinspire wiolence."

"The business, man," Mr Selwyn was quite pale and he snapped uncharacteristically. "Get on with it."

"If Your Worship an' the young gentleman would care to follow me, we 'ave hassembled warious felons for your hinspection."

We crossed the yard and I felt surrounded by hatred, although not a sound was made. Through a door into a long chamber and I froze, gripped by a sudden terror. At the far end of the room, more than ten yards from me, eight figures stood in line. But I could only see one of them. Short, sallow, with a wine red weal, angry and weeping, over half his face.

As an identity parade, it was a farce, for none of the others were similarly marked, but there could be no doubt. His face had been forever carved upon my soul in the still moonlight of Coopers Hill. I had to walk alone, the length of that chamber, and my light touch on his chest secured the noose that would choke the life from him.

Mr Selwyn brushed aside the Governors entreaties to join him in refreshment, and we departed as quickly as was seemly. To try and lift my spirits we walked around the city, through the cool glades of College Green and the wondrous, fan vaulted Cathedral Cloisters. We joined the pilgrims at Edward's tomb and gazed in awe at the Crecy Window[30].

For one so august as Mr Selwyn, the old Bishop[31] had been dragooned into acting as our guide. But he was woefully ignorant about his domain and seemed quite lost in the crypt, stumbling around the ambulatory with a spluttering candle, calling for the Deacon.

We walked along Northgate Street to the Debtors Prison, where inmates hang their pots from barred windows and howl for food. We fared better, for the New Inn laid us a table on the gallery, covered in fresh white linen, where we ate mutton and roast potatoes, and I furthered my education in the complexities of claret. There was an exhibition of wild beasts in the stable yard, and although we were high above, I devoured my food under the stern gaze of a glama*, which stood at least twenty hands.

We returned to the Cross where, to my great disappointment, the stocks were unoccupied. The berline was waiting in Eastgate Street and we hurried through the Barton turnpike, eager for the sanity of Matson.

---

* Giraffe

On the day of the execution there was a buzz around the Estate, a feeling of excitement, as though a carnival was about to start. I could not share in the pleasurable anticipation but Jud was impatient for the atonement to begin.

"I wonder if 'e'll be drawn and quartered," he mused, as if pondering the outcome of a cricket match. "Or perhaps they'll rot 'im in chains. I hope they don't give 'im to the surgeons, 'cause I want to visit him every week, until 'is bones are white."

We were all in our dormitory getting dressed. George studied his face in the mirror.

"I hear there's to be more than one," his eyes never left the object of his desire. "There's a woman to be turned off. Her old man knocked her about an' she took the carving knife to him."

"Well, hurry up then, you gert molly," said Tom. "We want to get a good view."

"You just want to pull your wire, you dirty little sod."

"I'd rather pull it than get it covered in scabs like yorn. They say you been pokin' Jane down at Larkham. She's 'ad more dick than Fanny Murray."[32]

George leapt at him. "I'll 'ave you, you little toad."

"'Elp 'elp, see I told you 'e wur a molly, 'e's after my arse now." The two rolled on the floor, and soon George was astride Tom's chest, knees on shoulders. He hawked and then curled his tongue around the phlegm. Tom's head shook from side to side.

"No no please George, I wur only jokin'." George's face was directly overhead and the phlegm began to trickle to the end of his tongue, but as Hannah bustled into the room he snapped his mouth shut and swallowed.

"Come on you two, you're like a pair of cocks, always fighting about nothing." We all sniggered but Hannah saw no joke.

She was dressed in her long Sunday frock with a lace bonnet and shawl and looked for all the world as though she were off to praise the Lord. Mr Selwyn had lent his coach and four, although he took his phaeton[33]. George and Job rode their own nags, but Tom and Jud and Sarah and I sat up behind the driver with the rest packed inside.

As we reached Port Way, the Prinknash coach went by in a tumult of halloos. Captain Howell fancied a race and roared his driver on, and even Jimmy, riding post horn, allowed himself a grin. We children heckled our driver but Hannah's forbidding tones were not to be ignored, and our progress remained seemly, even dignified. She was justified too, for where Westgate Street narrows to the bridge, the way was packed with people on foot, on horse, in carriage, all thronging to the party. The Prinknash coach was only just ahead of us and I glimpsed Mistress Smythe within. I tried to forget our purpose and think of the delicious pleasure of meeting Maria again.

Free of Westgate Bridge, the crowd surged along a causeway that crosses the wide flat marshes of Alney Island to Over[34], where ancient crumbling arches take the brave traveller to the Welsh road. On the river bank, at the side of the Ledbury road, the gibbet had been cleared of its loathsome remains and hung with three nooses. The multitude, as if attending a church service, settled in ranks around this hideous altar, laughing and prattling in joyous expectancy. Children played hopscotch and pestered their parents for sweets and buns, dogs barked, babies cried and even a tin whistle played as a girl in swirling skirts danced a jig.

An old willow, which had been called into use during the famine riots, stood near the gibbet, its topmost branches overhanging the crowd. It was a grandstand for the athletic and we climbed as high as we could to sit, like crows awaiting carrion. From this vantage I could look west, across the river, to Vineyard Hill and the brave little Leadon curling round the haunted palace, and to the Talbot Inn, emptied of its patrons, who lined the bridge to view the entertainment and piss over the parapets.

East was the City and Westgate bridge, and I could see a slow procession beginning to journey across the causeway. From this distance it seemed a carnival was approaching, with riders and followers pressing around a float. But as they neared, the lonely pulse of a muffled drum spread melancholy over us all. The wagon creaked down from the turnpike and ran the gauntlet of the crowd. Hurst was singled out for abuse and was pelted with any object that came to hand. The Holyoake boys were a rookery of hawking and spitting rage.

There were three bound figures standing on the cart, two men and a young woman. She was pretty and she was crying and I was sick with the awfulness of the goggling, gawking, lip licking animals that crushed forward to see her distress. Not even Ben Hurst, chained from neck to foot, but defiant as the spittle rained on him, deserved such an end.

The third stood aloof, head high, expressionless. He was a dissenter from Monmouth. Frenzied with righteousness, he had broken a few drunken heads in Northgate Street on a Saturday night. He had carefully divided their money bags, returned half and distributed the surplus in a workhouse. Nobody died and it would have been customary for his sentence to be commuted to transportation. But one of his victims was the Honourable Thomas Lyttelton[35], who was keen for an example to be made.

The two black cobs were led through the gibbet until the cart was in position. A boy shinned up to the crossbar and slipped knots for the hangman to adjust his nooses. A priest chanted, monotonous, sepulchral, a woman wailed, the crowd hushed.

The priest then spoke to the trembling girl who looked up at us, grey face, wild eyes, great heaving sobs. Ben Hurst next, no emotion, just his hard, livid face staring from the chain shroud, and finally the dissenter who stepped to the edge of the cart and surveyed the crowd, now silent, expectant.

In a high tenor voice he began to sing a hwyl[36]. The rich and rolling Celtic tongue was meaningless. But the fire and the passion scorched us all, leaving in its wake, a subdued and sulking throng, drained of festive spirit, impatient to be done. They were like naughty children after parental scolding, their fun had been taken away.

The Hangman took each noose in turn, tested the slip knot, then placed the longest rope around the girl's neck, the next on Ben Hurst and the other on the tall thin dissenter. The cumbersome knots were tightened under the left ear forcing the heads to the right. As the Hangman jumped from the cart, the three stood in line like a troupe of entertainers, heads cocked, waiting for the undivided attention of their audience, before beginning the song.

The hangman gave a sharp slap to the black cob's rump and the cart lurched forwards, leaving three marionettes, twitching and shaking and nodding.

"Well, they'm off," announced Tom, as if waving goodbye to departing guests. "Dancing down ol' Nick's stairs."

"Bet the Welshman gets there first," said Jud.

"Course 'e wont, yer daft sod. Ben Hurst's got the chains on. 'e must weigh twenty stone."

"What diffrence do that make?"

"'Is neck will 'ave broke like a twig. Bet 'e'm halfway there already." Blood poured from the girl's nose, staining her cotton shift. The dissenter's eyes were screwed shut and his mouth still moved as if in silent prayer. "Well I reckon the Welshman's enjoying 'imself. Carnt wait to get there an' give ol' Nick an earful."

"Twere a funny ol' song 'e sang."

"That were a yewel. I 'urd a preacher do one once". They might have been discussing the weather.

"Much o' that an' I reckon ol' Nick'll chuck 'im in the boiler."

The dance was slowing. Ben Hurst was still and the dissenter's long frame only twitched. The girl's movements had become relaxed and fluid, almost graceful.

"See, I told 'un. Ben Hurst's there already. I 'ope they're roasting the bastard. Whats the matter with Jo?"

I was crying and Jud nudged me, so that I almost fell from the branch. "You bloody gert soft lummox."

The crowd began to break up, the Talbot refill, a stage coach that had reined in for the fun, went on its journey. People strolled around the gibbet, farmers inspecting their fruit. Children returned to their games. Even Mr Selwyn, who had watched from the far river bank, drove his phaeton down to examine the swaying corpses.

We scrambled out of the tree and I ran, away from that depraved scene, trying to block it from my mind, knowing that it would follow me and haunt my dark nights. Away too from Jud and his brothers, for that was the time and place we reached the parting of our ways. I was to stay at Matson for some time, and the lessons, the play, the work, the trips, all would continue without discernible change. But on that terrible day by the Over bridge, I realised that I saw life through different eyes; that my future lay along a different path, a path that led first to the turnpike gate and the coach and four tethered nearby.

Captain Howell and most of the Prinknash party had adjourned to the Talbot. But withdrawn into the shadowed corner of the cab, I found Maria. Not my chattering porcelain angel, but a young woman. A young woman that took my breath, that stilled my tears with one winsome glance, that lit my dark thoughts, that rained sweet rain upon my thirsting heart.

I make no apology for this outbreak of unripe ecstasy, for this was indeed my Day of Revelations, when the two essences of my life were spawned, radicalism upon that evil gibbet, and romanticism in that perfect face.

I rose early the following morning, taking care to leave the brothers undisturbed, and padded down silent stairs. I crossed the yard to the stables and heard Bewitched nickering in her stall as I approached. I could ride a farm pony before I could walk and I vaulted up on to her wide bare back. With nothing but a halter to steer her with, we galloped across the meadows, scattering big brown hares and pretty green peewits. The spire of Upton church floated on morning mist which still clung to the hollows under Prinknash. The high beechwoods were clear against a china sky, promising settled weather.

We climbed Port Way and turned into the long drive, and in a great swearing confusion of horses and men and machinery, narrowly avoided certain death under the wheels of the Prinknash coach.

"Port to port, you damned jackpudding." The familiar roar, but not unkind. "You steer like a drunk Dutchman."

The coach had come to rest between two trunks and seemed unscathed. He gave me his wicked grin.

"And who, we must ponder, put ginger up your arse[37] so early in the day?" He called into the cab. "Elizabeth, we have the Matson macaroni to thank for that skirmish. Are you intact?"

Mistress Howell's ever cheerful, although flushed, face appeared. "If you refer to my virtue, sweet husband, you forget I am the mother of your child."

"How can I forget, my dearest, when only this morning you used me like a bilge pump?"

"The quarts of foul water you shipped last night left me no alternative."

"Pray do not think I protest, angel of the sweetest dawns, you are free to empty my magazine whenever and however you choose". He turned back to me. "Methinks the wild worm awakes in yonder tight breeches; and will soon be pointing at our youngest guest." The fairest face in all the Kingdom appeared next to Mistress Howell. I blushed scarlet and tried to hide my face in a gallant bow.

I am unable to commend this strategem to mounted persons, particularly those without stirrups. For the simultaneous acts of rising without an anchor and inclining the head can induce imbalance. I pitched forwards onto the flowing mane. Bewitched, quite properly, interpreted this unfamiliar disturbance as a directive and responded with characteristic vigour. She flew through the trees and I clung to her neck like a bayonetted hussar. When she jumped the ditch, tailed raised and farting with joy, I lost my grip and spilled into the malodorous depths.

At least the mud and duckweed and sharp spears of loosestrife ensured that my body suffered less than my dignity. I emerged from the ditch, monstrous with slime and frogspawn, to Maria's merry peals ringing around the beechwood. I hoped that she was not going to make a habit of witnessing my humiliations.

Jimmy set off in pursuit of Bewitched while I was taken to the house where, despite offers of assistance, I washed myself. Dressed in a medley of servant's Sunday best, I presented myself again to the Howells and their guest.

"When you interrupted us with your Cossack display, we were setting out for Newnham on Severn, to see the Maiden Dean. Would you care to join us? Or are your memories of the Kingdom's greatest river too soggy?"

"I would be pleased to join you, sir." I would be more than pleased. I would be enraptured. I would be transported on gossamer wings. I would be delirious with joy.

"You shall ride up front with me, for there is too much baggage in the cab."

We followed the route of the Bristol trip, past Quedgely and Hardwick and Morton Valence, past the Swan, its morning peace yet to be disrupted by George Ridler, over my bridge and Mr Kemmet's grand failure, through Frampton and Frethern and out onto the Arlingham Passage. Here the Severn swings in a great horse shoe bend around a five mile finger of broad flat pasture.

The Romans crossed the Severn here. They built their road, straight and true, right to the water's edge, then stormed across the wide shallows to conquer the Welsh; and thousands of travellers since have followed in their wake. It can be a perilous business, even at low tide, for there are long muddy sandbanks that dry out, and have to be negotiated on foot before the ferry can be boarded. The banks are prettily festooned with gulls, sheltering upriver from the estuary. They rise into the air at human approach complaining noisily, to wheel and dive overhead, shedding fluid shit upon the intruder.

On the far bank, red marl cliffs are topped by a bonny church with a conical spire. The busy little port of Newnham[38] is gathered about the slopes, and whitewashed cottages tumble down the Nab to the quay.

The tide was full and the river lazy, and my second crossing of the Severn a smooth and uneventful excursion. We disembarked at the new jetty. I held Maria's hand as she stepped from the wherry and melted in her smile of thanks. We had to thread our way through mountains of bark awaiting shipment, and I clung to that small white hand as a dog to a bone.

The boatyards were busy and full of noise, and heavy with the smells of pitch and varnish. Like half eaten carcasses, the ribs and hulls of two brigs stood high on the slipway. The Captain's new boat was out on the hard, complete with masts and rigging, shining with new varnish, glinting with polished brass.

She was a cutter, forty feet of bottle green hull with amber painted gunwhales. She had a fat round bow and a flat stern. Her bowsprit was half the length of her mast and high above, a burgee fluttered from the thin tapering topmast. A spiders web of rigging, too intricate it seemed for any man to comprehend, ran from mast to bowsprit, from spars to mast and from mast to deck.

The timber cradle in which she had been born was pushed by a gang of sweating men to the head of a slipway, where Captain Howell poured a bottle of claret over her bow.

"I name this boat Maiden Dean. May God bless her and all who sail in her." He aimed one of his most lecherous winks at Elizabeth. "May she be the second fastest little bitch in the Kingdom and may her arse be ever chased by Cumberland."[39]

He and Jimmy ascended a ladder and adopted noble postures, master at the bow, crew at the stern. With one final shove from the gang, the good ship Maiden Dean slid down to the sulking waters, where she bobbed on the flood tide, eager to be free of her tethering lines. The Captain waved a salute and we lined the quay to shout our huzzars as she was pulled alongside. Elizabeth, Maria and I clambered aboard and stood forward of the mast, while the Captain and Jimmy bustled like gleeful children about the task of fixing and raising the mainsail.

Jimmy heaved on the halliard, eyes bulging with the strain and an acre of white flapping canvass followed its yard arm to the masthead. The Captain scurried from side to side, barking orders, heaving lines, fending off, and then as the great sail filled he bellowed, "Cast off forrard."

Jimmy, surefooted amidst the debris of ropes and canvas and huddled bemused passengers, galloped past us to retrieve the freed line, and the bow began to move away from the quay.

"Cast off aft."

We were free and as we swung across the wind the boat heeled, first to starboard, then in a great smacking gybe[40], to port. Elizabeth clung to the mast, I clung to her and Maria clung to me. As the filling of a most agreeable pie, Midshipman Paget was cast upon the waters of England.

Jimmy, with scant heed for the wellbeing of his passengers, surrounded us with canvass to which he attached a score of snaking, snapping lines. When he had completed his seemingly random task, he pulled with all his might on the halliard, and the tangled mess rose into the air, to become a taut and graceful sail. We heeled further over, and gathered speed, and I heard for the first time a sound that will never fail to stir me: hurrying water on the hull of a yacht.

As soon as I deduced that our list to port did not signify imminent catastrophe, I began to enjoy the voyage. I made my way astern, slipping, sliding, clutching the gunwhales, grabbing the shrouds, a babe taking his first steps, to where the Captain stood, tiller in hand, humming a shanty, a rapturous expression on the perfidious jowls.

"Only two things in life are worth the effort," he announced to the sky, "a good ship and a good woman. And you need a fair tide to enjoy either of them".

The breeze was westerly and we reached down to Portlands Nab, then a broad reach to Box Rock and a run across to the far bank and Hock Cliff. This hump of sandstone guards the entrance to the Noose, where the river widens to a two mile lake. Jimmy dropped a plumb line from the bow. He walked to the stern where he reeled it in, called the depth, and returned to the front to repeat the exercise. The tide was beginning to ebb as we skirted the great expanse of water. We kept close to the eastern shore, although our destination was the wooded knoll of Gatcombe[41] on the Welsh side. I pointed this anomaly out to the Captain but he advised me to keep my counsel and watch for shallows.

Jimmy shouted, sharp and urgent. We turned to starboard, into the wind, and with sails idly flapping, floated on the tide across the lake. Jimmy now had a long pole, with which he kept the nose pointing north of the Gatcombe knoll, while the Captain poled the stern to keep our head to wind.

As the tide ebbed further, smooth glistening plains of mud and sand appeared to either side of us and I saw that by some miracle of navigation, we were following the course of a narrow channel that cut across the Noose. We neared the west bank by Poulton Court, turned to port and sailed a close reach down to the pretty little harbour at Gatcombe.

I think I shall never master the intricacies of navigation, and I shall retain, for those that do, my most profound humility.

The hamlet nestles in a wooded combe, sturdy cottages for the fishermen and foresters, with a large house on the quay where the business is conducted.

They build small boats, fish for Severn salmon and ship Dean timber to the Naval Dockyards. Gatcombe must have played a signal part in the defeat of the Spanish Armada, for it is here that Drake used to come to buy the best.

The hard was lined with stop boats, heavy black twenty two footers, that fish the waters down to Bristol with lavenets[42]. The brig *Martha* and a trow named *Farmer* were anchored off, laden with bark. But there was little sign of activity in the afternoon warmth, until the Captain's halloos brought a figure running down the quay to take our lines.

"Cap'n John," he called. "Cap'n John," and louder, "the Cap'ns come back to see us."

Doors began to open along the street and men and women and children and dogs were running and calling and waving and hallooing, as they swarmed down to the harbour. I deduced that the Captain was not unknown in these parts and asked him how this was.

"I used to get chased back to Bristol sometimes, by the Frogs and Dutch, but while they looked for me up the Avon I was hiding in here. I would slip past Beachley Point and up the Slime Roads, and even if they followed they could never find their way through the sands. I brought presents for the folk and my men would tup a few maids. We became celebrated visitors."

He disembarked to cheers and back slapping, and arm in arm with Elizabeth was escorted to the big house. I heard the bung being drawn, and suspected that we would soon be hearing the strains of the Accursed Oven.

The Prinknash coach had arrived via Gloucester, but it seemed that our departure would be delayed. I took Maria's hand and we climbed through the woods to the top of the knoll, from where the view can explain better than a volume of words, the complexities and depths of the Gloucester folk. For three countries can be seen from here, yet all are one shire. West, the wooded hills of the Forest of Dean rise, dark and mysterious, to brood over the vale. At your feet the river ebbs and flows down ever changing channels, through silky mudflats and chaste yellow sandbanks; and then the blossomed valley races away to a far blue Cotswold wall.

We sat in the high meadow, huddled close, for the afternoon had begun to chill, and watched a million sea birds rise like a mist over Frampton Sands, and then settle again as the danger passed. Maria kissed my cheek, soft, a mere brush of her lips, and then my ear which begat new and exotic sensations. She took my hand and placed it in her blouse against warm satin skin, and I cupped a small soft breast in my palm. She loosened the stays on my breeches and slid her hand within; and I have yet to master the words that can adequately describe the feeling, as her delicate fingers encircled my tool.

We sat, she gently amused, I quivering with ecstasy, and stroked each other in silence. Presently a tingling in my loins grew into an intense, but curiously weightless feeling, lifting and lifting and lifting me, until I exploded in shuddering shaking spasms. She took a silken kerchief and wiped her hands, but there was no seed, for I had been transported by the rising of my sap, but the reservoir was not yet full, and could not overflow.

We spent the night in the house on the quay; a forest house, built for a thousand years, with walls a yard thick and bare elm floors. I watched from my tiny weather proof window, as the evening river colours turned from blue to pale yellowing green, and then pink in the lowering sun. A skein of geese, honking across the sands, flew downstream, and as the tide began to fill again, the waters gurgled their way back into the harbour. Gentle lullaby sounds, but I slept little that night. My mind was full of the sweetest music, and my eyes, though closed, saw wondrous things. And my ears were assailed by a timber rattling, wall trembling snore, that was born somewhere deep inside the Captain, who lay where he had fallen, on the cold grey slate of the kitchen floor.

Chapter Four

I could have burst with excitement. I still quivered from Maria's touch, but the news that I was to accompany Pierce to London in the furtherance of my education transcended even her silken fingers.

London was the centre of my dreams – the most important place in all the world, where the great and famous walked the streets and my heroes rested between valiant deeds. Pierce had business in the Capital and I deduced from his transported expression, that it encompassed a meeting with the Marchesa. Even his poetic quotations were anchored in some of Goldsmith's more fervid lines:

> *'She speaks, 'tis rapture all and nameless bliss, Ye gods what transport e'er compared to this'.*

The warm August evening smelled sweet. The Matson carriage took us to Gloucester, where we caught Turner's double post coach from the Kings Head. Our fellow travellers were a rum pair. A fat bald man from whom odour escaped in great ripe farts, filling our small compartment, until Pierce, who wanted to sleep, was forced to light a cheroot as a counter attack. The other passenger was a tiny female, adult, but with the stature of a marmoset and little walnut face and lost eyes. She was a mouse in a cage, an object, a piece of fairground flotsam dragged from town to town and exhibited to anyone with a penny to spare. There was shame in her every movement and I doubted if the Over gibbet offered a worse fate.

I leant on Pierce and shut my eyes. Soon my ears followed suit and finally my nose escaped the torment.

I awoke to a tumult of shouting and a chilled dawn, as we pulled into the yard of the Kings Head in Oxford corn market. Our companions were leaving the coach, and as the fat man took up his bag I read a sign painted on the side, 'Maria Therese the amazing Corsican Fairy'. Pierce, who had been reading Selden's Table Talk, watched them preparing to leave. He passed the book to me pointing to a line on the page he was reading, twelve words that sometimes return to me in moments of melancholy:

'There was never a merry world since the fairies left off dancing'.

A hurried breakfast and we were off, with fresh horses and new companions – an earnest architect and his voluble wife who, upon detecting Pierce's accent, engaged him in debate on the splendours of Dublin. When he ventured that they were English splendours and thus should be reserved for London, our companions scoffed at such ingratitude.

Summer was at its richest as we thundered east, down the Thames Valley, towards the climbing sun. Another stop at Wycombe, with hardly time for lunch, let alone the good shit that I so earnestly desired; and on again as if our lives depended on arrival in London before evening. The main street of Uxbridge echoed to our clamour of straining horses, urged on by the crack crack of a long whip and the Coachman's hoarse halloos.

As we crossed the Brent, the reason for our haste became apparent, for through our window there came into view the outside rear passengers of Phillpotts London Flyer. High in the air, they sat in rigid terror, swaying and bumping to such alarming abandon that a capsize seemed not only inevitable, but welcome. We inched past them, our driver urging and hawking and whipping and swearing until we were broadside on and I could see the whites of their rolling eyes. I was John Gow[43] on Revenge and they were a French prize, laden with brandy and wine. One more fusilade and she would be ours.

Thus we raced abreast down the Kensington road, without heed for the growing numbers of travellers, first one then the other gaining the upper hand, past cattle drovers, Smithfield bound, and hog fields where the city debris is devoured; through neat and orderly market gardens, their martial rows stretching to the horizon: past long burning rows of fetid brick kilns, sulphorous stinking heaps that scar the country and spread their yellow stain for miles around; and finally down the Knightsbridge turnpike, where we were forced to slow, for the traffic became thick, and much of it the shiny crested carriages of persons with rank and distinction.

At Hyde Park corner our Coachman reined in to allow us a moment to recover and enjoy the view across the Green Park to the Duke of Buckingham's house. Then we progressed, with as much dignity we could muster, behind six wild eyed, flat eared, sweating nags, along Piccadilly, down the Haymarket, where I looked in vain for Jack Broughton's house[44], and along the Strand. I gawped from the window, unvoiced by the magnitude of wonders that passed before me.

The early evening streets thronged with humanity: flower girls and pie men and milkmaids selling adulterated milk; patterers and ballad mongers, street vendors and criers, strollers, urchins and beggars. There were young bloods and old rakes, ladies of quality and calling whores. And through this multitude charged a constant stream of phaetons, hansoms, chaises and carriages, all seemingly oblivious to the dangers of collision. And the buildings: tall graceful stone houses cheek by jowl with tenements and huts, churches on every corner, shops and inns and theatres and palaces along wide paved streets and fashionable squares.

We pulled in to the Bolt and Tun yard, Fleet Street, at precisely seven'o'clock, which was the time advertised by Turners. A man in olive livery awaited us with a halbberline in which we hacked in the fading light, back down the Strand, past Clifton's Chop House, St Clement's Church and the shiny new St Mary's, past the ancient arch of Somerset House and the splendours of the Duke of Northumberland's palace, around the Eleanor Cross[45], and down Pall Mall. We had expected rooms at an inn, or at best, lodgings in one of the less tasteful parts of town. Cleveland Court in St James was about as fashionable as one could be without a crown.

We arrived at an elegant house, four storeys high, abutting the Green Park to the west and the Royal Palace[46] to the south. Mr Selwyn was indeed a man of property, and it surprised me that his town residence was not here, but across the Park behind Shepherd's Market. For this was the home of Uncle Tom, my patron's sad and lonely old brother in law. He was the Honourable Thomas Townshend, once a thrusting and handsome politician and an artist of repute. But since the death, thirty years before, of his beautiful and beloved Albinia, he was a shell, acting out the duties of an empty life.

We were ushered by a disheveled footman, into a darkened hall and from there into an even darker sitting room. Our host rose from a high back chair and shuffled towards us. His back was bent and his head low, forcing him to inspect us as though through a keyhole. His round, red rimmed, watery eyes bore not a trace of welcome as he cleared his throat and extended a grey veined hand towards Pierce.

"Welcome to my home, Mister Creagh, and you too, Master Paget. Mister Selwyn told me of your visit and I have had a cold collation prepared for you. You are to use my carriage as your own for the duration of your stay. Forgive my shortcomings as a host but Charlton will attend to your needs."

We muttered our pleasantries, then silence hung in the air. Uncle Tom resumed his chair and the meditations that we had disturbed. The footman, whom I assumed to be Charlton, coughed behind us and we followed him to a curtained dining room, musty with disuse, where cheese and meats and bread and pickle had been placed at the far end of the table. After supper Charlton led us aloft to rooms on the second floor. My window looked over the inky black sea of the park upon which just one ship was afloat. There was a grand social function underway in Buckingham House. The crescent front of the building was lit, as if afire, by a hundred flambeaux held by coachmen, awaiting their glittering employers. It seemed that a flickering orange horned moon had fallen from the sky, and lay dying at my feet.

The morning came in a rush: Pierce hammering on my door and bawling to the household that modern youth was idle and unable to raise itself from its own arse: a timid little maid wobbling into my room with an overfilled washing jug spilling half of the contents onto the bed. Pierce humming a wild and emotional Celtic song as he cut his whiskers: and startling light flooding my room as the poor child tried to make amends by opening the elderly drapes, which tore on their rings and collapsed around her in a dusty mountain of velvet.

As the hullabaloo left little alternative, I rose and joined the distressed waif at the window. The sylvan scene before me and the abrupt elevation of my status, for I had never been attended by a maid before, however incompetent, wrought in me a feeling of benevolence. I patted her hand and showed her my warmest smile. To my horror she leapt upon me and kissed my lips with an ardour that recalled overheated nights in Mr Selwyn's bushes, watching his overheated guests.

I fell back on the bed and she fell on me, like a grappling iron with four limbs clamped around my inadequate frame. The door opened and Pierce grinned hugely at my dilemma.

"Would you look at the rat!" he announced loudly. "One night in London and he's up the first drainpipe he can find." My skinny little minx unhooked herself and fled in terror. I struggled to an upright position and puffed outrage at my tutor.

"The maid stumbled whilst filling my basin and I was merely helping her to rise."

"I think she was helping you to rise," his grin was even wider, "and you were about to fill her basin."

"You may think what you will, but I assure you I am innocent of anything save helping a poor female."

"Maybe," said Pierce, "but next time you feel inclined to gallantry, I advise more appropriate dress." I looked down and in an all enveloping blush, realised that I had retired unadorned.

Over a meagre breakfast, served on rattling china by Fanny, for that was the name of my bed wetter, I explained to Uncle Tom that I had demolished the curtains. My reward was to be followed by Fanny's dog like eyes, brim full of gratitude, for every step of the remainder of our London sojourn.

It did not surprise me that our first call was to be upon the Marchesa, who was residing at Mr Selwyn's house in Chesterfield Street, whilst he was away in Yorkshire. We walked across the formal lawns of the Green Park, gardeners kneeling in every flower bed, past the reservoir where lads fished from the jetty, and over Piccadilly, to the haughty streets around Chesterfield House.

Pierce rapped a silver gilt knocker and the black door swung back to reveal a sombre butler. He ushered us to a reception room and bad us wait. There we spent the next hour in silence, as though waiting in church for the service to begin. When the incumbent finally made her entrance, it was like a troupe of morris men arriving at a funeral.

We first heard her descending the stairs, abusing the maid for clumsiness, then the butler was deluged by a torrent of Italian in return for his mournful solicitude. But when the doors of our room opened, a shaft of sunlight found its way through the storm clouds to strike Milan's most precious jewel. The flashing smile, the earthy chuckle, the wondrous deep dark eyes were beamed upon us in their full glory.

"Amore mio, amore mio," and in a trice we were clasped to those soft and oh so lustful folds. We started to perform a tarantella around the floor, but Pierce was strangely reluctant and entreated the Marchesa to be seated.

She scoffed. "You are juss lika Bosky, an'my sweet ol' Billy. Always they wanna me sitting down or inna my bed. They don't take ame out no more, they don't kissa me no more, I theenka they don't love ame no more". A pout, and the upturned coquettish eyes. "Do you steel love ame, Pierce?"

"Oh my darling," breathed Pierce, and then, remembering my presence, "we have much to discuss, I shall arrange a carriage to take us on a tour of the City. But now I must insist that you rest." She stamped her foot and snorted, and patted her swollen belly.

"I 'ave bambino in 'ere, not gigante."

It had dawned upon me that her size was not entirely due to overeating but now the question of paternity crossed my mind. There was a Marchese, a wild and handsome profligate, who had accompanied his lady to England. But had he been undertaking the necessary exertions on a regular basis, surely his person would have been more in evidence? I had already concluded that Mr Selwyn was an unlikely candidate but I had no knowledge of Lord March. Her intimate references to him pointed to the likelihood of his being a visitor to her gate, if not a guest in her parlour.

Pierce was clear favourite in my book and I looked forward to the birth of a firebrand, for I could conceive of no more volatile integration than Irish seed in an Italian womb.

The days that followed are an indistinct page, a blurred voyage of discovery around the streets of London. We would rise early and take the halbberline to Chesterfield Street, collect the Marchesa, and the three of us, without a ha'porth of London between us, would aimlessly trot in whatever direction the pair of bay hackneys were inclined. I saw it all but saw nothing. The squares and markets, the churches and gibbets, the museums and monuments. We even circumnavigated Covent Garden but I was not allowed to alight.

But although I drank little, I had sipped from the well; and I was intoxicated by this teeming, vital, awful city. That I would return I had no doubt, although I could not yet know just how great a part London would play in my life.

The Marchesa grew pale and her eyes lost their sparkle. As Pierce became more attentive, she could tolerate him less. She puffed and she frowned and she sometimes wept a little, and her walk became a waddle. She would hold her back with both hands, projecting her great bulge so far that I was sure she would topple in the street. The pair were like a cross old dowager and her long suffering servant, she the afflicted, he the irritant. When she took to her bed I was forgotten, and left to find amusement with Fanny and Charlton and old Uncle Tom.

I had already sampled Fanny's idea of entertainment and decided to keep her at a benevolent distance. Charlton reacted to my attempts at flippancy by making it clear that he considered me one of the ruling class. Thus I was faced with the daunting prospect of days in the company of Uncle Tom; days that I anticipated with dread, realized with joy and recollect with fondness.

A breakfast of long silences, the old man and the youth struggling for common ground. He noisily sucking his tea to my discomfort, me tapping my spoon to his irritation. Each attempt at conversation interrupted by Charlton shuffling by. And then a contact, a spark that lighted his rheumy eye and fanned in me the ember that had already been lit by the halbberline trips.

"How old is London, sir?" It was nothing but a polite query, the answer to which was obvious, and about which I had no desire for further information.

"As old as man," he replied, and with the first suggestion of the warmth I was to discover, "even older than I."

I sought to encourage the conversation to limp a little further. "Why is it so big, why is it more important than Gloucester, or Bristol, or Oxford ? Why is the King here and the Government?"

A slow smile. "So many questions."

"Sir, I have spent three days touring the city and have understood nothing. It is all very grand and handsome but I would like to know London, not just see it."

"Then you must begin with an easel, a board, and some chalk. Your journey should start in the fount of all learning, the classroom. This wisdom is given only to tutors; pupils realise it too late."

I was singularly unattracted by the prospect of scholastic discipline, but felt obliged to indulge his new loquacity. He led me down the hall to a shuttered room wherein were all the accoutrements of a small academy: six desks with long legged stools facing a platform, which held an escritoire, lectern and blackboard. There were sketchpads on the desks, and the walls were adorned with examples of artistic licence similar to those that Jud and I produced for Pierce; similar but very much better. I took a seat and was seized with the unreasonable fear that Mrs Gale was about to examine my grasp of the Catechism. Uncle Tom stood on the platform and leant on the escritoire.

"This is where I taught my children, and now teach other people's children. It is the lessons they learn in this room that are the foundations upon which their lives are being built. I teach them not to read, not to add lines of figures, not to write prose in the style of Doctor Sam[47], but to open their minds in order that they may receive these teachings from others. Your intellect has a door. Closed it can welcome no visitors, but left ajar, with a lantern burning in the porch, it can give sanction to the wisdom of the world."

It would be untruthful to record that I found these profundities comprehensible, but I nodded and awaited mention of London.

"To understand anything, you must desire to understand it; to learn anything you must hunger for knowledge. This truth is so apparent to an old man, so obscure to a youth. You desire to discover the essence of London, therefore you will. I suspect that you do not hunger for mastery of syntax, therefore its complexities will forever remain a mystery to you." This much at least was right. He took coloured chalk from a box and turned to the blackboard.

"We shall draw a map of London and we shall begin with her heart." He drew, with practiced hand, snaking double lines across the board, wide apart on the right, converging to the left. "The Thames flowed a million years before we came and will hardly notice when we leave." He shaded the lines in blue and added streams running in. "The Tye Bourne and the Fleet and we must define Thorney Island."

He stood back and inspected his handiwork. "From Greenwich to Chelsea, nothing but water and marsh and mud banks and low cliffs; and in the forests beyond," he shaded all round the perimeter with green chalk, "roamed bear and wolf, hyena and rhinocerous, and even further out, mammoth grazed the plains. And then came man." He changed to pink chalk and marked some areas close to the river. "Hardly man to begin with, for these were little brutish naked savages, living in caves in the cliffs or holes grubbed in the woods." He turned to me and wagged a long bony finger. "But they were not animals, for they wanted to learn, they hungered for knowledge."

"Before long they learned to build mud huts so that they could live where they chose, and then make weapons, and poison the weapons, and trap the beasts. Then they mastered fire and made pots, and built their villages on the high ground, and made coracles to fish, and broke horses to ride, and worshipped idols, and buried their dead."

"Then at last, about fifty years before Christ was born, Caesar ran his galleys ashore on the beaches of Kent. A rabble of savages came hullabalooing at him out of the woods, brandishing their clubs and spears and jabbering in amazement at the sails and the banks of oars, the flash of armour, the sound of Latin; the miracle of civilisation." Uncle Tom raised his arm in theatrical salute to the solitary pupil he now held in the palm of his hand. "Behold, the Eternal City had sent to these poor wild creatures, Caesar himself, 'the noblest man that ever lived in the tide of times' . . . "

"Thus aboriginal London became Roman London". He now used red chalk to spread the shaded area around the river bends and add the line of a wall. "And when they drifted back to Rome, as our Englishmen will drift back here when the Empire declines, Saxon London, which saw no great change, for the Saxons lived in the Roman city as a hermit crab in an empty whelk shell. But the first St Peters would appear and Westminster Palace on Thorney Island and the first St Pauls on Lud's Hill," he marked the sites with purple chalk. "The walls too, to keep out the pirate Danes who sailed up the river, followed by the Saxons. Then the Normans, who came to conquer all."

He took up yet more chalks. "We shall use brown crosses for the river buildings, the Tower, London Bridge, St. Mary Overy, the Abbey. A line for the new Wall and its Gates will give us the medieval town. White crosses for the religious orders, Blackfriars, Whitefriars, the Charterhouse, the Minories". His efforts became almost frantic as he strove to keep pace with his commentary, and the map grew in a harlequin patchwork across the board. "Black for the Ghetto, old Jewry, Spitalfields for the Huguenots, Saffron Hill for the Italians, and for the love of Rome, Watling Street."

"Along the river and because of the river, the Strand, the Savoy and the other river palaces, and Billingsgate and the Temple and Horseferry Road and Lambeth; they all fall into place. We must mark the streets and buildings which owe their names and places not to chance, but to nature, or fear of invasion, or to trade. We must start with the river and let London grow under our hands. Only then will we know the essence of London, and understand the greatness of London."

With extraordinary speed, and what I later learned was great accuracy, a map of London had spread over the board, in a myriad colours, so that hardly a trace of the dark grey wood could be discerned. Uncle Tom was to leave his work of art untouched for his few remaining years, and I would return again and again to refresh the vision of his romantic city, whenever cruel realities perverted the dream.

The halbberline was made ready and we crossed the Park, threading through a cavalry of gentry, taking their constitutional: haughty horses with haughty riders displaying their splendidness to one another. We followed King's Road, through the meadows, down to the river at Battersea Reach, where uniformed watermen gathered around the stairs playing cricket.

Two stumps had been painted on a willow, and the batter stood before these holding an oar. The bowler lobbed at him a soft ball which he smote over a hedge, to the approval of his supporters. Money changed hands and new bets were struck, but before the ball could be found, Uncle Tom called for a boat and was immediately surrounded by both teams. Amidst much jostling and shouting he agreed a fare for the rest of the day, and we embarked, to conquer London, in a shiny high prowed wherry. Our big cheerful waterman had removed his jacket and he pulled us easily to midstream, hard bulbous biceps rippling like the brown waters under us.

The Thames is still a country river at Battersea. There are timber wharves and windmills, and cattle drinking in the shallows. It is the distant aspect of Lambeth Palace and the great Rotunda at Vauxhall that give notice of splendours waiting beyond the new Chelsea bridge.

We drifted downstream, with an occasional stroke from our pilot, and Uncle Tom was my guide. He told me of the bridge, being built to serve the vast crowds that flocked to the pleasure gardens of Ranelagh on our left, and Vauxhall on our right. I counted seventeen wooden arches as we slipped under the centre, still covered in scaffold poles and noisy with hammering and sawing and the clanking of cranes. I gazed in awe at the great Rotunda as he told me of its vaulted room more than two hundred feet in diameter and I could see it, alive at night with lanterns and music and entertainment of every form. He told me that the Gardens were devoid of morality, cess pits for the sin and the corruption of London, to be avoided by young or impressionable persons. He warned me to keep away, but did not doubt that I would ignore his advice. I too had no doubt.

Along Lambeth Reach, past the wharves and brew houses of Millbank; where two horses swam without concern around a timber laden trow: past sylvan avenues where sweethearts dally in the shade, to the granite bridge of Westminster. Uncle Tom, as though a maestro commanding the sections of his orchestra, waved at the brick red turrets of the Archbishop's Palace, then the towering Stone City, where a ghost of Edward walks on Thorney Island, and Westminster Hall, its massive roof shadowing the clustered chimneys of Parliament, and St Margaret's Church, a delicacy amidst the solidity of state.

I was already breathless as we rowed beneath the arches, dark, dank, echoing our talk, alive with water shadows, but nothing had prepared me for the sights and sounds of the Pool. Uncle Tom had told me that the river was the city's heart, but I had not understood that it was the highway, the port, the pleasure lake, the sewer, the engine, the lifeblood without which London would die.

Wherries and ferries and barges and barks crossed and recrossed the broad, sun dappled water, in a disorganised pageant. Larger trows and brigs struggled to catch the fickle wind that funnelled through ranks of tall buildings, clustering along the north shore. And along the south shore were warehouses and windmills and ramshackle wharves, guarding flat market gardens, as far as the eye can see.

We rounded the bend, where the river turns east, by the extraordinary facades of Adam's new Adelphi[48], with its wharves and arcades and subterranean streets and great Royal Terrace, still being built. All of the morning's lesson came to life. I could see the Strand behind Savoy Palace, and Somerset Water Gate and St. Clement's church. Uncle Tom pointed out the Temple and Whitefriar's Stairs and Fleet Street and the Black Lion Inn along Water Lane. We went under the new Pitt Tollbridge[49], which he said had cost one hundred and fifty thousand pounds.

He told me of the Apprentice Boy's riot the Sunday before. They gathered in St Georges Fields, about a half mile to the south, and marched to the Bridge demanding free access. But the gates were closed and the keeper refused to open them without tolls. They threw him into the river, broke the gates, and marched to Smithfield. On the way back, they entered St Sepulchre's church and pelted the kneeling congregation with sheep shit.

Then Wren's masterpiece on Lud's Hill, where the savages had camped, and the Romans had built, and the Saxons had slept, and the Normans had fought. And to the east, the Monument[50], where the Fire that engulfed the old city had started a hundred years before.

Before us stood the ancient London Bridge from Southwark to St Giles, narrow and low arched, with churning watermills by the shore. It has served centuries of travellers and pilgrims and marchers and players, but Uncle Tom paid it scant respect. He said it had been despoiled in the Fifties, when the houses and inns that stood on its roadway had been removed to accommodate traffic and replaced with fancy lanterns and carved parapets[51].

We squeezed under its central arch, past a cutter with stepped mast hauling through against the stream. The air beyond was heavy with the smells of the Billingsgate fish jetties. And finally the Tower, guardian, gaoler and executioner to the city for a thousand years; the history of London, and of England, written in blood on the venerable walls, and bound in stone.

We disembarked at the Tower Stairs and walked by the moat to the Navy Office, where the halbberline waited to take us back to Cleveland Court.

I knew Uncle Tom for just his few last years, during which we met only occasionally, but I have much to thank him for, not least an introduction to two of my dearest friends. For I spent the rest of my stay as his pupil, and with the help of his two most promising proteges, produced the much admired sketch of London Bridge that now hangs in the Drawing Room at Matson.

Jem Gillray and Tom Rowlandson were no older than me but, measured by artistic ability, they were decades ahead. Jem was as wild and dark, as Tom was fair and brilliant. They were day and night, ruby and jade, but bonded by a passion to draw. Against hypocrisy and injustice their young fires of indignation burned white hot, whereas mine was barely alight. They shared a humour that pricked and poked and outraged everything and everyone it touched, save Uncle Tom. For him they saved their love and respect, and in return he spluttered and flared like a dying candle, giving us glimpses of the man that Albinia had loved.

We stood in line by a wharf off Clink Street, one warm and dusty evening, easels perched along the bank, drawing visions of the venerable bridge that ranged from faithful to incomprehensible. One student appeared to have depicted a serpent crossing a turnpike. Uncle Tom congratulated him and mildly suggested that a little more attention to perspective would have improved what was otherwise a praiseworthy effort.

I had trouble with the water mill and the soaring tower of The Monument. Tom and Jem stood either side of me, and whenever my pencil went to my mouth, stilled by the complexities of the view, they would add a line here, a stroke there, and the vision that I so struggled to record, would be refreshed. But I paid for their help.

At the conclusion of our artistic outpourings, we stood in line, backs to our creations, awaiting the acclaim of our tutor. When Uncle Tom reached me, he studied my easel, over my shoulder, and seemed for a moment lost for words.

"Never mind," he murmured eventually. "Perhaps the subject was a little difficult for you."

This was hardly the response I had expected, for I was singularly proud of my masterpiece. I turned to consider my work in the light of this apathy and found that it had been substituted by a grotesquely accurate depiction of an erect phallus, soaring from a mound of bushy testicles, and entitled in flowing copperplate, 'The Monument'.

My embarrassment was complete when a party of young ladies, guided on their nature study by a watchful and stately governess, paused to inspect our pictures. The giggling, blushing girls gathered around my easel, and only when their protector barked at them with parade ground ferocity did they scuttle away down the towpath. One or two of them bestowed upon me flirtatious and admiring smiles. They must have assumed that I had been sketching from life.

I puffed with pompous outrage. I proclaimed my innocence to Uncle Tom, though he seemed not to care. I even shouted after the governess that the fault was not mine, but her imperious glare condemned me without trial to the fires of hell. Each protest fuelled the braying of my tormentors, so that when I turned to them and demanded an apology, they fell to the ground as if stricken with palsy, wheezing and choking with insane glee.

Later, as our wagon bumped across St George's Fields on the way to Westminster, Tom Rowlandson, of the fair honest face and sweet smile, begged my forgiveness and promised to be my friend. I found to my discomfort, when we arrived at Cleveland Court, that during this conversation, Jem Gillray, of the dark face and wicked grin, had been tying my breeches to the copses with a stout cord. When the others disembarked, I was left securely fixed to my seat. Uncle Tom interpreted my howls of protest as further petulance and I remained thus enthroned until well after dark.

The following morning, upon hearing the true account of my privations, Uncle Tom ordered the miscreants to make a full and abject apology to me. With exaggerated humility they knelt before me and I was so taken with their sincerity that I forgave them without reserve. My feeling of magnaminity was shortlived. They left the room, closing the door quietly and respectfully, and I would have been well pleased with my moral victory had it not been for the wild giggling that echoed down the hall.

I have struggled to find words that adequately define my feelings, following that first inauspicious acquaintance. When measured against the standards and rules that I had been taught, they were shallow, fickle youths, butterflies flitting from one enthusiasm to another. But I had never before been in the company of such fertile minds, and I found their wit and audacity intoxicating.

I had never known Pierce in such a parlous state. One minute full of bravado, singing his jaunty Irish songs, the next soft and dreamy with a foolish grin. Then his fair eyes would sharpen with worry and a deep frowning furrow appear beneath the wild forelock. Finally, indignant anger would burst in a crescendo of banging doors and thundering footsteps, and I would run after him, for my entreaties to be repelled with oaths and mutterings about the "fook'ninglish" and "barsturd eyeties".

It was clear that his business was concluded and no further reason remained for us to stay in London. We packed, or rather hurled our belongings into the chest, hurriedly said our goodbyes to Uncle Tom, Charlton and a tear stained Fanny, and caught the morning stage from the Bolt and Tun. Tom and Jem came to see us off, and it was their smiles and waves, given without a semblance of mockery, that persuaded me to vow I would see them again.

Pierce relaxed as the city turned to country and the paving turned to grass, and I began to feel a little less frightened of him. My timid enquiries eventually bore fruit, and amidst our rumbling, swaying progress, and to the discomfort of the matron who sat with us, he told me of the events that had led to our flight.

On the night before last the Marchesa had given birth, in a frenzy of screams, to a daughter. After the ordeal, Pierce had sat with her, and presently the washed and swathed infant was brought to her bed. But instead of suckling the babe, as a mother would, she handed it to Pierce and demanded a wet nurse. Pierce had spent the rest of the night rocking the infant in his arms, cooing at her little pink head, holding his breath as the tiny hands wrapped around his great fat forefinger, whispering gentle Gaelic lullabies until she was so still that he had to touch her lips with his, to discern her breath.

The morning brought him a note from Lord March, requesting his attendance at 138, Piccadilly to discuss a matter of some delicacy. He was received in the library of the grand new house by his Lordship, a birdlike man with a hooked nose, and the Marchese who, according to Pierce, would not have looked out of place on the gun deck of a privateer.

The interview was brutally concise. Pierce was given the option of accepting one thousand pounds in return for his immediate removal from England and undertaking never to return, or being dismissed from Matson without references and causing any further financial support of Jud and I to be terminated. He was handed a whimsical note from Mr Selwyn, in which he ceded any authority in the matter to his Lordship, and made it clear that despite their previous friendship, he was in no position to dissent.

Pierce put his arm around my shoulder and told me quietly that he had no choice, and would be taking the Liverpool post coach on Saturday. My distress was such that the matron forgot her distaste and wiped my tears with a large linen kerchief. She gave me a bun from her basket which I tried to eat, but coughed the whole mouthful over her. She smiled thinly and stood in the swaying vehicle to brush the debris from her skirts. A jolt, more severe than most, tipped her into Pierce's lap and his humour made a brave attempt to return.

"Madam", he said from under her ample arse, "if my talk of babies has overheated you, I apologise. But would it not be more seemly for us first to be introduced"?

On Thursday we rested from our journey, and Friday was the worst day of my life. I tramped the house watching Pierce collect his belongings. I rode

Bewitched up the hill and sat in the grass, gazing sightless at the nothing, hearing nothing, feeling nothing. I enwrapped her soft brown neck and sobbed into her mane. I searched for a present for Pierce, but could find none, not even a line of poetry with which he might remember me. And I slept that night not for one moment, heaving, tossing, then still, listening to Jud's steady breaths, and rattling snores from Tom, who had spent the evening in a vain attempt to drink a yard of ale[52].

When the brothers arose in the early morning, for this was the first harvest I had missed, I slipped into fitful dreams and awoke to Hannah's soft voice telling me that Pierce had gone. She had cooked me some breakfast, although it was not long to noon, which she left on a table by the bed. And she gave me a folded note, with my name writ large across the front, in my tutor's flowing, sloping hand.

> *'My dear Joseph,*
>
> *Now that I have gone you will learn useful things, the tools that you will need to build your life. Study your sums for my sake, master your languages, grasp your syntax, seek yourself in the history books. Above all, enquire. If the answer satisfies you not, enquire again. If the answer bores you, ask somebody else. Send me your drawings from time to time and do not forget that when the dawn is at its greyest, poetry can lighten the sky.*
>
> *Yours very truly,*
>
> *Pierce Creagh.*

As I write this journal, I have not seen or heard from Pierce since. I cannot believe that he would not write to me and suspect that his letters were intercepted. I think I have learned, during the years since his departure, why he was banished. But I will never condone the callous and summary way in which the privileged classes direct the lives of we, less upholstered souls.

Although I am English to a fault, Pierce left in me a piece of his bitter sweet Irishness, his inner rage, his gentle verse, his wild hibernian depths. Mie Mie is not yet five, but already I have taught her some of his poems. I shall visit him soon, and when she is ready, take her across the Irish Sea.

My distress was all too obvious, I stayed in my bed that Saturday, whilst every other man, woman and child on the Estate sweated in the fields until dusk. But when the brothers fell into their beds there was no reproach. On Sunday morning, despite the hated penance of having to scrub necks and clean finger nails and don church suits, they were eerily affable. Jud told me they were off to the boxing in Cirencester on Tuesday and urged me to come. I demurred at first, but then relented. Yet another decision that profoundly affected the course of my life, for it was at Cirencester I discovered that alcohol was not the only intoxicant available in this increasingly exciting world. Gambling too could lend wings to the spirit.

We filed into the little church, where we were subjected to the usual strictures against sins of the flesh. Not for the first time did I conclude that the Devil seemed to be having all the fun.

I must have learned to master my feelings when my parents died. I have the ability to close the door on unhappy memories, to shut them from my mind as if they had never occurred. Thus my misery had dispersed by Tuesday morning. Pierce had taken his place in my gallery of absent friends – Maria, my Parents, Captain Howell, Uncle Tom, Mr Selwyn – to be thought of in turn, when time permitted. I was free to savour the thrills of pugilism.

I rode with the brothers down to Jack Goss's shop, where the meat wagon had been cleaned and harnessed with four good nags. The two Jacks sat on the forehead with what appeared to be the entire clientele of the Kings Head saloon, including the Landlord, under the canvas. With three or four other carts and a handful of riders, we made quite a platoon as we rode up past Prinknash and through the woods to the Ermine Way. We galloped along the Roman highway, straight as a die, over the bleak and lonely wolds, where many a traveller is relieved of his purse, then down a fold in the hill at Daglingwoth, where the grey stone town spreads below around the massive tower of St John's, a beacon for miles across the high plain.

We turned the horses out on a pasture near the town and walked to the market place. The only activity was in front of two buildings at the bottom end, where Dyer Street begins. A crowd of several hundred had gathered outside the Fleece Hotel and despite the morning being only half through, were already rumbustious with ale. In a steady circular movement, foaming pewter pots were appearing from the Hotel entrance, being passed from hand to hand, and returning empty.

Next door was an altogether more patrician gathering, albeit with the same end. For these were the premises of the Bull Club, a society of sporting gentlemen responsible for the day's promotion. The front of the building was festooned with posters.

PUGILISM

The Noble Art

Under the patronage of the Bull Club a PRIZE FIGHT will take place in the Fleece Yard on Tuesday 2nd September 1771 at 2 pm between two renowned and feared hitters.

TOM "THE BULL" DINSLEY. v JACK "PIRATE" STANLEY

The contest will be according to Broughton's Rules and Cirencester's most famous sporting son will attend in person.

There will be a full supporting programme in which it is hoped to include a CONTEST OF AMAZONS.

I assumed that amazons were some form of exotic animal and found that exciting enough. But when Jud enlightened me, I could scarcely contain myself.

Our approach was greeted by cheering and shouts of "Good old Jack", and "Here comes the champ". Tankards of ale were thrust at us by beaming red faced hearties, eager to belong in our exalted company. I stuck close to JB and basked in the reflected glory. Although nearly seventy, he was still a giant. Not particularly tall, but heavy and thick, with hands like udders, and shoulders so wide that as we passed through the door he was made to turn sideways. He patted my arm.

"Stick by me young'un, and do what I do." He put his untouched tankard on a table. "You need none of that stuff to make a profit." The bar was packed and it seemed that everyone wanted to talk to their celebrated guest.

Jack made for the corner where a huddle of ferrets conversed in low voices, throwing the occasional furtive glance around the room.

"'ow do our Jack," said one, and they enlarged the circle to allow us in.

"What news boys?" They spoke from the sides of their mouths and Jack did the same.

"There's a Kingswood collier in the first, name o' Ben Brain, thats got the makin's of a champ." It was hard to make out the whispered tones and I wriggled into the middle of the circle. "an' they think ol' Tom Faulkners finished, but 'e's fighting a kid, an'll know too much".

"An' 'ows the Pirate?" The voices were lowered even further, so that the circle of faces closed over me.

"As well as 'e's ever been, but 'e'll need to look lively, for Dinsley's got a nobber that fair makes the air whistle."

We moved away and Jack said,"You'll be my mascot, I'll bet in guineas an' the shillin's for you."

Two gaudy men, patterned topcoats and powdered wigs, pushed into the crowd, followed by a villainous mountain who's towering presence quietened the bar. He was hairless, save for thick eyebrows, and his long nose, flattened by the rigours of his profession, flared in permanent anger.

"That's Tom Dinsley," said Jack, "'e looks fat to me." He looked fat to me too, indeed he looked positively overflowing.

"Well then, Jack," said one of the bucks, "come to see the execution?"

"Your man has the strength my Lord, but young Stanley's fast an' I reckon the Bull's basket is a bit too full o' bread."

The ogre paid no heed to this stricture and set about devouring a filled loaf and a quart of ale.

"You're welcome to fifty to twenty if your money has lost its attraction," said the buck.

"I reckon I'll do better than that in running, my Lord, but I'll take it in guineas against first blood." Notes were made of the bet and I followed my new patron's backslapping, hand shaking progress through the bar to the rear yard.

In the centre of the yard a stage had been erected with a post and rail fence around its perimeter. There was a further ring fence a few yards from the stage, beyond which were rows of forms and benches. They were already filling with as varied a collection of rascals as I had seen outside Gloucester gaol. There were ladies too, although I use the term only in its biological sense.

We stepped over the first rail, into the area reserved for gentlemen officials and honoured guests; and whips, who were local toughs armed with leather thongs with which they kept order. By midday the yard was packed with a laughing, swearing, shouting crowd and there was scarcely room for the fighters to enter the arena. A few cuts and slashes from the whips soon established a path, and the Landlord, tall and florid with mighty whiskers, strode to the stage.

"My lords, ladies and gentlemen," he boomed. "The Fleece Hotel, in conjunction with the gentlemen of the Bull Club, takes pride in offering, for your gratification and enlightenment, a battle royal between two of your favourite hitters, preceded by two absorbing bye battles and one," and he paused for effect, "Amazonian conflict!"

Much raucous cheering greeted this last allusion.

"The first exhibition of the fistic art will be between young Benjamin Brain[53], a miner from Kingswood, and your old friend, the Melksham Milkman, Billeeeeeeeee Doggett."

The two might have been father and son. One, not many summers older than I, callow and awkward, but solid and with a dangerous look in his eye. The other, balding, squinting, battle scarred, a wary old dog looking for a dustbin.

The two wound their ribbons, one yellow, one blue, around the post in their corner, and then sat on the knee of their Second. Umpires were chosen from the crowd and they in turn appointed a referee. A chalk mark was drawn at the centre of the stage and the fighters took their places, poised with fists raised, at the scratch.

"Two to one the boy," called a gent by the rail.

"Ninety to forty with me," called another.

"Guineas," shouted Jack, and the bet was struck.

There were bets flying in all directions, the weight of them on Brain, from betters who assumed Jack knew something.

The first fight I ever saw was also the shortest. A whistle blew, Doggett crouched and began to circle around the ponderous Brain, flicking a warning left. Brain lowered his head, as though to charge, then swung a punch which began its journey from below his knees, and ended deep in Doggett's mouth. The unfortunate recipient of this murderous weapon was lifted at least a foot from the floor before crashing into the corner post, from where he surveyed the young miner in toothless terror, and remained when time was called.

The preliminaries for the second fight followed the pattern of the first. Once again the contest was between youth and experience. Tom Faulkner[54] had been champion a dozen years before, but now played professional cricket.

When he stripped to his breeches, the evidence of the softer life, the slow bowling on the village green, the lumbering run of the middle order batter, was there for all to see. His belly boasted of the brews he knew, and the dangling of his chest was the envy of many a lady present.

His opponent, Spaniard Harris, was altogether a better example of the benefits to be gained from healthy pursuits. His swarthy muscles shone with oil, and although he resembled a dago, there was no denying his youth and beauty. An attribute not lost upon the females present, nor indeed was the possession of what appeared to be a codpiece in his breeches.

"What say you Jack, I doubt you'll want to bet the old'un this time." It was the gent that had lost the first bet.

"I might, if the price encourages me."

"Two to one Faulkner."

"What about the double, first blood and a win"?

"Seven to two."

"To a hundred guineas." The gent swallowed.

"Blast you, Broughton, d'you know something that I don't?"

"I suspect, Sir, I know a deal o' things you don't, but in this case I'm just backing my judgement. Harris is too pretty, 'e'll be a quitter."

The fighters came up to scratch, and on the whistle began to spar. They circled, testing, waiting, until Spaniard lunged in with a left that waved in the space recently occupied by Faulkner. A chopping counter hit his ear as a warning against carelessness. This pattern was repeated for at least five minutes and a cut on the swarthy temple was acknowledged by the gent as first leg of the double. But then the cricketer's reflexes let him down and he must have thought he had been hit with a bat. He was sent spinning across the stage to the cheers of the dago lovers, and he slumped to a heap at the feet of his own seconds.

They got him up to scratch for round two, but the fog had only just begun to lift, and he went down again before Harris could throw anything more than an insult. They wrestled round three, both trying to get the other in chancery, until a trip brought the pair to the floor. Faulkner had recovered by the time they began the fourth, and this time he abruptly ended proceedings with a cross buttock that had Harris's heels high in the air before the crash.

In round five, Harris was beginning to gain the upper hand as the tubby cricketer started to wheeze. But then the fight was won in an instant. Tom

Faulkner was wrestling for all he was worth, trying to soften the telling blows, when Harris slipped. Faulkner's arm went around his neck for a perfect suit in chancery. He locked the head under his left armpit and hammered with his right as if beating a tough steak. After a few minutes of this treatment Harris gave in. I suspect he feared more for his beauty than his health.

The much heralded war of the amazons was a bitter disappointment to me. The two contestants were well into their matronage and between them could have sunk the Maiden Dean. These viragoes spat and screamed at each other for half an hour without spilling a drop of blood. Far from the titillation I had anticipated, the feeling I experienced when they crashed to the floor, not a yard from my nose, was the terror inhabitants of Jericho must have known on the seventh day.

And then to the main contest. Dinsley, towering above his army of admirers, was the first to climb upon the stage. He wore a skin cloak, and upon his head a pair of longhorns. He walked around the rails, arms aloft, scraping his foot in the manner of an angry heifer, and uttering bovine bellows. A number of wags in the crowd began to moo in response, and as Jack Stanley entered the arena he must have thought he had been directed to a milking parlour in error.

To my untutored eye Pirate had about as much chance as Ben Hurst after the chain shroud had been locked. He was curly and handsome with long sidewhiskers. He had an easy smile which he beamed upon the ladies; but he resembled David when compared to the horned Goliath that strutted around the stage, and as far as I could see, he was not armed with a sling. But he did have two invaluable weapons, for JB was his second, and JG one of the umpires.

"C'mon, young'un," said Jack. "You're the bottle man, an' if I want a bet, you're to run like you bin figged."

We climbed on to the stage and Pirate sat on Jack's knee. "We'd better be fit, Pirate, for we've got some running to do."

He looked relaxed and confident. "Now don't you worry, Mister Broughton, I know what to do."

"Just keep goin' backwards till I tell you to stop. One to the face, then away. I want us to be a thorn in his flesh. Keep scratching 'im till 'e loses 'is rag. Lets see 'is claret afore 'e sees ours."

"If I didn't know you better I'd say you've had a bet on me getting first blood, Mister Broughton."

"Never mind about that, just concentrate on stayin' pretty. There'll be a present at the end."

The Landlord finished his monologue and the fighters came up to scratch. On the whistle David backed away from Goliath. An overladen man o' war lumbering after a frigate, firing an occasional broadside at the nimble opponent. Pirate, dancing, weaving, stalking his prey, would whack the bald head with a lightning left, and then be nowhere in sight when the club fist sought to execute him. Thus the contest proceeded, to the manifest frustration of the Bull, for fully ten minutes, until, red faced and blowing, he went down on one knee.

"We done fine, Pirate," Jack said as our protege returned to the corner, "Plenty more o' the same, jus' keep scratchin'." I gave him the water bottle and held the bucket for him to spit.

The next round followed the same pattern as did the third and fourth. By the fifth it seemed that a bloodless victory was within Pirate's reach, but as Jack's money was on first blood, no blood meant no money.

"We've got 'im where we want 'im now. Time to take a few more chances."

"He's still strong, Mister Broughton."

"Strong? 'e can 'ardly stand. Get in there an' draw the cork." The clock curtailed further deliberation and Pirate went up to scratch. At the whistle he began his familiar retreat, but then darted forwards and rattled five lefts and a sharp right cross on the Bull's strawberry nose. He achieved two rewards. A spurt of blood, which brought great satisfaction to his second, and a jarring, crunching clout in the ear, that momentarily deformed his head and hurled him against the rails.

We dragged Pirate's rearranged body back to the corner where I poured water on his head and Jack forced brandy down his throat. With his eyes open, but focused on a distant star, we carried him to the scratch, where the breeze from the Bull's first haymaker was sufficient to flatten him again.

"Three to one the Pirate," sang a gent by the rail.

"Fours," sang another.

"Get me that to a hundred guineas," whispered Jack, and I scampered off to do his bidding.

With another thirty seconds rest and a further gulp or two of cognac, Pirate began to realise that he was in Cirencester. At the start of the seventh he fell again at the mark, before damage could be done, but this time got up and walked back to the corner. He retreated throughout the following rounds, making the Bull blow and then dropping to a knee to gain the sanctuary of his corner, until by the twelfth, he was dancing again.

"Give 'im one in the basket, Pirate," advised Jack, as the pair rumbled by, "I think 'e might give birth."

At this slur, the Bull turned as if to smite Jack and Pirate seized his chance. He buried his right up to the wrist in the soft white belly, and as the Bull doubled, hooked his neck and wrestled him to the floor. Pirate's knee completed the coup d'etat by plunging in where his fist had just been.

Pirate was up quick and in his corner. The timekeeper began to call the seconds.

"Ten, eleven, twelve." The Bull had puked on the stage and lay grey faced and groaning as his seconds tried to shift the great mass. "Nineteen, twenty, twenty-one." The crowd now took up the count as the Bull fought to breathe through the torrent of water that poured on his face.

"Get up, Dinsley, you fat oaf," bawled his noble patron through the rails. He pushed himself to a sitting position.

"Twenty-five, twenty-six, twenty-seven." He made it to his haunches where he sat, a monstrous slimed toad, as the crowd roared "Thirty!" and began to throw money onto the stage. It rained silver for full five minutes as Pirate paraded the rails, waving, blowing kisses, flexing muscles – a prodigal son before his adoring retinue, a triumphant matador with the bull at his feet.

I am unable to recount, with any reliability, the events that filled the rest of that triumphant day. I know that Jack, pockets filled with banknotes, tried to empty the cellars of the Fleece. I know that Pirate got into an argument with a barmaid who knocked him senseless with a short uppercut. And I know that I lay on a bench that began to spin. It fell like a sycamore seed, into a bottomless void, swirling, drifting, ever downwards, until I erupted in a great fountain of glutinous liquid, and vowed never to drink again; and I know that somehow I returned to Matson, securely tied to Bewitched, to awaken the next morning and find forty pounds in my pocket.

Chapter Five

The expeditions of my childhood – the wide eyed voyages of discovery, when every sight, every smell, every sound, was a new wisdom – were coming to an end. But one sea remained uncharted. The Olympick Games[55] at Campden had thus far been out of bounds to the younger Holyoakes. At fifteen years, George decided that our struggle into puberty needed stimulus.

As soon as we gathered in the Matson yard, I could sense a difference about this departure. It was not just that the party was exclusively male, they had a bearing, a cut about them I had not seen before. All was cheerful banter and an eagerness to be off, and even their prancing, snorting horses felt the mood. There were two older men, George Holyoake and Bill Warr the Larkham farmer, a straight lean man of middle years, handsome with greying hair. And there were six youths: Bill's sons, Stephen and John, the Holyoake boys, George, Tom and Jud, and I.

We cantered down the drive in jovial mood, but had not reached the Cheltenham turnpike before the difference I had detected was made clear to me, and my obligations defined. George reined in at the side of the lane and Jud and I were surrounded by the rest of the party.

"There are certain rules to be observed by men in the company of men, written on tablets of stone and betrayed at fearful cost." George sat high on his black gelding, stern, magisterial. "A man that betrays the brotherhood of man can no longer be called a man, and for the rest of his life will be despised by man."

In much the same way as I had sat, in darkness, through Uncle Tom's overture, I looked attentive and awaited the daylight. "You may see and hear things during the coming days, that surprise you, even shock you." Dawn was beginning to break. "Men in the company of men are released from those obligations of society and behaviour, under which they labour for the residue of their selfless lives." He now fixed upon us his fiercest glare. "You must both give me your word, on pain of death and eternal damnation, that you will repeat nothing, save any innocent pleasures I authorize you to recount, about the happenings you may witness."

"I promise, Sir," mumbled Jud.

"I promise, Sir," I followed.

"Right." He seemed satisfied. "Our first release is from the proprieties of tongue." We had begun to canter again. He raised his voice. "Listen to our verse and repeat it loudly." He held his hand aloft and six voices roared in unison.

"On my trusty steed I sit, arse, bollocks, prick and shit.
I'm a man and I'm a wit, fuck, bugger, cunt and tit".

We stuttered at first, but soon mastered the couplet, and rode down the Cheltenham turnpike, shouting those delicious, forbidden words, in raucous celebration of adulthood.

We rode south of Cheltenham, on the rising ground, and it seemed that fashionable houses were growing there like elder. The town had doubled in size since our escape from the arms of Jesus. Even so I had no wish to rediscover its delights. We wound through the village of Prestbury, where thatch and timber of the Vale blend with hill stone, as if the cottages cannot decide upon their allegiance, then the monastic calm of Southam de la Bere[56], majestic stone buildings amidst cedar and shaved yew, and sycamore shaded lawns.

Climbing, ever climbing, ever steeper, the lane winding between hill meadows, oak and elm becoming hawthorn and ash, then beech. We were on the coarse turf of the heath now, racing, salt tears in the sharp clean air, hollow thudding hoofbeats as Bewitched flew in an ecstasy of freedom, head stretched out, nostrils flared, across the roof of the Cotswolds. I had no saddle, just my knees to guide her, but there was no contest. Jud and the others were left labouring in pursuit on their working hacks, elephants chasing a gazelle.

At our backs, far below, the blue grey distance of flat plain was broken only by the lump of Chosen Hill, and beyond that, the faint, misting outline of Robinswood. Ahead, as we crested the hill, the green and rounded combes of the Isbourne valley seemed close enough to stroke. We hobbled the horses and lay on our backs watching skylarks climb twittering stairs into the blue. We ate bread and cheese and drank cool green cyder from a leather bottle.

We had been invited to break our journey at Winchcombe, by Mr George Pitt, the man I had met with Jesus. He lived in London but owned Sudeley Castle[57], wherein there was sufficient room for an army to reside. Indeed, a goodly portion of Charles's army had resided there, until Massey's cannons encouraged them to leave. My head has since lain on many a pillow, but seldom have I endured such an eventful night.

There is a sadness about Winchcombe, like an old whore, no longer courted by the rakes, forced to scratch a living in menial service to the bucks that had feted her. Once proud and considerable, host to monarchs and clergy and peers of the realm, she is now mean and sluttish, full of mean and sluttish people. Inns and ale houses abound and the place is festooned with the totems of a society unable to restrain itself. As we approached the town, I saw two gibbets and a working scaffold, and in the main square there is a stone whipping post with four iron loops to clamp the victim's limbs. The pillory can accommodate seven limbs at a sitting, which is one more than Gloucester's; and the ducking stool, at the bottom of Duck Street, seemed more or less in constant use.

The remains of Sudeley Castle are about a half mile from the town, down a lane that crosses the Isbourne by stinking tanyards, where mounds of bloody skins, carpetted with a million fat flies, wait to be scraped and washed.

It is a sombre place. Gaunt, ivy clad, skeletal walls, elder sprouting from the gulleys, a dry moat, garbage strewn and rat infested, sweeping lawns of thistle and wild geranium and mallow; and rooks in the high elms, mournful sentinels of dead glory.

Only the north wing was occupied. A long grim sunless building, thick walls and small windows, it had probably been ignored by Massey; not worthy of his cannon. Under its sagging, neglected roof, was gathered a miscellany of the local fauna.

Where soldiers had billetted and servants had worked, pigs grubbed and sheep wandered and cows were milked and horses stabled. Dogs and cats lazed around the doorways, chicken scratched the bare earth and then searched for grubs in beady watchfulness. Blackbirds were warbling their evensong as we approached, and starlings squabbled in the eaves. The sun had long dropped behind the hills, but the evening was rosy warm, and wasps and bees and hornets and mayflies and crane flies and flashing green blowflies, still buzzed about their business; and as I was to later discover, the rodent population was well represented.

A thin, darting woman, trying to fill a pail from the dried udder of an aged beast, nodded at George's greeting and looked at some steps that led to an upper doorway. We all trooped aloft and found a long attic, white as a winter's morning with pigeon shit, on which had been thrown some straw filled palliasses.

"Welcome to the Hotel Sudeley," said Jud. "I 'ope it rains 'cause I need a barth." I looked at the roof, a chequer board of light sky and dark slate.

"Why's that?" said John Warr. "Winchcombe maids a bit fussy then?" He was a fat youth and he too had a boss eye. When Jud and he conversed, they seemed to face in different directions.

"'ope not for your sake," Tom said, lending support to his brother.

"I got all I need atween me legs. What you got then?" He lunged at Tom's loins.

"Mister Warr, your John's a molly," the familiar defensive whine. "Get 'im off me!" The two rolled in the droppings until Bill Warr lifted them, like potato sacks, and cracked their heads together.

In the brief silence that followed, I noticed the murmur of voices, not raised, just a hum of conversation, from the floor below. And then the smell of cooked food overcame its battle with the essence of pigeon. I sniffed, aware that too many hours had passed since the bread and cheese.

"You lot can roll in shit all night," I said. "I'm starving." I marched down the steps, turned the corner and fell over the outstretched legs of Captain Howell.

"Dear God ish the Mackson Materoni." His grin was unfocused and had lost its wickedness, he bore the expression of a naughty simpleton. He lay on the grass in a group of six similarly garnished rascals, each being cushioned by an ample wench, and surrounded by an orgiastic debris of animal bones and crusts and porter jugs and tobacco pipes. There was a large pile of money in front of the Captain, and now and then he would drop a coin between the scarcely concealed breasts of his pillow, who, with much giggling and wobbling and rearranging, would remove a garment.

Close to this Bacchanalian circle, the centre of which I now occupied, two men clad only in breeches, stockings and buckled boots, were performing a strange and silent dance. Each had his hands on his partner's hard muscled shoulders, and their heads were forward, foreheads touching. One head was shaven, its owner's skin glistening jet. They seemed to be watching each other's feet, as they circled, two scorpions seeking an opening to strike.

Like an adder at a rat Jimmy's boot struck, and with a howl the other man dropped to one knee, rubbing his shin.

"Five t' two the yokel," shouted the Captain. "Who wants fiffy shillings to twenny?" There was no response. "Three t'wun then."

"You cleaned us out already, you bloody pirate." The complaint came from a big bellied sour faced man.

"Watch your tongue, Sam Lucas[58], or Jimmy'll kick your arse." He leered at the nipple that had freed itself by his left eye. "An' if Jimmy kicks your arse you'll be shitting through your nose." He winked grotesquely at me. "John Howell ne'er stole from any man that was not a Frog." He belched. "Or Dutch." He farted. "Except the Spaniards."

"Well then, give us a chance to get our money back," said Sourbelly.

"An even pony the yokel gets his leg bust."

"How long?"

"Ten minutes."

"Done."

Sourbelly was beyond standing, but he struggled up on his elbows. "Tom, come here."

Jimmy's opponent walked across. "Yes father?"

"Now you 'eard the bet. Just stay out of trouble for ten minutes." The young man had worried eyes but he went back to Jimmy and the two squared up.

"Here, Jo, you're the umpire. Hold the stakes an' stop the fight when ten minutes are up. If a man falls, the fight stops an' you must add on the time he takes to square up again." The two gave me twenty five pounds each and a fobwatch.

Joseph Paget, man of consequence, strode to the fighters. "Are you ready?" I gravely eyed each of them. "Steady?" I held the pregnant pause, "Go!"

The two began again their silent stalking dance – a huge four legged beetle, half black half white, hunter and hunted. With a suddenness that made me jump, Jimmy hooked with his right leg, his boot slashing across the space between them, but the young man, his weight on Jimmy's shoulders, danced clear and then kicked the exposed black calf.

The pattern was repeated as the minutes ticked by, and I could see

Sourbelly getting happier as The Captain's frown deepened. The young man was dancing like Noverre[59] and there was desperation in Jimmy's wild kicks, as his Master's threats became ever more malevolent. "Kick him, you great blackpudding, or I'll have your hide for sailcloth".

Another minute went by with no improvement in the Captain's prospects.

"It's his leg or yours." This produced a flurry of kicks, but no contact. I held Sourbelly's big gold fobwatch aloft and called, "Eight minutes gone."

"You've not hit him once, you gelded gorilla. It's the slave ship for you, in the chains I found you in."

Jimmy started a kick with his right, but then hopped as the young man jumped. For a moment both men were in the air. Jimmy landed on his right, which flexed, leaning him to the side and lifting his left like a pissing dog. The young man landed on his right heel, unbalanced, his leg rigid and brittle. Jimmy's boot struck its target with the crack of a bullwhip, and the young man screamed as he rolled over and over, the lower half of his leg flapping. Jimmy knelt by his stricken foe, trying to calm him, pleading with his eyes for forgiveness, but the reaction of the backers was as pitiless as anything I had ever seen.

Captain Howell chortled into his porter and slapped his pillow's ample rump, whilst Sourbelly cursed and oathed, concerned for his money, but not his crippled son.

The evening mauve had deepened and the young man was helped away into the dusk by two weeping women. Most of the rascals had moved into the small room that called itself the Castle Arms, taking the wenches with them. The Captain had reached the slobbering stage, and so I picked up his money to keep it safe until morning, and straightened his legs and put a sack under his head. Sourbelly sat hunched against the wall, head down as though asleep, but watching me through his eyebrows.

The bar was full of the usual collection: red faced, half dressed revellers, too drunk to stand and too packed to fall over. I fought my way past bellies and breasts and all kinds of rumps, until I came upon the Matson troupe. They all seemed to be shouting at once, about nothing in particular, and I deduced that they had been there for some time. A jug of foam was pushed at me, sloshing over my shirt. Bill Warr had just began to sing. His deep baritone was so strong that the revellers fell silent, until the chorus, which they roared as if a thousand strong.

Euw 'appy a theung wur moi wedd'n,

'n 'appier still wur the bedd'n.

If only a farrmur could purrchus a woif,

fur cold winter noits, not the rest of 'is loif.

Chorus

To 'av 'er 'n 'old 'er, from Mickle mus dauy,

till young moids a roipen in April 'n Mauy.

But to 'ave 'er 'n 'ear 'er, when zhe's gett'n fat.

Big us a barrn, 'n grauy as a cat.

GOOD FAITH, MISTER PARSON. EXCUSE ME FROM THAT.

Oh dearo li dearo li dearo li doo.

Fertile ground for George Ridler and his Oven. I battled my way back to the door and out into the cooling night. The Captain's thunderous snoring rumbled around lifeless walls, now shadowed and fearsome, and I found another sack, which I threw across his body.

Around the thick stone corner of the North Wing, the noise was muffled, and the further I ventured the more I was wrapped in stillness. I found Jud sitting on the steps, motionless, watching the eaves. We put faces together and he whispered that an owl was perched under the timbers; I could see the hope in his eyes. I went into the stable, and by feeling my way along the nickering, fidgeting noses, I found Bewitched and patted her neck and tweaked her ears, so that she knew I shared these strange surroundings with her.

There was no light either in our dormitory, so I crawled on the floor until I found a palliasse, where I curled up and slept with the pigeons.

I had no concept of time or place when I awoke in the black stillness. I could see stars far above. A slight pressure on my stomach, as if a hand rested there, made me shrug and move my buttocks and run a finger round the waist band of my breeches. I stiffened in horror as I felt the soft furry flank of a rat scuttle up my chest and past my face. In the screaming, leaping panic that followed I was not to know that I owed my life to that rat. For, as I erupted, Sourbelly Lucas, grunting with rage, lunged at me with a butcher's knife. Another minute and he would have slit my throat at his leisure.

I stumbled across the floor until my head cracked on a beam, and then I crawled into a nook between the rafters. Sourbelly was crashing unaccompanied around the room and I concluded that my friends and protectors had deserted me for crapulence and a grass billet, in my hour of greatest need.

The crashing stopped. Silence, save the rasping breath of my pursuer. He was near and sensed his prey. The fox to the rabbit.

"C'mon out boy, I'll not harm thee. I just want my money."

I felt as I had behind the tree on Cooper's Hill, mortally afraid and sure that he could hear my thumping heart. Closer now, under the beam, crawling. I could smell the ale on his breath. "There's no need for fear boy, I've put down the knife. You shall just hand me the money and I'll leave."

I tried to push myself deeper into the nook and my shoulder dislodged a slate which slid, with grating, rattling clatter, down the slope of the roof. I might just as well have lit a lantern to advertise my presence.

"Well now, boy," he was beside me, but I could only smell him. "The money." Growling, full of menace. "Quick now, or I'll open your throat."

He must have grabbed at me in the dark, for his open hand hit my face, pushing me into the tiles and rotted timbers, so that my head crashed through to the night sky. He grabbed again as I kicked, this time finding my arm. In an avalanche of slates and choking dust, I fought with the fury of terror, kicking and flailing and screaming for help. He bellowed with pain as my boot found his soft underbelly. He lunged at me in savage, uncontrolled rage and we toppled from the eaves, falling, floating – a wrestling, writhing dive into a pitch black void.

We hit the ground still locked in our embrace, and the snap of his thigh bone was sharp and clear. To me it was as if landing on a cushion: my knees in his belly, an elbow in his neck, and my forehead with great force, on his broad fleshy nose.

And that is how we were found. The youth, unharmed save a few scratches, astride his bloodied and senseless foe. I was accorded a reputation that night, as a brave and ferocious fighter. I suspect that many reputations, in many walks of life, are gained by similar, fortuitous paths.

We left early in the morning, George Holyoake's waxen face and rosy eyes bearing witness to the night's excesses. We rode north east from Winchcombe, along a lane between banks of bluebell and cowslip and kingcups by a stream, then tall hedges of blackthorn and wild roses, winding down the valley beneath the escarpment. Bill Warr told that this was the path the King had walked in penance, five hundred years before, when he and his Queen, and the peers and bishops of the Realm, had buried Edmund. And along this same path, a million pilgrims had since come, to the monastery of the Holy Blood[60].

In a meadow scattered with oaks there is a sight to pierce the heart of any believer, for the great Abbey of Hailes, once the shrine of the most sacred relic in the Kingdom, has been reduced to an abandoned ruin of broken walls and solitary arches. It is as if the people of Winchcombe, not content with defiling each other, had conspired to desecrate these wondrous buildings that dared to proclaim the majesty of God. I must own that here I publish not my views, but those of Bill Warr, who was singularly moved by the pitiful scene. He rode down two men removing quoin stones, and then whipped them across the fields and through a thorn hedge to Didbrook, although they were clearly doing no more than a thousand had before them.

We bought cheese and bread and tart rough cyder from a cottage at Hailes and then climbed the escarpment. Bewitched pranced through beechwoods, pale green gossamer leaves of early summer, trembling in the soft airs, and out onto the uplands, to once again show her heels to all pursuers. We passed the quarries at Stumps Cross, where men are digging away the bowels of the hill, then followed Campden Lane to lose ourselves in the timeless stone country of the lonely Cotswolds.

No hedgerows here, just dry stone walls racing away to the fluent horizon, stone posts, massive, permanent, mottled with lichens, stone granaries balanced on staddle stones, stone barns and stone aviaries, and pretty stone cottages tucked from the wind into the folds and combes of the landscape. It is a limestone world, sharing nothing with the warm damp Severn shore, save oneness with this most diverse of shires.

The sounds are different, for here above the sighing wind, there is naught but bleating, ever bleating, of the Cotswold Lion[61], and the hoarse chorus of a million rooks. The people too. For these hills have bred an insular folk, bound by the toil of barren fields. Not for them, the latitude a great river brings, the mixed blood of a moving population, the colours and tastes of foreign lands. They are defensive, wary of visitors, and as shrewd as Scotch Jews.

And yet for all its wild and lonely miles, this Cotswold country does not slumber. We passed quarries and sawmills, manor farms hewn from the ground upon which they stand, shepherds and shearers, and drovers with long laden mule trains heading for the Thames and the greedy markets of London.

Campden is a shy town. She hides in a deep combe between two rolling hills, shrinking from the multitudes that engulf her at Whitsun, an English lady tolerating her violation by the hordes, as only an English lady can. Many travellers, intent upon their destination, hurry along the great Roman highways, Fosse Way and Icknield Street, which pass east and west of the town, without realising that in truth these wolds are mother of pearl, and in their depths lies a perfect jewel.

All the subtleties of Cotswold architecture are assembled in this warm honeystone town of handsome houses and green banks. Cottages and cool dark alleys, respectable gabled residences, majestic medieval halls, all stand to attention along a wide curving street, that leads to the haughty church of St James, aloof, apart, as if disdaining the Bacchanalian scenes below.

The town was awash with people. It was as if the surrounding hills had been drained of life and every serf and peasant, every child and youth, every farmer and his wife had flowed like logs down the Cam, to jam in the High Street. A clamour of human sound hung over the town, chattering and laughing and shouting and cheering; and at the centre, by the Market Hall, were gathered a throng of the queerest folk I had ever seen.

There were men dressed as geese and others as donkeys, buxom nymphs in garlands of flowers ushered by a pack of lusting, leering clowns. There were fiddlers in red hats and bagpipers in green, and all around, spruce lads and lasses, sporting yellow ribbons on their hats and bells on their legs. Tom Fool was there too, a shrunken dwarf in tricorn hat with a bladder on a stick. He waved this loathsome object at Bewitched who shied in terror, or perhaps it was horror, for the bladder was of equine proportion.

The focal point of this ragbag was a haycart bearing a gilded throne, upon which sat the Queen of the May, a fair tressed, red faced, plumply pretty lass, who watched me calm Bewitched, then gave me a smile I felt in my loins.

It is my experience that gatherings of this sort seem unable to function without the services of a self elected windbag, a human starling that chatters endlessly about nothing, and preens fine feathers for the perceived worship of its fellows. These birds are invariably short, thus needing a perch from which to sing; pompous, thus needing singular plumage; and obtuse, thus able to ignore ribaldry from the suffering audience. Edmund Postlethwaite, broom maker of Calf's Lane, was the nonpareil of windbags.

He appeared through the arches of the Market Hall, to the massed groans of his public, astride a broad white cob, so broad that his short legs resembled a second pair of arms, leaving his waist at right angles. He was bedecked in a plumed and flowered King Charles hat, which he doffed and waved to acknowledge his worshippers, and a suit of clothes that might have been discarded by Shakespeare. Ruffs and frills and voluminous pantaloons, they would have lent realness to these ancient proceedings, had they not been tailored for a much larger man.

I can recall nothing of his monologue, save that he welcomed us, exhorted us, warned us, and took nothing short of an hour to do it. The wait was made tolerable by the rustic courtship of my overweight queen.

At last the procession began and, in a confused noise of drums and trumpets and fiddles and pipes, the entire assembly shouted its way down the High Street. I stayed in the vanguard, encouraging Bewitched to prance romantically whenever Her Plumpness glanced my way. But many, including a few Holyoakes, paused for refills at each inn we passed.

At the corner of Hoo Lane stood a solitary preacher imploring the marchers to forsake the Devil. He had been pelted with so much dung that I suspected his true motive was to collect manure for the kitchen garden.

We climbed out of the town, into the sun bright, spring green, wind smooth meadows, leaving behind the blackbirds in their blossomed orchards, and higher still to the rim of the scarp. Here is the edge of Gloucestershire, her northern rampart, where she pokes her nose into the soft heart of England, from where the great rivers spring, to flow down the veins of this fortunate land. East, beyond Campden, flows the Stour, which feeds the Avon, which marries the Severn; and south, the first waters of the infant Thames, gurgle from the limestone hills.

There was such a gathering on these hills. Scattered across the wide acres were booths and tents and huts, and little spaces enclosed by straw bales, where hawkers hawked and pedlars peddled and gamesters preyed. There were stages erected for contests, courses laid out for races, even a castellated tower had been built on the highest point, but I doubted that war was going to break out. I hobbled Bewitched, so that she could graze but not wander, and joined the tide of humanity that surged and eddied through this transient town. Every colour I had ever seen, every smell I had ever smelled, every noise I had ever heard, poured over me in a pandemonium, drowning me, sweeping me away on a jumbling tide, so that for two hours I was jostled and bumped and kicked and cuddled to every corner of this rollicking carnival.

I watched bloodied cudgel fights and pike handling: pitching the bar, where great whiskered men, with arms the size of bellies and bellies the size of firkins, scattered tree trunks like chaff; shin kicking, where I cheered hoarse for the Winchcombe team; and coursing. But I could not share the glee with which the crowd greeted dismemberment of the hare.

I grinned through the horse's collar and won a toffee apple. I danced a passable jig and won a straw hat. I drank some gin, for which I cared not, and ate plum cake for which I cared greatly. In my literal innocence I thought I had deflowered a giggling nymph; although in truth I tweaked her twice and stole a few petals from her garland. And above all, I shared with that happy band of strutting swains and flaunting maids, the bountiful joy of being young.

Presently I found George Holyoake and Bill Warr lying on the grass by a wrestling ring, from which sweat and gore spewed in grunting spurts. They were betting with a walleyed villain, and wore the puzzled frowns of drunken men who cannot recall what has happened to their money. My approach seemed to lighten their load.

"Jo," said George, struggling to his feet, "where's that pony of yours? We think she might save our bacon."

"You leave Bewitched alone. She's mine and no one's having her."

"But Jo," now Bill Warr. "We got no money left. No money, no bed. No money, no food. It's twenty miles to Matson, you can have the pick of the farm ponies when we get home."

"Why Bewitched?" I felt the salt in my eyes. "Why not your horses? You lost the money."

"This gentleman wants her for his daughter." Walleye smirked and bobbed his head. "He will pay us twenty guineas."

I was desolate. I wept and pleaded and howled, for all to know the injustice that was being done to me, but George held sway. I led them to where I had hobbled Bewitched and watched with wretched grief as they loosened her fetters. She snickered with pleasure and sniffed the air. When she saw me, she tried to walk to me, but Bill Warr jerked her leading rein. I could have told him that Bewitched was a lady of breeding, used to courtesy and good manners. She planted her forelegs and raised her head in imperious contempt. Walleye grabbed the rein and tugged again, rough, irritable, and swore at her.

He would have been better advised swearing at Queen Charlotte. In regal and ferocious splendour, Bewitched reared; climbing into the air, flaring nostrils, snapping teeth, scything hooves. The rein was ripped from Walleye's grasp, and he was hit with a fetlock that would have floored Jack Broughton.

Bill Warr tried to run, but fell over the prostrate Walleye, and George backed into the heap. Bewitched completed her tour de force by raising her tail and shedding a plopping, steaming rebuke to her tormentors.

She cantered to me, looking smug, and although I surmised that her intended purchaser had lost enthusiasm, I mounted her and rode up the hill, away from trouble. There I found the younger set watching horse races, and they were clearly enjoying better reward than their fathers. Tom had just betted the winner of the farmers race at ten to one and Stephen Warr had a wad of banknotes like a slice of Hannah's cake. They too were pleased to see me.

"Fancy yerself as a jock, Jo?"

"Reckon y'could stay aboard f'ra mile?"

Windbag Postlethwaite, still in full flow, was seeking entries for the pony race. He bawled his message from the ramparts: one mile, open to allcomers not exceeding fourteen two, winner to receive a gold ring and a pair of embroidered silk gloves. Bill Warr and George, shamefaced, but happier in the knowledge of their sons' improved circumstances, had joined us, and Bill said, "Go on, Jo. I reckon you could win."

Thus I took a further step down the ladder of the profligate pit.

There were ten entries, mostly screws and pack ponies. A sway backed, parrot mouthed bunch of proppies, if John Warr's opinion was to be relied upon, but two took the eye.

Were looks to win the race, the showy sorrell mare, topped by a proud and fiery girl – leather boots, laced breeches, tulip silk blouse, willowy whip – would come home alone. But Bill Warr told me to watch the fat buttocked galloway and its fat buttocked yokel, who carried a stick and looked as if he meant to use it.

There was a betting post by the start and most of the farmers wanted odds about the yokel. Walleye had recovered and was in the thick, asking for evens. "Come along, you sporting gentlemen," he shouted. "There's ten runners, ten chances, an' all I want is evens about the yokel."

Earnest conversation between the Holyoakes and Warrs resulted in Bill's hat being filled with banknotes by disgruntled offspring. George Holyoake marched to the post, big, brave, confident.

"'E's four to seven with me." He disappeared in a forest of outstretched arms, all clutching cash. "Easy now, you'll all get on." He took a few bets, which Tom noted. "One to two now, gents." Still it rained money.

"Two to five this good thing."

Bill Warr was preparing us, stroking necks, tickling ears, patting rumps, giving me orders. "Just remember, you've no saddle, so knees in, arse out, take a sight between her ears, and look nowhere else. Don't use the reins, just hold them. Steer her with your knees, push her with your hips. Rhythm and balance. Rhythm and balance. Treat her like a lady. Roger her if she needs it, but be gentle."

I cantered to the start and heard Walleye call five to one Bewitched.

The course was oval shaped, along the top of the hill, sloping up to the north, with sharp turns at each end. It was marked by a stake every chain, with a furlong pole as the tenth. We lined up by Windbag's tower and he held a flag aloft.

"I want you to form a line, and then walk forward. When the flag drops, the race has begun".

I steadied Bewitched and patted her neck. We all watched Windbag, save the yokel, who was watching me. The sorrell mare was on her toes, the girl still and tense, but as the flag dropped she whirled into action and slipped the field, before the rest of us could draw breath.

The yokel cracked his stick across the galloway's rump, and after a furlong, was overhauling the girl. Bewitched, eager, straining, ears pricked, eyes darting, wanted to follow, but I eased her into the pack and even then she stumbled at the first bend. Down the back straight, past the six pole, then the five, Bewitched taking hold, my knees a vice on her ribs, forcing her way out of the pack, lengthening her stride, shrinking the gap, closing with the leaders, the sorrell on the rails, the galloway at her shoulder. I tried not to become transfixed by the slim arse above the sorrell, but John Warr had told me to sight through the ears, and the only other vision was that of a small fat arse on a big fat arse, a flying cottage loaf. I was with them before the four, but I eased her, giving them a length, letting them race each other.

Round the bottom bend, steering with my knees, the girl was beginning to work, pushing hard with long thin arms; the yokel, still at her shoulder, plenty in hand. Into the finishing straight now, uphill, three furlongs, the yokel going on, the girl kicking, slapping, not giving up. At the two, the yokel a length up, looking over his left shoulder, seeing the girl still there, cracking the heaving quarters with all his might. I saw the ears flatten, the tail swirl, as the galloway felt the pain. The girl switched to the outside, coming again, the sorrell's neck stretched, eyes bulging red.

I saw my chance and went for the inside gap. I still had a handful. At the furlong the girl and I were level, half a length down, either side of the yokel. He must have been expecting me on his right, for though he still had the beating of the sorrell, when it got to his boots he slashed its nose hard, once, twice, and then cracked the girl across the face. I was through, a length up, two, three, hands and heels, ears pricked, arse out, knees in, rhythm and balance, rhythm and balance.

The winner was greeted with sparse applause, save from a septet of wild buffoons, who whooped and shrieked and hullabalooed enough to wake old Dover. I dismounted from Bewitched, and at that moment, had she been Eclipse[62], I could not have loved her better.

The bets were settled, my prizes collected, an offer of seventy-five guineas for Bewitched refused, and Bill Warr, sprouting bank notes from every pocket, called us together. "We are now in some danger", we huddled around him. "We are eight, but there are gangs of villains on this hill, upwards of two hundred strong. By now they will all know the result of the pony race, and every horse thief in Campden will be after Bewitched."

Up to that moment, I had been basking in a glow of congratulation and such unwelcome thoughts were a pail of cold water. I looked around for Bewitched, frightened, suddenly aware of the dangers, but she was grazing where I had left her.

"And they will all know to the guinea, how much we've won," Bill continued.

"How much have we won?" I asked.

"I reckon we've more than five hundred pound here. Whoever won what, it's an eight way split." I still had Captain Howell's wad. With all this money, and the County's finest pony, I concluded that my hide was under threat.

"Let's go home".

"*Home*?" they chorused.

Young George spoke, "Well you can go 'ome if you like. Me, I've got a few quarts to drink, an' a maid or two to tup."

"We'd 'ave to ride all night, an' that'd be worse than stayin' 'ere," said Bill. "We'll be right as long as we stay together."

"All night?" George's plans did not include the rest of us.

"All night."

"Well, that'll be 'andsome. What are you goin' to do, stand at the foot of the bed an' watch?"

"Wouldn't want to watch you anyway," said Tom. "Jane down at Larkham says you're no bloody good." Stephen Warr went red. "That ol' scrubber's got one like an' 'orses collar. She wouldn't know a good shag from a ride on Arthur." Stephen was purpling, and he jutted his jaw. George and Tom continued their defamation of his beloved.

"I thought you was sweet on 'er."

"Sweet on 'er? I'd sooner shag a sheep." Stephen clenched his hairy fists.

"What's it like? They tell me you've 'ad 'er a few times."

"Not bad," said Tom. "Long as you mind she's bin dipped. There's nothin' worse than a tick in yer tool."

"Bet it don't 'urt like 'er teeth."

In a whirling fury of fists and boots, Stephen, who had long worshipped, in dreams, the virginal Jane, launched himself at George. Disfigurement of the beauteous profile was his aim, a kicked arse from his father his reward.

I have recorded this piddling quarrel at some length because of the effect the emnity between Stephen and George was to have upon my fortunes that night.

"We've two rooms reserved at the Green Dragon", said Bill and we'll pay the ostler to put a guard on the horses. George an' me will sleep with the young'uns, and the rest on yer can fight an' fornicate all night for all I care. I'll keep the money safe until we get back to Matson."

Before we left the hill we watched the ladies' race for the prize of an embroidered shift, which Windbag held aloft and waved from his ramparts, and felt inside and lewdly winked. Six girls tucked skirts into drawers and lined up at the start. There are milestones in our youth which mark significant steps in the mysterious journey to manhood. I first enjoyed that most pleasurable of sensations – ogling, lip smacking lust – at that exhibition of twelve pink thighs, tensed, primed for action, crouched for combat.

One pair of thighs stood out from the rest: great honeyed hams of blushing milk, smooth, powerful, libidinous loins. I sat on the grass, squirming in wonder, transfixed by desire. I saw her buttocks beneath the gathered skirts, plump and naked, submissive to my manhood, her broad back, damp and downy, her pendulous plums, ripe and fat, full of the juice of life. Her long fair hair was tied back with a ribbon and her plumply pretty face smiled at me, then poked out the tip of a strawberry tongue.

"If you don't bed that tonight," said Jud, who was laying on his belly next to me, chin in his hands, stalk in his mouth, "it's the molly 'ouse for you."

"Don't be daft," I said. "She's the Queen of the May."

"There's no *may* about it. She's a certainty."

The race was won by a long limbed lass, tall, straight as young elder. My baggage came in last. Whatever her name, and I never did find out, I christened her Dawn there and then, for her face was a morning pink sun, round and happy, and her brow, and her chin, and her bare shoulders, and her legs, had been kissed all over with dew.

Windbag eagerly helped the winner to don her shift and presented ribbons to the also rans, which he insisted on fastening to their chests. He fumbled several times, and when he reached Dawn, his hands were shaking, and he was forced to put them inside her blouse, to protect her titties from the pin.

She dawdled to where we sat, smiling, watching me sidelong, tongue on teeth. "You stayin' in Camden tonight?"

"W..w..why, yes, m..m..miss." I must have sounded like Jesus. "We have rooms at the Green Dragon."

"Might see you there, then."

I felt Jud's elbow in my ribs and heard him snigger. She took the loose end of ribbon that hung from her breast, and sucked it. "There be cockin' tonight. I like the cockin'. D'you?"

Jud burst. "'e loves the cockin' miss," snorting like a porker in a trough.

"Might see you there, then." My plump paramour left us rolling in the ground, as I tried to force grass down Jud's throat.

We rode back to Campden, the gang of eight, watchful, fearful of pursuit – Stephen and George sulking each side of the lane – and stabled the horses at the Green Dragon. It is a large and comfortable stone building, with mullioned windows that overlook the High Street. It has an industrious yard, with stables and saddlery and livery and coach houses, and brew house and malt house and wash house and bake house. There is even a rope factory, where fat drums of hemp and flax unwind slowly at one end, and snakes of cord and twine wriggle from the other. By the back lane, set apart, shunned by the rest, stands a round squat windowless building, devoid of any features, save a door, and a drain for the blood that is spilt therein. For this is the slaughter house by day, and the cockpit by night.

Bill Warr paid the ostler and gave us five sovereigns each. "I shall hide the rest", he said, "'an you'll get no more till we're at Matson". This stricture was ill received by the brothers, but arguing with the big farmer was not to be undertaken lightly. We spent the darkening hours quaffing Whitsun Ales in the Live and Let Live, then the Kettle, then the Rose and Crown and the Barley Mow. When we regained the Green Dragon, the door was smaller. At least it seemed a damned sight harder to pass through.

A banquet was in full and riotous swing: red faces gorging red meat and swilling red claret; big bellies, big arses, and big bouncers on the serving wenches, that seemed to fall out at random. I concluded that Mr Hogarth must have come to Dover's Games and sketched a cartoon on this very spot. We ate beef and plenty of it, and then repaired to the Pit, where a main of cocks, between Gloucester and Warwick, was about to commence.

I have to report that I find the spectacle of cock fighting no more uplifting than the blood letting at Over. But the gambling is another matter altogether.

There is a circular stage inside the Pit, about twelve feet in diameter with a cross at its centre, over which hangs a chandelier of candles. At the apex of the roof is a cage about four feet square, attached to a system of pullies and weights. There are seats by the stage for the gamblers and principals, and there is a raised platform around the wall for onlookers. Only the gamecocks are allowed on the stage, with their handler, who is termed the cocker.

We squeezed on to the packed platform amongst a murmur of voices, hushed, expectant, eager for blood. But first Windbag Postlethwaite had his way: "My Lords, ladies and gentlemen, tonight we offer you a Welsh main, between the honourable houses of Gloucester and Warwick. Ten guineas a battle and one hundred guineas the main. All bets to be settled before the next contest begins. All welshers," and he looked to the hanging contraption, "to be caged. The first bout between Izod's gray and the Lyttleton duckwing."

Two cockers, bearing linen bags alive with kicking, struggling contents, came to the stage. With practiced hands, they produced the cocks, as a conjuror would a rabbit. The sight of these proud and furious birds stilled the crowd, for these were no dunghill cocks. Thin heads with full eyes, wicked, crooked beaks, long thick necks and short hard bodies. But it was their bearing that took the attention. Stout thighs, placed well up the shoulders, and thick yellow legs gave them an upright gait, stately, almost regal. Sharpened steel spurs had been strapped to the hind part of their legs, but otherwise they were strangely devoid of ostentation. Bill Warr explained that they were in fighting trim. Their combs had been sliced off, necks scraped, wings clipped to sharp points and tails short.

The cockers held the birds at the centre cross, beak to beak, firing their beligerance, feeding their hostility, until they quivered with rage. The betting began and seven to four on the duckwing was taken all round by a tall, arrogant buck, wigless, with dark fine habit and shifting eyes. Bill Warr whispered that this was the Honourable Thomas Lyttleton, and I recalled the name of the man whose word had noosed the Welsh Dissenter.

A referee called for the cockers to ready, and then a whistle blew and the birds were released. Slow at first, but in magnificent rage, they stalked each other around the mark, exotic warriors in a ritual display. Breathless quiet around the Pit, waiting, waiting. Then there was an explosion of fury, slashing, screeching, scratching fury, as they ripped at each other with beak and claw, and flashing, razored spur. The crowd bayed, shouted, urging, as if the fighters were human, as if Pirate was maiming the Bull. Blood spurted, feathers flew. And then the gray was down, jerking, flapping, its chest gashed open, its eyes dulled.

The duckwing was held, then carried aloft from the arena, to the cheers and huzzas of his backers. The gray's cocker collected his charge and with a practiced twisting pull snapped its neck.

And so proceeded these cruel diversions: eight contests, then the winners were matched in four more bouts, then two, and finally the Battle Royal, so that only one bird lived to fight another day. I would have left, were it not for the Gloucester cocker in the third bout. It was a young woman, fair tressed and buxom, and as she crouched to set to her red pyle bird, I saw again the shape that had made me squirm on Dover's Hill.

Even I cheered as her bird won its contest, by pecking the eyes of the black red from Leamington. It won its second bout, and third, although feathers flew about the ring like snowflakes. The Lyttleton duckwing too had beaten all comers, but when the two were put to the mark for the Battle Royal, they were more dead than alive. Dawn's bird was cut almost to mincemeat and the duckwing had lost an eye. But when they were set to, their loathing for one another was such that from unplumbed depths in their small frames they summoned the will to fight to death.

The duckwing finally succumbed, and I saw the Honourable Thomas strut from the Pit, his face contorted with anger. The victor was left blinded, gashed, matted with blood, and fit for little but boiling. He was carried aloft and cheered and feted, as if he had defeated the French. When his backers had done, and were streaming back to the drinking, Dawn sat on the side of the stage with the exhausted bird on her lap. I approached her. Just the two of us remained in that house of death.

"I saw you watching," she said. "I 'ope you 'ad a bet."

"Five guineas," I lied. She handed me a jug.

"Can you fill that for me?"

"Where's the water?"

"Not water, you gert daft lummox. I need 'ot yourin[63], an' I don't think I got none." She was parting the bird's feathers, exposing the wounds. "'urry up". I turned my back to undo my breeches. "You don't 'ave to 'ide it, I seen 'undreds afore. Any roads I don't expect there's much to 'ide." I turned and faced her. She was sucking a wound on the bird's neck, and she watched me through its feathers as I half filled the jug. She spat and then gently licked the ripped flesh with her wet strawberry tongue, her eyes still on me as I shook the drops. "More'an I expected," she murmured.

I was rock hard. It was the blood stained mouth that did it. And the insolent, lusting eyes. And the overfilled blouse. And the thought of those libidinous loins. I was on her in an instant. The poor flapping gamecock cast to the floor, the skirts drawn like curtains, the drawers ripped from their moorings. It is somehow appropriate that my first consummation was on a stage, for I have recently been told by an obliging friend that my powers in this regard deserve an audience. Whether in farce, tragedy or heroic drama, she did not make clear.

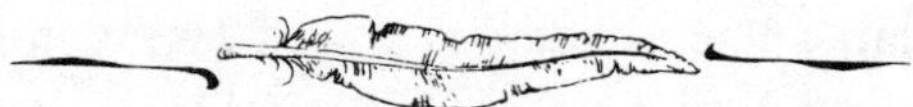

During the three minutes it took to reach manhood, my spirits rose even faster than my sap. And when I left the Cockpit, they had never been higher. I was a man. I had left a girl with shining eyes and what more did a man have to do? But in the following three minutes, they dropped further and faster than a whore's drawers. For my face was grasped from behind by a ham of a fist, evil smelling and hairy. A snake like whisper told me that any sound would result in a knife in my gizzard. I was bound tight with cord, gagged with a bloody rag, and thrown, there is no other word, thrown into a black void. I am indebted to Jud Holyoake for the following information.

The Holyoakes and Warrs had retired from the Pit, leaving me to my inauguration. They had fallen to giggling at the bar over Jud's observation, that Jo 'had to be up at the crack of dawn'. Walleye and an even more sinister companion had engaged George Holyoake and told him that I was in protective custody, and could be exchanged for the afternoon's winnings. Stephen Warr and Tom Holyoake were for immediate retreat, but the rest thought my hide worth saving.

Whilst Bill Warr was away getting the money, the feud between Stephen and young George erupted into violence. They rolled on the floor, breaking tables and pots, they kicked and they scratched and they bit and they punched. George ran through the door with the righteous Stephen in pursuit, and down the yard they crashed and yelled and swore and spat.

John Warr caught them up and, in trying to restrain them, was punched in the mouth. He responded in kind and then there were three in the fracas. Round the yard they went with frenzied momentum, collecting bodies, first Tom, then George senior, even Bill Warr joined the mayhem. Jud followed their progress from a respectable distance, into the stables, horses whinnying, neighing, rearing in their stalls, the ostler shouting unheeded abuse, into the brewhouse, bottles and pots smashing, a river of ale through the doorway, and then the wash house where I lay, bound and bloodied, on the floor.

It was George senior that spied me, thrown in a dismal corner with the dirty linen, as he was trying to drown his eldest son in the boiler. The discovery stilled them, reminded them of Walleye, and the threat to their money. I was untied, and we huddled around Bill Warr.

"Keep fighting," he whispered, "and make way slowly back to the stables. I'll take Jud and Jo and we'll untie the horses. When we're all in, grab your horse and don't stop till you're in Matson."

Under a huge white hunter's moon, we raced twenty miles across the silver wolds, stopping to rest in slumbering beech coppices, descending Cleeve as the black valley greyed, and was then washed pink by the coming day. We returned to Matson tattered and torn, like a troupe of Jacobites the day after Culloden[64].

Chapter Six

Just north of the tribal city of Venta Belgarvm[65], where the roads from Sorviodvnvm and Calleva, and Noviomagvs and Corinium meet, the Itchen turns south and enters a broad flat valley of rich water meadows. It must have been a mighty river once, for the bed of the valley would take the Thames. The tiny Itchen is so confused by the vastness of the watercourse, that she splits into a hundred rivulets, as a shower on a window, crossing and recrossing in a whimsical journey to the sea.

We had followed the Roman legions from Glevum, Captain Howells, Elizabeth and I, with Jimmy riding post, and a liveried coachman. Across the wild wolds and high plains that feed the Thames, Ermine Street runs straight and true, sixty miles south east to Calleva. We turned south at Wanborough, where the chalk downs of Wiltshire begin, and retired early and sober in the Castle Inn at Marlborough.

I rose early on a noisy market morning, and walked along the grand street from St Peter's church to St Mary's; which glare at each other from either end, as if competing for sinners. I reflected that these Wiltshire folk must be in perpetual awe of Our Lord, for wherever one stands in that pretty town, He frowns from His towers on the smallest indiscretion.

A short detour to see the Wansdyke[66], then through the Royal forest of Savernake, where to my disappointment we saw not a footpad nor a highwayman. Captain Howell said they were probably hiding behind the trunks looking for easier prey. I had to concede that the sight of Jimmy, blunderbuss in one hand and pistol in the other, would have given Turpin second thoughts.

Then came the rolling rounded chalk downs: broad rhythmic land, swelling and flowing to far horizons, and our road, unerringly straight from hilltop to hilltop, discordant among the harmonies of these hills. Finally, with the westering sun on our backs, down long gentle slopes to the dark earth of Hampshire.

Can there be another corner of this world where landscape and flora mix with such infinite variety, in such limited space? It is as if Mother Nature keeps a closet wherein are all the powders and pomades and rouges and dyes that enhance her beauty. Her jewels too, scattered around the packed shelves, and exotic perfumes hanging on the air, and sumptuous dresses of silks and brocades in rainbows of colour – summer riot, autumn hue, winter stark, spring fresh. Our short journey, but a fraction of the length of this island, took us through three countries, three landscapes, three shades of green: yellow green Cotswold fallow, blue green Wiltshire distance, deep green Hampshire plenty.

On the banks of the Itchen, a few miles south of Winchester, at the end of a half mile avenue of limes, stands Brambridge House, seat of Walter Smythe Esquire and home of the Kingdom's most beauteous object. It is a modern house, symetrical and elegant, in the style of Nash and Adam, and the parks and farmlands that it commands stretch as far as the eye can see.

My heart galloped faster than the hooves as we cantered down the drive twixt towering limes. I leaned from the carriage to see the house grow as we approached: first a doll's house framed in trees, then the chimneys and uniform rows of windows, then the raised terrace and pillars of the verandah, then soft lawns shaded by giant cedars, then a figure in a flashing red dress, calling and waving and running towards us.

I have described previously in these journals heartstopping, breathtaking encounters with Maria. But that afternoon at Brambridge I knew the adoration of a lap dog for its mistress. Had I a tail I would have wagged it in frenzy, had she offered her hand I would have licked it, had she beaten me I would have been transported with pleasure.

I also knew, in a stab of wretched perception, that she might never be mine. For she was a woman. A high breasted, full hipped, dew eyed, honey lipped woman. The lustful wink bestowed upon her by the Captain, and the coquetry with which it was received, were strident alarms to both Elizabeth and I.

In a welter of kissing and hugging and handshaking and formal bowing, we met the Smythes young and old. They had gathered on the lawn in their Catholic profusion: Maria's parents, brothers and sister, grandmother and several cousins. A large dark severe man was announced as Edward Weld. Each of the three men – Walter Smythe, the Captain and Edward Weld – shared the intimacy that comes from long acquaintance. When the introductions were complete, they moved apart from us, a knot of deep conversation that brooked no intrusion.

Later when tea and cakes were served on the lawn we chattered and laughed, the two Elizabeths joyous in each other's company, the three men loud and jocular, the brothers and cousins competing, like any family, for attention. I listened to Maria in wrapt silence. She told me of her school in France, of serene nuns and cool cloistered calm, of Paris, of sophistication, of noblemen, even of Louis XV, who had caught her eye at a banquet and sent her a dish of sugar plums and a single red rose. She had told her parents of the sugar plums but I alone knew of the rose.

"*Et tu, mon cher, ca va*?" She laughed at my discomfort. "*Tu est un sot, un garcon hebete*". She prattled in this strange tongue and I could but marvel at her gifts. Chestnut curls tumbled around her long lashed, pretty nosed, laughing mouthed, perfect face. I noticed that although she spoke only to me, her eyes would flicker to her father's two friends, and theirs to her.

Maria had a sister and four brothers, all younger than her, and I was to sleep with Wat and Jack. Unlike the sisters who had inherited their Mother's slenderness, they were big boned overweight youths, saplings of their Father's seed. They seemed amiable enough. After I had washed and dressed, on Jack's advice in boots and canvas breeches and coarse shirt, that had been laid upon my bed, we stepped out to explore the grounds. And I entered the moist, muddy, magical world of an English river.

Beyond the lawns at the back of the house runs the Itchen, crossed by a lichened stone bridge that leads to the Navigation. Between the two streams is an island, a sliver of land, twenty yards wide but more than a mile in length: a wet wild wilderness of tangled willow and thick grasses, of worts and mosses, of bright fragrant orchids and ragged robin, and pools and thick marshy turf wherein lurk newts and frogs and fat lazy toads.

From dawn to dusk I spent the days that followed in that acquatic Eden. Not the Smythes, not the Howells, not even Maria could find a place in my mind as we stood on the bridge for hour upon hour, tossing bread and watching trout rise in silver ripples on glossy water. We put meat in jars and held them on strings, to trap fierce red sticklebacks that stared malevolently at us from their glass prison. In the golden evening, when wood pigeons murmured to their mates in the high elms, and cows lowed across water meadows, and dragonflies glittered in and out of sunbeams on the limpid river, we sat on Jack's legs, still as statues, while he leant out over the stream.

With fingers spidering like a moving crab, he would slowly put his hand into the water, deeper and deeper until his shoulder was submerged. Not a movement, not a breath. Then in a sudden splashing fountain that never failed to knock me flat, he would jerk upright and throw his hand high. Usually he caught nothing but water, but twice a wildly flapping trout flew through the air to land on the bank, where it lay in open mouthed astonishment.

As the evening dimmed, our return to the house, happy as only bedraggled boys can be, was greeted with horror by the ladies, humour by the men and disdain from Maria. She was at pains to ignore me, but snorted when I seemed not to notice. When I did notice, she engaged Edward Weld in banter, fluttering and teasing and allowing me the merest glance. She was not to know then of the desires hidden within this joyless man[67].

On the far side of the island, opposite the bridge, is a lock, a deep brick lined pond with thick tarred gates at each end, where the level of the Navigation is raised and lowered to allow barges to pass. The gates are operated by oak beams, a foot square, that extend out over the towpath; their sluices by a ratchet that is cranked up to let the trapped waters escape downstream. We would perch on the beams, straining to hear the jingling brasses and slow plodding tread of the great white shires that pull boats from Southampton to Winchester. When they hove into view, we would stand to our stations and wait for the bargee to guide his long black loaded hulk into the lock. Sweating and straining, as if labourers on a shilling an hour, we would close the gates, then run to the top end to fight for the honour of the sluice handle, dogs chasing a bone.

When a downstream barge passed through, the traps below the bottom gates writhed with slippery eels, which Jack caught and held by the tail, till they tied a knot in themselves and expired.

Close to the lock, a cut led to a boat house large enough to store a brig. A wherry was moored inside and a small skiff. I was puzzled as to the need for such a structure, for it was at least twenty yards square, with eaves as high as three men. The roof timbers were buttressed as though they were used to support a hoist. There was a curious wooden assemblage, leaning against the wall at the far end, a rectangular timber frame, about twenty feet by ten, with a shallow planked hull. I first assumed that it was some kind of raft, used for cutting weeds; but in the course of a game I crawled behind it to hide from the others, to find the underside felted and festooned with lumps of coal. They were of such density that the entire surface was covered and the whole resembled an inverted fuel heap.

I asked Wat to explain. He winked at Jack and told me to mind my business. Later I asked Captain Howell, who seemed irritated by my question, but then recovered his humour, clapped me on the shoulder and promised to take me to the cricket on the morrow. Even Maria was evasive, and I retired that night convinced that Jo Paget was the only soul at Brambridge in the dark.

We were woken early, and the lure of cricket dispelled my misgivings. The Captain and Mr Smythe were in high spirits, and a rumbustuous breakfast was followed by an even more rumbustuous journey. The dozen or so miles to Hambledon, through Owlesbury and the wooded lanes and rippling wheatfields of Hampshire, were covered in less than two hours of thundering, swaying, dust flying exhilaration. Flowered meadows were fat with heifers, chalk streams tumbled with trout, thatched cottages peeped from forests of hollyhock.

There were six on the chaise: three men, two youths and Jimmy, driving four fine cobs so fast that I suspected the Captain had bet on the time of our journey. Led by Mr Weld, who seemed reborn in male company, we sang as if we intended the whole of Hampshire to hear. What the sleepy burghers of Corhampton must have thought, as we bowled down the seductive slopes of the Meon Valley, roaring our Dorset ditty, is beyond my conception.

Be oi 'amshur, be oi not zur,

Oi cums up from Ware'um,

Where all the gurls wear calico drawers,

an oi kneows 'euw t' tare'um.

There is nothing outstanding about Hambledon, a warm brick and flint village, tucked into a combe below Broadhalfpenny Down. Nothing that is, save a cricket team envied throughout the civilised world[68]. How these plain peasants and yawning yeomen managed to sire the likes of John Small and Dick Nyren, Tom Suitor and Bill Hogsflesh, is one of the deeper mysteries of our universe. Captain Howell says they must have stumps between their legs, and leather balls.

We had rooms at the George, the village coaching inn. After we had left our bags and paid the ostler, a cab took us up a winding climbing lane to the heights above the village, where the breeze from the sea, not a dozen miles south, cools the warmest day.

It seemed an extraordinary place for the cream of English cricket to assemble, and even more extraordinary was the multitude gathered on the Down, more people than could possibly reside in the whole of Hampshire. It was as if Dover's Games had changed their venue and doubled their attendance. Ten thousand bodies gathered around a field, and in their midst, a couple of acres of green sward, empty save for thirteen men dressed in white, with black stove pipe hats and knee length gaiters. The match had begun and the swains of Hambledon were batting against the might of England.

At least John Small was batting against the might of England. When we arrived, Hambledon had lost three batters in scoring twenty five notches. He was still there when Billy Barber hit his wicket, on seventy eight from a total of one hundred and forty six.

With the likes of Shock White and Jeremy Fuggles and Tom Minshull and Jack Miller, it was plain that England would score more. At the betting post the best price I could hear was two to one on first innings lead. I was therefore surprised to hear Mr Smythe taking seven to four from all comers. When England had reached sixty eight for three at stumps, with Shock on thirty five not out, I concluded that Mr Smythe knew less about cricket than I[69].

There were a number of booths and tents around the field, from which, as the evening relaxed, came the all too familiar sounds of reverie. The central tent, a striped wigwam topped by a banner of St George, was Billy Barber's wine booth. It bulged with occupants like a bag of marbles. Entry was controlled by a pair of yeomen with knobbed sticks, and all but Quality were being turned away. Whether or not we belonged to that exalted rank was not material, for at Mr Smythe's approach, knobbed sticks touched forelocks and we were ushered in.

A corner of the tent had been roped, and there sat my heroes: Shock White talking to Jack Miller as though they were ordinary mortals and even Lumpy Stevens, the greatest bowler in the land, drinking claret like the rest of us. Not only drinking it, but spilling it, and spraying it, and dribbling it, in the manner of a body that is brimful of it.

A cask bound in wooden hoops was rolled from behind the bar, and in a display of puzzling ceremony, Mr Smythe invited to breach it. With a mallet he drove in the tap and then loosened the bung. The perfume of the clear liquid that splashed into his jug hung in the air, heady and strong. He filled the jars of the England team and then dispensed less prodigious measures to the rest of us.

"A toast," he shouted, "to tomorrow's sport."

The England team drank deep, but Billy Barber and Tom Brett and George Lear sipped, between conspiratorial winks. I too sipped, but that was enough to introduce into my throat the sensation that it was being savaged with a ripsaw.

Shock levered himself aloft. "A very fine brandy, Mr Smythe. Have you left some for Farmer George[70]?"

"We've already drunk his, Shock, so we might as well see it off." This *bon mot,* obscure though it was to me, was greeted with guffaws all round and the jars were refilled.

Jeremy Fuggles, fat and red, climbed on to a chair, where he swayed in precarious isolation until a hush crept over the throng. He cleared his throat with an eructing rumble and I feared that the Oven was about to be resurrected.

If I wur a bowler, I'd parlish my ball.

The tune differed little from George Ridler or Mister Parson, but the words were new to me.

Then throw it at Nyren, Tom Sueter 'n Small,
'n when it did 'it 'em, atop o' thur rump,
They'd fall over back'ards, 'n sit on thur stump.

I once watched my Father felling an oak tree in Robins Wood. He dug a trench and cut the roots, and the more he cut, the less purchase the tree had, until the giant of the forest was reduced to a hulk, without support, prey to the gentlest breeze. Jeremy Fuggles swallowed another gill of brandy, which severed the last of his roots.

If I wur a batter, 'n 'Ogsflesh wur on,
I'd smite all 'is balls back down to 'Ambledon.

This dubious couplet was roared from an angle that defied the laws of geometry.

'n if all my notches wur counted up right,

They'd think 'e'd been bowlin' all day 'n all night.

He must have forgotten that he was in a tent, for he leant on the wall for support and the canvas, not having the stern qualities of lathe and plaster, flapped. The oak tree, in a majestic finale, crashed to the table, which itself collapsed midst fountains of broken pots. The rest of the England team, who had been supporting their heads on the surface thereof, fell around him like wreaths on the grave of a loved one. Mr Smythe nodded to the Hambledon men and bad them sleep well. We returned to the George where some heavy bets were laid on the home team.

The morning saw a dishevelled Shock White take guard against Thomas Brett. I would rather face the French infantry than TB's first over after a good night's sleep. He is a farmer from Catherington, with titanic arms, and is the fastest bowler that I have ever seen. He runs to the wicket with a queer, sidelong gait, clutching the ball in both hands. At the bowling crease, he leaps into the air, punching at the ground with his left fist, so that the right, wherein the ball now hides, swings aloft behind his back. From its apex, which must be seven feet from the ground, this mighty engine plunges earthwards, releasing its missile at knee height.

Shock never saw the first two and the third hit him in the groin. He looked mightily relieved when the last one broke nothing more crucial than his stumps.

England were all out for a hundred and nine, the only resistance coming from Palmer and May, who had not been in Bill Barber's booth. Hambledon shambled out for their second innings and John Small resumed command, but even his genius could not disguise the parlous state of his comrades. They may have consumed less than the England team, but only marginally so. They batted with the enthusiasm of passengers on a deportation boat, and were all out for seventy-nine, leaving England a hundred and seventeen to get, with a day and a half to do it.

White and Fuggles emerged from the pavilion to open the second innings, and I thought they would collapse on the long walk to the wicket. TB's first ball clipped the edge of Shock's bat and flew like a hare being coursed, to disappear in the undergrowth by the lane. Smouldering under the insult of six notches for a lost ball, TB marched to the limit of the field and began a thundering run of such velocity, Shock's trembling form was two yards from the stumps when the ball hit him in the stomach.

There are few more intimidating moments in sport than to march to the crease at number three, passing the stretcher laden with your opening bat on its way to the surgeon. Tom Minshull scored one, Jack Miller a duck. Apart from a pause for further resistance from Palmer and May, the procession continued until there were no more, leaving the Hambledon men fifty three runs and five hundred guineas to the good.

There can have been little sleeping done in Hambledon that night. Dick Nyren[71], captain of the team and landlord of the George, left his doors open till dawn. Even when he finally put up the shutters, the celebrations went on in High Street, where pretty cottages climb the slope to the squat flint church, as if queuing for the hereafter, and folk are used to rising, not falling down, at sun up. We gathered around another of Mr Smythe's evil casks and sang anthems to our heroes. And relived, with drunken inflation, the deeds of the day.

I now come to an episode in my life that I recall with great relish, but if the true nature of my contribution were revealed, would cause me some inconvenience. I have already referred to the wealth of amphibious fauna that frequents the long island. It was difficult to catch the newts, for they are swift shy creatures, always scuttling under stones and deep into pools. The frogs were hardly more accommodating, leaping when you least expect it, or swimming with contemptuous ease away from the clutching hand. But the toads – the fat, warty, spotted blobs, waddling in procession along their secret paths, flicking their sticky tongues at passing flies, grinning stupidly at friend and foe. The toads seemed to welcome capture, to enjoy abuse, to expect humiliation.

So we caught them, bucketfulls of them, and threw them at each other, and tied corks to their legs and raced them down the river, and coursed them from the middle of the lawn with the tom cat that lived in the stables, and dropped them, from high in the overhanging willow, on the heads of the bargees.

On the first fine day that follows the feast of John the Baptist, or to those of an older faith, the Summer Solstice, it is the habit of the Right Reverend John Thomas, Lord Bishop of Winchester, to reinforce his proprietorial rights over the Navigation, by travelling its length in an appropriately sombre craft. Appropriate, for the bargees and watermen are sorely resentful of the dues they must pay the Bishop.

A dark canopied wherry, crosier in the bow, rowed by a dark liveried waterman, and bearing the enthroned prelate with his lady aft, plies the stream from Blackbridge Wharf to Bishopstoke. Along the route the faithful gather at bridge and lock and riverside inn, to be chilled by the old Jonah's austere smile.

The lady, at least thirty years his junior, and as comely as Elizabeth Howell, fluttered in the stern under a parasol, a butterfly on a tomb, with decolletage I can only describe as uneccliastical. Jack whispered darkly that this was not his wife Helen, but a widowed niece called Hester Chapone who brought comfort to his years.

We had been aloft in the willow for three hours, but the sport that day was sparse. Only two barges had passed, and our aim had been poor on each occasion. The toads were flaccid and beginning to stink and my arse was numb.

"C'mon Jack, lets go and catch some 'backs," I sniffed.

"Shhhhhh."

"Oh, c'mon, my arse hurts."

He was peering through the leaves. "Listen."

Voices, faint at first, growing nearer. I recognised the Captain, and Mr Smythe, then Maria's tinkling laugh.

"What do they all want?"

The two families had gathered on the banks and were chattering and laughing as if at a picnic. The sluice was raised and the churning, rushing waters escaped from the lock. I heard Wat and his younger brothers swinging the gates open and the waterman calling his thanks.

I first saw the crosier, then the bow came into view below us, then the waterman, not rowing, just guiding the boat on the surge from the lock. It was when the black hat of the Bishop passed, that my cramped leg twitched and hit the bucket, balanced so carefully on the branch at my side. Like a swoop of swallows, the toads were launched from their home and, although I caught the bucket, its late contents were already landing with muted plunks on the aft planking and stern passenger of the wherry.

With an oath of which Fanny Murray would have been proud, the

Bishop's lady leapt aloft, ripping at her corsage like a bagnio keeper's daughter on her first assignment. Before the assembled Smythes she revealed that three, not two amorphous lumps lurked within her decolletage. She resembled a wild and naked harridan, a Siren shedding apparel to fuel the desires of the Argonauts on the bank. She screamed and shook – sooth how she shook – and waved and swayed, and the boat rocked in ever more alarming gyrations, and the waterman shouted, and the Bishop held tight to the gunwhales. And the water tipped first over one side, then the other.

The effect of elevating a significant proportion of a cargo, without stemming the tide, is well known. It was most graphically illustrated when the *Mary Rose* sank in Portsmouth Harbour[72]. The wherry followed this time honoured tradition by resigning itself, its howling waterman, its stoic prelate and its shameless baggage, to the Itchen depths. The shoal of toads swam lazily away to tell their children of the great adventure.

Unlike the toads, neither the Bishop nor his lady were at home in their new environment. The waterman, apparently guided by some celestial pecking order, grabbed the Bishop's floating robes and dragged him, gasping, towards the bank, leaving the pink Mrs Chapone to flounder in the depths.

I am not sure what prompted my heroic dive into that churning stream, but I suspect that Jack was not guiltless. If so, I owe to him gratitude, for being, in part, responsible for my present comfortable circumstances.

I have known four benefactors in my short life: my Father, Mr Selwyn, Captain Howell and the Bishop of Winchester. The first sired me, the second raised me, and the third, as I shall soon record in this journal, has been overwhelmingly generous to me. The fourth, out of gratitude to the Lord for sending me to rescue his dear niece, has opened the doors of respectable society to me.

I held her head clear of the surface until the waterman returned, and then splashed to the bank where I was greeted with applause from the Smythes, and a shining eyed, proprietorily proud hug from Maria. The scurrying Brambridge servants wrapped us in woollen blankets, the Bishop fell to his knees and we all, Catholic and Protestant, felt obliged to follow.

"Oh Lord, who giveth life and taketh away, we thank thee for restoring to us thy servant Hester." No thanks to you, you old fraud, thought I. "By sending thy messenger in the body of this brave and selfless boy." Precious few were due to me either, I had to concede. "To pluck her from her watery grave so that she may serve thee and worship thee all the rest of her days. Amen."

Maria sat with me at dinner and put her hand on my thigh, under the white linen cloth, and smiled at me as on the hill at Gatcombe – secret, intimate, daring. Later we walked in the grounds, where woodcocks called across evening damp lawns, and I felt as I had at Prinknash, when my porcelain angel had led me through the arbours of the old mansion. We went behind a cedar tree and kissed, her sweet soft mouth open, her tongue darting, teasing, my hand at her breast, her's on my breeches.

"There you are, Maria." Cruel interruption. "I've been searching the grounds for you." I felt the passion drain to my feet. Edward Weld stepped from the dusk of the shrubbery. "I thought you might care for an archery class before the light fades."

He had taken to teaching her the sport of bows and arrows. A coiled straw target with a gold bull's eye had been set up at the back of the boathouse. Here they would spend hours, her laughing and sighing at her inability to master the ancient sport; he, behind her, arms encircling her shoulders and guiding her hands. It all seemed so innocent, but his groin spent an unwarranted amount of time pressed to her rump, and I suspected that his concern for her sporting prowess hid a deeper design, in which I featured very little.

Maria hesitated, I now think she expected me to demur on her behalf, but at fifteen I had yet to master such subtlety. She sighed and half smiled at me. A forbearing smile, as an adult to a child that does not fully understand.

"Coming Edward?" still looking at me. "Jo and I had finished our talk." They walked away, silent at first, then her laugh, bright as ever, tinkling and fading into the shrubbery. And I knew for the first time the loathing of the inept for the adept.

The days returned to their familiar pattern: fishing and toading and working the lock. Jack and I became firm friends, to the exclusion of Wat and the others, and I shut from my mind the continued mating dance of Maria and her ageing beau.

When the the cotton clouds turned grey and swelled with rain, and fat drops fell from the willow, scurrying the surface of the river, we would run for the boat house. Cedar lined walls hung with ropes and oars and sails and spars, and a skiff that bobbed on the rippling floor. Here we were pirates, or sometimes King's men, or privateers in sleek black brigantines. We were the Hawkhurst Gang[73], attacking the Custom House in Poole, or Speedwell[74], prowling the southern waters.

One evening, as we lay on the floor of the skiff, musing about our lives and listening to the rain on the shingle roof, Jack said, "Would you like to see some real smuggling?"

"What do you mean?" I was not entirely taken with the idea of running before Speedwell.

"There's a smuggler's hide, the richest in all Hampshire, not forty yards from your feet." I studied his face, seeking the joke, but his eyes showed only excitement at the prospect of revelation.

"And I suppose you've got the key?"

"There's no key. The door's open. Come on."

The rain had eased but the trees still dripped as we skirted the lawn and entered a small thicket, where a privy stood, unwanted since water closets had been fitted in the new house, a graceful little building, flint with a stone mullion over the door and a conical roof. It had received the droppings of the masters of Brambridge for generations and passed them to the gardeners, as night soil to nurture their charges. Inside, it was dank and dark, domain of spider and louse, a room six feet square, with a mother and daughter[75] seat along one wall.

I was momentarily concerned about Jack's motives. I thought he might be a closet sodomite. He put his finger to his lips and listened for a moment. Satisfied that we were alone, he raised the seat and hinged riser, and secured them to the wall with a latch. A cellar stairway led down into the earth and I reflected that digging it, through a century or two of shit, must have taken determination. Just below ground level, a brass lamp and a tinderbox hung on the wall. Jack took them down and sparks flicked along black walls, as he worked the flint and steel. When the candle was lit, he beckoned me to follow his stuttering shadow along the passage.

The privy was about twenty yards from the house, and I judged we had covered this distance, when the passage widened into an arched vault. Along each wall were neat stacks of boxes and crates marked with strange symbols and foreign script, and row upon row of casks bound in wooden hoops, identical to the one that had contributed so much to Hambledon's famous victory. The air was stale, pungent with spices and perfumes and aromatic oils, and our footsteps echoed as we walked along the rows, menaced by long leaping shadows, distorted on the curving walls.

"Let's go back," I whispered.

Jack chuckled and the sound seemed to surround us. "There's no one here. There's only one way in and anyone that enters brings the lamp with them."

A scamper between the barrels – I jumped. "What was that?" Terror crawling up my spine.

"Just rats. I'll let the tom down here tomorrow."

I was torn between dread of staying in that place, and even greater dread of leaving the pool of light thrown by the candle. Jack, like a shopkeeper with a valued customer, took me on a tour of his warehouse, pointing out the treasures that he commanded.

"Spices from the Indies, Chinese silks, cognac of the highest quality. But of course, you have already sampled the cognac. Tobacco from the Colonies, darkest, fiercest rum, and enough tea to satisfy London's thirst for a year."

We reached the end of this vast oriental bazaar, where a blank wall barred our way. A movement at the far end. A footstep.

I froze but Jack muttered "Bloody rats!" and continued his discourse. "The wall is a yard thick. We are under the main house, but when it was built, this vault was so designed, that it cannot be discerned from inside."

"But how does all this stuff get here? And why?" Jack put his fat face close to mine. It was creased in a smile, a goblin in the candle's jumping light.

"You really don't know, do you?" Another movement, closer now, and even Jack paused, alert for a moment, but he continued. "Farmer George charges duty on all these goods when they are brought to England, in order to pay for his German bumsuckers. He also expects to be paid for the wool that is exported. My Father and your Captain and Mister Weld don't agree with him, so they take out Cotswold wool from Bristol, to pay for the goods they bring back here. They make a big profit going out and a bigger profit coming back. And they keep the money themselves."

I heard a sudden scuffle of footsteps, smelled the sweat of a man, and a blinding roaring crash on my head, brought all conversation, all fear, all consciousness, to an abrupt close.

I was at Prinknash, cradled in Elizabeth Howell's soft arms, soothed by Elizabeth Smythe's cool murmurs. At the foot of the bed, the Captain, pacing this way and that. Jimmy stood in the corner, impassive as the dark oak wardrobe.

But why was Mr Smythe in the room? And Edward Weld? And where were the whorls and fans and pendants on the ceiling? And why did my head, rather than my leg, throb with cutting, remorseless pain? And why was I adorned, like some potentate, with a white turban?

The aching mist reluctantly receded to the corners of my brain, where it lurked, still potent, a wildcat spitting from a cage. Acrimonious debate in muted tones flew around the room, angry wasps, stinging where they landed.

"That black ape has gone too far," Elizabeth Howell hissing venom. "He must be caged, or put on a slaver. I'll not have him near my son any longer."

Jimmy's eyes, round, pleading.

"Hold your tongue woman," the Captain said, suppressed fury purpling his face. "He was doing his duty. He stays." Elizabeth Howell opened her mouth to protest, but wilted in the fierceness of his glare, and closed it again. "His fat little arse should be birched till it pours with blood, for this treachery."

This abuse was directed by the Captain at Walter Smythe, in whose shadow I discerned Jack, snivelling and red eyed.

"Hold there," whispered Mr Smythe. "The door should have been locked."

"A lock might have alerted the Preventives. We agreed that long ago."

"We'll get nowhere fighting," Edward Weld added, calmer, steadier. "We must decide whats to be done." He glanced at me. "And be careful, he's coming to his senses."

Fourteen eyes bore upon me, some more malevolent than others, and I shrivelled under their scrutiny. Elizabeth Howell wiped my brow with dampened silk, her eyes at least, deep with care. The Captain raised his voice, making the pain stab inside my head.

"You have the luck of the Devil, ye damn pest." No humour, just the evil I had seen when he had planned the Kingswood manhunt. "Jimmy saw your face as you fell and did you no more damage. He thought you were Preventives and would've opened your necks. As it is, the thump he fetched you would have broken most men's skulls. You must be bone from ear to ear." I thought it prudent not to dispute this calumny.

Walter Smythe hauled his son forward by the ear. "What's to be done with them, John?"

"We agreed long ago," said Edward Weld. "Anyone that sees, must become a party. He must be as guilty as the rest of us, so that his neck will stretch just as far, if we get caught."

"You can't mean to send the boys on a run." Elizabeth Howell had summoned the courage to speak again.

There followed the lowest point of my relationship with Captain John Howell. I enjoy moments of the greatest affection for this boisterous, rollicking, generous man, but his black depths will erupt from time to time with unrestrained savagery. He moved, with a swiftness that belied his bulk, along the side of the bed and, as the terror leapt into Elizabeth's eyes, punched her mouth. Not a warning smack or a playful cuff, but a crunching, disfiguring blow that sprawled her across the bed, wetting the coverlet with her spittle, staining it with her blood. I hated him then and, despite all of his kindnesses to me, whenever I recall that awful moment, I hate him again.

In the silence that followed, as she was helped from the room, I saw his anger die, drowned in welling tears of remorse. He reached a hand towards her shoulder but was stilled by Elizabeth Smythe's bleak rage. When she had left, Walter Smythe and Edward Weld stared at their feet until the Captain recovered his composure. But then, as if the interuption had not occurred, the three continued to plot the fate of Jack and I.

"So be it," said the Captain. "They can crew on the next run. We'll take them to Lulworth Friday next and if Jo ain't mended by then, he'll just have to work with a bad head."

They left Jack and I in a state both of apprehension and excitement. Not knowing if we were punished or rewarded, looking forward to the danger, but dreading it too.

Friday morning, still bandaged, but greatly improved, I was kissed by a tearful and swollen Elizabeth Howell, while Jack was hugged to the bosom of his Mother. The same coach bearing the same party that had so jovially travelled to Hambledon, set out in tight lipped silence from the elegant house on the Itchen. We crossed the small bridge, then the larger one over the Navigation and galloped through river mist to Otterburn, to join the turnpike for Romsey.

Over the River Test, we glimpsed Palmerstone's great house[76] through the beeches – the art of Capability Brown in all its riotous extravagance, stark contrast with the Bridewell nearby. Surely one Englishman should not live at such advantage to another?

Through the New Forest, long straight lonely miles watched over by silent oak and lordly elm. Out onto the meaner soil of Dorset, where gorse and sea grasses creep across the land. Through Lychetts and Bottoms and Minsters and Puddles, through Wimborne so pretty and Wareham so ancient. I suppose we were no more than fifty miles from Brambridge, and yet we might have been in a far country. For yet again this extraordinary island had changed her clothes, discarding the grandeur of the Downs and the richness of Hampshire for the secrets of the heath, wizened oak woods cowed by sea winds, rounded knolls and shadowed combes hugging warm brick farms against the mists; everywhere a sense of smallness, of hidden corners and quiet.

Along the way to Wool we turned south from the turnpike towards the sea, an untamed landscape, remote and mysterious, lurking, waiting, as if watching our progress, holding back until we had passed. I have experienced the same feeling when blustering into the society of a country inn, as the murmur of conversation dies and secret eyes appraise the intruder.

We glimpsed the sea, at Worbarrow Bay, and the cold grey towers of Lulworth Castle, high above its oak strewn park. This was the home of Edward Weld and I could see that its sunless battlements were hewn deep into his soul – tall, sombre, without humour or whimsy, pompous, efficient, and deadly dull. Huge in its graniteness, with four keeps soaring to five storeys, and a fearsome castellated roof silhouetted against the sky. It has no enemies and has never known attack. It defends no one against no one and serves little purpose other than to shout the wealth of its owners to the people of Dorset. Its church, a mighty structure in its own right, built, I concluded, to the glory of the Weldgod, is dwarfed by the monstrous castle. The stables and coach houses, which also lurk in its shadow, are sufficient to house the population of a small town.

It was to these stables that Jack and I were directed by Edward Weld.

"You're collier crew now," he said, "and you'll live like it till the runs done."

Walter Smythe marched away from his son without a word, but the Captain, twinkle restored to soften the evil eye, cuffed me on the shoulder and said.

"Sleep well, pest. Don't breathe too deep, for the grass is bad in these parts and the horses fart a lot." He chuckled at his own joke and as he walked with the others, up wide balustraded steps to the statued and frescoed portico, called over his shoulder. "Sail training tomorrow. If you're not sharp, I'll have your backs like raw steak."

A groom led us to the stables, where a cold picnic awaited us, with jugs of beer. We sat on the straw, with Jimmy and the coachman and several of the stable lads, and ate until our heads drooped. I remember Jimmy picking me up, as he had on that first journey at Prinknash, and laying me gently on a paliasse. His eyes, big and deep and soft, seemed to be trying to thank me, for what, I know not. Perhaps he thought I had saved him from the slaver. Perhaps I had.

The next morning, buffeting wind and big woolly clouds racing across the wide sky to Devon. Jack and I, with Jimmy and the Captain, striding down rabbit scampered turf, to the sea at Arish Mell. There, moored against the tiny quay, a sleek blue cutter, nervous, tugging at her lines, impatient to be running; a greyhound eager for the slip.

"You'll work hard today," the Captain shouted above the gusts, pointing to the cutter. "She's Mister Weld's racing yacht and even Cumberland can't catch her. She's a thoroughbred, hard to handle and about as forgiving as Lizzie Brownrigg"[77].

A waterman stood by a pile of oilskins on the shingle, waiting for us, a skiff beached by the waterline. We dressed in the heavy garb, big flopping sou'westers down to the eyebrows, thick woollen socks and boots that would have accommodated both feet, and I was soon hot and fetid inside. I puffed, to which the Captain shouted, "Worry not, pest, you'll not be hot for long." We clambered onto the quay and clumped along the timbers to the cutter.

Everything about the *Lulworth Queen* was similar to the *Maiden Dean,* but better. More brass, and shinier too; softer lines, not hemp but boltrope, stitched and supple, sails furled as if by clothiers, pine decks as clean as the floor at White's.

Once aboard, the Captain and Jimmy moved around the decks, touching the equipment, stroking the lines – stage coach drivers inspecting a phaeton. They checked the stays and the long thrusting bowsprit, Jimmy swung on the shrouds, and the Captain attached sheets to the sails with a twist of his hand that produced bowlines as if by magic. They cast off the lashing around the sails, cleared the sheets and halliards, unfurled the foresail and laid it on the deck ready to hoist, and hauled out the jib on the bowsprit.

When they were satisfied, the Captain took the helm, applied his most fearsome face and bellowed at Jack and I, "Now, my fine hearties, you're about to find out what sailing really is. One mistake and you'll feel the lash of my tongue. Two and Jimmy's monkey fist'll stroke your shoulders. Three, and you'll swim back. Take'em forrard, Jimmy."

We were led to the foot of the mast and Jimmy showed us, with actions clearer than any words, how the halliard ran from the foot of the gaff to the top of the main mast, through a block and back down to a second block at the bottom. He pulled a little on the halliard and the gaff went a foot or so up the mast, taking the mainsail with it. He passed the end over a cleat and gave it to me. He placed Jack at the foot of the mast and demonstrated how he should haul the halliard away, and then release it while I took up the slack. He nodded to the Captain.

"Hoist the mainsail!"

A clear and piercing call that sent shivers up my back, exotic music of the sea, full of promise, of voyages to unknown lands, of adventures that only the brave can know. Jack hauled and I took up; and the main billowed into life, flapping and snapping above our heads like a hunting bird, still tethered, but impatient to be free. As Jimmy showed me how to belay the halliard to the cleat, the Captain roared, "Hoist the foresail!"

We jumped to the other side of the mast and this time I hauled and Jack took up, as the smaller, triangular foresail slid up its stay. There was cacophony of flapping sails and whipping lines all around us, the Captain and Jimmy unhurried and unconcerned.

"Cast off forrard!" Louder, even more piercing.

The waterman let go the rope at the bow and ran to the stern. The foresail filled and ballooned to starboard.

"Cast off aft!" The boat moved slowly away from the quay, nodding on the choppy water.

"Hoist the main peak!" We performed our *pas de deux* on yet another halliard and the main taughtened and then bloomed into a huge white petal. The boat heaved to starboard and I slipped on the tangle of ropes around my feet. I crashed to the sloping deck and slid, at fearsome speed, to crack my forehead on the gunwhales. My cranium was thus violated both fore and aft, but sympathy was manifestly absent.

"Get up, you jackpudding. There's no sleeping on my ship." The sails no longer flapped, and his voice was unchallenged as it reverberated around the decks. "I want the foresail set fair, the jib run up, the main tack howsed down and the halliards coiled. *Neatly*!" This last word rang in our ears like the noon bell at St Pauls.

We scampered round the deck, under Jimmy's direction, pulling, pushing, lugging and heaving, until all was shipshape and we could collapse by the mast and take stock of our surroundings.

We were out of the bay and reaching across the wind and tide. I have known great excitement in my few years and I hope to know much more; but I doubt I shall ever recapture the thrill, the pure unfettered exhilaration of that first reach on the *Lulworth Queen*, heeled over to starboard, slicing the spume topped waves, our bowsprit dipping into their crests to send foaming, fizzing, glittering spray high over our heads – no sound save the rushing of the sea and snatches of a shanty, sung by the Captain and being whipped away on the wind.

Moments of such joy must be transient, for if they are prolonged, we become sated with pleasure and begin to seek their flaws, and thus diminish them in recollection. This one ended as abruptly as it had started.

It is difficult for me to recall, with any accuracy, the following sequence of events. They were a bawling, swearing, soaking jumble, in which I skinned one hand, lost my hat, spent more time on my arse than my feet and was crowned by the boom to such effect, that I lay unconscious and unattended in a heap under the taffrail, whilst the boat continued its maniacal progress towards St Aldhelm's Head. For those unversed in matters maritime, I should explain that the process of beating to windward is the most chaotic in the sailing manual. I have learned since to love it. But my distaste for it on that day was exceded only by my loathing of what followed.

I have yet to gain control of the mysterious functioning of my digestive system, when running before the wind on a quartering sea. Somewhere off Kimmeridge Bay, we turned and headed east, so that the wind was on our backs, and the waves, building and piling as they entered the trap of Weymouth Bay, came from over our left shoulder. A boat on this point of sail will wallow up and down the troughs, in a corkscrew motion that never fails to reverse my gastric flow.

The awfulness begins with a feeling of nauseous debility. The ruddy glow of reaching, the fiery blood of beating, drains from the cheeks to leave a tragic greenish countenance – sunken cheeks and spaniel eyes, a corpse in an oilskin shroud. The sufferer grows cold and wizened, retreating into the folds like an old crone; and tired too, yawning and swallowing, a trout on the bank. Then, deep inside the bowels of the being, there begins a rumbling, erupting sensation that cannot be denied. It begins somewhere down by the pancreas. A feeling that air is being pumped into the stomach from below, a bubbling, a churning of the contents. The rear exit is closed to this swelling tide of lava. Thus it is forced upwards, ever upwards, along the oesophagus, until it reaches the pharynx, where it is bravely opposed by a frantic swallowing. This rearguard action can only stem the tide and allow the victim time to reach the guard rail.

As I hurled myself to the gunwhales, the Captain murmured, without compassion, "I see Hugh and Ralph[78] have joined us." Then louder. "One drop on the hull, pest, and you'll lick it off."

I have a naturally optimistic outlook on life: I believe that, whatever my difficulties, there are persons in far worse circumstances than I. It is a view that has always sustained me in moments of anguish and will, I trust, succour me to the grave. But at that particular moment, ten thirty-five ante meridian, Saturday the eleventh of July, seventeen seventy two, it was difficult to imagine even the most abused of souls feeling lower than I.

The last drop of bile slobbered down my chin and I could retch nothing more than a primeval groan. I knew how a soiled smock must feel, rubbed raw on the washboard by a muscular charwoman, then twisted and squeezed until every drop of moisture has been expelled.

My maiden sea voyage held one final revelation. Some distance west of our starting point at Arish Mell, we turned north to reach back again across the wind. At once the motion of the boat steadied and I felt the blood flow again in my poor limp frame. My spirits improved and I began to take an interest in our progress. My new found confidence was shortlived, for as we closed on the forbidding rocks of Dorset, neither the Captain nor Jimmy made any attempt to change direction.

The prospect of imminent destruction is an acknowledged bowel loosener, and had there been anything left in my innards, it would have been discharged there and then. We seemed bent upon a glorious suicide, about which I had not been consulted. With a shanty on his great bewhiskered chops and the light of battle in his eye, our mad helmsman steered us straight and true at the cliffs, which rose above us in stoical indifference. Just as we reached their foot, and I was trying to recite what I could remember of the Lord's Prayer, an orifice appeared in what had seemed impenetrable. A refuge in that foaming graveyard, a gap in those fearsome teeth.

As we sailed through, the Captain, brimming with childlike glee at my discomfort, said, "Welcome to the arsehole of Dorset, boy," and we were bobbing across an idyllic circular bay, of calm clear water playing on a shingle beach.

We dropped the sails as we came alongside the jetty, threw lines to the waterman and were at peace in a Dorset summer's day, watching rabbits hoppity hop on the steep turfed chalk down. A coach and four stood where the stream tumbles down from the combe, and a liveried footman brought us goblets of port wine for our restoration. The rigours of the morning were already a memory, when I fell fast asleep.

Chapter Seven

My first experience of the Preventives was sudden and violent.

Dawn light flooded into the stable, as doors were slammed back against walls. Men running – grim, determined – hammering, crashing, shouting. Bleary faces, helpless in the half light of waking, struggling to comprehend the chaos – kicking, shaking, punching. Bayonets thrusting deep into straw bales, paliasses, mangers. Roaring red faced dragoons lining us, faces against the wall, threatening our shivering huddled bodies with musket and blade – and a short strutting bantam cock of a man, sneering at our discomfort in a flat nasal voice.

"Now then." A pause for effect. North[79] in the House. "Captain James Wicks, His Majesty's Preventive Officer at your service, gentlemen. Some people call me Wicked Wicks, a title that I have earned by diligence and relentless pursuit". Another enamoured with the sound of his own trumpet, I concluded. Windbag Postlethwaite would have made an excellent Preventive. "Now then. I am reliably informed that illicit goods have been secreted upon these premises and I'll know where the store is afore I leave, or one of you'll be shot trying to escape."

Silence, save for the creak of his leathers and the soft footfall on straw. I faced the wall but felt him near. A hand on my shoulder, tightening, digging into the flesh, making me twist around whining with the pain. His face close, no higher than mine, foul morning breath, veined yellowing eyes. "Now then. This young beauty'll do, be good target practice Sergeant."

I was propelled across the straw to the arms of a tall dragoon, who laughed and held me by the scruff, wriggling, feet off the ground. Wicked continued his soliloquy, "Now then. I might want to know where the store is, but the men'll be disappointed if you speak. They want some sport, they get bored shooting rabbits." Still silence, but Jimmy looked round, and Wicked faltered in the murderous threat of the glare. He looked up at the mountainous shoulders and beyond to the huge shining head. "Take the slave as well, he needs a lesson."

None of the dragoons moved for a moment, doubting the wisdom of the Officer's instruction. They followed their Sergeant, not the Preventive Man, and waited for the order to be confirmed. "You heard what the Captain said,"barked the Sergeant,. "Chain the blackie." Four men, one bearing leg irons, tentatively approached Jimmy, dogs baiting the bull. They should have known that a slave, once free, is devilish difficult to tempt back into irons. The bull turned to face its molestors, snorted and launched itself into their dismayed midst.

They may have been dragoons, disciplined riding men, versed with sabre and musket, but they were not the cream of their species. They had not been at Wolfe's side, nor Clive's, nor even following Eyre Coote[80] to glory at Wandewash. They were used to pursuing villagers and labourers, who, armed with little but sticks, melted into the night with their meagre booty. Frontal assault by a demented foe was an experience they had been spared until this moment, and it showed. They fell in disarray before Jimmy's scything limbs: the crunch of knuckle to temple, of foot to groin, the woof of an imploding solar plexus.

Jimmy crouched over the fallen heroes, wary, watching the other dragoons, a wolf guarding its kill. The Sergeant hesitated, not knowing whether to shoot. He looked to the Officer for direction. Wicked Wicks was dumbfounded, eyes darting from group to group, no more the bantam cock, now the startled hen. It was the moment before the curtain rises, as the players have taken their positions and stand motionless, awaiting the footlights and the applause.

Alas, the audience were in no mood to applaud, for into this tableau marched a furious Edward Weld, a purple Captain Howell and the smoothly fat Walter Smythe puffing like Tom Newcomen's[81] pump. The downfall of the bantam cock was completed by Edward Weld, who roared, "Wicks, you airbladder, you damn bawbling dunghill! What d'you mean by invading my property, abusing my men, defiling my air?"

"M – my duty Mister Weld. Only doing my duty."

"Duty"? He could have been hailing the Lundy Queen. "What duty is it, that demands the violation of law abiding homes? Where in your orders are you given the duty to abuse young boys?" The Sergeant dropped me abruptly on the straw and I crawled towards the freedom of the open door. "Which of the subjects of that overstuffed German sausage are you empowered to arrest without reason? "Wicked chose to ignore this treasonable reference to His Majesty.

"We are conducting a search and seize raid on Lulworth and have reason to believe that some of your workers have been illicitly importing goods."

I saw Mr Weld's eyes flicker to the Captain. "Illicit, you wine soaked fribbler? The only illicit goods you'll find in Lulworth is the port sloshing around your fat belly." I had no liking for Edward Weld, but I conceded that when he took the offensive, he did so to great effect.

As the onslaught continued, the Captain bent to me and, with uncharacteristic solicitude, helped me to my feet. He shepherded me through the door and when we were beyond earshot whispered, his eyes watching the doorway, "Run to the castle and find Bastard. Tell him you're to have a horse and the bell. Then ride like the Devil to the village and ring the damn thing. Quick now!"

I hurried across the meadow, then along the carriage drive which curved through a landscape as alien to Dorset as the Castle itself – soft sward, shaved to a green velvet and dense shrubberies of foreign fragrance. I bounded up the wide steps to be grasped by a bewigged footman intent on hurling me from whence I came.

"Out o' here, you tyke, or I'll feed you to the dogs." I had forgotten that my dress and bearing were those of a collier boy.

"I have to see the Bastard," I squealed. "I've a message from Mister Weld." He smirked. Clearly Mr Bastard was his better and he was not averse to my sacrilegious use of the proud old Dorset name. He released his grip.

"Wait." He walked away from me into the dark cavern of the hall, footsteps echoing in still depths. I was left on the granite terrace, under the soaring granite towers.

As far as I could see, the raised terrace upon which I stood, with its intricate carved balustrade and decorated paving, girded the entire building. John Bastard, dark and bearded, warm as the Dorset soil, appeared around the corner of the west tower, at which distance he was of everyday proportion. But with slow measured tread he grew larger and ever larger as he advanced towards me, until the waistband of his thick cord breeches seemed to be the limit of my horizon.

He was a giant, bigger even than Jimmy. He soared above his surroundings just as the Castle did, but whereas the building that was his charge inspired awe, he inspired trust. It repelled, he welcomed. He smiled through the great hairiness of his face and rumbled from deep in his belly.

"And who is this mite that disturbs my labours?"

"I am instructed to ask you for a horse and the bell." He took my arm.

"Why?" The same urgent tone the Captain had used. I told him of the intrusion by Wicked Wicks and the dragoons.

Still holding my arm, he turned and strode along the terrace and I was forced to run, or be dragged. He descended some steps and I tumbled in his wake to a cavernous cellar, wherein were several hacks, used I assumed, for estate business. He led one out, all of sixteen hands, and saddled it in a trice. He gave me a leg up with such force that I flew straight over the broad back and landed in a winded heap on the grass beyond. He shook with volcanic laughter as he lifted me with one titanic arm and placed me in the saddle.

The bronze handbell he thrust at me must have weighed ten pounds. As I wrestled with the problem of holding it in one hand, with the reins in the other and trying to secure my feet in the stirrups, John Bastard smote the broad rump. The nag and I flew headlong down the drive – he, ears flat and angry eyed at the outrage to his bruised quarters; I, a terrified tangle of harness and limbs, sure that my last moment had come.

He must have been watching over me from His Church tower, for only Divine intervention can explain my adherence to that mighty engine of charging flesh. We careered across the parkland, a blur of green and hurrying trees, past the granite lodge house and through massive gate pillars, at a speed I have never since attained. It was only when we reached the lane my conveyance slowed, and I was able to observe that we were passing between thatched cob cottages, pretty as teapots in their cosies. I began to wave the arm that carried the bell and the response was as instantaneous as it was extraordinary.

Doors all along the street opened and yokels in varying stages of dressing ran from them, as though the plague had been discovered in their parlour. There was no shouting or confusion; they all knew their business. Two box wagons, with teams of four, materialized at the end of the lane, and from every corner of the gardens and privies and orchards and sheds, men women and children carried casks to the waiting transport.

I have observed ants in their labours, orderly legions, fetching and carrying loads twice their size, without apparent command or direction. I have concluded that if, by some mutation of nature, these minute insects were to grow to human dimension, they would inherit the earth. On that morning I was tempted to the thought that the process had already begun, and thus far they had attained the form of Dorset villagers.

The teams were whipped up and the piled high wagons creaked and swayed from the village. A cask fell from the latter wagon and smashed in the lane. A stain spread across the dust. The heady perfume that had filled Billy

Barber's wine booth drifted on the breeze. It pervaded the thatch and cob, the waving pink hollyhocks, the neat hawthorn hedges, the gentle bank by the castle gates, and the park over which I had lately flown.

A mounted villager gathered the debris of the cask and galloped in pursuit of the wagon. Another took the bell from me and helped me down from my warhorse. A third led me along a path between the cottages to a spinney, where I was instructed to climb a willow and hide in the bowl of the stunted trunk. The rest returned to their cottages and, but for the smell, Lulworth resumed the easy rhythm of rural life.

There was, though, a tenseness about the place; a sense of waiting; of anticipation. The cottages seemed to crouch in their gardens, rabbits knowing the stoat is coming, but unwilling to take flight, frozen in their foreboding. And the stoat did not keep them waiting.

The sweet scent of sin, much diluted, but still potent to the nose of a thirsting dragoon, reached the stables. Shouts were followed by the martial sounds of jingling brass, barked orders, and the steady pound of a cantering troop. By the time he reached the cottages, the abbreviated figure of Wicked Wicks had preened away the ravages of Mr Weld's assault. He perched in his saddle, pert and stiff, jerking first one arm and then the other, in theatrical husbandry of the dragoons, surveying the village with sudden movements of his head, in the way of a rooster deciding which hen to mount first.

From my vantage point I saw them dismount and stand to attention in a line across the lane. On a command from the Sergeant, they drew singing glinting blades from their scabbards. Then, in chaotic stampede, they ran in pairs to the cottage doors and smashed their way inside.

I have great regard for the military mind, its efficiency, its certainty, its bravery. But these unquestioning qualities can wreak terrible wrongs upon those labelled as hostile. Guilt or innocence matter not to the soldier ordered into battle. The objective is all, and woe betide any that obstruct the path.

As the search progressed without prize, for the Preventives are paid by reference to their seizures, the mood of the searchers darkened. The sniggering villagers, the strutting Wicked Wicks, the shouting Sergeant; the stink of brandy that mocked their efforts, all were darts, pricking their anger, goading their violence.

At first they were irritated, kicking doors, cuffing children. Then I heard breaking glass and the crash of furniture being overturned, thrown out. I saw a man clubbed with a sabre handle, blood oozing from his ear, a lurcher beheaded in mid bark, a saddleback gilt, let out of its sty, squealing defiance at the men who surrounded it and stuck it to death with a dozen cuts.

I saw a farm girl, eyes bulging in terror, run from a cottage along the path towards my tree. Three soldiers caught her and punched her to the ground. They ripped her drawers and two held her down, legs wide. The third dropped his breeches and stood, hand to his tool, stroking it, holding it for her to see. And when he was ready, he knelt between her legs. When her screams of pain became sobs of shame, they left her to find more spirited prey.

And then they were gone, recalled by the Sergeant, sullen in the indignity of failure. They mounted and galloped from the village as if bound for Newmarket. The villagers, surprisingly jocular after such an ordeal, set about the task of repairing the damage. I walked back to the Castle leading the dashing dobbin upon which I had arrived.

Had Isaac Gulliver* designed it himself, the stretch of coast between St Aldhelm's Head and Portland, could not suit the smuggling trade better: a wild deserted shore, of ledges and rocks and hidden coves, and treacherous waters where the Revenue Cruisers venture at their peril.

West from Chapman's Pool, where a beck trickles down a steep fissure off Matravers, and Egmont Bight, a wooded gwyle, which covers the run to Kingston, there are four bays – Kimmeridge, Holbarrow, Brandy and Worbarrow, tucked down behind the high coastal ridge. They are easily defended from landward. For the Dorset country beyond these hills is flat heath, soft vulnerable land of purple and brown and sombre green, without cover, the domain of one man with a good spyglass. Wareham is out of sight to the north, and Weymouth a few distant lights in the east. There are no towns of nosey folk to overlook moonlight landings, just the close, secret village folk, kindred bound and not a family without at least one involved in the business.

Jack and I lay on our bellies in the hot afternoon. We had walked down the slopes from the Castle, through Monastery Farm, and climbed to the ancient fort high on Rings Hill. Snowflakes of thistledown drifted on the breeze, out over the cliff, to soar up and ever up, on currents of warm air. Below us the sea, milky white where it washes the chalk, lapped over grey shingle, in absent minded, trifling ripples. We could see clear across Worbarrow Bay,

* King of the Dorset smugglers.

from the Knob, to the line of teeth that are Mupe Rocks. The Mupes guard the entrance to a little cove called Bacon Hole. There is a deep cave in the cliff here, under Bindon Hill, where the Preventives concentrate their meagre resources, laying in wait for night after night. But although it is often used as a sprat, the mackerel usually lands elsewhere.

The fort marks the descent of the Purbeck Ridge[82] down to the sea at Arish Mell, where a rift has allowed the sea to wash a cove from the chalk cliffs. This is the only point of the bay where the way from landward is but a gentle slope. There are no buildings on the hills, and from the sea only one can be spied through the Arish Gap. It is as if the Welds had hewn the gap themselves to allow their own private sea view. I was soon to discover that a far more practical use had been found for this facility.

We threw thistle heads at each other and caught little blue butterflies that fluttered in our cupped hands and left the dust of their wings. We talked of smuggling and sailing and fast Revenue cutters. But when I recounted, once again, the tale of Wicked Wicks and the hateful dragoons, Jack gave me the same knowing, crafty grin, as the night in the cellar at Brambridge.

"Surely you weren't fooled by Wicks and his strolling players?"

"Fooled? I was near killed by them."

"They wouldn't have harmed you. They're part of the team".

"Team! What team? How can they be part of a team? They ransacked and abused and broke heads. They even raped a poor maid."

"Raped? She gets raped every week. She can't wait for Saturdays. Her Father's always threatening that if she don't work harder, he'll send the soldiers to Lizzie next door."

"I don't believe you."

"Please yourself."

"But if it's all a farce, why do they do it?"

"Because Mister Weld tells them to."

"What has Mister Weld got to do with it?"

"He pays their wages."

"I don't believe you."

"Please yourself."

"Why would Mister Weld arrange a raid on his own workers?"

"As long as the Customs House in Poole knows that Wicked has his beady eye on Lulworth, they're happy. They send an officer with extra dragoons to most raids, and he always reports that Captain Wicks is too zealous in his treatment of the law abiding villagers."

"How do they feel about it?"

"They only have to put up with a bit of pillage each week. In return they get all the brandy they can drink and a small share of the profits."

"I don't believe you." In truth I was beginning to.

"Please yourself."

We walked down the steep incline to the beach at Arish Mell and threw grey chalk pebbles in high arcs, so that they fell fast, entering the water with a glottal stop. The cove was in shadow, for the sun had already lowered behind high chalk cliffs. So we strolled up towards the Castle, where the heat of day had not yet died. The slopes beneath the south face are wooded, stunted oaks that crouch under the towers, hiding from winter winds. Our approach through this toy forest was unseen by the party that sat on the terrace, but the faces that I saw between the twisted branches, were graphic testimony to Jack's tale of perfidy: Captain Howell and Wicked Wicks, John Bastard and Walter Smythe, Edward Weld and a dark handsome man, no more than twenty five, with wild black hair and dense beard. This, I was to learn, was John Darling, master of the collier brig Clevedon and custodian of my voyage into villainy.

The six were in deep conversation, poring over a table scattered with charts. From time to time Mr Weld would point seawards for them all to look up, as if searching the horizon for a sail.

Jack and I returned to the stables, following the aroma of the evening meal, and gobbled bowls of rabbit stew, with fresh baked bread and Blue Vinny. Later in the evening we were summoned to the castle and this time the footman nodded respectfully, as we walked through those fearsome portals.

Whenever I call to mind the great hall at Lulworth, I can think only of death: a huge darkened vault, walls of carved mahogany hung with lifeless armour and faces of sombre men, and the heads of savage animals, seemingly decapitated in the moment of attack, snarling, watching me with wild eyes as I passed. But nothing moved and there was no sound, save our echoing footfalls on stone flags and a sparrow, frantic to be free, beating the round gothic window. Evening light, cold and dead, frosted the high ceiling.

We entered a room directly from the hall and could have stepped into another house, intimate, cheerful, with patterned drapes and floral decorations, and the somnolent fog of a village inn – murmured conversation, warm odours of flatulence and tobacco, the brandied fume of France.

The Captain, beamed at us, expansive, flushed with his usual evening excess. "Come in, come in, my jolly little pirates". A conspiratorial leer to his fellows. "Tonight we have work for you. Tonight you shall strike a blow for the downtrodden imbibers of this fair isle. You shall take from the thieving Guelph[83] that which is rightfully yours".

It sounded ominously like another exposure to the delights of the deep, and I felt the sludge of rabbit and vinny begin to simmer. "You have already met Mister Bastard." The eyes laughed and the great beard thrusted at me. Seated, he was taller than I. "But you may have gained a false impression from your introduction to Captain Wicks." Wicked smiled in the way of a lurcher showing its teeth. I concluded that my first impression of him had been not at all false. "And this is my good friend John Darling, master of the Clevedon, your employer for the run to Brambridge." The dark wild haired man held out his hand to me and although he bore no physical resemblance, I was reminded of Pierce Creagh. They shared the same quiet depth, thoughtful eyes, they both wore wisdom beyond their years. "You're to go fishing tonight with Mister Bastard and Captain Darling. Fishing for tubs. The finest, sweetest food the sea can provide."

We followed John Darling and John Bastard to another smaller room, where we all dressed in heavy jerseys, cord trousers and sea boots. Each carrying a set of oilskins, we went out into the night. At the side of the Castle, where John Bastard had thrown me clean over Dashing Dobbin, four estate hacks were tethered. We mounted and galloped away, along the lane to West Lulworth. I felt as I had when our troop set out from Matson, fired by the mysteries of the night, alight with the prospect of conflict.

The cool black air took my breath. My eyes watered, and I saw nothing, save the giant rump of John Bastard's mount heaving its great load along the lane. We followed down the slope towards the sea, past cottages with lighted windows and the sound of a stream tumbling through a mill. It was still dark, but there were shapes and voices ahead.

We rode into the cobbled yard of a small coaching inn, and there must have been forty men waiting in groups under the stable eaves, some smoking pipes, some talking, but none drinking. I reflected that the landlord of the Red Lion must have other sources of profit that night.

The horses were taken to the stables and the men gathered around John Bastard. He stood a foot above the rest and his deep voice rumbled over them. "We've two extras tonight, men, but you need not be concerned. They're sent by Mister Weld." I felt eighty eyes judging Jack and I. "Matthew Downe and Uncle Job are the decoy. Wicked must have his prize to show them in Poole."

A ring of faces flickered in the lantern light, the strong faces of independent men, hard, determined. Had the Preventives arrived to do battle at that moment, my money would have been on the smugglers.

"Away to your boats then. There's a good wind and we'll make the Mell within the hour."

We followed the brook that gurgles down the combe – a small army, silent save for the muffled footfall of soft soles on the lane. Where the brook widens, its journey done, sliding silently across the shore to its death, we donned our oilskins. I will always hate those heavy alien garments – hot, uncomfortable, restrictive – and even today, just the smell of them brings a cold sweat to my brow. In the blue black dimness of the cove I could make out the shapes of a score of luggers drawn up on the shingle. John Bastard led me to one which, with the help of a waterman, we pushed into the water.

Thus began my second sea voyage. I trembled at the prospect of being sick again, but had I known what was in store, I would have welcomed sickness as a brother.

We hoisted lugsails fore and aft and dipped and nodded our way past a coal brig anchored in the cove, to the open sea. We turned east and followed the just discernible line high above, where grey cliff becomes black sky. Sailing at night is daunting enough; on a lee shore in dangerous waters it is awesome. A sudden squall, an eddy, a freak wave, any one can take the unsuspecting helm on to the rocks. But our Waterman seemed unconcerned, so I sat in the bow, pulling ropes when instructed, and tried again to recall the Lord's Prayer.

After some time I became accustomed to seeing rocks on my left, but when I spotted a large broken tooth around which the sea boiled, not twenty yards off our starboard bow, I am ashamed to say I screamed.

"Tis only the Mewps," called the Waterman, as if that morsel of information was sufficient to calm me. "Bless me, we'd take another quarter hour if we had to go round that lot," Fifteen minutes seemed a meagre investment for the lives of two grown men and a promising youth, but I was in no position to argue. So I screwed my eyes tight shut and awaited the inevitable.

The inevitable did not present itself, for in a trice we were out across Worbarrow Bay. The chalk shingle of Arish Mell can never have welcomed a more devoted admirer. One by one the other boats slipped out of the night and beached alongside us.

We sat in our boats listening to the sigh of the waves as they died on the shore, the soft murmur of conversation between boats. The occasional shriek of an owl brought Jud sharply to my mind. It was just possible to make out the grey cliffs that tower on either side of the Mell, and beyond them the blackness of a clouded sky, no stars, no moon.

"Good night tonight,"said John Bastard to the Waterman. They were the last words I heard him speak.

"I wooden a comed had the night been clear," said the Waterman. "That Speedwell 'e bin stickin' 'is nose in 'ere too much a' late."

Just then I spied a flash from out at sea, then another. As one, the armada was launched. Twenty boats rowing from the shore, then hoisting sail without commands or shouts and pulling them hard in, to sail to windward. We tacked and tacked again, heeling one way then the other. It was at that moment that sailing took its grip upon me.

I am not able to convey the exhilaration I felt as I sat in the bow of that shabby, fish reeking old lugger, leaping over a sea that crashed and splashed beneath me, tasting salt on my lips, sniffing the sharp wind. But I know now, that this world offers few sensations to compare – a good woman perhaps, a bottle of finest claret, a thoroughbred at full stretch.

Twenty boats, beating to windward, racing for the honour of first tub, tacking left, then right, then left again, not a pageant, not an organised parade, but an intoxicating tapestry of boats, criss-crossing each other's frothing wake. Each turning to steal wind at the whim of its helmsman, each careering at another on collision course, but never touching.

I looked back at John Bastard and the Waterman, eager faces of men at home on the sea, and beyond them to a single star that hung low in the sky. I shouted that I could see the North Star.

"That be no star me lad," the Waterman called back. "That be the Bastard Light. John show it when coast be clear so the Frenchies come in close. It be at the top o' west tower. Dang bugger it. That be too much torkin,"

The boat to our left had tacked across our bow, and for a moment our sails flapped as the wind dropped in their shadow. I heard a laugh over the water, deep and harsh, not a southern laugh, as they scurried away to starboard. And then we were under the lee of a tall ship, no lights, no movement, just the creaking of her timbers as she wallowed on the swell. I heard John Darling hailing her and the reply; muted, fugitive, foreign. And then lines coming over her side, with casks attached each couple of feet.

We had dropped the sails, and the Waterman nudged up to the side of the ship using an oar as a sweep. I grabbed one of the lines, and an unseen French hand began to pay out. One by one the casks came down to me and I laid them, as instructed, in the bottom of the boat, still attached to the line. I was puzzled by the large cork floats attached to the casks, but I was soon to bless them. I asked the Waterman their purpose.

"I hopes you never 'as to find out." I asked again.

"Well. The stuff we'm loading be more valable 'n you 'n me. So they put floats on it 'n weights to keep it under. If'n we sink, they can still come out tomorrer 'n collect it."

Before we had finished loading, another boat pushed off, hoisted sails and headed south west. "That be Matt an' Uncle Job. Off with a couple a' barrels fer the Farmer. They'll get arrested by Wicked and chucked in the Bridewell at Poole fer a couple a months."

"Don't they mind"?

"Mister Weld'll pay 'em well".

We were full and I pushed the bow away from the Frenchman. We hoisted sail and this time let them right out to run before the wind. Several other boats were leaving with us when I experienced the most startling moment of my young life.

A spurt of flame, searing amber aginst the still dark western sky was followed by a thundering crack that knocked me to the bottom of the boat. I lay on the tubs and the eerie whistle of a missile passed across our midships and rushed into the water, a tall spout of spume, not ten yards from our gunwhales.

The Waterman and John Bastard seemed not to notice. They sat in the stern, staring ahead into the night, tense, silent, and we began to gather speed as the wind filled our sails. It was as though an ant's nest had been kicked apart on the Frenchman. Sailors swarmed the rigging, the lines of casks were cut. Big sails, grey in the growing light, rose like disturbed swans, angrily flapping, hungry for the air. And then she heeled to port, away from the Revenue Cruiser, towards St Aldhelm's Head.

Another flash, another crash. This time the whistle seemed to hang in the air. I knew it would hit us. It called my name. It was as if my Mother were coming from the sky to fetch me, embrace me. I had no fear. I watched the sky, looking for her, wanting her. I saw the ball smash right through John Bastard, scattering him in pieces, through the starboard timbers, splintering, destroying; so that the boat collapsed upon itself and folded into the water.

I floundered in the cold black waves, trying to keep my head up. I swallowed mouthfuls of salt water as I tried to shout. I was coughing, choking, unable to breathe, being dragged down by the heavy oilskins, submerging as I gasped for air, filling my nose, my eyes, my throat, my lungs.

Something floating bumped my face. I grabbed at the cork, but it slipped away like the soap in a bath. I lunged again and this time stuck my fingers into its spongey surface and gripped so tight it would have taken Arthur to pull me free. I put my chin on its edge and sucked air into my bursting chest.

I lay across my tiny raft, coughing and retching and gasping, without idea of time. But when I had recovered sufficiently to take stock of my situation, I was entirely alone. I could hear gunfire cracking over the water from the east, where the sky was already bruised with the coming dawn, but I could see nothing but water wherever I looked – featureless, impassive water, deaf to my cries, blind to my fate, a slab of fluid marble, waiting to entomb me.

Whether my deliverance from that bedraggled end was due to Divine intervention, I cannot say. Perhaps my Mother still watches over me, or my Father has been reincarnated as a seagull. Or perhaps some force of nature, as yet unsuspected by any of us, succours us until our time is due. All I can do is record what happened and leave interpretation to future generations that may read this journal.

The rigours of the night – lack of sleep, coldness and the dead burden of my oilskins – seemed to drain my resolve, numbing my limbs, weighing my eyelids. All spirit and fight curled inside me, a dog before the fire, resigned to drift wherever the tides of sleep determine. The depths beckoned me, warm, seductive, my Mother's breast.

The harsh skirl of a black backed gull disturbed my reverie. I saw a wicked hooked beak, surmounted by two malevolent eyes, considering me, as though deciding which piece of this delectable morsel to peck first. It was sitting on the sea, as bouyant as I was porous, mocking me. I was in its element and it was my master. With considerable effort I shouted at it, a sort of coughing bark, but it merely opened its wings, hung for a moment on the air and then resumed its lordly throne. We glared at each other for a minute or two, before the drowsiness overcame me and I began to slip again into the twilight.

This time the damnable thing rose again and alighted on my head, gripping tight with the claws at the end of its soft webbed feet, and inflicting agonies upon my cranium. I was overcome with anger. I felt that this vulgar bird was interfering in my heroic death. I swiped and although I achieved my goal, by cuffing it several yards across the water, I lost my grip upon the float, which scudded off like a pondskater. The odious fowl, ruffled but defiant, circled me for a moment, as I began to fill again. It then landed by the cork and, in a welter of squawking and flapping and nudging, directed it back to me.

I will forever be ashamed for the lack of gratitude I displayed on that soggy morn. I hurled abuse at my avian friend, using terms that would have earned congratulation from Jud. I waved at it, splashed it, I even threw the cork at it, but this it merely returned in the manner of a farm dog retrieving a stick. And much of the morning passed in profane badinage between us. For despite his lack of English, he gave as good as he got, in a series of cackles and squawks and hisses and shrieks.

In the mysterious ways of wind and tide, I was returned to Worbarrow Knob and deposited on the beach, in the little inlet of Punfell Cove. I should have been just another corpse, for many find their final resting place along these rocky shores. But anger had kept my blood surging and the efforts of my feathered hound had kept me afloat.

I slept where I lay for much of the afternoon, but when the chill of the evening revived me, I sat up; then found that with a little effort, I could stand. He was still there, sitting on a sharp rock, mean eyes, hateful beak, watching me in the manner that Mrs Gale reserved for the class, when one of us had farted.

I have since come to know that gulls are the most arrogant of birds – handsome scavengers, loved by few, beast or fowl. They neither taste nor sing well, they are in habit rude, insatiably greedy and gratuitously cruel. But I will never see one again without feeling deeply sad. For I did not acknowledge his going, never thanked him for my life, never even waved as he took his leave.

As I walked unsteadily away from the beach, he rose in the air, circled me and with one squawk soared up over Gad Cliff. And I made yet another of my sodden and unexpected returns to Society.

There was a distracted air at the Castle. My absence had been noted, probably regretted, but nothing had been done to resolve it. I was assumed to have perished with John Bastard, and as tears would bring neither of us back, the shedding of them was superfluous. A more pressing problem was the need to prepare for the run to Brambridge, for I learned that the Jamaica Sun was due that night. Her presence off the South Coast, loaded with spoils, would take a deal of explaining to a Revenue Officer, and the Captain was anxious for her cargo to be transferred to the Clevedon without delay.

I thus began my third sea voyage with precious little notice, and even less thought as to the state of my health.

The Clevedon, a collier brig of about three hundred tons, plies the coastal routes delivering Kingswood coal to the ports of southern England. She is a fat, friendly old tub, black as her cargo, reeking of Stockholm tar and the mud of a hundred harbours. She carries two masts and enough rigging to string up the entire Hawkhurst Gang. In my short spell as cabin boy, I was to hear, but never master, the names of her stays and guys and gammon and hounds, her booms and fids and futtocks and rattlings, her jibs and staysails and stunsails and royals.

Her crew of twenty consider it their right to curse her roundly, but woe betide any stranger that agrees. Her captain, John Darling, was a cabin boy from Blyth, who had served his time on Baltic traders since the age of twelve. At twenty-six, he was already a consumate seaman – and I suspect that he would have made an equally good physician, for he nursed his ancient charge through storm and tempest and the mountainous seas of North Devon, with a devotion to her frailties that would have made him a fortune in the Temple of Health[84].

Her crew quarters were under the forecastle deck which opened and closed like bellows with every plunge or roll she took, giving the impression she was splitting in two. Here hung a dozen or so hammocks, with oiled tent covers to fend off the worst of the constantly dripping deck. Here also lived the windlass, several spare kedges and anchors, mooring hawsers, grease tins, paint pots and casks of Stockholm tar. When the anchor was weighed, the cable chain was coiled in the corner, looking and smelling like an immense pile of dog shit. Despite the residue of weariness from my exertions on the previous night, I resolved to go without sleep for the duration of my duties aboard the Clevedon.

The only other accommodation below decks was the Captain's cabin – a tiny oasis of refinement amidst the squalor – and the Galley, from which steam and gruel and rock hard biscuits issued, as a substitute for food. Everywhere else was coal. At least, everywhere else should have been coal, but when I peered into the airless depths of the hold, I saw nothing but dust, black choking dust that invaded every nook, every crevice of the boat and every orifice of the human body. This, I was to discover was the ballast, free from the traders of Kingswood, but sufficient to pass inspection as a legitimate cargo.

We set sail from Lulworth Cove as the sun was sinking over Portland Bill. We sailed due south for a mile or so, then east for two miles until we could see the Bastard Light winking through Arish Gap. There we hove to and aided by a series of pullies and hoists and ropes and chains, the ship's company set to dumping the ballast. It came up out of the hold in buckets and was swung out over the sea on a projecting arm. The lack of breeze allowed much of the dust to float upon the air, and a goodly proportion of it seemed reluctant to leave the ship. It settled back on the decks, where it mingled with the evening damp to a black slime. Long before the hold was empty, the entire crew were covered from head to toe. We must have resembled a well stocked slaver on passage to the Bristol market.

And then we waited, sitting around the decks in the black night, no sound save a groaning timber and the kindly wash of the sea, nothing to see save the glow of a clay pipe and the Bastard light beyond the stern. It disappeared once and we hoisted a sail and crabbed to starboard until it winked again.

It was after midnight when they showed. First a flash, as the Frenchman, then a golden carved figurehead atop a sleek and graceful bow, sliding out of the void. I had forgotten how big she was, this greyhound of the sea. She dwarfed us, five hundred tons that could outsail anything afloat. An elite ship with what must have been an elite crew. For she came alongside, made fast fore and aft with springs bow to stern, without an audible order being given.

Her holds were opened and the perfumes and spices of the East filled the air. Bales and boxes and oaken casks were swung across in nets to be hooked to our hoist and lowered slowly into the coal hole. The work went on for an hour and when we were full, she slipped away into the night, as stealthily as she had come. I was filled with wonder at her beauty, with longing to sail on her and fervour for the adventures that she could tell. She was simply the most exciting thing that I had ever seen.

We too were not long in setting sail. We headed east around St Aldhelm's Head, then east north east for the Needles. John Darling called me aft where he took the wheel. I stood between his arms and held the spokes, feeling the surge of the ship as the breeze took her sails, feeling her slow if we came up to starboard; labour if we went off to port. Learning how to keep the sails working, but not fighting.

As a pale sun, still cold in the mists, came up over the Isle of Wight, we passed a merchantman out of Poole, bound for Newfoundland, three tall masts, with every piece of canvas that she possessed hanging in sullen idleness, as she tried to beat around the Head. I asked John Darling how it was that the wind was filling our sails and not hers, and he explained that we were reaching, with the wind on our beam, our sails like bags catching every puff.

"She's beating, sailing at the wind and she'd like a better blow than this to make her course. She'll take an hour to get round the Head, but then she'll reach all the way to America."

Those words were like a dart, piercing my heart, filling me with the romance of the sea. I would dream that night, and on countless future nights, of the sun rising through feather soft mist and my ship taking leave of its home port, to sail wild and lonely oceans to the New World.

We passed the Needles at ten, Jack and I sitting on the gunwhales, sipping scalding salty gruel, watching the jagged white teeth that have savaged so many mariners, snarling from the mouth of the Solent. We had caught the tide and were swept into the land locked waters on a current so swift, that we made four knots with not a sail filled. The sea is always flat in the Solent and the air this day was still. The sun gathered its strength, and the morning greys became blue, the soft dove hills of the Island cleared and sharpened, the dark forests down the Hampshire shore lightened to a rich green.

Southampton Water was reached at two, and a breeze to push us north. Merchantmen and men of war, coasters and cruisers, all nodding at anchor, waiting for the tide. A new ship of the line, three decks high, a floating fortress of New Forest oak, making ready to quell the natives in some distant land. I counted thirty-two gun ports[85] as we slipped by in the lee of her towering decks. I marvelled at the Roman soldier, carved on her bow under the long raking bowsprit, helmet and shield glinting gold, sword raised to strike – three masts, mighty columns, straight and true, bedecked in a foliage of rigging. The Captain's Walk was set into a gilded stern, under an ornate canopy of bare breasted nymphs; and brass lamps that would have graced St James's.

A second tidal surge pushed us past the mouth of the Hamble up to where the Itchen and Test go their separate ways. The tide was turning as we nosed into the Itchen, but there was enough breeze to run along the slack, past docks and wharves, to where the river slips shyly into its country clothes.

Here at Northam, where the river bends east, Mr Smythe owns the coal wharves. Three barges, all full, but one riding higher than the others, were rafted to the bank. With only mizzen and main aloft, and John Darling at the helm, we reached across the stream, gathering way until it seemed that we would plough a furrow right up to the bargee's hut. As our bowsprit cast its shadow on the jetty, we turned sharply to starboard. The sails fell, the lines snaked ashore, and we came alongside with the calm unruffled air of a dairy cow stepping into her parlour.

The decks and the wharf sprang to life. An old and creaking crane swung its scrawny finger over the hold and dipped a grab down into the depths. Two sailors, squirrels in a wood, scampered up the rigging to the topmasts, where they surveyed the river for movement. Then the cargo of the barge that rode higher than its fellows was raised, like a top hat before a lady, and one of the many mysteries of my young life was resolved, for I perceived the purpose of the strange, coal bedecked craft I had encountered in the boat house at Brambridge.

Up came the grab, with a net full of trophies. I remembered my Mother telling me that babies arrived swinging in their swaddling clothes, from the beak of a stork. The Clevedon gave birth to twenty fine plump children, which were all delivered to the belly of the barge. And then the holds were secured and Jack and I said our goodbyes to John Darling and his crew.

The last leg of our voyage, along the Itchen as it narrowed from a tidal creek to a stream, then along the Navigation from Woodmill, was a peaceful journey in a sylvan setting, towed at a steady plod by a game and massive shire. We sat on the stern, watching the whorls of our wake on the evening smooth water, and I concluded that crime was an altogether more pleasant path to one's fortune than commerce.

Chapter Eight

M*atson, Autumn 1772.*

The leaves are dying again. They fall, light and brittle, before rain littered winds, pirouetting on eddies that dance around the Courtyard, fluttering in the damp airs, then flopping, cowpats on wet cobbles. My life too is entering its winter. The safeties and certainties, the unpolluted pleasures, the steadfast friendships, all must be reviewed, questioned, probed, and those that fall must be swept away to clear the decks for new adventures.

Jud and his brothers were the first leaves to fall. For I had become a stranger in their midst. I know now that the fault was mine, that I was changing my spots, shedding the slough of my childhood for a many coloured coat, whilst they were merely progressing through adolescence to a life of estate work, determined for them at birth.

I was uncomfortable in their company. Their conversation seemed to me vulgar; their bearing, oafish. When I told them of my adventures – of London, of sailing, of cricket, of smuggling – they paid no heed, preferring to fight, and giggle when one of them farted.

George was twenty-five and his fine features had coarsened, cyder and fresh air setting them into a yeoman mould. He was engaged to a village girl and soon she would be Hannah, he would be his Father, and from them would spew another gaggle of Holyoakes.

Job was twenty-two and already looking after Mr Selwyn's accounts. He, if any, seemed destined to progress in the commercial world.

Tom, at nineteen, had outgrown them all, a young oxen with a fearful temper. He drank prodigiously and had to be treated with humility when he stamped into the dormitory during the night hours. He considered it his beholden duty to protect Sarah from the young men that sniffed after her, for she had grown too, in all the right directions.

Jud's features had not been improved by the passage of time. His face seemed ever more squashed. It was as though he were carrying a mighty weight upon his head, slowly flattening him, widening his nose, slitting his eyes. His hair still belonged to a hog, but now he wetted and brushed it, which was worse, for it stood out from his crown like a besom broom.

He remained fond of me and I tried to return his affection. We walked the fields, and climbed Robinswood Hill. We rode down the long slopes to Gloucester and the Severn. But I could only wish that Jem Gillray and Tom Rowlandson were with me, or Jack Smythe, or Maria.

Maria – whenever I thought of her, there seemed a leaden lump within my stomach. I was sure I had lost her and blamed my own stumbling ignorance, my preference for stupid games, for childish adventure, the damned, wretched, unjust, affliction of youth. Had I indulged less in my own turmoil, I would have realised that Jud too was churning the same wake, that we are all cast adrift on a bemisted lake of adolescence, and can do nothing but rage against the clouded waters until they clear. Only then can we perceive our course.

"You'd best stay clear o' Sarah." We were sitting in the hayloft of Larkham barn. Rain drops ticked on stone tiles, nervous winds gusted under eaves, the dust dry smell of dead summer hung in the air. We were musing about girls.

"I haven't touched her."

"Try tellin' that to Tom. 'e thinks you'm after 'er. I 'eard 'im tellin' Job yesterday that if 'e catches you with 'er, 'e'll geld you."

I protested at the injustice of such calumny, but in truth thoughts of Sarah had filled many idle moments since my return from Brambridge. Her gaunt, vulnerable face, big brown eyes, high cheekbones, smiled softly at me when we met around the house. And I found it difficult to ignore the contours that lurked beneath her working clothes.

"That brother of yours belongs in Bedlam."

"Maybe, but it'll take more 'n you to put 'im there. An' she's a right little prick teaser, is our Sarah. I sin 'er turn 'er eyes on you, an' from the way you looked back, she could 'ave your breeches off with one wink."

I continued to puff my innocence whilst making a mental resolution to keep an eye peeled for Tom, whenever Sarah hove into view.

I should have known that, faced with the female form, my powers of concentration are prone to polarisation. And at my next meeting with Sarah, there was more than sufficient female form on view.

Our dormitory was a long attic room with elm plank floors and dormer windows. There was a door at each end, one into the corridor that led to the main staircase, and one into the next dormitory wherein George and Hannah slept, which in turn had a door through to the girl's sleeping quarters. It was this route we took to reach the back stairs.

I awoke late on All Saint's Day, alone in the long room midst a jumble of clothing and pillows and scattered nightshirts, debris of the brothers' departure for church. I hurried on my shirt and breeches, wiped my face and slicked down my hair, pulled on my best boots, and ran through the attic rooms, clumping on the bare timbers sufficient to wake the dead.

The dead and Sarah. She too had overslept and been left by her sisters. As I slithered to a halt in the doorway of her dormitory, she was in the act of emerging from her blankets, a butterfly from its pupa, one slender foot touching the boards, a bare arm raised as she stroked hair from her face. She showed no sign of sharing my embarassment. She smiled, a slow, waking smile, and stretched – cotton shift taut over her breast – and swung her other leg to the floor, bare to the thigh, pink with night warmth.

"Too late, Jo. Service'll be half over." Lazy voice, laughing eyes.

"But Mister Selwyn's there. He likes me to attend." In eighteen years I have uttered nothing more feeble nor pointless.

"He won't miss you, but I might." A sidelong glance, daring, teasing.

It was then that the image of Tom should have sprung into my mind. But if it did it was drowned by the sight of Sarah, now standing, hands on hips, legs astride, before the bright morning light of the dormer window. It was as if her shift had melted, the outline of her form clear and sharp, a smudge of curls rippling the cotton where it fell over her pubis.

I kissed her mouth, my tongue deep in her wetness, her eyes, her ears, her throat. I pulled her to me, my hands under the shift, gripping and pulling her arse apart. I felt her hands at the buttons of my breeches, ripping them open, sliding down inside, stroking my thighs, cool darting fingers kneading my arse. Then slowly, teasingly, round my hips, scratching the creases of my groin, tickling the hair, knuckles just touching my tool as if by mistake, then at last, holding it, tighter, moving now, slow rhythmic tugs, until I began to move with her, pushing, harder, harder.

For a moment I thought the dragoons had arrived as the door crashed open. But the sight of Tom, six foot two of athletic savagery, purple face, wild eyes, was infinitely more fearsome than Wicked Wicks and a whole troop of cavalry.

He roared like a bull in rut and charged down the room. A bucket of cold water could not have doused my ardour to such effect, but in the panic of trying to disentangle my hands from Sarah's shift, her hands from my tool, my breeches from my knees, I fell to the floor. With satanic glee, he launched himself, a flailing engine of destruction, upon my meagre frame.

I have only one clear recollection of the following few minutes. It stands like a beacon in a sea of gory mist, of crunching numbing blows to my head, my ribs, my stomach, my legs. It is of Tom's awful, devilish face, as he held my poor shrivelled penis in his left hand, and with his right, brandished a gelding knife. Whether he intended the foul deed, I shall never know, for a strident shriek from Hannah froze him, and the crack on the side of the head she gave him with the stone hot water bottle sent him sprawling across the elm boards in whimpering, bloodied shame. Her children might have outgrown her, but they did not yet outrank her.

"Dress yourself, and get out of this room." Her venom was directed not only at Tom. I dragged my dishevelled self aloft, trying at the same time to pull up my breeches. I had not the coordination for such a task and collapsed on to a bed where I sat, legs akimbo, pointing the remains of my manhood at her. The breeches collapsed around my legs, and I kicked them off, resigned for all to see my humiliation. Sarah snickered and was rewarded with a cuff.

"You, my girl, will be dealt with by your Father." The look of terror that sprang to Sarah's face was testimony to the legends of George Holyoake's belt. It was said that once removed from his domelike belly, it could not return 'ere it had tasted bare arse.

One eye had closed and I could taste salt blood from a split lip. Barbs of vicious pain shot from ribs to stomach and back. But my agonies were nought to Hannah's rage.

"You think you're a gent. Well, let me tell you. You're no better than the dogs in the yard. You treat my boys with your airs and graces, you think you can ravish my girls. We want no more of you. I shall tell Mister Selwyn this morning, either you go, or we do. And I don't care if you rot in the gutter." As she hurled this torrent at me, she was crying, tears of rage or remorse I know not, but when she was done she raised the stone hot water bottle, and unfettered by breeches, I scuttled for the refuge of the door.

I was summoned to the presence of Mister Selwyn later that day. He stood with his back to the fire, as he had when Jud and I had met Jesus. He tried hard to look stern, but I could see in his eyes that he considered my crime no more than that of being caught in flagrante delicto. And he rather envied me.

"I am far from happy with you, Joseph. You have enraged the Holyoakes, impregnated their daughter and made a very dangerous enemy in young Thomas".

"I do not believe I have impregnated any Holyoake, sir."

"I really do not wish to know where you put it, Joseph, suffice to say it was discovered in young Sarah's hand and that, as far as Mistress Holyoake is concerned, is conclusive evidence of impregnation."

I had a sudden recollection of Sarah tweaking it when I was being bathed in the kitchen, on my ninth birthday, and Hannah laughing at our play. Extraordinary the difference a few years can make.

"You are no longer welcome in the Holyoake's dormitory and I have therefore arranged for your belongings to be transferred to the top of the main house. You will sleep in the room next to the classroom where you will attend closely to your lessons for the remainder of the winter. We are doubly fortunate in that little Maria Emily is coming to stay, and her nurse, Miss Tuthill, is an accomplished mathematician."

"Who is little Maria Emily, sir?"

"She is the daughter of the Marchioness Fagnani. She is fifteen months of age and the sweetest, most exquisite child you will ever see".

"And will her mother be accompanying her, sir?"

"The Marchioness has other engagements."

"And her father, will he be here?" The soft pink face flushed, the kind eyes fluttered and the rouged lips pursed demurely. "I hope so Joseph. I do hope so."

So my winter progressed. Solitude save for the inescapable company of Miss Tuthill, who looked and sounded like the mathematician she was – earnest, owl like, and blushingly naive – and the gurgling, cooing, enchanting little personage of Maria Emily.

If it is possible for a man to fall in love with a fifteen month old , then I did. I alone could hold her in my arms when she was red and angry, and coax from her a sunny, toe wriggling chortle that would light the whole room. I alone could keep her attention through long rain soaked afternoons, by crawling behind the furniture and leaping upon her from unexpected corners. I alone could lullaby her to sleep in minutes, by softly clicking like a trotting horse, with an occasional coachman's chirrup.

And I taught her to walk – faltering, swaying steps that ended on her bottom, which I concluded was fashioned from rubber, for she never tired of falling upon it – and talk, toothless words that only she and I recognised. Miss Tuthill was *mee tata*, Mr Selwyn, *mee cewa*, I was *cho cho* and she christened herself *mie mie*.

I can even claim to have been her first riding instructor. When January winds eased and the rain clouds grumbled by, I would perch her on Bewitched and lead her around the courtyard, followed by the fluttering Miss Tuthill, a mother hen trying to restrain her errant chick.

Poor Miss Tuthill. I dismissed her from my mind as soon as my need for her was ended. But she taught me mathematics with infinite patience, she bore my adolescence with fortitude. Although the lesson took a few years to germinate, I now understand that humility is an asset, not a burden.

I was to spend my sixteenth birthday at Cleveland Court, from where I would travel with Mr Selwyn to Newmarket for the Craven meeting. I left Matson without regret, for the winter had been long and mathematics hard. But had I known that more than a year would pass before I saw my childhood home again, I think I would have shed a tear or two, and I think I would have sought out Jud to say goodbye.

Spring time in London: the great city sparkling as a new season comes alive; gardens tended, and neat with young plants; railings shining in new coats of paint; buildings clean and spruce like children in Sunday best; trees trimmed and lopped, ready for their summer extravagance. Even Cleveland Court smiled as Charlton ferried me in the hallberline down Pall Mall and past the ancient brick of the Palace.

Uncle Tom, even more frail, fluttered his hand for me to take, parchment skin stretched over grey veins. His voice hesitant, stumbling over some words but full of pleasure just to see me. "A young gentleman, Charlton, how two years have changed him. How tall he is, how slender."

"You have certainly grown, Mister Paget," Charlton said. "When you were last here, you were no higher than Fanny. Now you are as tall as me." The greetings were so warm; so different from the grudging welcome that had been afforded to Pierce and I. Charlton was at ease, for our places in Society were now more clearly defined. And Fanny blushed and curtsied whenever I glanced at her.

At dinner Uncle Tom told me of the progress of his pupils. Pride quavered his voice as he spoke of Tom and Jem. "Those boys will be my epitaph. They are sorcerers both, wicked and wilful, but with the tiger of genius caged within. Those tigers are slavering for the blood of the idle, and the gorgers, and the rich, and it has fallen to me to release them into the world."

"Will I be able to see them?"

"When they heard of your visit, they insisted on being present for your birthday celebration. I must warn you that the causticity of their humour has not yet been tempered with responsibility." I cared not a jot. They could inflict upon me their whole repertoire of humiliating japes; nothing could dim the brightness of their friendship, the dazzle of their wit.

I leant from the wide bay window and breathed misted air, moistening my birthday morning. The park slumbered under its grey blanket, its black rootless trees still gaunt in their winter nakedness. A timid cough and I turned to see Fanny with the jug of steaming water.

I had been careful to don my nightshirt on retiring and was thus respectable, but the light in Fanny's eye was anything but respectable.

"I fought you might like your birfday present early, sir." She put the jug on the washstand and advanced towards me.

"Now, Fanny," I tried to look imperious, but the effect must have been diluted by the hue of my nightshirt, which unfortunately was pastel pink with blue velvet bows. I was trapped in the window bay and wondered if Fanny's passions were being inflamed by a view of my person, in the way that mine had been by Sarah's translucency.

"You doan 'arf look luvley, sir, like a big pink toffee apple. Can I 'av a lick?"

Short of crying for help I was at a loss. I sat on the sill, arse half out of the open window, an action she clearly interpreted as one of complicity.

"Juss you sit there, sir, an' Fanny'll 'av you spurtin' in no time." She licked her lips like a hungry man faced with a leg of mutton, and advanced towards me.

"I didn't mean *now*, Fanny," I spluttered. "I meant, *now Fanny*, Fanny."

"Doan you worry 'bout it, sir," she said, kneeling before me and looking up at my face with ill disguised wickedness.

"But, Fanny – ."

As she slid the nightshirt up my thighs, my resolve must have melted into my tool, for as the one softened the other hardened. Thus I received the first present of a memorable birthday.

After such a start, breakfast, even with Unce Tom's wheezing and Charlton's shuffling, was a languid affair. Mr Selwyn had sent me a brocade dressing gown in which I lounged over toast and tea, and fresh rolls with marmalade. If Uncle Tom noticed the secret grins and knowing glances that Fanny aimed at me when she cleared the table, he said not a word.

He showed me the classroom, where his map of London still adorned the blackboard and the efforts of his students were pinned around the walls, and he gave me a parcel, which proved to be my drawing of London Bridge, mounted on vellum and framed in gilt.

At half past ten, whilst I was idling at my toilet, ogling the mirror, transfixed by mine own comeliness, a berline, bursting with laughter and shouting, pulled up at the front door. Four youths, making sufficient noise for forty, tumbled up the front steps. Half dressed and half washed, I raced along the landing and down the curved staircase, to arrive in the hall as they were being ushered in by Charlton. In gleeful, backslapping bedlam, I renewed my acquaintance with Tom and Jem.

"Happy birthday to you, Joseph." Tom had grown taller and fairer and even more godlike. "Jem and I have brought you a present." He handed me a flat parcel which I accepted with a tremor of trepidation, uncalmed by Jem's dark wicked grin.

"Go on then, open it".

Eager black eyes glinting beyond a hooked nose, I felt like a rabbit walking into a fox's earth. "How kind of you both, but first, may I be introduced to your friends?"

Tom swooped in front of his devilish companion. "Your manners, James, are of the Scotch piggeries from which you spring." And then to me, with much theatrical gesture, "This, my dear Joseph, is Master Jack Bannister, artist and bon viveur."

The two were no older than I, and the thin one, a nervous boy with big soulful eyes, stepped foward and bowed.

"And this is Harry Angelo, a dago to be sure, but we daren't tell him, for he is a famous man with the sabre." This one was tall and aristocratic, with an aquiline nose that flared a little, as though he had smelled something disagreeable. He too bowed.

"I am honoured to make your acquaintance," he said, in a tone that suggested he was not at all honoured.

"You must make allowances for Harry," said Tom. "He's at Eton".

This was a new term to me and I assumed it referred to a gastric disorder. "I hope you will soon be better."

My solicitude was received with wild guffaws from Tom and Jem and little Jack, and even Harry Angelo smiled thinly.

"You see, another wit for our company of bucks," said Tom. "I told you that anyone who had lived with Bosky Selwyn would make us laugh."

"Now open the parcel," hissed Jem, a dog waiting for its dinner.

I could find no other reason for delay, so I began to tear away the paper wrapping. It was a picture, framed, though not as expensively as Uncle Tom's present, and its back was first revealed. A verse in familiar copperplate hand read as follows:

Can botanists find out the cause,
That contrary to Nature's laws,
Some people can abuse it,
North claps it up the Farmer's bum,
Walpole fingers it, and some
like Selwyn,never use it.

It is almost superfluous to record that the subject, now lovingly coloured, in lurid pink and angry mauve, was that object of schoolgirl tittillation so proudly displayed at London Bridge.

The braying of my fellows brought Fanny running up the stairs from the basement. Her intrusion was met with shuffling, embarassed silence – pupils caught by Matron, playing with themselves behind the Pavilion. She collected the wrapping paper, strewn across the floor, and then demurely took the picture from me. I never saw it again. I like to think that it resides at the bottom of a cupboard in a room in Southwark, or Islington or Mile End, and in lonely moments she takes it out and remembers me.

"We are your champions for the day," said Tom. "We are to dress you, guide you, and instruct you in the ways of London. Your patron, the Divine George Augustus, has offered to meet our expenses and we intend to thank him by making the fullest use of his kindness."

"So do your pants up, there's drinking to be done. You can open them again later in the Shakespeare." Jem was fortunate in not being hidebound by the rules of etiquette.

"I must first complete my toilet, then call upon Mister Selwyn to thank him for this exquisite gift." I twirled my robe.

"Mister Selwyn has already left with Lord March for Yorkshire, from whence they will make their way to Newmarket. We are to take you there on Wednesday next."

"Or the week after," added Jem. "If you catch the pox tonight."

Friday morning, streets already thronged with traffic. We trotted down Pall Mall to the Haymarket, and thence to Charing Cross, where we stopped for Jem to buy tobacco. Looking down Whitehall towards Parliament Street, we counted three stage coaches, an ale dray, two dung carts, ten waggons, seven private chariots, and five saddle horses. Fifty-nine horses in all, and enough shit to sink the Agamemnon.

We called first at a mercer in Fleet Street, a fluttering bonbon who measured my intimate parts with the enthusism of a rutting pigeon. I paraded before my ribald audience, dressed in satin waistcoats, velvet breeches, silk stockings black and white, and a selection of fashionable coats. I added a gold watch, a tortoise shell snuff box with a picture of Betsy Coxe[86] on the lid, and a gold headed cane. I arranged for the account to be sent to Mr Selwyn and the wardrobe to be delivered to Cleveland Court on Monday morning. We then made for the Devil Tavern.

If I carry to my grave only one memory of London, it will be the roar of Fleet Street: a discordant choir of hawkers and traders calling their wares; rabbits and carpets and clothing and baskets; fat red cherries, hot bread and cats meat. There were mackerel sellers and milkmaids, potato carts and oyster stalls. And outside each shop, competing with this cacophony, 'prentice boys bawling of the wonders that lurked within. There was an orchestra of bear wards with drums, ballad singers and tumblers, and dancing girls with pipes; and a percussion of ponderous waggons, rumbling carts, scraping sledges and rattling chariots.

To those of you seeking a life of probity for your children, I earnestly advise discouragement from the Devil Tavern. But if you seek to enlighten them in the wickedness of the world, I can suggest no better academy.

Entry, for the intrepid, is gained via a urine stained alley, dark and hushed from the bedlam of the street. The tavern, even darker, is filled with furtive people. They do not stand at the bar and sit around the tables, as in any inn. They lurk, watchful, suspicious, and when they converse with their fellows, the words are quiet, indistinct, spoken from the corners of their mouths.

This is a meeting place for bankrupts and creditors, the greedy and the hapless, the jackalls and the carcases. And it is possible to discern one from the other without a word being spoken, for the eyes of the debtors are without hope, and the eyes of their pursuers without pity.

At the far end of this sad room is a door, upon which has been painted the word Apollo. Tom shepherded us through and it was like walking from a tomb into a tattoo. A long room, fitted out like a small theatre, with a round stage, upon which a few players shouted their lines above the hubbub. They were dressed in Elizabethan costume and I assumed they were performing Shakespeare, but the words were unknown to me. Jack Bannister shouted into my ear that the play was *Cynthia's Revels* by Ben Jonson, and that the whole room was devoted to his memory. He must have been a rake, for the pictures around the walls were of flimsily dressed women and mightily blessed men, consorting in a multiplicity of positions. His portrait, big eyed and bearded, glared from every alcove, and his sayings, inscribed in gold, adorned every panel.

At some time during that drunken afternoon, I saw Jem, pipe billowing, being harangued by an old man on the ills of smoking. Above their heads were two inscriptions:

> *Tobacco is good for nothing but to choke a man, and fill him full of smoke and embers*
>
> and
>
> *Talking is the disease of age*[87]

By five o'clock the floor was strewn with bodies, some alone in blissful dreams, others in pairs seeking to emulate the pictures – rumping, grunting beetroots. A new set of players were performing *Sejanus*, but tragedy was not their forte. They were so overcome by the anguish of the plot, they began to fight. One or two bystanders, persuaded by the power of the performance, climbed upon the stage and joined in.

The fire spread, and soon the room became an orgiastic turmoil of broken glass and splintered wood. The whole ensemble, men and women, set about each other with a dreadful violence. Lovebirds became fighting cocks, cardsharps became pugilists. And I became an athlete as I ran through the door, sprinted the length of the debtors' bar, flew along the alley, and gained again the happy hubbub of Fleet Street.

The others, dishevelled but intact, caught up with me. We chased each other down the pavements, children again, bumping indignant merchants and pushing shocked ladies. We passed by St Dunstan's Church, with its statue of Queen Betty and great clock that glares up and down the street, seeking late worshippers. At Temple Bar[88] I asked the purpose of the row of little black knobs, high above the arch. Jem derived considerable pleasure from telling me that they were skulls of Jacobites, executed after the rising in '45.

We feasted at Clifton's Chop House, on steak and oyster pie, and then walked down the Strand to the back of the Adelphi, from where we followed Southampton Street to Covent Garden. I felt as Orpheus entering the abode of the Furies.

On first acquaintance, Covent Garden is a quadrangle of fine buildings, gathered around a soaring column, which supports a four faced sun dial and a stone globe. There are arched cloisters on two sides and a church in the style of a Grecian temple. If the people and the noise and the animals and the stalls could be sucked away on a whirlwind, it would be the noblest of residential squares. But it is as if Old Nick himself has colonised the core of London and emptied his bowels therein.

For on Friday evening it is the waiting room for Hades, final stop on the slimed path to purgatory. Here is gathered the city smegma; the filthy, the infested, the lewd and the profane. They all appear drunk, regardless of the hour, and wanton. Before I had ventured twenty yards into the square, I had been propositioned by whores, both male and female, and mollies, who leered at the prettyness of our youth and opened their breeches at us.

In the centre of the square, gathered like jackals around the decaying column, was a ramshackle litter of sheds and tents and makeshift stalls.

"Here you can buy anything you cannot buy elsewhere," said Tom, as he guided us between rows of fetid merchandise, where fat harridans shrieked at us and foxy men flickered in and out of the shadows. Harry Angelo bought some linen cundums, and I smirked, although I had scant idea of their purpose. Jem found a pair of fullams, crooked dice that land as double six whatever distance they are thrown.

A number of kiosks openly displayed obscene prints and books. Jack Harris's *List of Covent Garden Cyprians* was in well thumbed evidence, as was *Essay on Woman* by John Wilkes. Tom and Jem stopped at a hut that had a hole in the front, and dirt encrusted windows on each side. Within these windows were pictures of such pornographic excess that I should have found them grotesque. But I cannot stoop to hypocrisy, I devoured them in the manner of a starving man with a pork chop.

Tom conducted a conversation through the hole with the lower part of a squirrel face. "And how has our week been, Mister Spindle?"

The squirrel evidently had a cold, for it sniffed between each sentence. "Bloody awful, Mister Thomas." Sniff.

"Sold many?"

"Just a few." Sniff.

"How many exactly?"

"Bout six." Sniff.

"That's one pound ten you owe me, and fourteen prints."

"But you only gave me ten, Mister Thomas." Sniff.

"I left twenty here last week."

"I don't think so. What's that smell?" Sniff sniff. Smoke had begun to curl from the rear of the kiosk.

"Jem has just set your little home alight." A squeak and then the door began to rattle. "And I've locked your door." The windows shook, the sides bulged as the frantic Spindle tore at the walls of his prison. "Unless four pounds, that's sixteen drawings at five shillings each, comes out of this hole, you'll roast like a Christmas goose."

"But Mister Thomas, I haven't got that much on me." He was whining now.

"Then you had better tell me where Mistress Spindle should spread your ashes."

There was no further resistance. A few banknotes appeared through the hole which Tom grabbed and counted, to the accompaniment of the sounds of a broken man within. Jem appeared, wickedly gleeful, from behind the kiosk, holding a tin of shavings, from which acrid smoke curled.

"Thank you Mister Spindle," said Tom.

"My Partner and I place great value upon your custom, and shall not trouble you for the outstanding balance until a week has passed. Please convey our kindest regards to Mistress Spindle."

They both bowed low, and then collapsed to the cobbles, in giggling, choking convulsions, that left them purple faced and exhausted, so much so that Harry, Jack and I had to convey them to the Shakespeare's Head for a draught of medicinal port.

"And how much do you charge?" I was having my first lesson in commerce.

"Five shillings for an original Rowlandson, and four for a Gillray. They're not as good."

"No, but they're dirtier," said Jem.

"Dirtier, uglier, more distasteful in every way. Mine are works of art. The sort of thing a man can show to his mistress. When I draw a penis it is an expression of power, a magnificent harpoon, thirsting for the depths of woman. Jem's are excrescent cysts, the product of a warped and savage mind."

"We sell more of mine." Jem's evil grin widened.

"That is because you are a prostitute to profit. Artists of my excellence must guard our reputation above all else."

"Its because I draw my pricks from life, at Bethlem. I reckon you see yours down at Clare Market. You'll be putting flowers on them next."

"Must I carry the weight of this scotch dangler for ever?" Tom's hand soothed his forehead, and he sighed deeply in mock resignation.

"Scotch dangler is it? I'll give ye scotch dangler, ye lily sassenach." The manner in which his grin had died, leaving nothing but dark anger, in the way a sun will scurry behind clouds before a storm, reminded me of the Captain. I felt that Tom should beware for his own safety, but he too had seen the signs, that doubtless he had seen before.

"Now my friend," he said in softer, understanding tones, "save your anger for the easel, don't waste it on me. Your brush is a sword, your pallette a shield. Thus armed you can attack the world." The sun peeped again from behind the clouds, delinquency flickered again across the dark visage.

"Well, nae more o' your scotch dangler, or I'll trade ma brush for a claymore."

At seven we made our way to the Theatre Royal, where Doctor Goldsmith's new comedy was playing to packed houses. I remember little of the dialogue, but concluded that I was very much like Tony Lumpkin - handsome, witty and misunderstood – and I fell in love with Mary Bulkely, who played the part of Kate.[89]

Jack Bannister's eyes shone like stars as he sat in rapt silence throughout the performance, oblivious to the continual uproar of conversation and coughing, of guzzling and giggling that surrounded him. His mouth moved as the players spoke their lines, for he knew every word from every scene. Not just the men, but the women too. He knew Mr Garrick's prologue, he imitated Kate Hardcastle's flutter, he even joined in the *Song of Three Pigeons*, with the gentlemen of the alehouse.

The comedy had only recently been published, and to master it was a feat of staggering dedication. I concluded that he belonged, not in an art academy with Tom and Jem, but on the stage with Mrs Bulkely. I told him so when we returned to the Shakespeare's Head, or rather bawled my views into his ear, for the clientele therein were on the flood tide of alcoholic evolution. He shouted that his father was an actor, who had set his heart against his son pursuing the uncertainties of a stage career. I screamed, with what proved to be singular foresight, that sooner or later he would have to ignore his father.

We had turtle soup in the Shakespeare, rich consomme to which had been added a gill of old madeira, and drank port wine, sweet blood of the sun. We lost our money in the Hazard Room, and then won it all back again, Harry emerging with a hat full of guineas. The Whores' Club was on the first floor, and my friends tried to drag me up the stairs, but I decided that this broiler was not quite ready for the old hens that perched aloft.

There were many gentlemen in the tavern. Young bucks and old rogues stood arse to arse with pimps and sailors and all manner of jetsam, for alcohol is a great leveller. We roared London songs, and the sailors sang shanties. Then we stood in ear ripping awe, as La Galli[90] stripped the paint from the walls with an aria *di bravura* from Alcestis by Christoph von Gluck. I know this because it was writ in letters large on a board, which her assistant held aloft and waved in concert with the music.

When she was done, Harry, awash with guineas and port, stood on a table and announced that his lifelong friend the Hon. Joseph Paget was celebrating the anniversary of his birth, and would be pleased if the assembled company would take wine with him. It occurred, even to my befuddled brain, that the avuncular proprietor, Mr Packington Tomkyns[91], would seek my incarceration in the spunging house, when he discovered the limited means at my disposal. But then I saw Harry emptying handfuls of coins down the deeply cloven front of a serving girl and concluded that whatever he had eaten, he could be a friend of mine.

I acknowledged the thanks of the stampeding tide that swept over the bar and I was then hoisted table high to the massed huzzas of my public. I gave them a rendering of the only song that came to my mind, *"The stwons that built George Ridler's Oven, And thauy quem from the Bleakeney Quaar"*

When I was eventually sick, Tom dragged me into the chill night of the Square, where the halbberline, Charlton on the box, a carbine over his knees, waited to save my life. He took me back to Cleveland Court and put me to bed. As far as my life is concerned, the weekend of Saturday the twentieth, and Sunday the twenty-first of March, seventeen seventy-three, does not exist.

On Monday my wardrobe arrived, ushered into the morning room by the Fleet Street fondler, who insisted upon a fitting for every garment, and smoothed the creases around my groin with boundless enthusiasm. I dined at Mr Selwyn's house, with Miss Tuthill who had brought Mie Mie down from Matson, and retired early, unblemished by the night sins of London.

I spent Tuesday morning in the Classroom, where Uncle Tom armed us for our Newmarket trip, by instructing us in equine bone structure and muscular formation. He gave to Tom his own copy of *The Anatomy of the*

Horse by George Stubbs[92]. He ensured that our sketch pads were filled, our pencils sharp, and he made us promise to forego the fleshpots for at least long enough to visit Ely.

In the afternoon Miss Tuthill brought Mie Mie to visit. I cradled her in a satin shawl and we sat on the box with the coachman, to trot through St James's. I told her of the great buildings in Whitehall, the implacable clod of Kent's new Horse Guards, and Westminster, of the Abbey and Parliament. I held aloft her tiny hand and we waved at our subjects, the Sovereign and his Lady.

We stopped under the trees at Millbank, and while Miss Tuthill laid out a cold collation on a linen cloth, Uncle Tom and I carried Mie Mie in a wicker crib down to the water's edge. We cooed to her and gurgled, and made gargoyle faces at her – the old man and the youth, leaping about the shore as though they belonged to Bedlam, and all for the chortles of a toothless mite.

On the verge of my greatest adventure, I slept little that night. The pillows were too soft, then they were too hard, then my nightshirt twisted around me like a straightjacket.

I was watching from my window, the early light hatching over Pimlico and down King's Road to the river, as the mantel clock chimed six, and Charlton knocked on my door.

Fanny had cooked a breakfast for three, at least that was my assumption, until I saw that only one place had been laid. When I had finished and Charlton had gone to fetch my luggage, she kissed me full on the lips and gave my breeches an affectionate squeeze.

She murmured in my ear, "Jus' remember, its fast 'orses and slow fillies you want. The other way round and you get the clap and the turnkey together." I reflected, not for the first time, that she had come a long way in two years.

Charlton drove me through waking streets. Clip clop clip clop echoing from silent buildings – the polished emporiums of Cheapside, the scholarly bookshops of Poultry, the Bull in Bishopsgate, where bustle of morning departures filled the yard.

My fellows waited in an excited knot of chatter at the back of a post chaise. Their bags were being loaded by the coachman and four nags harnessed to the shafts by an ostler. Tom flourished his fob watch at me.

"It is the late Mister Paget," he announced. "Methinks he has been *shafting* already this morning." He winked at the others. "A little *Fanny* for breakfast is no bad thing for a growing lad."

"A little *figging* more like," said Jack. "If we entered him at Tattersall's looking like that, we wouldn't get a bid." The sleepless night must have been evident in my demeanour, for this quip was greeted with roars of laughter and a good deal more ribaldry.

My bags joined the others and I bad farewell to Charlton. We crowded aboard the chaise, jostling and laughing and fighting for the window seats. At the Coachman's cry to "Walk on", we creaked our way through the arch and off into the Tudor splendours of Bishopsgate.

We fought a tide of market wagons, bringing their produce to fill Mayfair's rich white bellies, to Shoreditch, where the Roman highways meet. Jack told me that this was the home of the English theatre. For here they built the Globe, and Will Shakespeare learned his art, and so did Ben Jonson, and Bill Kemp, and Dick Burgess, and they grew to love the building so much, they moved it plank by plank to Southwark.

And then we emerged, as from a darkened theatre into a Spring afternoon, to the lanes and wild hedgerows of Essex. But not a meadow, not a copse could we see, for regimented market gardens and orderly orchards had laid seige to the capital, and were encamped across wide marshy fields to the horizon.

At Hackney, the new wealth of city merchants is flowing into the little town. They build houses that chart their enrichment: modest villas for the starters, country houses for the runners, mansions for the winners. The marshes have been drained and the great Roman causeway left high and dry. I suspect that its antiquities will soon be carried away, and the builders of Hackney will triumph where more than a thousand years have failed, for many of the new houses have walls of suspiciously ancient stone.

We crossed the water meadows to Leyton and the isthmus of rich pasture between the Lea and the Roding, and then turned north to pass a daisy chain of villages: first Wanstead, where Campbell's great mansion, the finest in England so they say, beams over its acres[93], then Woodford and the Chingfords and pretty little Loughton, dairy villages all, where slow suspicious cows meander on the road. The finest butter and cheese in the World are produced there, and all to be gorged in the coffee houses of Pall Mall.

And then we were plunging deep, ever deeper, into the dappled forest of Epping – sudden sunlit glades, slanting shards of light in the evening of the trees, hornbeams towering over us on their smooth grey columns. The wailing woods of Waltham they call them. Here came Boudicca[94] to die by her own hand when all was lost. Here too they laid the body of Harold[95], the last king to die defending this soil.

Harry told us that a thousand footpads earned a living from robbing the travellers through these woods, but our coachman had a carbine and Jem produced an ancient flintlock pistol which he waved from the window. Harry brandished his sabre on the other side and we must have resembled a man o' war as we sailed through Epping village.

North of the forest is malting country. In front of us were rolling wheatfields and plump little towns: Harlow and Sawbridgeworth and Bishop's Stortford, clustered around the seductive banks of the Stort, with their malt houses – curious chapels where the barley is steeped and couched and kilned – and granaries, tall as London houses, gaunt unsmiling buildings, flat roofs, flat walls, great brick crates scattered across the landscape.

We were refreshed at the Star in Newport, and crossed the Cam over Uttlesford Bridge in Littlebury.

At Stump Cross, a mile north of Great Chesterford, we forked right to begin long straight miles across the land of the Iceni[96], an ocean of plough and wheat, soothing land, gently swelling and falling away to misted distances.

Fresh horses, cantering true – growing excitement as the landscape flattened and the trees grew sparse and the crops gave way to grass: paddocks enclosed with neat white palings, gallops worn by a thousand hooves, tree plantations to break the winter winds. And the names ringing with racing resonance: Six Mile Bottom, Westley Bottom, Four Mile Stables.

We arrived at the Racecourse, a wide track over the treeless heath, marked with furlong posts, breasting the rise to our left, then curving to run alongside our road to the top of the town.

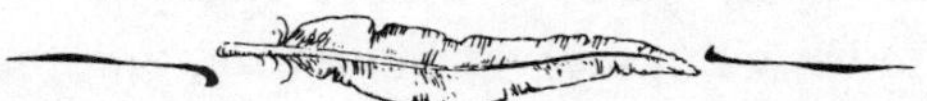

Newmarket is remarkable for its ordinariness. I had expected that this playground of kings, where Edward jousted and James hawked and Charles raced and his son debauched, would bear its royal pedigree in style. I thought that the noblemen of the Jockey Club, who maintain sporting lodges in the area, would have demanded that Tunbridge or Bath be built on the Heath for their diversion. But no. One street leads from the Heath to the Heath, and is a collection of inns and lodging houses and mean shops and stable yards. The house of Lord March, at the top of the hill, is elegant but unpretentious, which is surprising for his Lordship is anything but unpretentious.

There are a number of lodges on the slopes below March House, but none that would stand out in St James's, and the only building work in progress is the enclosure of the Jockey Club rooms and Betting Court[97]. This is the heart of Newmarket. The training establishments are the organs, the horses the muscles, the gallops of the Heath the veins. The Betting Court is an engine that pumps the lifeblood of money around the arteries: massive wagers, thousands of guineas, enough to feed a family for a lifetime, resting on the nod of a nose, the fall of a playing card, the beak of a fighting cock.

We had rooms at the Ram, a friendly hostelry at the far end of the street. We drove through its gated arch, to an enclosed courtyard, wherein was a knot of the familiar felonious fellows that foregather, wherever the scent of pickings is fresh. I asked the ostler their business and he told me they were touts[98], off to the evening exercises.

My room was at the front of the inn from where I could look beyond the town, to the rising ground that was Warren Hill. I could see strings of mounted horses, some sharp against the skyline, some blurred by the browns and mauves of the evening heath, some walking slow, some galloping free. I would have watched those moving patterns until the light died had my gaze not been drawn to the pretty building that stood next to the Ram, on my right: delicate bow windows with neat white shutters, boxes of spring flowers around the door, a gilded coat of arms. It was ironic that such innocent walls should shield such barbarity, for this is the Newmarket Cock Pit, the most famous in the land.

Thursday passed in innocent pursuit. We walked up Warren Hill for the morning exercises and watched in awe muscular thoroughbreds thundering over lissom turf: long backed, small headed flyers, necks stretched out, sweating flanks, swollen veins.

We called at the livery yards and hired strong bay geldings, which we raced around the town with raucous enthusiasm, and then climbed them up the Devil's Dyke to run along the ridge to King's Gap[99].

In the afternoon we presented ourselves at March house, where Mr Selwyn had arrived with his Lordship. There were others in the party and we were introduced to them all, bowing, stiffly formal, trying to ape their sophistication, but hampered by the apple cheeks of our exertions and the sweat of our horses. I resolved to discover why gentlemen never seemed to smell of such things.

There were two other men of middle years: James Ogilvy, the Seventh Earl of Findlater, bluff and ruddy cheeked, white lumpy knees under a tartan skirt; and Mr George Pitt, the owner of Sudeley Castle, too tall and regal to recognise me. But it was the two young men that drew us like pins to a magnet. For their humour was flippant, sometimes outrageous, they chided and laughed at us, but without malice. In our eyes they were princes of fashion, pinnacles of culture.

They were Freddy and Charles, bucks of flawless perfection: Freddy, pale hollow face, shadowed eyes; Charles, fat and dark, a porpoise with an oiled smile.

"Yearlings Charles, yearlings," murmured Freddy, inspecting us all closely.

"Damn jadey yearlings at that. Never stay a furlong. Not flat out." Charles sniffed. "Might just have a few bellows to mend. Smell like they've done the Beacon on Pantaloon." He addressed Tom. "You, sir, reckon you could run a furlong in a minute?"

"Depends if I was the hound or the hare, sir. If the latter, I think a few rows of bared teeth might make me gallop that fast."

"If the former I suppose it would depend upon the shape of the hare's arse."

"The nature rather than the shape, sir. If there were a couple of pills slung underneath, I would probably go lame."

"Why do you wish to know, sir?" I asked.

"Freddy and I need some athletes for Saturday, eight to be precise."

"And what fool wager have you struck this time?" Lord March had overheard. A thin man, watery eyed with a long nose that flared when he disapproved. He stood next to Harry. They could have been father and son.

Unlike the rest of us, Harry was relaxed. He was at home in this company, laughing at their jokes, but not overloud, sharing their conversation without stuttering or blushing. I heard Eton mentioned more than once and concluded that most of the men in the room had been educated there.

"We bet Jimmy over there," Charles nodded at the scotch earl, "a thousand guineas that we could send a ladies garter home from the ditch without a nag, quicker than him." He pouted. "He says he's hired a team of runners from Edinburgh and won't let us off."

Freddy too, effected to look like a wronged child. "We have to report for our beating on Saturday morning and we've only four footmen to run for us."

"Why don't you two run sir?" Jem asked the question with mock innocence, but Charles's smooth face took on the expression of a man eating snails, who has just bitten into a slug.

"Run?" His thick black eyebrows knitted. "*Run*? A gentleman never runs. A gentleman may walk briskly between White's and Almack's, he may instruct his sedan to hurry, he may even drive his phaeton like a charioteer. But run?" He took an acre of shot silk from his breast and wiped his brow. "I wish to sit down," he said.

"A garter you say. Do you have it?" Lord March's eyes had narrowed, greedy, a fox sensing prey. Charles produced a blue satin frippery and my lips dried at the thought of the thighs it must have caressed.

"Jimmy has the other one, first home gets the owner."

"May I enquire as to the identity of the lady?" He inclined a large ear towards Charles who whispered a name into it. Lust joined the greed in his eyes. "I might be willing to accept your obligations."

"Never laid off a wager in me life," said Freddy. "But if you've a scheme I should like to hear it."

"A third then," said his Lordship. "But I get the lady."

"And if we lose?"

"A Douglas never loses, sir. A Douglas either wins or suffers an impermanent disappointment."

"Then we shall be the three Muses," said Charles. "Joined as one to defeat the wicked earl. Freddy shall be Hope, I shall be Charity and you, sir, must be Faith. I suspect that you alone command that particular commodity."

"Jimmy!" boomed his Lordship. "I've joined Saturday's bit of sport. Let's make it worth getting out of bed. What d'ye say to five thousand?" He could have been talking about five thousand pence, for there was no change of expression upon James Ogilvy's fierce highland face.

"I am obliged to your Lordship. I and my team shall be at the King's Gap at nine o'clock sharp."

"How many men?"

"As many as you want. I shall have eight, each doing a furlong and a half. If you have eight hundred you'll do it no faster."

I recall this encounter with great clarity, for I regard it as another milestone in the gestation of my views upon life. It occurred to me, in that elegant drawing room of March House, that the gulf between rich and poor, between those at the trough and the queue outside, is a moat. It surrounds a fort wherein the treasure is stored, and the few lucky souls within have pulled up the drawbridge. Until that moment I had assumed that Divine intervention marked some for eminence, that a natural order determined our station. But we are all the same. We lust, we grasp, we envy the next fellow, and our bodily functions, fore and aft, are identical. Some buckets may be canvas and others finest porcelain, but the shit we deposit therein smells just as much.

I suspect that Freddy and Charles used buckets of diamond encrusted gold. They were not only at the trough, they owned a share of it. For this was Frederick Howard, Earl of Carlisle, kin of England's most powerful family; and Charles James Fox, darling of the Whigs, scourge of the King, soon to become the hero of the nation. A mantle he would be unwilling to wear.

On Friday, Harry informed us that he had been asked to spend the day with Lord March. The rest of us were to deliver notes from his Lordship to the incumbents of a number of country churches. My route took me north to Snailwell in Cambridge, where the little river, so aptly named, is born. I followed its track, sleepily slipping across the Fens, to Fordham – a grand maternal Church, clutching cottages to her skirts, and the River Snail, struggling through water meadows where King James hunted hare.

Back into Suffolk, to Freckenham and Worlington and Barton Mills and ancient eerie Mildenhall, delivering folded papers sealed with blobs of his Lordship's red wax to puzzled parsons, who read the contents and bad me tell my master all would be well. It was a long ride, nearly twenty miles along flat friendless roads, and I was not a little relieved when the sharp spire of St Mary's pricked the dusk to guide me home.

The evening was spent badgering Harry over supper, about his new found patron – lewd references to his Lordship's leanings, much talk of mollies and fondlers and Sodom. Harry was as bewildered as the rest of us, but happy to be the topic of the day.

"He is simply a kind man who has taken a shine to me. We are both persons of quality, and of wit. He has grown bored with old George and seeks the refreshment and stimulation of the young."

"Stimulation of the young what?"

"My Lord March may have many faults, but I do not believe that sodomy is among them. His preferences are well known and his appetite legendary."

"What then attracts him to a youth so callow?"

"We talked of Eton, and of fencing. He has been a pupil of my Father. We spoke of Italy, he asked me to convey his regards to my Mother." He paused, a shadow crossed his face. The rest of us exchanged glances. We all felt that we had probed a little too deeply[100].

The conversation turned to the morning contest and we speculated on the scheme that Lord March would employ.

"I reckon he has a greyhound trained to course without the hare," said Jem.

"Not much good if a hare pops up and runs in the other direction," observed Jack.

"There's a windmill at the back of March House. Perhaps he can wind a line in with that."

"Oh yes," said Tom. "Very practical. He would need a two mile rope, and even then he'd be a distant second if the wind didn't blow."

"He could tie the garter to an arrow and get the Scorton Archers to fire it along the course." This was my contribution.

"They'd probably lose it." said Harry. "In any case they'd take an age to aim it and collect it." We came to no conclusion, save a certainty that the old fox had a trick hidden somewhere upon his person.

I was awakened early on Saturday by the rumbling and clopping of transport coming into town. From my window I observed the extraordinary sight of a blue harvest wagon with a dozen men aboard, six seated along each side, all wearing black stove pipe hats. Following behind was a chaise carrying four men, similarly attired, and then about half a dozen riders. They too wore tall hats, and I could see that their breeches were knee length with white hose and black buckled shoes.

I hurried on my clothes and wiped my face, then ran down the stairs to find the others gathered. An ostler had harnessed our horses and we galloped out of the Ram yard, a troop of young bucks as fresh and noisy as the morning – down High Street, past the new Jockey Club Rooms, where the Betting Court was already filled with gamblers, eager for early odds about the morning sport. Shops were opening and sleepy 'prentice boys hung produce in rows under the canopies, the front of the butcher's hidden behind a gibbet of hares.

Cantering, line abreast, we climbed the slope to March House. A footman stood in the carriage drive, holding the head of a handsome grey cob harnessed between the shafts of a high flyer. His Lordship and Mr Selwyn strolled down the steps in languid conversation – no sign of concern for the outcome of the contest – and climbed aboard the graceful little chariot. Mr Selwyn took the reins, laying the long leather thong across the flanks of the grey and clicking it to a trot. We rode across the London road, on to the springing turf of the Heath. A crowd of yokels, rugged men with big bellies and thick arms, two hundred or more, milled around the King's Stand. A herd of heifers waiting for their hay – every man jack of them sporting a tall black hat.

From our mounted vantage they were a flotilla of small black boats bobbing at anchor, waiting for the calm. His Lordship was the eye of the storm, for as he neared they were all removed; sunk without trace. He stood in the phaeton, the general addressing his troops.

"Yeomen of England," he roared. "Today we shall play the game as we have never played before. This fair sward, this soft and glorious field shall witness your finest hour. Your eye will be sure, your hand secure, and your arm strong and fast. Dick Nyren himself will hear of your feats today and be proud to be one with you."

Mention of Dick Nyren was the first hint that this was a gathering of cricketers. My bewilderment was complete when they began to limber up, throwing balls to one another and running on the spot.

"To battle then! There's five guineas for every man that catches and throws true, and tonight you'll eat and drink till you burst." His Lordship drew himself to full height – Henry at Agincourt. "You all know me, I am the

Earl of March, a man of the Fens, one of your kin." A dubious claim, but not one worth challenging. "Together we shall defeat the Earl of Muckraker." He sneered the ridicule slowly, emphasing each word, and his army responded with raucous glee. "Take your positions, ten a furlong. Leave all the balls here, for there's only one need concern you now. Let the blood of Hereward flow in your veins, let none pass, even though they walk upon your dead." The hats were replaced on ruddy heads, and with set jaws and steel eyes the men marched to their battle stations.

The Emperor and his Guard took the salute as we began a proud and stately progress along the racecourse: two cricketers at every furlong pole, a catcher and a longstop, then nine with a chain between each. They cheered as we passed, and waved their hats, and I felt like a cavalry man, riding with Clive, as he inspected his troops before Plassey.

There was a knot of people at King's Gap, mostly mounted, but a group of eight stood apart from the rest. They were on foot. At least they were whilst they were not airborne, for they leapt and bent and stretched in an obscure ritual that seemed bound to exhaust them before the contest began. Their dress too was distinctive. They wore identical uniforms of harlequin reds and yellows and blues, with hunting caps to match.

"That's Jimmy's performing fleas," shouted his Lordship as we neared the group. "Damn fool's got'em done up in his silks."

"Good morning, your Lordship," called the Seventh Earl. "I have been observing your preparations. I am inspired by the multitude willing to support your cause, but may I remind your Lordship that our wager depends upon a race, not a game of cricket. I suspect the only time we shall see your stout fellows run will be when you open the tap room."

"Good morning, Jimmy," called Lord March. "I suggest you postpone your Scotch rutting until we meet in the Betting Court tomorrow. The experience of paying me five thousand may geld you."

Mr Pitt was there, elegant and aloof. Freddy and Charles wore immaculate riding habits on shining steeds; even their horses didn't sweat.

"Good morning boys," said Charles. "Come to see Culloden? Bonny Prince Findlater's all done up for battle."

He was too. The Seventh Earl was resplendent in tartan plaid with a claymore hanging at the side of his steed. Jem also was wearing a tam o' shanter as a mark of solidarity with his kin, for he was the only one of us to have betted the Earl.

A dozen or so other gentlemen had come to see the sport, and bets were shouted from one to the other, a hundred here, fifty there. Most of them wanted their money on the athletes.

The Seventh Earl stood in his stirrups. "To your positions," he called, raising his arm in noble gesture.

The Edinburgh athletes, trained professionals, calm and assured, no banter, no laughter, went to their posts. One remained at the start and the others trotted easily down the Course. They stopped each three hundred yards or so and left one of their number to stand, eyeing the cricketers that lined the far side.

"We are ready, sir," shouted the Seventh Earl. "Do you wish to address your team?"

"They have their instructions."

"My garter is contained within this cylinder, which will be handed from one runner to the next, in a relay to the winning post. Where is your garter, my Lord?"

With some ceremony Lord March held up his opened hand and Mr Selwyn placed a red leather ball therein. "I have had the garter stitched inside this cricket ball." He tossed it to Harry. "We are ready to start."

Mr Pitt had been appointed Starter and he called the contestants to their mark. Harry drew back his arm. There was a chorus from the watchers. They were trying to cancel their bets, as they percieved the innovative form of transport Lord March was about to employ.

Mr Pitt held a kerchief aloft, asked Harry and the athlete to make ready, then dropped his hand and the race was on.

There is little more to report. We galloped after the garters: to our right, lean and muscled athletes striding across the Heath, baton in hand, an inspiring sight of human endeavour. To the left a row of corpulent rustics, shouting at one another and lobbing the ball from hand to hand. The athletes had the romance, and the pride, and the nobility, and the grace. But the ball was never headed and it passed the finishing post a hundred yards ahead.

Among the crowd around the King's Stand was a pretty little chaise with an open top, decorated with a proud dark lady, who sat in the shadow of a parasol. The ringlets, the liquid eyes, the wide scarlet mouth, there could be no mistaking the Marchioness Donna Constanza Fagnani. I knew at once that only she could be the owner of the garters.

"My leedle bambino," she shrieked, to my acute embarassment. "You 'av grown into Adonees."

"Hallo," said Tom. "Young Joseph has been keeping secrets."

I blushed and approached the chaise. "Your Ladyship," I inclined my head, "It is a great pleasure to see you again."

She chuckled. "A gentleman too. I 'ope you 'ave won the race, Joseph."

"I fear not, Madam."

"Ees ol' Bosky looking after my leedle Maria Emily?"

"Oh yes, Madam. She is the sweetest child in the kingdom. She will be as beautiful as her mother one day." The Marchioness purred with pleasure.

"'av you seen my lovely Pierce?"

"I have heard nothing of Mister Creagh since he left the employ of Mister Selwyn."

Lord March swept into our conversation and the marchioness squeaked. "My dear ol' Billy, 'av you won me?"

With theatrical flourish he sliced the ball with a sabre to reveal the blue satin within. The ancient roue licked his lips. He was wet with lust. "Indeed I have, Madam. And I will brook no delay in claiming my prize." He climbed aboard the chaise and squeezed her thigh. She giggled and pushed his hand away, but not far. She took the garter from him and tossed it to me.

"Take thees to Pierce with my love. Tell 'im to be steef for me."

The massed cricket teams of Fenland kept the entire population of Newmarket entertained all night, and thus it was a dishevelled self that breakfasted early on Sunday morning. Of my companions, only Tom found the strength to join me. We were mounted by seven, pencils and sketchpads in big leather saddle bags, and on the road to Ely.

Your first view of Ely will never leave you. You ride through this flat wet land, where ditches of lazy water, straight as Roman roads, seep away to the horizon; where placid windmills, black against a huge sky wait for the breeze; and slowly you become aware that a giant is brooding over your progress. A grey silhouette of soaring pinnacles and lofty towers floating in the mist, clearing as you approach, hardening, sharpening, until the sky is filled with massiveness. The Queen of the Fens, they call her and how she deserves it –

one of England's greatest glories, enthroned upon the Isle, majestic in the nothingness that surrounds her[101].

We never saw the town. We spent hours in the water meadows by the Cam, sketching with fevered intensity Then we climbed Cherry Hill for a better view. Tom, stylish and fluent; me, pencil chewing and frenetic – how I envied his skill, his calm flowing lines, his living trees, his deft shades. But he helped me without swank, guiding my efforts through the intricacies of the turrets and gables and great flying buttresses. I am very proud of the picture I include with this journal, although half of it could fairly claim to be an unpublished Rowlandson.

When we returned to Newmarket, Warren Hill flowed with people. This was the eve of the Races and the afternoon exercises were turned into a parade – a carnival of colour, each string of horses bedecked in the silks of its noble patron: the sky blue of Lord Farnham, the dark blue of the Duke of Grafton, Freddy's scarlet and grey and Charles's green and white stripes. Every horse had been polished and clipped. The riders too, every button had been fixed, every cap was straight – the grooms and the lads in best livery. The crowds, which must have been half the population of Cambridge, were all in their Sunday clothes.

But to Tom and I, the rigours of Saturday night and the exertions of our long ride dulled the colour of it all. I was yawning by seven, and by eight, deep in the hollows of dreamless sleep.

Monday morning. Dull and bitter. A wind from the steppes howling through the town. Slanting rain burning cold on the face. Ruts and holes brimming with muddied water, sloshing under the wheels of hurrying carts. How perverse the English weather can be: capricious, taunting, alluring. She is the ultimate prick teaser. Lock yourself in a room to add your sums or write your letters, and she will dance at the window in her most radiant costume. But parade in the fields, have pageant and pomp in the streets, and she will conclude that you take her for granted, and sulk and cry and scream abuse till you run for shelter.

But in this petulance lies the strength of the English. They had to be resilient to emerge from their caves. Once in the open only the stubborn survived. With thrusting jaw and bellicose eyes they clung to the land through storm and tempest and they developed belligerence to a science. Small wonder the Frogs are punch drunk; they simply do not have the pedigree.

The qualities of the English under attack were evident in the Betting Court. We had made our dripping way down the street and stood by the gated archway gazing therein. Gentlemen, their finery hidden under capes and oiled canvas, stood with their fellows in haughty disdain of the downpour, studying bedraggled lists of the racers and calling bets as morning cockerels in a farmyard.

"I want six to four Firetail, six to four anywhere?"

"Here's eleven to two Pythia."

"What price Nancy?" This last request was from a short strutting man with a moon face and pretty lips. On his arm was a boy dressed in satin, and together they paraded like a bride and groom around the Court. They were both uncovered against the rain, for two footmen, holding aloft a tented canopy of tasselled scarlet, walked on either side of them.

I had heard much of His Royal Highness the Duke of Cumberland, but as yet, nothing complimentary. Mr Selwyn had referred to him as a pompous boil, good only for pricking, and my first view of him did nothing to discredit that reflection. Harry Angelo told me that the boy was Prince George, heir to the throne. I have long held vaguely republican views and I think they were born on that squelching morn, watching two German chichis trying to be English.

Most memories of the rest of the week have sunk into a Fenland bog: a quagmire of fetlock deep mud, of shivering wet on a wind blasted heath, of evenings with my feet thawing in bowls of hot mustard. We followed the races as best we could – dawdling processions of steaming nags ridden by soaking lads, emerging from the half light of a storm to sprint home midst the huzzas of their owners, who sheltered in brick grandstands, and were warmed by the Tuscan grape.

We saw Firetail win the Craven, with Cumberland's horse sixth. We saw Charles Fox lose a fortune when his filly dead heated with Giantess in the sweepstakes, and another fortune when Trentham was stuffed by the outsider of three. He recovered when Zamora and Pantaloon won their matches, but then Pantaloon lost it all again behind the pea green silks of Augur.

We went coursing on the Wednesday. Or rather we stood in the rain for hours at Hare Park with two whimpering dogs on leashes, whilst the beaters scoured the fields for prey. I concluded that hares must be French, for they had all taken shelter. Even my own stoicism had been diluted by the end of the day.

The Earl of Findlater, well used to such weather, had a servant prepare a tureen of hot toddie. I believe this fearsome drink has been inflicted upon the English by Jacobite survivors intent on redressing the reversals of '45. It is sweetened vitriol, liquid embers. I felt that the inside of my mouth had been scarred forever. The anaesthesia induced by the first made it possible to drink the second, and the third, and so on.

Charles Fox, plumply radiant and fired by this wicked Scotch brew, took issue with the Seventh Earl about the qualities of one Pincher. The dispute centred upon the aforesaid horse's gameness and willingness to race under pressure.

"He's the best horse I've owned," said the Seventh Earl. "Equal to anything you've ever had, and a stone better than the mules you ran on Monday."

"You forget,sir, that Trentham ran on Monday."

"I include Trentham."

"Pincher couldn't beat Trentham over the Beacon if he started now."

"Are you suggesting a match, sir?"

"I am suggesting more than a match, sir. I am suggesting that you deliver the ailing Pincher, for he could never walk that distance, to the Beacon start after racing tomorrow. He can race against Trentham at level weights, and any other horse of your choice currently stabled in my yard. I shall bet you five hundred guineas that Pincher will be last."

"Your generosity, sir, does you credit. I can only assume your conscience troubles you after the affair of the garters. And you wish to return some of the ill gotten gain."

"I shall be returning nothing to you, sir. I shall be removing a further five hundred from your sporran."

"I nominate Pyrrhus as your second string."

Charles's thick brows knitted in a thunderous frown. "You are aware, my Lord Findlater, that Pyrrhus is no longer a racer."

"He is currently stabled in your yard and is my choice."

"Then I shall see you on the morrow, sir. Good day."

We rode with Charles back to Newmarket and he sulked the whole way. But as we cantered down the slope past March House he asked us to follow him to his stables.

His yard was at the back of the town on the Moulton road, a quadrangle of warm brick stables around a well. There were piles of steaming dung outside each open door, for the horses were at exercise on Warren Hill and mucking out was in progress. Only one stable was occupied, a bay horse with big kind eyes watching the activity in the yard with casual interest. Charles tweaked the horse's ear and patted its neck.

"Permit me to introduce Pyrrhus. The most deluded horse, and the most delightful, ever to gallop on the Heath." We each tentatively patted the nose. "Unaided that is, and never in a straight line, nor a circle. We have tried him over the Round Course, the Long Course, the Ditch Mile, the Beacon, even the Five Furlong sprint. He simply refuses to race with his fellows. He wants to be free." He held out a sweet and the waxy grey lips scooped it from the palm of his hand. His fondness for the delinquent horse was undisguised. "We have concluded that, shown a racecourse, he develops a loathing for mankind. Give him his head and you will be rewarded by the most glorious sight of Pyrrhus at full stretch. But he may fetch up in Swaffham Prior, or Burwell, or even Wicken Fen. Certainly not at the winning post, and certainly not in the company of his rider."

Charles opened the stable door and led him into the yard. He looked amiable enough, and I patted his withers and his belly. His skin shivered with each touch, but otherwise it could have been Bewitched that I stroked. I took his bridle and led him myself, tentatively at first, then quicker and quicker, until I was running and he was trotting. We circled the yard four or five times, and then I stopped him in the furthest corner from the others.

"Now, old fellow," I whispered in his ear. "You may not like this, but if you throw me off, I shall like it a deal less." And I gripped his bridle and swung myself up, as I had a thousand times on Bewitched. I held the bridle as if it were a bag of gold, and cracked walnuts with my knees. But he stood, to my utter amazement, and his eternal credit, he stood. Stock still, as a brewery dray outside an inn. And when I clicked and asked him to walk on he walked on. He could have been a Lipizzaner from Vienna[102].

Charles and the rest stood open mouthed, as my agreeable conveyance and I walked past them, through the archway and away across the meadow at a Sunday canter.

On Thursday the rains eased. All was emerald green on the Heath. The sky was still low and fierce, great rushing clouds from the sea. I thought that this being April Fool's Day, we would be tempted out of our burrows, far enough for Poseidon to call down one final deluge. But no. Muffled against the wind, red nosed and wet eyed, we witnessed the final races.

Last of all was the match in which the team of Trentham and Pyrrhus were to run the full Beacon Course against Pincher. We had all ridden down to Four Mile Stables where the horses were being saddled and the riders dressed in their silks. Charles was there with Freddy Howard, and the Seventh Earl of Findlater had once again donned his tartan skirts.

The groom led Pyrrhus out of his box with a saddle slung over his back, but not fixed. The horse seemed as amiable as ever, but when his girths were tightened, he fidgetted and became nervous, prancing, tugging at his leading rein. He was led to the start, where Pincher and Trentham stood ready, and grey sweat began to show down his flanks. His rider grabbed the reins and cocked a leg for a lift into the saddle. Terror showed red in the big brown eyes, but he allowed the boy to mount. They danced a circle tangling the leading rein, to which the groom clung with ill disguised distaste. Charles approached with comforting, clicking sounds, but when he tried to check the tightness of the girth, the patience of Pyrrhus finally ran out.

He reared as Bewitched had on Campden Hill, scything, flashing hooves, trumpeting his displeasure for the whole of Cambridge to hear. The rider thudded to the ground and the groom tossed the reins aside in both panic and relief. Before the horse could run, I lunged for the rein and held on while his temper subsided. He was still on a razor edge, twitching, whinnying. But I talked to him, softly, sweetly, and the red began to recede from his eyes.

Very carefully, slow as an old man, murmuring all the time, I reached under the leathers and loosed the girth buckle. The girth fell away from his belly, and it was as if a fire inside him had been doused. He relaxed, he reached round to where I stood and nuzzled me. His eyes were brown again, his ears pricked.

"He has a pain in his belly, Mister Fox," I said. "The girth causes him agonies. If your rider can manage without a saddle, he'll probably run the Course as true as any."

"Beggin' your pardon, sir, but I ain't never rid wi'out a saddle."

"No more 'av I," hurried the groom, before anyone had the idea.

"He runs or I must insist that you forfeit." The Seventh Earl had been enjoying the preliminaries. "I leave for Cullen this evening and cannot allow time for a rematch. You must either put up a rider or five hundred guineas."

"How much do you weigh Joseph?" Charles was contemplating me, as though I were the next lot in a sale.

"About nine stone, sir".

"Will you accept a change of rider, carrying overweight?" This was addressed to the Seventh Earl.

"Your nag'll not complete the Course with a dragoon on his back. Put up who you will, but hurry".

Thus I reached the pinnacle of my riding career. No doubt many have ridden a race at Newmarket whilst still sixteen, but I suspect that few have ever ridden one bareback.

The Beacon Course starts near Hare Park and runs straight across the Heath for two miles north east, where it meets the Devil's Dyke at right angles. A narrow gap has been cut through the ancient earthwork, and beyond, the racers must turn sharp right and run east for a mile or so towards Cambridge Hill. As they near the London Road, they swing north east again for a five furlong sprint to the finish at the top of the Town. It is four miles one furlong and one hundred and sixty-eight yards from start to finish, but the Cambridge road takes a more direct route. As we lined up for the off, Charles Fox and the Seventh Earl and Freddy Howard and my four companions galloped away to the east, to be in at the death.

The sport and the cheer of their presence went with them, and I felt abandoned, drained of the bravado they had fed, clumsy in the company of seasoned horsemen.

We started at a gentle canter, none willing to make the pace: Pincher's rider, a wee Scotch lad, watching us both; Chifney on Trentham, easy and polished; me, intent on Bill Warr shouting in my head, *"Arse out, knees in, rhythm and balance, rhythm and balance."* A cold wind, tugged our clothes. In single file we followed Trentham, divots of wet turf flying past my face. Pyrrhus, head high, looking about him, enjoying the run, the freedom from pain. Pincher behind us, out of sight, just the rattle of his breath to remind me of his nearness.

Approaching the Dyke,still cantering, a green wall across our path, seven yards high. But there was the King's Gap, where Charles himself had raced through the hole. Out beyond the Dyke, past half distance, now we could see St Mary's, far over the flat nothing of the Heath. And then the turn. And then the disaster.

At the furlong pole where the garter race had started, we turned sharp right. At least, five of us did: Trentham, Chifney, Pyrrhus, Pincher, and the wee Scotch lad, all rounded the corner in line astern. I went straight on. I hit the pole with my left shoulder, and the pain could not have been greater had it been cleaved with an axe. I got to my feet, for below my waist I was undamaged, to find that the upper part of my body had been redesigned. The right shoulder was now level with my ear, and the left with my nipples. And my left arm hung, a unilateral member, over which I had no control.

Pyrrhus had stopped. He was cropping grass a few yards from me. I stumbled to him and rested my right arm on his neck. Despite a surge of pain that made me shriek, I managed to swing my right leg over his rump and get my arm far enough round to grip his throat. Thus we hacked towards the King's Stand – a farm horse carrying a sack of potatoes.

At the Turn of the Lands, where Cambridge becomes Suffolk, we entered the finishing straight. Through the thudding hooves and pounding pain I began to discern another sound. Shouting, cheering. I heard the name of Pyrrhus being called. And Jo. And young Paget. I raised my head from where it banged rhythmically against Pyrrhus's neck, and saw that we were being followed by the troop that had left us at the start. And all but the Seventh Earl were hallooing and huzzahing fit to wake old Rowley[103].

We passed the stands, and our arrival at the winning post was cheered long and raucous. They were the last sounds I heard that day. I could grip no longer and I slid from my bier to the grave below, and what candles that remained alight after the fall, were doused.

I awoke in the Surgeon's house, entrapped in a scaffolding of poles and bandage. As was becoming the habit, a knot of well wishers stood at the foot of the bed.

Tom smiled and spoke softly to me. "Well, old son, what a hero you are."

Jack's eyes were their most soulful, and even Jem's dark visage had lost its wickedness. All I could recall was falling off a horse, and as there is little heroism in this, I asked what I had done.

"You not only saved the day for Eton's favourite son," said Harry. "You won a pony for each of us, and a thousand for our patrons."

"But how?" I asked weakly. "I must have finished ten minutes behind the others."

"Indeed not, sir". Charles Fox had bounced into the room, his colour high, his brows black, and a chortling grin all over his fat face. "You finished second – Trentham first, Pyrrhus second, the rest nowhere. And I have brought your reward. A hundred guineas from me, and the same from Lord March and the same from Freddy Howard. When you have recovered, I would like you to call upon me in London. I shall have a surprise for you."

After Charles had gone, Tom described to me how Pincher, challenging for the lead as they passed the plantation, had shied, and tried to jump a shadow. The wee rider had been dislodged and Pincher finished the race unaided. Caught in the High Street, he was being hacked back, for a revival of his partnership, when Pyrrhus trotted by. At first the watchers assumed him to be riderless, but when they saw me laying along his back, they all rode down the Course and escorted me home in triumph.

I could easily become accustomed to this adulation.

Chapter Nine

Fanny was sent from London to nurse me. I stayed in the Surgeon's house for three weeks, smothered in her tender care, comforted by her cool hands, drained by her warm mouth. I then spent a fortnight at March House, from where she promenaded me, enthroned upon a grand wicker perambulator, up and down the High Street. My bones knitted together, but not with the conformity they had previously enjoyed. To this day one shoulder remains higher than the other and my gait is slightly hunched. I think it lends me a worldly air, a strong man of hidden pain, of mystery and promise. I am rather pleased that I fell off Pyrrhus.

It was May when I returned to London. But the sweet airs and scented blossoms were soon snuffed by news that Tom had left England for Paris, and Harry had returned to Eton – and I knew that Jem's blackness would deepen at his friends departure.

A note had come from Jack Bannister asking me to dine with his family on the twelfth. So the expansion of my social horizon was left in the hands of a dreaming youth, years younger than I, and without a vestige of life beyond the fables of art and theatre.

Deptford is a plain little town down the Dover road. Plain that is, save for a graveyard that embodies not only bodies, but all that is best, and all that is worst, in the art of the architect. On one side is the wondrous church of St Paul, and on the other, a rector's house of ugliness beyond words. The town grew around King's Yard, where Henry VIII built his ships, and Red House, which is the stomach of the British Navy. Here they victual the men o' war.

There is no mouth to the Ravensbourne. It just loses itself into a creek, which is all at once the cold grey Thames, quarter of a mile wide. The salt marshes can grow little, no crops, no pasture for a beast. Yet there is abundance here. Long brown warehouses hug every inch of shore, like milch cows along the water's edge, and to their teats come ships of the line to gorge on salt meat and flour, on butter and cheese, on oatmeal and raisins and suet and oil, on mountains of biscuits and rivers of rum.

The Yards take their name from the Victualer's residence, a large red house with a white observatory on its roof, a beacon to ships upping the tide along Greenwich Reach.

The Red House is a warren, a haphazard jumble of rooms reached along creaking passages, all inhabited by the Bannister genus, young and old. The Patriach of this private army is George Bannister, fat and jovial grocer to the Admiralty. He came to Deptford in '45, already the father of six, and for fifteen years, with the regularity of a ticking clock, he sired an annual addition. When his wife Anne finally lost her womb, I suspect that she, thin almost to invisibility, was greatly pleased to see it go.

Elder children that had survived the battleground of adolescence were now churning out their own stock. Infant cries echoed down long dark halls, and every chair was taken by a young woman, babe at breast. It was like entering the Foundling Hospital[104] in Guildford Street.

But here was their home, all of them. Here they returned when troubled, for comfort in their defeats. Here they came to celebrate their victories. Here they were loved, and forgiven no matter what they had done. How I came to envy Jack his membership of that warm and human refuge. More than I covetted Freddie Howard's wealth, or Charles Fox's fame.

Jack met me at the door, shy, unsure of himself, not knowing what I would make of his disorderly home. He led me down a stone flagged passage – panelled walls covered in theatre bills – to a large parlour, wherein the family table, big as a cricket pitch, was housed. There were at least a dozen people around the table and all seemed to be talking at once. At the far end sat his Grandfather in a high back carving throne. It was as if Falstaff had walked along the banks from Southwark to reign over the Bannisters.

"Welcome, welcome," he rumbled, when Jack introduced me. "We don't see many of our John's friends deown yur." I was surprised at the country burr. "Where you frum boy?"

"From Gloucester, sir."

"Glarster is it? Eow be things in Glarster then? Oi be frum Glarster you."

"Gloucester was very well, sir, when I left," I replied, but it had not been a question, for he had already turned to attend to one of the others.

Jack then walked me down one side of the table, and back along the far side, introducing me to aunts and uncles, gruff beery men and rosy ladies, and finally his parents.

Charles Bannister was the pride of the Family. He had brought his Gloucester wit to London and made them laugh, first in the dockyards, where he learned to imitate the tongues that came to Deptford from the Empire, then in the little local theatre. And now his name was on the bills at Drury Lane, and he walked the boards with Garrick and Ned Shuter and the beauteous Bulkely. He took my hand in his big meat fist and beamed redness at me.

"A pleasure, Master Paget. A pleasure indeed. I have not met John's schoolfriends before. I wager you're all proud of him." He ruffled Jack's hair. "He'll paint the King one day. He'll be as famous as Mister Gainsborough." Jack looked singularly embarrassed.

"As famous as you, sir"? Ingratiation was becoming my forte.

"Bless me. His left toe'll be more famous than me." He was right of course, but easels and brushes were not to be Jack's utensils.

The birthday party was a rampage. A continuous supply of food dumped upon the table and devoured by a throng of Bannisters and one Paget. My belly was as tight as a tambourine when the puddings began to come, but I still managed a bowl of spotted dick.

After the orgy we all had to sing for our supper. Grandfather Bannister and I put our roots to good use by rendering the Anthem to the Oven as a duet. Jack sang, still and clear, a song by Doctor Goldsmith, and his aunts and uncles danced and whistled and recited verses. And then the room hushed, all watching the door at the far end. It opened, and King George, glittering in brocade, with powdered periwig and blue satin sash, walked slowly across the end of the room. He looked neither left nor right, so that the watchers could see only one side of him, and as he walked, he sang with a heavy accent:

"I'm George the turd, your farmer king,
Who's word no man relies on.
I never said a foolish thing,
Nor ever did a wise one."

He reached the far side of the room, and in an instant turned completely around to face the door. I was astonished to see that he was now a mean eyed dark faced man, with long black hair and rough clothes. The voice too had changed, it was now a rolling drawl:

"I'm Boston Bill, and I've 'ad my fill,
Of a big fat German king.
I'll drink my tea an' I'll pay no fee,
Now just you 'ear 'im sing.[105]*"*

The last line was roared as he reached the door and turned again. And it was the King again. We all cheered and banged the table and sang with him at the tops of our voices. *"I'm George the turd, your farmer king . . . "*

It was the performance of a comic genius. He threw great leering winks at us, then stopped for what seemed minutes, half way through his walk. Still as a statue until our laughter reached a crescendo, when he would start again, and we would follow his song, slaves to his every movement, an orchestra following its maestro.

And none followed more closely than Jack. He watched his Father with the intensity of a hunting cat, mouthing the words, miming the actions. When the song was finished Charles Bannister turned to face us and take his bow. We saw two halves of different persons in his elaborate costume and painted face.

Two wigs, two faces, two coats, breeches with different coloured legs. Even his shoes were odd, and the staff he carried was a gilded mace on one side, and a hunting gun on the other.

How we cheered, and shouted for encore after encore, and both the King and Boston Bill beamed their delight at us. Applause is fresh air to an actor, and the more we shouted, the more he strutted, and pranced, and swooped in long sweeping bows to the floor.

Jack too breathed this heady brew, for when his Father had finished, he climbed onto the table and held up his hands for silence. When he had our attention, he began to sing. Not Dr Goldsmith's song, but George Ridler's Oven. And not in his voice, but mine. The lower pitch, the Gloucestershire vowels, even the arm waving that I thought theatrical, but he interpreted as writhings on a gibbet. It was as if I had stepped aside from my body and could observe myself with detachment. And I concluded that I should never stand and sing before an audience again.

He gave a tour de force. He mimicked his aunties and uncles, even his Grandfather was not spared, and each new voice was greeted with braying and shrieking and pointing at the victim. If Garrick had been there, he would have whisked Jack away to Drury Lane that evening. But he was not, and Jack would have to struggle through the Royal Academy, wasted years of daub and scribble, before his talent finally burst over the citizens of London.

Summer drifted by, and Autumn too, whilst I laboured under the benevolent eyes of Miss Tuthill and Uncle Tom. There were occasional outings: sketching with Jack and Jem, cricket at Islington, long walks down the river banks with Mie Mie. But I can recall only two with any clarity.

On a Wednesday night in July, Jack and I went to see *The Bankrupt*, a new comedy by Sam Foote[106]. Charlton took us in the hallberline, just the short distance down Pall Mall, so that we could be deposited like gentlemen, under the pillared canopy of the Little Theatre[107]. On the bills outside, Mister Samuel Foote was writ large across the top. Jack allowed that this was fair, for he not only wrote the play but managed the Theatre. Thomas Weston[108] was next, which Jack also conceded because of his eminence. Third on the list of actors, in letters only a little smaller, we read and read and read again, MISTER CHARLES BANNISTER.

I cannot begin to imagine Jack's feelings. Even I felt as proud as a cock. I was a friend of the players. Had I not dined with one of them, but a few weeks ago?

The Pit was already filling, and candles flickered in tiers of private boxes each side of the stage. There was expectation in the chattering faces, eagerness, the air tingled with anticipation. This was my first taste of that singular moment before the first performance of a new entertainment, when neither the audience nor the players know if garlands or bad fruit will be thrown, if the author's new child will be hissed to a still birth, or saluted with huzzas.

I followed Jack to the side of the stage and along a passage to a long low room at the back. I felt as though I had entered the throne room of King Mob. There was riot all around me. Men and women, some dressed, some defrocked, some painted like clowns, running this way and that, shrieking to deaf ears, exploding with rage. It was a riot without a cause, a war with only one army.

"These are the players," shouted Jack above the din. Two ladies, one with her breast bare, screeched at each other from either side of us, as if we did not exist, and then the clothed one ripped away the blouse she was wearing and flung it at the other. "Just a few first night nerves," he yelled. "They'll be happy when the play begins."

At the far end were three doors with names written on cards affixed. We went into the third, no more than a closet, to find Jack's father wedged before a mirror, painting his lips. He was a youth, a perky tousle haired youth. Farmer George had shed a score of years and now wore the uniform of a servant: striped waistcoat, green breeches and a kerchief. He greeted us without turning, still intent on his toilet, and spoke with his mouth stiff and open.

"I nust not snudge ny haint," he said.

"Your what?" asked Jack.

"*Ny haint*," he said, jabbing a finger at the red weal of his lips. "*I cannot close ny nouth*."

There was a crash from the room next door and Jack's Father, still with lockjaw, got up. As he pushed past us, he said something like. "Hoor old hugger can't get his leg on." We followed him to the next room where a white haired man, in a black frock coat, lay writhing on the floor, unable to rise, an upturned dung beetle. His one leg was raised in the air and the other was not. Neither was it not raised in the air. It was laying on the floor across the room. It was dressed in the leg of his breeches, it even wore a buckled shoe identical to his, but it lay several yards from the point at which it should have joined his hip.

His face was contorted with rage. "A pox on the cursed thing," he rasped. "Pox, pox, pox!" Jack and I helped him up and he leant on my shoulder. "Keep still boy," he shouted at me, purple face a foot from mine, and then to the room, as if an audience. "Dear Lord, why do you mock an old cripple so?" Hand to brow. "When I need oak you send me string," and louder. "Keep still boy."

Jack's Father retrieved the errant limb and bent to the task of strapping it on. The old man continued to grumble and I was on the point of letting him go when he pushed me aside, with scant recognition of my services.

"Get away from me, ye buffoon. Charles, why am I surrounded with cretins?"

"These are not cretins, Samuel. This is my son John and his school friend Joseph."

"God help you, Charles. Now get the little snots out of here. I must prepare for my public. Have you seen Tommy?"

"Not yet. I hope the old scoundrel's here soon. The house is nearly full."

"Naturally. Any new play of mine is a great event."

I could not take my eyes away from his leg. Not just because it was false, but there was something else amiss. Jack too was staring at it, and his Father's eyes, though directed towards the old man, began to flick downwards. As one we realised that it was fixed on the wrong way round. One shoe pointed at us and the other at the door. Jack and his Father began to splutter and I regret that my manners were even worse. I became hysterical. I giggled so much that I had to lean on the dressing table for support.

The old man followed our eyes and, upon perceiving that only one of his feet protruded, hopped around the room trying to wrench the offending limb away from his person. He became distracted with rage and pulled so hard, that although the leg came away in his hand, the force was sufficient to throw him again to the floor.

At that moment the door opened and swaying on the threshold was a thespian of old. Purple cape and long powdered wig, a feathered plume upon his tricorn hat. He stood with noble stance, feet wide apart and a stout knobbed staff held out as though he were being followed by the Artillery Band.

"Weston is here," he bellowed. "Pray do not fret, for soon ye shall be in my debt. I shall perform your little farce, without once falling on my arse." He swept off the hat and bowed flamboyantly. A little too flamboyantly. For he overbalanced and tumbled into the room.

Charles Bannister, still open mouthed, said, "Allow ne to introduce ny hellow layers. Nister Reston and Nister Hoote."

"That one's Tommy Weston," said Jack, pointing to the thespian, who had closed his eyes and was beginning to snore. "And that one's Samuel Foote," he nudged me. "He used to be Samuel Feet." My giggling became uncontrollable and I felt the wisest course was to make my exit.

Jack followed me and fuelled my hysteria by observing, "I hope Mister Garrick's not in the audience tonight because the players may not be at their best. One can't speak, one can't walk and the other's blind drunk."

"Oh well," I sobbed. "We must thank the Lord it's a comedy."

And a comedy it was: Sam Foote, splendidly avaricious as Sir Robert, strutting around the stage as if he had three legs; Charles Bannister, his paint dry, the sweet apple of every lady's eye; and Mister Thomas Weston, noisily overacting as the loathsome Pillage. All three were word perfect and outshone the ladies of the cast by moving faster, shouting louder, and squeezing out applause with noble gesture and heroic stance.

We watched from the wings, and as the performance progressed, Jack explained to me the art of the comic actor. Humour has little to do with it. Timing, experience and selfishness are the tools with which the professional fashions his performance, and Samuel Foote was the nonpareil of his profession. When he spoke, he was always full face to the audience, but furthest back of the players, so that he could be clearly seen. His voice was louder than the others, and harsh, and his face was an ever changing contortion, lop sided grins, leering winks, then squashing to an evil lip licking gnome with hunched back and spidery hands. The butt of his jokes was Pillage, who wore an ill fitting coat. Each time he spoke a line, Sir Robert would cup a hand to his ear and ask the audience if they had heard what the gent in the sleeves had said.

The players took their bows and cheering shook the chandeliers. Mrs Williams and Mrs Jewell, and naughty Nancy Ambrose, all received bouquets, and when Sam Foote spoke the epilogue, I was convinced that I had wronged him. For he was wreathed in smiles, his manner was that of a kindly uncle, and he even shed a tear in the emotion of the moment. My conversion was shortlived. As he walked off the stage he saw me and snapped, "Will someone remove that brat from my theatre?"

Thus ended my first experience of actors and their world. Insincerity and shallowness are their stock in trade. They are fickle, self seeking charlatans, strutting foibles, fragile as daisies. But they are the possessors of a Divine gift – they must have been touched by Our Lord. For no matter how palsied, how much they have sinned, they appear to be able to take up their beds and walk at will.

We went to Bartholomew Fair in August – Harry, Jack, Jem and I – and there we met the Mohocks[109], and lost. We had breakfasted late at Clifton's and walked through Gough Square on our way to Smithfield. Leaning on the railings at the back of St Andrew's Church were four young men who greeted each passer by with loud and malevolent contempt. They were a strangely assorted bunch. Their leader, tall and angry, was what Pierce would have described as a Cromwellian: red hair, hard blue eyes, harsh military voice. He was a crusader, he never laughed. His friends did, but only in taunt, only to insult and embarrass. One of them was American and another looked Italian. The fourth was a fop, brocade and silks proclaiming his wealth. He was harshly English and, I guessed, banker to the others.

As we passed them, the Italian hawked and spat phlegm in our path. We tried to ignore them but Hamilton, for that proved to be his name, said, "Well now, here's four little mollies for us. We can have an arse apiece." Jem, who was leading us, stopped and I cannoned into his back. "We'll have to hurry though, they're trying to get up each other." I pushed Jem on, fearing that his temper would break our heads. "I want the pretty little one at the back," and he grabbed Jack's arm and twisted it.

In an instant, Harry pulled the short sword that he carried and held it to the Irishman's gut. "Release him, or I'll open you wider than your mouth," he hissed.

Hamilton's eyes never left Harry's face. He slowly released his grip and Jack darted away. Hamilton, soft voice now, disguising a towering rage, said, "No man can do that to me, let alone a mummy's boy."

Harry inched away, sword still up, and the four stood motionless, stalking him with their eyes. We started to walk across the square, looking back, but they were not following.

"Enjoy the fair, little boys," called Hamilton. "We'll be waiting for you."

My enjoyment of the day was tempered by thought of our homeward journey, but I have to record that Bartholomew Fair is the most rumbustious, jollified exhilaration, I have ever experienced. And unexpected too. For the steep winding climb up Snow Hill, allows no view of what is to come until, on rounding the last corner, a great wave of babble and riot washes down the street.

This is no country fair. None of the simple pleasures of rural life are celebrated here. For the folk that flock to Smithfield have more worldly tastes. Not for them the fiddler and the puppet show: here there are string quartets and theatrical booths with Drury Lane productions. African animals of extraordinary shapes are caged next to shows of legerdemain and tight rope walking and fire eating. Contortionists bend to bone breaking shapes and I watched in amazement as a dog counted to ten.

In one of the freak shows sat the fat man who had ridden with Pierce and I to Oxford. Standing at his side the sad little sparrow nodded at the passers by when he prodded her, curtseying when he pulled her arm.

Garrick had a booth, though he was not appearing. But Charles Bannister was. He was playing in The Beggars Opera and as we squeezed in at the back of the crowd. The Beggar was finishing his prologue. Polly then danced onto the stage singing a pretty song, and soon we were all singing and whistling at her. Jack's father was a young highwayman, then an old salt, then a prisoner in Newgate, and each time he appeared we shouted and waved, but he seemed not to notice us. Towards the end I hoisted Jack onto my shoulders. He put two fingers into his mouth and let out a screeching whistle that would have stopped a stagecoach.

It certainly stopped the players. They stood, hands cupped over eyes, peering from their lighted stage towards the back of the booth. As he recognised his son, Charles Bannister laughed aloud, then held up his hands for silence.

"Good people of Smithfield," he announced, "please make room for the principal player at this afternoon's entertainment." He waved us forward and I carried my load down the aisle that had opened before me. Jack, perched aloft, saluted the cheers, a matador entering the arena, Harry and Jem his picadors.

When we reached the stage he dismounted, patted my head, and joined the cast. The rest of the Beggar's Opera was played with an additional actor. He mimed, he danced, he sang, and everything he did was greeted with roared approval. There were probably two hundred witnesses to Jack Bannister's first public appearance, but only one that played his horse.

If I needed an antidote to the euphoria of that performance, I found it next door in the booth that contained Mrs Salmon's Waxworks. The old girl died about ten years ago, when she was ninety years of age. I'm surprised they haven't pickled her as an exhibit. If I live as long as her, I think I shall never be more revolted. They had the execution of Charles I, complete with blood and brains, a man suckling his daughter's breast, a lady on a bed, having just given birth to three hundred children, and a clockwork gibbet upon which the chained victim was destined to twitch forever.

I may have been repelled, but Jem was like a child in a sweet shop. He stood before the tableaux, enchanted by every gruesome detail, pointing out with anatomical descriptions, the tortures and sicknesses that were depicted. He even suggested that I join him on a visit to Bedlam[110], where he considered the displays more stimulating, because of their animation. Had we not dragged him away, I think he would be there now.

If I am not to inflate like Charles Fox I must never eat as much again. There were pigs a'roasting in every corner of the square, and great dripping slices with a dollop of apples, could be had for a penny. There was an oyster frying booth and another selling hot sausages, and there were puddings black, puddings pease, puddings cherry and puddings suet. Like a honey bee I visited all the blooms, then returned to each one for a second taste.

Late in the dusty afternoon we took our leave. It was our intention to walk down Snow Hill, then along Holborn to Fetter Lane, which would take us to the anonymity of Fleet Street without crossing Gough Square. Rhoan Hamilton had anticipated us. As we rounded the corner of Cock Lane he was waiting with his fellows. They had placed five beer barrels across the street and were sitting on four of them, watching us approach. On the fifth was a lighted lamp, although the day had not yet died. I wanted to run, and I am sure Jack and Jem would have joined me, but the avenging Angelo was having none of it.

He drew his short sword and shouting for his hesitant troops to follow, marched towards the Valley of Death. They waited. They waited until we were almost upon them. Presumably in order to see the whites of our eyes. And then as one they rose. And each had a sword that had been concealed behind the barrel. And each sword was longer and looked horribly sharper than Harry's. And before we could turn they were on us. Men against boys. Armed men against boys.

We were lined up, bloodied faces to the wall, each with a sword point in our back.

"And now my pretties, we'll see your pretty arses." It was Hamilton, and I knew Harry was first in line. "Give me your breeches, Mummy's boy." There was no move from Harry, but then a slap as the flat of the blade hit him.

"Hurry now! Ossie's getting impatient." I heard the American laugh.

"And the rest of you, knickers down!" The point in my back pushed, arching me. I fumbled with the fastening of my breeches and as they dropped, felt the evening chill on my legs.

"Everything. All your clothes." For a moment I did nothing. The sword was eased from my back and then I heard a swish of air. It was as if a red hot poker had been drawn across my buttocks, searing, burning. I wanted to scream. I bit my lip, tasting blood. I couldn't hold the tears.

I ripped off my clothes and sensed my companions doing the same. I could smell burning, hear taunting, sneering. I stood, trembling naked, not knowing what was coming.

"Spread your legs." The sword, between my thighs, slapping them apart. The cold sharp point, pricking my arse hole, as if to enter me.

"Wider." I felt the steel slide between my legs, touching my testicles, stroking my tool.

And then it was taken away, leaving me uncut, and I was so flooded with relief, I would have kissed my captors had they wished. Fortunately they did not wish.

"Face the front now my darlings, pray do not shiver. We have made a fire to warm your little pricks." The barrel that had held the lamp was ablaze, there must have been faggots and paper inside. I saw Hamilton pick up my breeches and throw them on to the fire. He had a tin of powder, and when he threw a pinch at the flames, they flared and cracked. We stood and watched, flickering pink in the glow, babes from the womb, held against the wall by three swords, while Hamilton burned our clothes.

"Ossie, are the carriages ready for our young guests?" The American nodded eagerly.

"Just itching to roll," he said.

"And are their new garments laid out?"

"Si, signore," said the Italian. "I 'av a pretty red dress for each of them."

"Well then, let us see them safely off on their journey".

The point of the sword was again in my back, and I was forced to walk, with the others, towards the barrels.

"In," rasped Hamilton. At least I would be covered, and I jumped over the lip of the barrel. It was about as high as my stomach, and I stood erect watching my companions clamber in. Harry was reluctant and singled out by Hamilton for some hefty blows, fist and sword. "Down," was the next order and I saw Harry punched to the bottom of the barrel. I needed no second instruction to crouch in the depths.

What followed were the worst moments of my life. I heard the rattle of a milkpail and then a thick red glutinous mess was poured upon my head. It stank and I gagged in horror as I saw entrails sliding down my chest[111]. But that terror was soon eclipsed by pandemonium as the barrel was overturned and rolled, slowly at first, cream in a churn, round and round. Faster now, head banging on the sides, whirling red, splashing and slurping. I pushed at the sides, trying to steady myself, now bouncing and crashing down again and spinning like a top. Nausea, sickness, a clamouring, screaming, thundering nightmare.

I know not how far I rolled, nor how long, but as I slowed, my course became erratic. I swerved increasingly, hitting walls and railings, until I came to rest with a final shudder against a lamp post.

I heard hooves and carriage wheels coming near. They stopped. Footsteps running to me.

"Great Heavens!" A man's voice. "The poor boy. He must be dead. Keep away, my dear. Don't look."

"My God!" a woman's voice. "That cannot all be his blood."

"Come away, my dear, it is no sight for a woman. I shall call for a constable."

"John, he is still alive. Bring me a blanket, we must get him to Whitechapel." There was something familiar about the voices.

"But, my dear, the upholstery." A ripping of cloth.

"I shall bandage him with my petticoats."

"My dear, cover yourself this instant."

"Bring me the blanket," she shouted, "and help me remove him from this barrel".

"HE IS UNCLOTHED!" Go to the carriage. I order you to go to the carriage." I raised my head from the gory depths and came face to face with my Lord Bishop of Winchester and his comely niece.

I was surprisingly unharmed. Unnerved yes, unadorned, save for a few lumps of sheep's intestine, but on the whole, unscathed. And considering the happenings of the previous few minutes, that was a miracle on par with the Itchen deliverance.

Mrs Chapone searched my nakedness but could find nothing that deserved her intimate bandages, and so I was wrapped in a blanket and bundled into the carriage. Jack and Jem were similarly treated, but Harry was swathed in torn petticoats before he joined us. Thus we were delivered, like parcels from the butcher, to Cleveland Court and Fanny's eager ministrations.

Before he left, the Bishop asked Uncle Tom about me – my upbringing, my circumstances – and he recounted the saga of the Itchen. He left instructions that I was to write to him when I had recovered from my ordeal. I did so, and although his reply at first disappointed me – for it contained no cash, and on the face of it, precious little else – it proved, in time, to be most fortuitous.

To Joseph Paget, Esq.

Dear Sir, We were troubled by your recent misfortune and thank God for your recovery. When you have attained the age of eighteen years, we trust you will be able to dine with us at Farnham. Your progress shall ever interest us in the sincerest manner.

We are &c.

Cheerless November rains, day after day, soaking the streets and the mournful buildings. No wind to vary the tempo, no sun to lighten the grey, just relentless, monotonous, drenching rain. We huddled in our mildewed classroom, trying to draw with damp pencils on damp paper, and when forced to venture out, hurried back to steam around the kitchen range.

Nothing marked the change to December, save the cold that seemed to venture further under my bedclothes each morning. The prospect of Christmas, even the arrival of Tom, with parcels of wickedly delicious chocolate, did little to rouse us. But he did warm us a little, with wild tales of Paris, of sewer taverns and ghetto cafes, where revolution was breeding.

And then a silent morning. Nothing to hear from the deep dark of my bed. Nose escaping from the blankets. Misting breath on the crisp air. The hush of death. Gone were the rumbling carts, the clattering hooves, even the birdsong. Shards of brilliant light stabbed from behind the drapes.

It might have been another city, another country. All was rounded, soft sensuous whiteness, plumply piled against walls, pendulously drooping from trees, blurring the hardness, shrouding the ugliness. Six inches of snow had fallen in the night, and the sky was pregnant with more.

Two months it lasted. Two months in which we regained our fast disappearing childhood, sledging down the King's Road, skating on the reservoir. We built a snowman twelve feet high at Hyde Park Corner and for days the coachmen had to steer around it. The Thames did not freeze over for she was flowing too fast, swollen by the rains, feeding a swirling brown lake above London Bridge, where the waters were forced through narrow arches to boil past Billingsgate.

There was nothing gentle or gradual about that winter. Even the thaw was violent. Temperatures rose as March was born, snow became rain, trickles became torrents, and the Thames burst its banks from Windsor to Westminster. We drove along the Strand, and every street to our right had been shortened by the waters. Stinking muddied ditches led straight into the river. Houses at the far end were half submerged. Flotsam bobbed past upper windows. Dogs and cats, even a monstrously swollen cow nodded on the tide – wherries free of their moorings.

Along Lud's Hill and down Eastcheap to the Monument, where we climbed gloomy winding stairs to an eyrie seventy yards above the ground. Jem had scampered aloft, a rat up a drain, for he came here often to sketch, but the higher Jack and I ascended, the more nervous we became, clutching at the walls, dragging weak legs from step to step, leaning forward in terror of falling back.

When we reached the railed platform Jem warned us not to look down, which we did. It was as if my feet had been nailed to the floor, whilst the rest of my body wanted to fly, swaying in terror, no thought but to grasp something safe. Everything moved, even the building: shrinking railings, lower and lower, a force pulling me over them, toy buildings below my feet, insects scurrying along tiny streets. And then Jem pulling my coat, trying to drag me back into the doorway, my hands locked on the railings, so that he pulled me down rather than back, and I sank to my knees, facing west. There I remained rooted for ten minutes, and thus my description of the wondrous view is a blinkered one.

Blinkered but nonetheless remarkable, for out beyond Battersea and Wandsworth lay a silver sea, and on that sea floated a thousand islands. We could see twenty miles in the westering sun: hilly islands of Wimbledon and Richmond, and between them the palace at Hampton. Anne Boleyn's house at Feltham[112] caught a ray of sun, and we could even make out, on a far horizon, the castle at Windsor. But wherever the land was low, glittering fingers of water had claimed it. There is a Chinese landscape by Motonobu[113] hanging in the Morning Room at Matson, and he could have painted it from the top of the Monument that afternoon.

I have dwelt upon these floods because they were the instrument that caused me to visit Strawberry Hill.

A few days later I dined at Chesterfield Street. There was one other guest, a small neat man that could have been a clerk of works, or the secretary to a bishop.

"Joseph, I feel that I have known you for years." As he stepped towards me and offered a hand, I noticed that he limped. "Mister Selwyn has kept me informed of your progress." A precise voice, soft and clear. A female voice but not effeminate.

He shared Mr Selwyn's air of languorous boredom, and my evening was spent listening to them lampoon with mournful glee, the great of England.

"The present state of England, Bosky," drawled Mr Walpole, "is that she is drowned and dead drunk. All water without, and wine within."

Mr Selwyn swigged his claret and nodded. "No restraint."

"No restraint, no principles, no genius, no character, no friends. Overrun with robbers and horse racers."

"The Government does what it can."

"Government you say? Farmyard fowls scratching around the dunghill."

"Steady on, Horrie. I attend sometimes in person."

"I do not include you, dear old George. You have no responsibility for the Westminster winds, for you are invariably asleep."

"It is so hot in there. Enough to melt your rouge and shrivel your nosegay. But young Charles Fox speaks well, and much sense."

"I went to see him the other day and agree with you. He spoke passionately on the side of the American colonies. But I am told he had been at Almack's[114] till four and was leaving for Newmarket at twelve."

"He has recently moderated his behaviour. He never bets more than one hundred thousand pounds he does not have."

"I understand that his Father has been persuaded to die this year."

"That'll be good news to his creditors."

"And my Lord North. I may be lame, but I shall never be a duck."

"He gains great comfort from being applauded."

"But does he infect you with his oratory? Can he interest you in his policies?"

"He is as interesting as a revolution in Sweden."

"He has justice, but no bowels."

"They say he has a quarry of gall stones instead".

"The rest of them are either gentlemen, all beautiful negligence, or placemen voting for their dinner."

"But surely, Horrie, there are good men among us?"

"Well, where are they, George? The Catholics? I hear the King is going to visit the Welds, so short of quality is he."

I thought of Maria. "Do you know the Welds, sir?" I asked.

"I would be unwilling to admit it in public."

"I shall raise Mie Mie a Catholic," yawned Mr Selwyn. "It is her Mother's wish. And I shall ensure that she attends well, for the only thing more tiresome than a zealous Catholic is a doubtful one." This wisdom took some time to digest.

"I read that the crew of monsters at the East India Company were shocked by a mutiny of our Indian subjects."

"I don't expect our Indian subjects were shocked. They've been hacked, hewed, lamed, maimed, tortured and worked to death. I suppose the poor devils will now have to love their masters too." The topic widened, as did the river of claret.

"It is the same at the theatre. Whores with nothing more than ambitions to have pretensions, parading before us as actresses. They wear diamonds that should be exchanged at Betts for a dozen strong beer glasses. And they dance like turnpike menders."

"I saw Nancy Ambrose last week. She was dressed in a white domino and did little else but stand still with her left hand erect as if in blessing. I was reminded of Nancy Cavendish, when she got drunk in the bathing tub."

"She will be forgotten in a month as if she were the pattern of last year's coat."

"They say that Garrick's buffoon is the best there has been. But he had the advantage of knowing the part at birth."

"Your friend March is little better, George. I hear that his mistresses have to keep him alternately diverted and drunk each hour."

"I have no knowledge of that, Horrie, but I do know that his maid has left him because she could no longer undergo the fatigue of making the bed so often."

"And then there is the absurd bombast of Dr Johnson."

"He had sense till he changed it for words."

Pauses between the bon mots grew longer and longer, until they would each have a short snore before beginning again. When the decanter was empty they fell to ruminating in tutts and grunts and I tiptoed from the room to find my bed.

George Selwyn and Horace Walpole had known each other since their days at Eton, and in the morning my Patron was concerned that his friend was proposing to brave the floods and drive to Twickenham. I suggested that I would accompany him and report back on his safe delivery.

We had to keep north of the river, for we had heard that the bridge at Kingston was near collapse. We kept to the high ground, through the town of Hampstead and the little farm hamlets on the way – Willesden, Twyford, Drayton Green. But then we were forced to descend, for Twickenham is on the river bank. The Brent was full and the Crane in flood, but the bridges had held and we crossed them both. Much of our way was under water, but it was possible to discern the route by hedgerows and hillocks. We squeezed onto the box with the driver, for at times our axles were covered and the pair of bays that pulled us were up to their bellies.

At Kingston, the Thames swings north to wind around Richmond Hill. The broad meadows of the Ham allow her to spread and flow in benign mood past the treasures of Twickenham[115]. Castles and villas and Grecian temples smile from leafy lawns, salmon ripple the lazy waters and willows trail long fingers in cool clear pools. At least that's how the guide books have it.

When we arrived at Strawberry Hill there was little more than a crescent of land on the Middlesex side, and marooned thereon a few bedraggled residences besieged by the gorged river. Their defences were gone, their skirts raised, but they were somehow indomitable – English ladies defending their honour against brown hordes, one of them absolutely bristling with indignation.

Pinnacles and spikes, arches and turrets soaring above the trees in splendid gothic rage – a spectacular folly, ignorant of style, indifferent to taste, but wonderfully, Englishly eccentric. This was Mr Walpole's house, his *'pretty bauble set in enamelled meadows and filigree hedges'*.

We were met by the butler who ushered us to a baronial stairway – armaments clinging to the walls, heraldic antelopes crouching at every turn, fierce carved lanterns leaping from alcoves, and a ceiling that flew in great vaulted leaps as if it were heaven itself. I followed him aloft in reverent silence.

"Your company has brought me great pleasure, Joseph, but there was no need for you to come."

"Mister Selwyn is concerned for your wellbeing, sir."

"He is concerned for everyone's wellbeing but his own." He led me into a library, where brown and gold bookcases, carved as rood screens, lined the walls. It was a chapel to the printed word. Polished leather volumes stood to attention in wild Gothic cabinets, delicate traceries of stained glass under pointed arches. He limped to a chair by a window overlooking a sea that had been his lawns. Rain was falling again.

"Your patron has been my dearest friend since the dawn of time, but we dedicate our decline to very different occupations. I comfort only myself, and the few old women with whom I rake, whilst he nurses babies, and educates youths, and opens his purse to anyone in need of a shilling."

"He is indeed a generous man."

"He is more than generous. He is possessed with a determination to rid himself of the meagre fortune he commands. I perceive that young Charles Fox has learnt at his knee, and the two of them are the toast of every gamester at Almacks."

I bristled a little. "I know, and wish to know, of nothing but good about Mister Selwyn. I hold him in the highest possible esteem. I have had little contact with his circle in London, but in Gloucester there are few men, women or children that are not indebted to him in some way."

"Your defence of George does you credit, but he has no need of it in my eyes. I am simply concerned that he keeps enough money for his dotage."

"Your fears would be eased were you to see Matson. It is a well run, profitable estate, with two efficient farms and control of the water supply to Gloucester."

"I visited Matson a score of years ago, soon after George inherited."

"He has wrought great changes, sir. You should come again. I would be honoured to be your guide."

"George asks me every year, and I promise to come. Then I find a reason to stay here, and promise to come next year."

"Then don't promise me, sir, and perhaps you'll come soon."

"Perhaps I will." I helped him rest his leg on a stool. "But not until the summer. Not until the sun can dry this accursed gout." He gazed from the window, a mournful captain on his bridge. "Were I the master of the good ship *Strawberry*, I would give the order to weigh our anchor, and with a following wind we would be at Ranelagh before nightfall."

"But first you would have to collect the animals, two by two sir."

He smiled a little smile. "It would seem that Mister Selwyn's wit has not been wasted on you." He turned from the window. His eyes reflecting not the pain of the gout, but the tedium of it. "I should not mind the beasts, nor even the fowl. But I should not be at all excited by the thought of the things that creepeth upon the earth."

Chapter Ten

June. Leafy, lustrous, lovesome June. Midsummer month of marigolds and meadowsweet. And Maria.

As in any life, there have been peaks and troughs in my eighteen years. The first fortnight of June seventeen seventy four was the summit.

On the first day of the month, a splendid invitation arrived, requesting the pleasure of my company at Wimbledon House, to celebrate the wedding of His Grace the Duke of Devonshire, to Lady Georgiana Spencer. On the second, a note from Brambridge announced that Mrs Smythe, with Maria and Jack, would be residing in Bond Street for a few weeks, and would be pleased to see me.

The invitation had been expected, for I had visited Charles Fox in May. The surprise he had promised me, when I lay in state at Newmarket, was a whole wardrobe of fashionable finery. Coats and sashes and ruffs and buckles, and enough embroidered silk to fill the holds of the Jamaica Sun.

"Remember Joseph", he said, "the society to which you aspire will judge you upon your appearance and your wit, not upon your quality. Wear these clothes until the fashion changes, then discard them. Give them to your servants, or to the poor, but on no account be seen in them. It takes but a moment for de riguer to become de relict." He allowed himself a smile at this bon mot, which no doubt he would be repeating at Almack's. "There is nothing so ancient as last season, and to wear its clothes is the mark of Cain. You would do better to attend a masquerade naked, like Her Grace the Duchess of Kingston[116]."

"When should I wear them, sir?"

"Shed blood for invitations Joseph. Ranelagh and Marybone are all very well, but the balls and masques of great houses are the keys to the Kingdom. Be seen at one and you will be invited to another. Shine at that and a further door will open."

"I shall ask Mister Selwyn to help."

"First you shall ask me to help. I have imposed upon my friendship with the Right Honourable the Earl Spencer to wheedle you a place at his daughter's nuptials. Georgiana is the loveliest thing in all London, seventeen in a day or so and already banged up by Willy Cavendish."

"You are more than kind, sir."

"I know. There will be a thousand guests but ten thousand would kill to go."

Saturday was the King's birthday and I spent the morning strutting up and down in front of the mirrors in my room, preening my new feathers, a peacock in rut. Did indigo clash with rose? Vermillion with mauve? Does eggshell suit my complexion better than midnight? Was hose stitched or plain this year? Wigs were out and the problem of whether my hair should be back or forward occupied at least an hour. Fanny tried to help, but her heart was not in it. Only when I removed my breeches did she show interest.

By mid afternoon I had donned and discarded every garment that Charles Fox had bought me, and convinced myself that nothing I possessed could transform me into a gentleman of fashion. Charlton discreetly knocked on my door at three thirty and suggested that the lady would soon have finished her tea and would not see me in coronation robes if I was much longer. This advice persuaded me that the midnight coat with pearl buttons, silk breeches and violently embroidered crimson waistcoat would have to do.

Slow and sedate, we climbed St James's Street, where coffee and chocolate houses bustle with business, over Piccadilly and along Bond Street, to Number 148. A plain box for such exquisite contents, a simple house, so like its fellows, unadorned, unpretentious – I had half expected it to shine. But then only I knew that Number 148 harboured an angel.

A Brambridge servant answered the knock, and that was enough to set my heart racing. I was ushered into the drawing-room across which Jack strode to greet me and Elizabeth Smythe smiled her empty smile. But they were nothing – furnishings, background scenery, members of the cast whose name you cannot recall – for by the mantle stood Maria. I can recall every wisp of her dress, every chestnut curl, every inch of her delicate face, but I cannot find the words. It is as if that picture of her was frozen, and then somehow transposed to a branding iron and burned into my brain. If I live to a hundred, I think it will remain with me, clear and bright.

It might have been my clothes, or perhaps I had grown up. For this time we met as equals, not the speechless boy and the porcelain angel of Over, nor the lumpish youth and pretty flirt of Brambridge, but a young buck and the doe for whom he thirsted.

I shook Jack's hand, but parried his joviality, nodded to Mrs Smythe, and then stood before Maria, consuming her, breathing deep her perfection. Her eyes did not mock, as before. A new light danced within them, warm, pleasurable. Even now, I hardly dare admit it, but as they flicked down to my feet then back to my face, and as she grinned a huge smile, she was admiring me. I took her hand and kissed it, holding her eyes. "Your servant ma'am," I murmured. I swear that she blushed.

The servant rattled in with a tea tray and the moment was broken. A few seconds that will last all of my life.

Jack, fat and hearty, wreathed in smiles at the renewal of our friendship, seemed stuck in time. He chortled about the toads and the trout tickling, elbowed my ribs endlessly about smuggling, and repeated and repeated and repeated what fun it was to see me again. His country clothes were coarse beside mine, his ruddy face belonged to Hampshire, not London. I was courteous to him, but cool, and after a while he fell to silence, realising that our bond had gone, that we were no longer chums. It was a great mistake of mine, for in the months that followed, an ally at Brambridge would have served me well.

I promised to be their guide on a tour of London, taking care to regret that I was otherwise engaged on Tuesday. Fortunately Maria enquired and I was able to sigh of my obligation to attend his Grace's nuptials. Even Mrs Smythe's cool eyes widened at this. I was to join them at the theatre on Wednesday, and Marybone on Friday.

When I left, Charlton was waiting, and I rode in the hallberline. But there was no need, for without it I think I would have flown.

Tuesday afternoon, buffed and polished, dripping with silk, frothing with lace, I waited in the morning room at Clarendon Court. Uncle Tom inspected me whilst Fanny tugged and straightened and smoothed as if she were sending an infant to its first class.

"Langour, my boy. Langour is all you need. Be in no hurry to speak, and when you have to, do it slowly." He put his hand to my chin with a little pressure. "You must relax your lower lip, and hood your eyes. Then raise your nose a little." I did so. "There. If you can master that expression and speak only badinage, every eyelash in St James's will flutter at you."

I considered myself in the mirror. "I look uncommonly like a chicken. Perhaps I should scratch the ground, and eat worms."

At three Mr Selwyn's new chariot, a landau imported from Germany, called for me. This splendid equipage has hoods made of harness leather, fore and aft. The day was warm and still and both hoods had been lowered, so that I felt at least a Lord Mayor. I had to restrain my hand from waving as we flaunted our splendour across the Green Park. We collected Mr Selwyn at Chesterfield Street, and then headed down the King's Road, two fine gentlemen of fashion.

Putney is a modern retreat for City brokers. The little church by the river has been surrounded by villas, not extravagant like Twickenham, nor mean like Islington, comfortable abodes for comfortable families. The village sits at the southern end of a reach and has been a crossing point since time began. A wooden bridge was built about fifty years ago by the Spencers, who seem to own everything and everyone. Wimbledon House, gaunt and castellated, perches like an owl on the hill, looking down on its domain, watching for prey, missing nothing, particularly those that try to cross without paying a toll.

We alighted from the chariot and I took care to walk a few steps behind Mr Selwyn, so that I could ape his walk, hold my hands as he did. Thus master and pupil entered the Hall.

Dressed in Charles Fox's finest, I had expected to be an object of attention, even desire. In the event I felt like a pullet in a peacock run. There must have been a million pounds scattered around that rotunda: jewellery that flashed and fired in the glitter of a hundred chandeliers, great domes of powdered hair standing as high again as their owners, cascades of silk and taffeta and lace, and gold and gold and more gold. I did not doubt that frankincense and myrrh were there too in abundance.

We were greeted by a funereal footman, who announced us as though we were about to be buried – a mortician calling aloft for two clients to be admitted. And then a queue of fearsome splendids had to be negotiated. I am nearing six feet in height, and some of them were less than five. Yet I swear I had to pass under all their noses. I followed Mr Selwyn, and to each of them I inclined my head, and received but one greeting. An eyebrow twitched here, a merest nod there, but only when I reached the end, where a girl of my age stood, fresh and oh so pretty in that row of effigies, did I find a smile. And what a smile. Almost a laugh. Full of fun and friendliness. The unsophisticated, unspoilt, unqualified cordiality of youth.

"Mister Paget, it is a pleasure to meet you. Mister Selwyn and Mister Fox have spoken of you." She had been married just an hour, but Mr Selwyn had bowed low and used her new address. I followed suit.

"Your Grace, may I be allowed to congratulate you, and offer my sincerest wishes for your happiness."

I heard Uncle Tom whispering in my ear. *"Lower lip, eyelids, nose up half an inch."*

"I am beginning to suspect, Mister Paget, that you and I are the only people here under eighty. I shall therefore call you Joseph and you shall call me Georgiana."

"Badinage", whispered Uncle Tom. *"Slowly."*

"Your Grace, I – "

"I shall not listen until you call me Georgiana."

"Lady Spencer," murmured Mr Selwyn. "Orders men, sir. But sufficient the wish, of a Cavendish." He had stolen my limelight and I realised how players must feel when appearing with Sam Foote. I paused.

"Not so slow as to look simple," urged Uncle Tom.

"I have not the wit of Mister Selwyn, madam, nor the nerve of his Grace. For if I did, I should call you Georgiana and ask you to dance."

"You shall do both, Joseph. Are you familiar with the minuet?"

"Of course, madam." No pause, quick as a hare.

"You damn fool," whispered Uncle Tom. *"Slowly, I said. You can no more dance a minuet than speak Turkish."*

"Yardim edin," * I muttered.

The first entertainment was a grand masque for which Doctor Arne had written the music. This was to be performed in the gardens. The guests were being ushered through to a wide terrace at the rear of the house and there they preened at each other in the sunshine: ladies standing in their gushing silks, gentlemen moving amongst them with balletic extravagance. I ask you to imagine a few hundred roosters loose in a field of marigolds.

An entire orchestra had been assembled on the lawn, and a canopied stage

---

* Turkish for "Help!"

built by its side. This had a backcloth painted with the most wild and lavish creatures, serpents and dragons and red eyed bulls. The music began, conducted by a dilapidated man with long hair, whom Mr Selwyn informed me was Michael Arne, son of the composer. Players began to walk across the stage, some uttering verse, some dancing a few untrained steps, some simply giggling with embarassment and hurrying to the wings. They were dressed as harlequins and all wore masks, and I think that the boys of the Charity School in Cheltenham could have put on a better performance. Yet each appearance was greeted with shrieked enthusiasm from the gathered ranks. Even one player who managed nothing more than to fall over, was rewarded with wild applause.

The performance lasted for an hour – sixty minutes of artless extravagance. I recognised nothing save the final tune, in which players joined with the guests to trumpet the words of Doctor Arne's song, *Rule Britannia*[117].

After the masque, French wine was served in silver goblets and I followed Mr Selwyn on his perambulations among the marigolds. We were presented to His Pompous Boil the Duke of Cumberland[118], and I marvelled at Mr Selwyn's grovel, in the light of the sniff he normally employed when his opinion of the King's brothers was sought. I recognised many faces: Lord March, with near closed eyes and immense beak, the non pariel of Uncle Tom's chicken look; cool Mr Pitt and pale Freddie Howard; and the irresistible Georgiana talking to Charles Fox.

"Joseph, my boy." The fat and florid darling of the House beamed at my approach. "Allow me to compliment you on your choice of costume."

"Why, thank you, sir," I replied. "I shall pass on your good wishes to my tailor."

"Her Grace and I were discussing the American colonies. We both think it is only a matter of time before the Boston Massacre is repeated. What do you think?" I could hardly maintain my fowlish trance in the light of such a question, and badinage seemed inappropriate, but my knowledge of the Americas was on a par with my command of the minuet. Then I recalled Jack Bannister's tour de force.

"I think it is foolish to charge Boston Bill for drinking tea."

"That is precisely the view of my Party. I shall leave your Grace in the capable hands of a young Whig."

He moved away and Georgiana said, "Have you ever visited America?"

I decided that confession was preferable to falling on my arse. "About as many times as I have danced the minuet, ma'am."

She chuckled. "But your name is already on my card. Look here." She produced a list of names and halfway down I saw Mister Paget in neat and girlish hand.

"If your honour depends upon it, ma'am, I shall be pleased to become a laughing stock."

"Come with me, Joseph." She took my hand. "We must polish your pirouettes."

She led me through the rotunda, collecting a violinist on the way, to a chamber. She locked the door behind us, commanded the musician to play minuets until we expired, then faced me in the centre of the room.

"Bow to me, Joseph," she said. "Bow to me as though I were the most beautiful woman in London."

"I do believe you are, ma'am." I swept low and she replied with a pretty curtsey.

"The minuet," she began, "is the most polished and cultivated of all dances. It is a display of chivalry, and of courtesy, and of ceremony. It is eloquence and grace, the languishing eye and the smiling mouth. There are a hundred movements with a pause between each, and these pauses must be filled with neatly turned compliments. This at least you have already mastered." Raised eyebrows but laughing eyes.

"Ma'am – "

"Georgiana."

"Georgiana, I cannot hope to master such savoir vivre, no matter how beautiful my tutor."

"Come. If your partner expects little, there is little to master." She stood at my side and held aloft her hand. "First the coupee, then the high step, then the balance." And we gambolled around the room as a pair of lambs – the new first lady of Society and the boy from under Frome Bridge.

The dance was a triumph. We stuck to what I could manage, but our very simplicity was seen as innocence, the freshness of youth. Uncle Tom was right. I noticed the fluttering of many an eyelid when we left the floor.

The final entertainment was a ballet dance performed by Mr Slingsby's entire Company. They called it dancing, but there the similarity with my efforts ended. For this was elegance incarnate: lissome ladies in skirts so short they scarce covered the knee, muscular men who leapt so high as to be winged, the whole performance in a woodland scene of such authenticity, live doves flitted in the branches of real trees.

As we drove back, Mr Selwyn told me that he soon had to return to Matson. "I grow older," he said, "and the prospect of embalming myself in Gloucestershire clay is ever more odious."

"But surely, sir, there can be few more agreeable times than summer in the Cotswolds? The seasons at Cheltenham and Bath are in full swing, the countryside is as lovely as any in England, and Matson is such a friendly house." He sighed a deep melancholic sigh.

"It is a prison to me. I must sit therein and wait upon a multitude of bores who will harangue me with petty problems, implore me to attend their beastly dinners and expect me to beg for their piddling patronage."

"Why must you receive people you do not choose?"

"Because of our great and glorious democracy, Joseph, and an attachment I have fostered for the income that a seat at Westminster commands. It is election time, and the burghers of Gloucester will exercise their right to vote for Charles Barrow and I to represent them in Parliament."

"How can you be so sure of winning?"

"We are the only two candidates, which reduces the whole thing to a charade. But I must play my part in order to secure my income for a few years more. The only sunshine in my summer will be the visit in August of Mister Walpole."

"If Mister Walpole is coming, then I too shall be there, for I promised to be his guide."

"Come by all means, and bring your friends. Their laughter may brighten my darkness." He paused. "Friends are very important to you, particularly those you make as a young man. You made friends today that will serve you well for the rest of your life. I am very pleased with you. Georgiana is already the Queen of Society at seventeen, and Charles will be the King's First Minister one day, if the bailiffs leave him alone."

I too was pleased with myself, but already my thoughts had turned to the morrow.

We took a box at the Little Theatre on Wednesday – Maria and Jack and Mrs Smythe, Jack Bannister and his Grandparents. And I took Uncle Tom. We saw Sam Foote and Thomas Weston do their usual pas de deux in The Devil upon two Sticks. The rest of the cast were simply butts for their jokes, and the two of them kept up a dialogue caustic enough to scour a bullock. But we all loved it, roaring at the indiscretions, shrieking at the great lewd winks. I sat at the back, as close as possible to Maria. Our fingers touched a few times, and once when no one was looking, her hand brushed my thigh. That was enough to cause me uncommon discomfort, for Charles Fox's breeches are fashionably tight, with no allowance for an enlargement therein.

We talked during the interval and discovered to our collective delight, that we would all be in Gloucestershire for August. Jack and his parents were taking the old folk to see their home village, and the Smythes would be at Prinknash.

The last and most delectable dish of that June banquet was our visit to Marybone on Friday night.

If you follow the Tyburn brook, and go a mile or so past its grisly tree[119], you will come to the pretty little country church of St Mary's, and on the far bank you will see a dark and brooding house of nodding gables. This is the Manor House Boarding School where the sons of Quality are taught to look down upon the rest of us. Once Henry VIII's hunting lodge, it commanded the forests over Hampstead and Highgate and Holloway. But now it has been reduced, and the trees have been cut to make way for villas, and most of the formal gardens turned into pleasure grounds.

The gentlefolk's loss is certainly the common folk's gain, for the pleasure grounds are the most famous in London. They are wildly expensive – admittance for one is two shillings and sixpence – and I was not displeased when Mrs Smythe offered to treat us all. But they are worth every penny. For I can imagine nowhere else in the Kingdom that offers so much entertainment in one evening.

A grand walk between lime trees covered in lanterns leads to an ampitheatre for contests and sport. There are discreet alcoves along the way behind latticed walls of honeysuckle, where lovers can drink each others eyes. As we walked past them I exchanged wicked glances with Maria. The Assembly Rooms have a balustraded balcony upon which an orchestra plays the melodies of the day. *Rule Britannia* is played at least once every hour, which is not surprising as Doctor Arne is the resident conductor.

After we had viewed the arboretum and floral displays, and drunk chocolate on a verandah, we took our seats for the concert. Some symphonies by Joseph Haydn were first and I was soon tapping my foot and nodding in half interest. After a couple of movements I saw Maria whispering to her mother. Then I felt her breath on my ear.

"Mother will not object if we walk together."

And walk together we did, until we were out of sight, and then we ran. The first three alcoves had coats hung across the entrance to advertise occupation, but the fourth was empty and we slipped behind the honeysuckle into a nest as cosy and private as any fledging can have known. I hung up my coat as she loosened my stays, I raised her skirts as she lowered my breeches. From the way she rode me you would have thought Bill Warr was at her side whispering instructions: arse out, knees in, rhythm and balance, rhythm and balance. The orchestra was playing a post horn gallop, and I won in a canter. My engine had such a head of steam that no sooner had it entered the race, it was on the short strokes. And a furious eruption ended the competition before Maria's cheeks were pink.

Our second movement was to the strains of a sombre oratorio by Mr Handel, and this time I was in control. Slow and languid, deeper and ever deeper, bringing little gasps and grunts from her. I licked her eyes, and her mouth, and kissed the hot skin of her neck. I found the hard wart of her nipple and sucked it into my teeth and could scarce restrain myself from biting it clean off. And then she gripped me like a vice and the whole of her shuddered as though in death throws, stabbed to the heart by my plunging sword. And then she flowed, and I floated upon her, a warm deep river, luxuriously silken, langorously sated, murmuring soft obscenties to me as I worked the pump.

A romantic would report that the rest of the evening was an anticlimax, but it was not. For Signor Morel Torre introduced his new exhibition that night.

The concert was ending as we rejoined the others. Mrs Smythe must have known, for we looked nowhere but at each other, and spoke to no one but each other. And my manly bearing had turned to that of a simpering youth, and Maria's sharp eyes to those of a well fed calf.

At nine thirty precisely, Mars and his warriors thundered into the ampitheatre midst a terrifying display of fireworks. Streaks of coloured flame lit the sky and the flashes and crashes of a thousand cannon exploded all around. On the far side of the arena, a mountain had been built. This was Etna and it reached to the roof and was painted in greens and browns and even had snow atop. At the base there was a dark cavern, as high as two men, and on the slopes above, a smaller cave, glowing red. This was Vulcan's Forge, from where he could call upon the Fires of Hell to vanquish his enemies.

Mars stood in his chariot, taunting and shouting, brandishing a burning torch, his men throwing lighted fireworks up at the Forge, in long arcs of brilliant sparks. Smoke and flames began to belch from the cave. And then Vulcan appeared, his entire body seemed alight, flames licking his bare arms, smoke billowing from his head. He screamed a terrible oath and from the cavern below spewed the mighty Cyclops: giants, hideous figures, at least three yards high, bald shining heads with one eye in the centre of the forehead.

Their followed a battle royal. All around the arena, the warriors of Mars and the Cyclops of Vulcan were fighting, stabbing, clubbing. It was so realistic Maria buried her head in my lap, which sharpened the excitement as far as I was concerned.

Mars seemed to be winning the fight, when Vulcan, raging on his platform high above the battle, pointed with magnificent evil to the top of the mountain and began to chant. The Cyclops ran for their cavern with the warriors in pursuit, and the top of the mountain glowed a fearsome orange. The whole edifice rumbled and shook, and then in a crashing, ear splitting explosion, half of the hillside was consumed by fire. The lava began to flow. A river of molten fire swept down upon Mars and his men, and they died in an orgy of writhing agony that would have done credit to Sam Foote and his Company.

As the lights were lit again, Vulcan and his Cyclops paraded in triumph, then Mars was resurrected to take a bow. And the audience, captivated and terrified for an hour, cheered long. Some from delight with the performance, some from relief that it was all over.

I arranged for the Bannisters to stay at Matson and we all took the stage from the Bolt and Tun early on an August morning. We were full of excited chatter: Jack's Grandparents, for they were heading home for the first time in three decades; his parents, happy by nature, and me, fearful of my reception by the Holyoakes, but astir with memories tumbling in my head.

The King's Head yard at Gloucester was empty save for the Matson carriage. Tom Holyoake looked immaculate in green livery – not a sign of recognition, eyes forward, fixed as a guardsman. A porter loaded our bags, and when we had boarded we were conveyed along the streets of Gloucester and through the Barton turnpike.

I expected change. It seemed that I had been away so long. I had changed almost out of recognition, but nothing along the Upton road was different; and when we climbed between the elms, past the lower lake and kitchen gardens, it could have been ten years before. Everything had shrunk, as though I now viewed the world through an inverted lens, but nothing had been added, or taken away.

The Courtyard echoed with the clatter of our arrival and George Holyoake emerged from the kitchen, with Hannah a few paces behind. Tom opened the carriage door, still silent, and we all got down to the cobbles. The Bannisters were chattering and laughing and asking me questions, but I had only eyes for Hannah. She too was staring at me, uncertain, twisting a cloth in her red hands. I held out my hand to George, still watching her.

He took it, embarassed, downcast, and mumbled, "Welcome home Master Joseph."

I did not reply, but looked at Hannah and said, "I hope that you can forgive me."

The log jam broke. I was engulfed in a tidal wave of emotion. First Hannah enveloped me in her heaving breasts, fat wet tears staining my brocade, then George clasped again my hand, this time pumping me as though I were a hydrant. Jud appeared, his squashed grin wider than I had ever seen, and even Tom, gruff, shamefaced, put out his hand for mine. This last gesture surprised me, but when Sarah came out, the reason was clearly and proudly protuding from her belly. She must have been eight months gone. Pregnancy without marriage does not feature in the Holyoake creed, so I assumed she was wed and Tom had relinquished his post of protector.

I turned to Jack Bannister, still with an arm around Hannah. "Meet the family, Jack," I said with proprietorial pride. I introduced all the Holyoakes to all the Bannisters, and could see from the first that they were soulmates. They trooped into the kitchen, where Hannah had prepared a meal, but I loitered in the yard, impatient to explore, eager to taste again the flavours of my childhood.

The stables first, but most of the horses were turned out. I took a bridle and ran across the bowling lawn, past the canal, where even the carp were not the giants of my memory, through the arboretum and out onto the lower meadows. Under the chestnut tree where Pierce had taught me to draw, a few horses stood in the shade whisking flies from each other. There was only one palomino amongst the bays, and when I called she raised her head and sniffed the air.

You must forgive me if this manuscript now descends for a few lines, to the doggerel of the penny dreadful. For I have tried to record my feelings in unemotional prose, but there are no passive words that are adequate. As I walked towards the chestnut tree, Bewitched gave a snicker and cantered to me. I put my arm around her neck, right round, for now I was taller than her. She put her face to my cheek, and I swear that we both cried. Tears of deep feeling, neither joy nor sadness, but of shared life. Part of me is lodged in those big gentle eyes, and although Maria can claim to have been the first love of my life, Bewitched was certainly the second.

She seemed not to notice that I was heavier, or that my legs dangled at her sides. She flew across the meadow in long rippling strides, racing the breeze, and the larks, and the flashing fluttering butterflies. Through Larkham farm, cantering now, then walking up the rutted track that Father and I had slithered down on the Oxford wagon. I could smell the woodsmoke again, hear his chuckle, and see the fat round flanks of Arthur undulating before us. At the top of the hill I left Bewitched cropping grass, and walked along the ridge watching the sun slip down behind the Welsh Mountains, and the blue valley greying with evening mist. And I could hear Pierce reading by a spluttering lantern and see two boys chasing fireflies.

In the morning we rode to Prinknash, Jack, Jud and I, and the Captain welcomed us as a prisoner would a liberating army. He barged past the footman that opened the door and clasped me to him as though we were Frogs. He treated Jud much the same, and when introduced to Jack, lifted his small frame into the air like a prize puppy.

"I cannot tell you what joy it gives me to see you, Joseph. I have sailed every sea there is, and none have defeated me. But Gloucestershire will drown me in boredom afore long. There are only two things to do, drink or fornicate, and even they must take their turn, for I could never manage them together. In any case I must drink with bores, or fornicate with whores, for Elizabeth bears fruit again and has lost her taste for gin." He sighed. "And sin."

"I am sorry to find you unhappy, Captain. You share Mister Selwyn's disdain for the Gloucestershire folk."

"But now you are here we shall go sailing. And then we shall watch some cricket, and you can take me horse racing, and I hear there's to be a grand boxing match in Cirencester next week." He was alight with enthusiasm, a child with new toys. He was more of a child than any of us.

"I look forward to your company." I said. "But there will be other demands on my time." He pouted, an incongruous expression for a face of middle years. "The Smythes will soon be visiting you and I hope to spend some time with Maria, and I have to act as guide for Mister Selwyn's friend Horace Walpole, and I have to show the Bannisters around the village from which they came."

"Maria will be perfectly happy with her mother and Elizabeth, and Bosky can look after his own friends. As for the Bannisters, if they came from the village why can't they find their way back to it?"

"I have given my word to Mister Walpole, and the Bannisters are my friends. Maria might well be happy without my company, but I am not at all sure that I would be without hers." I looked at him straight, but blushed nevertheless. He narrowed his eyes, and for a moment looked petulant, then he roared with laughter and pointed at my breeches.

"I do believe yonder worm has found his tunnel. He'll not be up for air for some time. You win, Joseph. Maria can come too, and your friends. But the Maiden Dean is in Monmouth and we are going to sail her down the Wye on Sunday. I refuse to entertain further conversation."

My first duty was to the Bannisters and the next day we set off for Tewkesbury. There were so many of us we took the haycart. All of the Bannisters, most of the Holyoakes, and even the Warrs came for a ride. We followed the lanes through summer villages to Wainlode Hill, where the river is pushed west before it swings down to Gloucester. North of Gloucester the Severn has lost her maritime flavour. She winds through fat orchards which suckle her banks like piglets on a sow, nourished by her plenty, but sometimes punished by her caprice. For her floods can be sudden and angry, and can cover this whole valley.

There is a saying in these parts that nothing is surer than God's in Gloucestershire. I suspect it was coined by one who stood on this small summit: the view south is dominated by the great cathedral, whilst north is venerable Deerhurst[120] and the massive Norman tower of Tewkesbury[121].

The Severn and Avon meet at Tewkesbury, and the cultures of Warwick and Worcester meet the Gloucester folk. So the old town, fed for centuries by barges headed for Bristol, is a mingling of stone and timber, of thatch and slate, of tall crooked houses and squat Cotswold cottages. Shakespeare would have felt at home here, but so would Whitefield, and probably Cabot too.

Our destination was the pretty little church of St Nicholas, in the fields at Ashchurch. This is the centre of a group of hamlets that farm flat damp meadows east of the town. We must have resembled a wedding party as we all trooped down the aisle to the chancel. George Bannister, fat and red and wheezing from the walk, held Anne's thin white hand as they stood before the altar, quite still. Their silence affected us and we all fell quiet. It was as if there were another presence that demanded respect. I have said before that I have yet to suffer the joyless bonds of religion, but if I wish to retain this happy state I must visit fewer churches, for some of them possess an extraordinarily persuasive air.

When they turned to face us they were both crying. They hugged each other tight, then walked slowly back along the aisle, two sweethearts on their wedding day. I reflected on the warmth, the oneness they must feel, to share such emotion after thirty years and twenty children.

Down a lane that follows the Carrant brook, both of them wandering through Jethro fields[122] as though lost, to the village of Aston, where shy white cottages peep from thatch bonnets through forests of flowers. George found his old home and Anne found hers, then we turned south along a daisy chain of hamlets that shelter under the lee of the escarpment – Oxenton, Woolstone, Gotherington – and the smug village of Bishop's Cleeve.

Thus to Matson and a party in the barn that must have woken folk in Upton. I can recall George Holyoake and Bill Warr rendering Mister Parson as though fire had broken out. I dimly remember a command performance by His Majesty and Boston Bill, and I believe I witnessed an impersonation of Captain Howell by Jack. But from then on the memory has faded. It was sunk in several yards of strong ale and wrapped in the moist dampness of Larkham Jane's underclothes. I am pleased to record that the calumnies uttered in previous chapters are without foundation. No horse could wear a collar so small; a Welsh pony perhaps.

On Friday my Patron was all of a dither. Word had come that Horace Walpole was on his way and would arrive that evening. The day was spent in frantic preparation. You would have thought the Queen herself was due. Everything had to be cleaned. Each Holyoake had a polishing cloth and from the top of the house to the bottom, no chattel was left unrubbed. A regiment of gardeners clipped and mowed and weeded and sprayed, and armfuls of flowers were brought in to stand in every alcove. In the afternoon Hannah was consigned to the kitchen, where she immersed herself in an extravaganza of culinary witchcraft, bubbling and boiling the produce of the fields, burning great sides of flesh, and baking soft white pies into crusty golden masterpieces.

The cellars were opened and the finest claret uncorked, the dining table groaned with silverware, a string quartet from Booth Hall arrived and George Holyoake, bedecked in gilded livery, stood to attention in the entrance hall for more than an hour.

Mr Walpole and his servant arrived at this breathless house just after seven. He complained of a feverishness brought on by the tiresome journey, asked for a hock and seltzer, and was in bed before eight.

At breakfast he told me he planned to call upon Bishop Warburton that morning. I talked of my friendship with the Howells and he asked that he be permitted to call at Prinknash on Sunday. I invited him to join the voyage down the Wye, but he rolled his eyes to the ceiling and said, "My dear Joseph, rivers exist to nourish the land and please the eye. Floating upon them is usually a prelude to immersion in them, an activity enjoyed by Hindus, but not elderly Christians."

I took this as a refusal. "I am at your service, sir. Is there any part of the county that you particularly wish to see?"

"A castle or two perhaps. These venerable bones have much in common with ancient monuments."

"Berkeley Castle is the finest in Gloucestershire," said Mr Selwyn, "and Thornbury the most poignant."

I promised to facilitate Mr Walpole's visit to Prinknash and arranged to meet him at Thornbury on Monday afternoon. I was then released from my obligations and hared upstairs to pack a few clothes.

Not more than half an hour later the three of us were panting at the door of Prinknash: Jack and Jud from the exertions of scrambling in my wake, me from the prospect of seeing Maria.

This time she greeted me with a kiss on the cheek. Her hair was tied and the closeness of her pearl white neck and edible ear dried my throat. French perfume too, only a hint, a whispered promise. I asked Elizabeth Howell to welcome Mr Walpole and we were gone, hullabalooing down the drive, children off to the seaside, the youngest fifteen, and the eldest about forty seven. Thus began yet another eventful excursion.

We started through Gloucester and across the Severn at Over, where corpses still swing, blackening in the sun, then along the Welsh road to Huntley and the forest trail which winds down to Dean Magna.* Then we climbed the rocky scarp, steeper and steeper until the horses snorted with effort and we had to walk before the carriage, for fear of it rolling back.

But every drop of sweat was an investment, for atop Plump Hill is a grassy plateau, cooled by Atlantic breeze, from where the emerald valley stretches away to infinity, and a serpent writhes through the tiny fields. No hint from this distance, of the treacherous tides, the petulant floods, just a stately stream of silver blue smiling in the sun.

Down long western slopes, through oaken woods with bracken carpets, a road of disturbing contrasts, green dark forests of mossy land and mothering trees, then great wasted quarries where the oaks lay piled like bodies after a battle, and brush fires blacken the sky, and ant men burrow into the hillside, ripping out its heart. Can man be so foolish as to destroy in one year that which nature has taken a million to fashion? And for what? To pamper some soft arse, or make war on some poor savage.

Where the forest dips to the Welsh border, we followed a winding track down coppiced ridges of the Kymin – tantalizing glimpses of sweet Monmouth, queen of the Wye.

It is not twenty-five miles from Gloucester, nor much more from Bristol, yet a different race again, a different land: cosy wooded hills, soft and rounded meadows, with here and there savage teeth, bare rock, torn from the earth's bowels in primeval agony, snarling at the sky – bleached walls that mark the progress of mountain rivers, the Monnow and the Trothy, as they tumble into Wye Valley.

A market town of white houses and black gables, clustered on a tor around an ancient fort. A town of which I had never heard, but a name that must stick in every Frenchman's throat. For it was Henry of Monmouth that led his tired bowmen into battle at Agincourt, at odds of four to one against. In three hours they lost a hundred dead and killed ten thousand Frogs.

---

* Mitcheldean.

I had expected to lodge at an inn, but I think that Mrs Smythe had a hand in the arrangements. We were accommodated by a fearsome lady in a large house overlooking the Chippenham field. When we arrived, she fastened a claw upon Maria's wrist and I swear she did not let go until the morning.

We were up at first light, the Captain stamping around the house, urging us to look lively, to shake a leg, threatening to keelhaul us if we missed the tide. A hurried breakfast. Maria, without makeup, pink and fresh, chattering with excitement. Then to the *Maiden Dean*, tethered with long warps and secured with springs, riding on a flood tide that lapped the top of the jetty. She seemed so much larger than before, her gunwhales higher than our heads. We scrambled aboard. No Jimmy this time. Joseph Paget was first mate. I showed the others how to raise the main, prepare the jib, belay the lines, coil the warps.

Then that haunting moment of casting away bonds, filling the main and heeling with the wind: the freedom, the adventure, the sense of oneness with the elements that comes at the starting a voyage. It will never fade. It matters not if the voyage is across an ocean or a lake. The umbilical cord is severed and your survival is in your own hands.

The Wye below Monmouth is surely the Kingdom's fairest river: soft and sensuous, she slips between castled tors, silent tombs of long forgotten wars, where salmon leap and tumbling streams feed her flow, and green velvet banks are strewn with molehills.

We sat in the bow, Maria and I, whilst the others had lessons with the Captain. They each had poles to fend off, for the flow was quickening as the tide began to empty, and it is never easy to steer a boat downstream. We passed several pleasure boats returning from Chepstow, hurrying against the turning tide, six oars apiece working harder and ever harder as they struggled to reach Monmouth before low water. And it was one of these pleasure boats that brought us all the pain.

As we rounded the bend below Brockweir, the great abbey of Tintern, in all her fragile death, came into view. Unutterably sad, she stands stark and skeletal above the river, a majestic reproof to the savages that violated her. Roofless arches perilously balanced upon solitary walls, sightless windows, crumbling sandstone. I gazed in silent awe, reflecting on the anger that lies within the peace of God. How can a creed that preaches the love of all men, sanction the desecration of such beauty[123]?

The others must have been deep in similar meditation, for the chorus of shouting was too late, and with a splintering crash we hit the pleasure boat amidships as it frantically tried to avoid our assault. Maria and I were thrown forward, I to land with excruciating pain astride the bowsprit, Maria to execute a screaming dive that would have won applause at a bathing resort. Unfortunately, as she sunk beneath the brown waters, it was all too clear that she was not practiced in the art of swimming.

The boatmen and Captain Howell were engaged in hurling ever more obscene abuse at each other, and I seemed to be the only witness to the imminent demise of my beloved. I saw her break the surface, threshing and choking, and I dived in despite the genital agony that consumed my lower body. But the strong current had by now carried her too far and there was little hope that I could overhaul her. I swam to the bank and by miraculous chance ran towards the only thing I could see, the lonely parapets of the Abbey. Within yards I was stumbling again into the river, for at Tintern, she describes a loop and near runs back into herself. As the waters came up to my chest Maria came threshing along and I dragged her sodden body to the shallows.

On the far bank the village of Tintern prettily hugs the river, a mix of cottages and mills and ale houses. All was still. No wheels turned, no smoke came from the forges, and there were no villagers. There might have been a plague. Then came faint voices from high up the wooded hill: shouting, running footsteps, growing louder, nearer. Then the whole village was alive, men shouting, women waving, children shrieking, and all of them dressed as though it were Sunday. And of course it was. They had been worshipping in the little Church of St Mary, high on Chapel Hill, when Maria's screams had disturbed their devotions.

The object of my devotions was puking mud, as I rhythmically pummelled her back, in the way of the Newnham trader that saved me from the Severn Bore. With a shuddering cough she came back to life and rolled onto her back – clothes sodden, face muddied and weeping, hair a tangle of rat tails – but, oh how lovely. Never will I have a more enchanting picture of her in my mind. I held her tight, mumbling into her neck, telling her that I loved her, that she was safe, that I would always fend for her. And she pushed my face a little away and kissed my lips, then hugged me to her and whispered that she was mine and would be for ever.

An armada of gesticulating villagers had crossed the river to where we lay. We were loaded with chattering ceremony into the belly of the biggest boat and rowed back to the Beaufort Inn. The ladies of the village patted and sighed over us, and Maria was taken to a cottage to be cleaned and dried. Then we were wrapped in blankets and carried in state to the bar.

The naval battle had been settled with money and the damaged craft towed into dock. The *Maiden Dean* had no holes below her water line and would be ready for the morning tide. Captain Howell was already singing with the boatmen and upon our arrival called for more ale. Soon the heroic deeds of Joseph Paget were flowing into legend.

We all flowed into legend the following morning. Red eyed and furry tongued, we watched Chepstow's fearsome castle glare down at us from the cliffs. It is surprising the river is not red, for a thousand years of blood have been spilt down those soaring turrets. The Romans butchered the Silures and the Normans butchered the Welsh, and for centuries the Welsh have tried to bugger the English. In the Civil War, ownership of the Castle went back and forth between Cavaliers and Roundheads as a ball in a tennis game. Even today, whoever holds the ramparts holds the bridge, and whoever holds the bridge holds South Wales. Not a singularly attractive prospect. The folk in these parts seem permanently angry, and the delapidated state of the bridge is a tribute to their parsimony.

But there was no time to dwell on the ghosts of Glendower, the stream was flowing fast and we had to navigate through the rickety arches. The Captain was in confident mood and promised that the only danger lay in the bridge falling on us. In the event we slewed on our approach and tried to go through sideways. The crash must have been heard in the castle ramparts, but no cannon was fired; no boiling oil was poured. Surprising too, for although the damage to *Maiden Dean* was slight, we managed to demolish an entire pier, and deal boards an inch thick rained upon us as we emerged to seaward[124].

Perilous our passage may have been, but I would sooner pass under that bridge thrice than cross the damn thing in a stagecoach.

Our navigation of the Lower Wye was completed at an uncontrollable speed. As if in a final rush to the arms of her Mother, the ebb tide scurries past shipyards and dockyards and forests of rigging to melt into the wide cold waters of the Severn. We were propelled out of the mouth at Beachley like phlegm from a docker, but once free of the sheltered land we picked up a westerly breeze and were able to head up river against the tide. It is a strange sensation to be sailing well on a broad reach, heeled over, foaming gunwhales, canvas straining, sheets taut, but moving not an inch. I should think we were making five knots, and the tide was sweeping down to Bristol at about the same speed. Thus we enjoyed an unchanging view of Aust Cliff for the best part of an hour.

As the flow eased we dropped an anchor and waited in the peace of low water. The shining flats of Oldbury Sands surfaced like a huge whale, and fog of a million gulls settled thereon. Nothing but their cries and the mournful bell of St Tecla; and Maria's whispered pleasure as we sat by the mast, away from the others, stroking each other. All of each other.

When the tide began to flow, we headed north for an hour or so, then ran up onto the mud at Oldbury Pill. This time we anchored fore and aft to keep her from swinging on the high tides, then a boatman ferried us to the quay. The Prinknash coach stood ready with Jimmy on the box. He nodded to us respectfully, and smiled, but I felt ashamed that I had threatened his position as first mate.

We followed the Pill through damp cyder orchards, to the village, a ramshackle place of huts and mean hovels, many of which must float away to America when the Severn bursts her banks. I suspect the local builder is a wealthy man. It is extaordinary that just beyond the village is a hill, and perched thereon, the Church of St Arilda[125]. Logic dictates that the substantial structure of the church should be at the bottom, where it could withstand the floods, and the hovels should gather on the dry hill. Not for the first time did I conclude that logic is but an occasional visitor to Gloucestershire.

We climbed the hill. Cow Hill it is called, which merely serves to underline the bovinity of those that planned the village. It is not particularly high – it would be dwarfed by Robinswood – but the surrounding orchards are flat and low. Thus it commands a ten mile reach from the mouth of the Wye to Lydney, and can observe all river traffic, however small. It is said that a Roman fort was here before the Church, which does not surprise me, for shepherds and bullies have similar needs.

By the Church we found Mr Walpole's coach with his funny little foreign servant asleep thereon. We walked around the tower, and sitting among the gravestones was Mr Walpole. A white linen cloth laid on the grass: salads and cold meats and a jug of lemonade, a notebook and pencils and a ship's spyglass. He was utterly at peace, smiling softly to himself, humming without tune, and watching with ever moving eyes the broad reach of the river that lay at his feet. I coughed and he looked up, then consulted a pocket watch.

"I have been here four hours, Joseph, and have watched each yard of your progress. I am rather sorry that you have finally arrived, for if you had not, I think I should have stayed until the sun dropped into the river. I may have had no option, for I fear my bones have set. Without the assistance of my servant, who has disappeared, I should probably have been consigned to rest here with these other poor fellows." He waved around the gravestones. "Rigor has already invaded. Mortis would surely have followed."

The Captain made his feelings clear. "Your servant sleeps in your coach, sir. He should be whipped."

Horace looked alarmed. "Please, dear sir, do not offend him. He is the most congenial servant I have known. He is loyal and trustworthy and above all, quiet. He is from Switzerland, you see, and has little English."

"My man has little English," growled the Captain. "But I would still kick his arse if he slept when I needed him."

"I do not wholly approve of corporal punishment," murmured Horace. "In any case I suspect that my gout would suffer more than his buttocks."

We drove in tandem the few miles to Thornbury, little lanes through wide low orchards, gnarled old trees green with cyder apples. The town comes as a surprise in this marshy land. For it is much like a Cotswold town. High stone walls abound and the church is like a wool church, tall and noble. But it is the castle that stirs the blood. For this is Buckingham's palace, this is the great house that was to be the heart of his power. He started it in 1509 and it was from here that they dragged him ten years later to be tried for treason.

The buildings share Tintern's silent testimony, they brood, they accuse. A naked monument to awfulness. But in their case Henry left them to rot, perhaps as a warning to all pretenders. They were unfinished and could never harm him. It was their owner that he violated[126].

We walked around the grounds, then sat with the others in the shade of the crumbling walls to finish Mr Walpole's picnic. He knocked on some doors and finally found a divine to show us around the apartments, but I was too hot to join him, Maria too tired, Jack too bored, Jud simply not interested, and the Captain was already filling the Thornbury airs with stone rattling snores. So Mr Walpole went alone.

I kissed Maria goodbye amidst the grey impotence of Thornbury, for Jack and Jud and I were to travel to Matson with Mr Walpole, and she was to return home in the morning. She whispered that I should come to Brambridge soon and that she cared for no other, but I could not stop the shadow of Edward Weld crossing my mind, and I was as forlorn as I had ever been at her going.

Mr Walpole wanted to take the waters in Cheltenham on his final day. So for the first time in seven years I put my head back into that cyclopean cave of my dreams, wherein lurked Mrs Gale and the hornets from the Charity School, where tortured screams of Erasmus and Cato echoed down dark caverns.

I had to admit that Cheltenham had come a long way in seven years, and the bustle of building work was evidence that she intended to go a good deal further. A grand assembly room had been built at the spa, where a curious little bonneted lady pumped the foul brine into metal cups, for the unwary to sample. Most cottages in the main street were being destroyed to make way for emporiums, and avenues and gardens were being laid out in the fields. But the Grammar School remained, even more stained and crumbled, Schola Grammatica still etched in the dirt. I hurried by, an inmate passing the prison.

Our day was spent in idle contemplation of the idle. For the town is full of wastrels, overweight awfuls with less to do than donkeys in a field. They ponderously perambulate up and down the avenues, braying to their fellows as they pass.

"They are here," observed Mr Walpole, "to avoid the more expensive pleasures of Bath. Not the pleasures, just the expense. They would die for the sight of a duke, even an earl would transport them with delight. But I fear I am the most famous personage they will see today, and I have not yet been recognised." He bowed to a group of walkers who ackowledged him with dismissive nods. He rolled his eyes in mock resignation. "Popinjays with empty purses," he sniffed, rather too loudly for my comfort. "Boors who would be beaux. Can they not see that Horace Walpole walks among them?"

After he had consumed a third glass of the vile waters, I admitted to mild surprise that he was still alive.

"One of the penalties of age," he said, "is the abdication of Prince Lust, and the coronation of King Bowel. He is now my liege, and I am but his servant. My life is dedicated to his movements."

"And do Cheltenham waters assist these movements?"

"They are so poisonous I suspect they are capable of moving an entire army."

"Perhaps we should return to Matson, sir, before the evacuation begins."

Chapter Eleven

Autumn. Back to London. Nothing much to occupy my time during the day, but the nights offered compensation: Ranelagh on Monday, Vauxhall on Wednesday, the theatre on Friday, and in between, the ale houses and bagnios, the occasional ball at which I polished my minuet, and the evil pleasures of Tuttle Down.

There is nothing in these withered fields behind Westminster to suggest their glorious past. The chivalry has long gone, the pageantry swept away. Where knights of the Round Table jousted and medieval kings held their Courts, plague victims have been buried in pits and dead of the Civil War shovelled in by the thousand.

It is as if their misery has driven joy from the place, for it is now host to all that is blasphemous: mountains of refuse alive with rats, mean eyed pigs that roam at will, and a dismal grey bridewell, where debtors are locked without food for days on end. The sports that are celebrated amidst this squalor are a mirror of the awfulness: cock fighting and dog fighting, rat killing contests for sharp little terriers, and bull baiting, which is the cruellest spectacle that I ever wish to see.

It was Jem's delight in the obscene that led me to the place. He called at Cleveland Court one day and suggested that I needed some manly entertainment. His grin was as wicked as I had ever seen it, and I really should have known better.

"Ye need a rest from Jack's sweet innocence," he said. "A bit of flavour on your meat will do you no harm at all." I assumed that he meant bawdy entertainment, and I had to admit that young Jack was not the ideal companion for wenching. Ladies usually thought him to be my young brother and wanted to mother him, and make sure that he got home safely.

Harry Angelo came with us. He was hardly older than Jack, but his height and the sword he carried and the languid manners of Eton lent him maturity.

It was not far, and we walked across St James's Park – fallow deer so tame as to take titbits from the hand – and down to the tidal canals of the Chelsea Waterworks[127], where two of Newcomen's mighty engines clank a ponderous pas de deux. They stand perhaps fifty feet high, great heads nodding, as if in endless salaam to the palace across the meadows. They billow with smoke and steam, and hiss with fearsome rage. They resemble some avenging Messiah, and I believe they must possess biblical powers, for they turn water into wine. At least they turn thick brown river porridge into the spring water that emerges from our kitchen pump.

There is a tavern by the reservoir called Jenny's Whim, where we stopped for a few pots of ale. It has an extraordinary garden. Behind every bush lurks a monster, or a harlequin, or a goblin covered in warts. The unsuspecting walker along the paths and glades somehow triggers a spring engine, and one of these gruesome objects will leap from its lair. I am not sure how many seizures have occurred in those gardens, but I do not propose to go there when I reach my dotage. I suspect, though, they serve a purpose. Any maiden confronted by such an apparition in the evening dusk, would be sure to dive into the arms of her swain, and it is but a labour of love to convert a terrified maiden to a satisfied madam.

Early afternoon, but trade was good. On reflection, good is singularly inappropriate. A great deal of ale was being drunk and commensurate coinage finding its way into the Landlord's coffers, but as a decriptive adjective, good could hardly be ascribed to the clientele therein. It was as if the Covent Garden Parish had arranged an outing for their most villainous residents. I have never seen a more furtive bunch: secret, stooped men, with shifting eyes and stubbled jaws.

"An honest pickpocket would starve in here," observed Jem. "There's too much competition."

And at least half of them had fearsome dogs tethered to their wrists, by a short chain; squat and powerful brutes, with wide undercut jaws and menacing eyes. The dogs shared their master's malevolence for society at large. They slobbered and growled at any approach and I do believe that if one of them had got loose, my bowels would have been evacuated with greater efficiency than a gallon of Cheltenham waters could beget.

At a table groaning with empty jugs and a platter piled with bones, sat a group of bucks. Their manner was jovial. They slapped thighs and roared at jokes, and threw bones to the dogs, but it was not an agreeable humour – barbed ribaldry that mocked and derided those unlikely to respond. I recognised one of their number. He was the man that had lost his cock in Campden, the same that had sent the hwyl singer to sleep. Such was the reputation of Thomas Lyttleton, that at the age of thirty he had already entered the folk lore of the nursery. Round eyed infants heard tales of his dark deeds and were threatened with the vengeance of Bad Lord Lyttleton, if they neglected their sums or picked their nose in church.

Jem seemed quite at home in this company. He was greeted by several of the ruffians, and Lyttleton called to him, "It's the kilted dangler. Over here Jacobite, and bring your lasses with you."

I recalled the time that Tom Rowlandson had called him a dangler, but there was no anger this time, no talk of claymores. Jem's mouth smiled, but not his eyes. I was none too happy about being labelled a lass, but sensed the virtue of discretion.

Unfortunately obeisance is not taught at Eton. Harry flicked back his coat to show his sword. Lyttleton gasped, theatrical, mocking. Then in falsetto voice said, "Save me, save me, it is a footpad." He peered at Harry. "Or is it a hardpad?" The rest guffawed and Harry's colour rose. "Or a footnote?" Harry drew himself to maximum height and directed the full Angelo glare at the reptile.

This glare has been known to wither water lilies, but in this case Lyttleton added, "Perhaps it's a notepad," and turned his back.

Harry was used to more gallant opponents. "I demand an apology, sir," he cried in ringing tones. Jem took his arm and tried to lead him away, but Harry shook him off and repeated his demand. The crowd were now taking an interest, and the dogs sensed excitement, straining on their chains, some up on their hind legs. Lyttleton still had his back to Harry, but his shoulders had tensed, his mood changed.

Harry was unstoppable. "I'll have an apology, sir, or I'll have satisfaction," and he drew his sword.

To say that I was dismayed is a statement so far under as to be subterranean. Here was a fifteen year old youth with two companions, preparing to do battle with a man twice his age, and a retinue of at least fifty malefactors who looked as though they were preparing to share pieces of us between their dogs. And I was one of the two companions. I felt as though I had chosen the wrong side.

"Steady on, Harry," I said. "The gentleman was only joking."

"Stand aside, Joseph," said the imperious one. "If he was only joking, let him say so and apologise."

Now one of Lyttleton's cronies took a hand. "The lad wants satisfaction.

Tom," he taunted his friend. "Perhaps you're not man enough to face him." Stirring the pot, eager for violence. "What's the matter, Tom? Eaten your tongue?"

Lyttleton turned slowly, still seated, to face our hero. "If I stand, boy, you'll be offal before an hour's out". He was well dressed, a man of some means, but he had the face of a felon. Dark purpling rage that reminded me of Ben Hurst. I saw Harry's eyes flick with fear, but the gauntlet was down and Eton demanded that only the foe could pick it up. For a moment, not a word, not a movement. Then the scrape of the chair leg on tiles, as Lyttleton slowly stood up. "On the Down," he said. "We'll fight on the Down."

It was as if a fairy had waved a wand, and animated a Catholic graveyard. Villains smiled and ale began to flow again, and chatter was all around. Bets began to be shouted, four to one the lad, five to one, eleven to two. There were precious few takers. Even I, to my shame, kept my money dry, but I saw Harry backing himself.

It is but a few hundred yards from Jenny's Whim to Tuttle Down, and we three had an escort of fifty for every inch. Had there been a chance I would have run, but from the way Harry strode purposefully towards his doom, I suspect he would not have followed.

We reached a spot on the Down that seemed a regular haunt for most of them, a hollow in the slope that formed a natural arena. Harry and Lyttleton took off their coats, and the Landlord of Jenny's Whim opened a case in which two broadswords lay in gathered silk. Harry took one, then stood, stock still, as if at attention, whist his adversary swished and thrust his weapon at the air. Harry seemed remarkably calm for a boy about to die.

The Landlord, who had appointed himself referee, held a cloth high and the two faced each other: Harry, back straight, long legs wide apart, left hand held to his waist like a molly, right straight out, sword slightly raised; Lyttleton crouching forwards, bouncing on the balls of his feet, like a pugilist, weaving, poised to strike.

The cloth dropped and Lyttleton charged, slashing and stabbing as though he faced a regiment. Harry, calm and lightning quick, parrying, darting away, a matador playing the bull. Around that evil ring of braying men and snarling dogs, Harry in reverse but in control, dancing before his raging foe, defending, avoiding, not striking. I recalled Tom Rowlandson introducing Harry to me as a famous man with the sabre, but I had not realised that he was an artist. A maestro, a will-o'-the-wisp who flitted and hovered and nipped, and laughed at Lyttleton's clumsy efforts to punish him.

Then I saw a foot come from the crowd and trip him, so that he stumbled back and fell, and as he fell he dropped his sword, out of reach. No one moved to help. Quiet now, silent anticipation of death: Lyttleton standing above him, panting, sweating, savouring the triumph, raising his sword to behead the stricken youth, the blade slashing down to bury itself deep in the soft flesh of the neck.

But there was no neck. Just the hard rutted ground. There was no Harry. For he had been waiting for the strike, and he rolled and leapt up in a single movement that was the nimblest thing I ever saw. In a flash he had his sword and had taken his stance again.

Lyttleton's rage had turned to terror, for his sword had snapped and he now had little more than a dagger with which to defend himself. He looked round wildly for an escape but the crowd had closed in. Most of them might have betted him, but their priority was to see someone's guts and anyone's would do.

"Kill," they began to chant. "Kill." Slow and rhythmic, louder yet louder, as Harry stalked his ashen faced prey. A thrust to the shoulder. "Kill, kill." Lyttleton gasping with pain. "Kill, kill, kill." A cut to the knee, and then a lunge straight at the middle, executed with such precision that the blade pierced his blouse and drew blood, but stopped short of running him through.

He fell to his knees, whimpering before his youthful conqueror. He did not plead, for he had shewn no mercy and expected none, but it was clear his courage did not extend to dying like a man.

Harry held the sword at the trembling gut, and in the cultured tones of Eton asked, "Will you now satisfy me, sir, with an apology?"

"I am t-truly sorry, sir."

"Louder."

"I – I am t – ttruly sorry, sir."

"You are truly what?"

"S- s- sorry, sir!" he shouted, and to the dismay of his audience Harry withdrew his sword and stepped back. Lyttleton could not walk, for the tendons of his knee had been severed, and he hobbled away, hanging between the shoulders of two cronies. I resolved to enlist at the academy run by Harry's father, for without doubt pugilism is an infantile game, compared to mastery of the sword.

Harry might have denied the crowd their taste of blood, but the spectacle that followed must have slaked the thirstiest of them. I shall describe the event, for I wish these journals to be a truthful picture of my times, but I urge sensitive readers to pass by the few pages that follow.

Close by was a stone post, higher than a man, with an iron ring at its middle. Stone lips above and below the ring left it free to move round, but neither up nor down. An area around the post about thirty feet across was worn bare – lifeless dusty earth like the floor of a barn.

The crowd now turned their attention to this post as three men arrived leading the most noble beast I have ever seen. It was a bull ox with monstrous shoulders and massive head, but pretty curling hair and eyes as kind as any mother. It had long curved horns to which metal knobs had been attached, and ribbons too, as if joy awaited the poor animal.

"Now we'll see fun," said Jem, his dark face working with excitement. "The bull bait is the most thrilling sport in England."

A rope was taken through the ring, then tied to the base of the horns.

"What are they going to do?" I said, fearing the answer.

"They're going to kill the bull. They'd slaughter it anyway, with a poleaxe, but this way they get some fun, and some of them win enough to drink for a month."

"But why do they want to kill it?" asked Harry. "I've not seen a finer bull in my life."

Jem sighed, a teacher with two obtuse pupils. "Most of these men are meat traders and the taverns pay well for baited beef." He nodded at the bull. "There's a few hundredweight of the stuff on those hooves. They never eat anything else at the Beefsteak Society[128]. The owner of the dog that pins the bull wins the sweepstake and a quarter of the carcase."

The Landlord called for attention, "Five shillings a dog and eightpence a run," he announced. "The bull will be peppered after ten minutes."

"That's to encourage everyone to enter early," said Jem. "As soon as they pepper him it'll take a good dog to pin him."

The men with the dogs pushed forward to crowd around the landlord and pay their money.

"One at a time, gents," sang out the landlord. "You'll all get a chance. He's a fine beast. I think we might be here some time."

A ring of faces, all intent, most of them eager, but Harry and I disturbed. The bull placid, uncaring, lazily flicking flies with a matted tail. The first dog paraded, frantic to be free of its chain, pulling its handler around the ring. The usual bets, hair raising sums, roared between bucks and roughs alike. Two to one on a throw, twos against a kill, eight to one a pin and twenties a pindown.

"The bull is free to move anywhere in the circle," explained Jem, "and the dogs will only be released one at a time. We all bet on each dog's chance, whether he's killed, thrown, or pins the bull. To score a pin the dog must clamp the bull's nose. A pindown is when the dog throws the bull, but I've never seen one."

"But surely no dog's a match for a bull?"

"Just you watch. These are butchers dogs, they call them bulldogs these days. Once they get a hold, they'd hang on if you cut off their legs."

The Landlord rang a bell and the first dog was released. It hurtled at the bull, snarling and snapping. But the bull was almost scornful, lowering his horn to ward away the pest, as he might a persistent wasp. The dog then tried to get beneath his belly, and the bull, with rising anger, scraped the ground with his hoof and put his head low. The dog rushed again, and this time the horn went under the dog and flipped him like a pancake on Shrove Tuesday. High in the air he went, yelping and kicking, but as he fell, several men dived under him to break his fall. Jem explained that owners paid threepence for saving a dog, and many men made a living as a professional catcher.

The next four dogs met the same fate, the bull becoming more indignant with each invasion. Then a dog was gored despite the metal knobs. It flew through the air, entrails dribbling, and no one tried to catch. It hit the ground with a thump, already in its death throes.

The landlord then walked forward armed with a pair of bellows. Four other men held the bull by the horns and the nozzle of the bellows was pushed into his nostril. At a signal, the landlord pumped the bellows and the five men jumped back as though stung. The bull snorted in a terrible rage and charged to the limit of the rope. For a moment I was sure he would break free, but the rope held and he was jerked back, almost falling. He charged in the other direction, desperate to get at his tormentors.

"He's peppered now," shouted Jem, wild with excitement. "It'll start raining dogs in a minute."

The shouting became a hubbub as everyone wanted to bet at once.

"Two at a time gents," bawled the landlord, and a pair of dogs were released. The bull, now a savage and dreadful engine of destruction, bellowing with terrible rage, rushed at the hapless dogs. He stood on one, breaking its back, and tossed the other so far that the catchers were sent scampering, like fielders when John Small is at his most majestic.

Faster and faster, the dogs were released, ripping at the bulls legs, his belly, his flanks, but each time they let go, for it was his head they were after. Now and then one would get a hold on his cheeks, or his ear, but not secure enough to hang on. The more that came, the quicker the bull despatched them, trampling, tossing, charging around the post, his anger turning to frenzy, and as exhaustion slowed him, to blind incomprehension.

The poor bewildered beast, blood flowing from a hundred wounds, staining the dust, splashing the faces of the onlookers, began to sway. To a mighty roar of approval, one dog rushed the bull and seized his nose, as he was trying to disengage another from his horn. The dog's protruding underjaw clamped up into the roof of the bull's mouth and, although the mighty head shook from side to side, and nodded so low that the dog was smashed on the ground, there was no escape. There must be a mechanism within the jaw of a bulldog as powerful as the strongest lock, for in the chaos that followed, of cheering and guzzling and settling of bets, it took three men with staves to prize open that murderous mouth.

The last act of this awful spectacle was the clubbing of the beast to death. Even this was undertaken with relish, the executioner being rewarded with the testicles.

In October we suffered election fever. Charles Fox was returned for Malmesbury, and Mr Selwyn was unopposed at Gloucester. Most boroughs were represented by placemen who purchased the votes, and country polls caused few sparks. The fireworks were reserved for London.

John Wilkes, hero of the people, but the Antichrist to all Tories, was once again standing for Lord Mayor. He had been clapped in the Tower for writing what he thought and banished to France for writing what he did. But here he was, back again, still pricking their flesh. This time, if the crowds that surged along Pall Mall could be believed, he was set to become the Capital's first citizen. *'Wilkes for Liberty'* was their cry, and they plastered it all over town, on bills and posters and huge coloured banners[129].

Voting took a week to complete, and daily polls were published. There were four candidates: Frederick Bull the existing Lord Mayor, Sir James Esdaile, Brackley Kennet, and Wilkes. After a few days it was a contest between Bull and Wilkes, and in the end this Bull fared no better than the poor beast on Tuttle Down.

On Saturday, Wilkes was declared elected and the riots went on till Monday morning. The 'prentice boys ruled the streets and the rich put up their shutters. They could have taken over that weekend. If the working class heroes of England had been abroad, if Tyler had marched, or Cade[130], or Wilkes himself had not been drunk, Cromwell's commonwealth could have risen again. But there was work to do on Monday, and hangovers to be cured, and the English never could harbour a grudge. They are adept at expressing their feelings with the utmost violence, but they quickly lose interest. They drown grievances and pleasures alike in the ale house.

A month later saw the crowning of the people's king. I doubt that London has ever seen such a day. It nearly killed Wilkes. His unhappy face was a red nosed gargoyle with squinted eyes peering malevolently from under a tricorn hat, as his flotilla of barges nosed their way through perishing grey November fog. They sailed upriver from London Bridge to Westminster, and by the look of him they should have gone straight on to Chelsea Hospital; then back again to Blackfriars, wallowing on the slack tide, where he had to be helped up the stairs to the waiting procession. He was suffering from ague when he started, and looked ten years more than his fifty. But by the time he paraded down Cheapside to the Guildhall, in his dazzling golden coach, he resembled a deceased monarch on his final journey.

He appeared at the Feast, but only briefly, propped at the head of the table, doing his best to appear alive. He left early, as I should have done. Six hundred dozen bottles of wine were consumed at that Bacchanalian orgy. A week later, when I had recovered, Mr Selwyn told me that I could be proud of my contribution.

The newspapers that came to Cleveland Court were full of reports from the American colonies, of the ungrateful people of Boston, who were now mysteriously called Canadians, the pathetic disarray of the Philadelphia Congress, and the terrible retribution that would surely fall upon them from the Empire[131]. There was scant mention of any grievances, and Uncle Tom either knew of none or would speak of none, for he was loyal to the King, and the King's enemies were his enemies. So I sent a note to Charles Fox seeking enlightenment. I received more than I bargained for.

I knew from gossip and papers and occasional meetings with Mr Selwyn, that Charles Fox was experiencing a turbulent year. He had fallen foul of the King and been sacked as a minister. His attacks upon the Administration had become more and more virulent, and his support for the colonists had brought him powerful enemies. He had also lost his father, mother and eldest brother, and paid his gambling debts with the inheritance. But he had time to write this reply:

> *My Dear Joseph,*
>
> *You ask for my views on the Colonists. I will answer with questions. You are a Gloucestershire man. How feel you if Gloucestershire were part of France? Well the Colonists are Gloucestershire men.*
>
> *I am a Londoner. How feel I if the Lord Mayor is a Dutchman, and the sheriffs and all the juries, citizens of Amsterdam? Well the Colonists are Londoners.*
>
> *Freddie Howard is a Yorkshireman. How feel he if he must pay his taxes to the Scotch? Well the Colonists are Yorkshiremen.*
>
> *They are English. As arrogant, as aggressive, as truculent children of this isle, as you and I. But they have suckled for too long, and their Mother's tits are dry. They wish to leave home, and will, whether or not we approve. We should bless them on their way, and help them if they stumble. That way they may feel obliged to keep us in our dotage.*
>
> *But the die is cast. The King will have his subjects, and North knows not east from west. A war that we can neither afford, nor win.*
>
> *I am sir,*
>
> *Your friend &c*

That night, after I had consumed far too much in the Shakespeare, leaning on Tom Rowlandson, who was leaning on me, I proposed a toast. I held my glass high and shouted, "To Boston Bill. God bless him." The room was packed, but at least half of them stood and drank with me.

This unhurried maturing of body and mind continued throughout the winter. I spent Christmas with the Bannisters and greeted the dawn of seventeen seventy-five in the arms of La Galli. Fat and fifty she may have been, but she was a powerful haven from the frost. I learned more that night than Mrs Gale taught me in a year. I also caught the clap.

It is a profound thing to awaken on a January morn with the sensation that a fire has been lit between your legs, and upon inspection, espy a member that you do not recognise. Like a strip of boiled beef it hung there, angry and red, between two uncooked faggots. When I got out of bed, I had to walk in the fashion of a man that has just ridden from Glasgow. At breakfast I was forced to sit on the left buttock, and support myself on my elbow. It is deuced difficult to apply marmalade to toast with one hand.

Uncle Tom must have noticed, but he said nothing. Fanny, on the other hand, watched my efforts with ill disguised glee, and when I tottered back to my room, she followed, carrying a small black box.

"Tsk tsk," she said. "We've been a'dipping it where we shouldn't."

She lay the box on a table and opened it to reveal an arsenal of medicaments.

"I know not what you mean, Fanny," I said, drawing myself up as far as my bandy legs would allow.

"Come along, breeches off," a governess to an infant.

"I believe you are mistak- " I had reached the bed and turned to face her, and she pushed me in the chest so that I sat down, abruptly and very painfully.

"There now, you've sat on your eggs. Lay down and we'll see what we can do."

There is little point in arguing with a female when her surgical feelings have been aroused. She bustles and clucks like a mother hen, and treats all objections with the same infuriating bossiness.

She removed my breeches and exposed my suffering member which she inspected in minute detail, lifting it and peering under it, and prodding it until I squirmed.

"Good job I spotted you in time," she said, speaking apparently to my member, not to me. "I've heard that you can wither and die if you don't get treated. And that'd be no good now, would it?" She patted the sorest part and I whined. "You men are all the same. Babies, the lot of you." She was still adressing my groin. "But we're going to be brave now, aren't we, 'cos I've got some ointment here, and some true love leaves, and they might sting a bit." We were not feeling at all brave, but I was pinned to the bed with my breeches about my knees and flight was simply not an option.

She applied thick brown cream to all the sore parts, and tied evil smelling leaves around my tool. She massaged the soreness, and the soreness became a largeness, and a small tree with brown trunk and pale green foliage rose bravely from the bushes.

"You'll be lucky," said Fanny to it. "No more exercise for you this month."

"Pleasure hunts alone, woe takes both his hounds", was one of Hannah's more obscure sayings, but as so often, a truth lay within. A truth that was made abundantly clear when Walter Smythe came to see me, with Wat and Jack. For he certainly brought me woe. And thereafter I came to think of his sons as dogs.

February was spent, and even more appropriate than Hannah's homely philosophy was the line that Shakespeare gave to Caesar, *"Beware the Ides of March"*.

I had written thrice to Maria: to the convent in Paris, to Brambridge, even to Lulworth in case she was there, but had not been concerned about the lack of a reply. I had assumed that her studies and her travels had busied her. In any case there were facets of my education that were better carried on in her absence. When I heard nothing at Christmas I confess to a little petulance, for I had sent her my sketch of Tintern Abbey, of which I was paternally proud. I wrote to her again, assuring her of my undying devotion and seeking leave to visit her on my birthday. It was but a week later when her kinsmen came to call.

The three of them appeared fat and jolly as ever, and the pleasantries were pleasant enough when I introduced them to Uncle Tom. But there was something in their manner that did not rest easy. The boys looked to their father too often, and Walter Smythe carried a weight in his eyes. When Uncle Tom had left us, these eyes were fixed upon me in the manner of a judge pronouncing sentence of death. A black cap would not have looked out of place, and in the light of the news that he brought, would have been singularly appropriate.

"I have seen your letter to Maria," he said. "It was opened in error." It did not occur to me then, that my previous letters had suffered from similar mistakes. "I am concerned, sir, that you should write in such intemperate terms to my daughter, particularly as she is betrothed to another."

The words were so repugnant to me that for a moment I could say nothing. The four of us were frozen, as in a painting, each waiting for the other to speak. "B – b – betrothed sir? That cannot be. I love her." A torrent of words now. "Don't you see? I love her. There can be no other, for she feels for me too. Who is this other? How can you tell me such lies? I must see her. I shall ride to Brambridge tonight."

"Damn you, sir. Did you not hear me? My daughter is betrothed to another, and you shall not speak of her in this manner." The boys clenched their fists, menacing, truculent. "Mister Edward Weld has asked for Maria's hand and I have consented to the union. There is nothing more to be said. You shall not see her, you shall not write to her, you shall not talk of her."

"I shall ride as soon as you have left, and you will not stop me."

"It will serve you no purpose, for you will not be welcome at Brambridge, and in any case, Maria is elsewhere."

"Sir, I beg of you. You are mistaken. Maria and I are lovers." As I said it, I knew that I should not. Wat's large fist hit my cheek bone with crunching effect, and Jack's buried itself in my solar plexus.

I gasped on the floor beneath Walter Smythe's furious fatness. "At least you have shown your true colours," he shouted. "You are a knave, sir. A knave without honour. A knave without prospects. If you dare to seek my daughter's company again, I shall have you whipped."

I could not help reflecting that whipping was probably less painful than the blows I had just suffered. They marched from the room, slightly comic in their corpulent indignation.

I took the stage that afternoon for Winchester. It was full inside and I had to ride on the box. I wore three coats and a hooded oilskin, and thick mittens and a woollen scarf, but still the wind scratched at my face, and the rain soaked through to my skin. I cannot describe my route, for I saw nothing, ate nothing, and thought of nothing save Maria. I know that we stopped at Farnham, and I slept in a bed with three other men. At least I lay in a bed with three other men, and listened the whole night to a lullaby of snoring and coughing and hawking and spitting.

I hired a horse at Winchester, and rode it without mercy down the Twyford road. As the lights were dying, I came to the edge of the estate, where the long ride between the limes begins, the ride that had been such a joy on my first visit. I prayed then. I prayed to a god I had never known. I prayed to any that would hear. To the Bishop of Winchester even. I offered my soul in exchange for Maria.

I came to the house and luckily the footman recognised me, for I was unshaven, unwashed, and he would have turned me away for sure, had I been a stranger. I was shewn to a small ante room across the hall. Before the door was closed behind me, I heard urgent whispering, female whispering, from the floor above. When Mrs Smythe entered, I could see at once that she was as set against me as her husband. Her empty eyes held no warmth for me.

"Joseph, I have consented to see you because you have come a long way, and I will allow you refreshment in the servant's hall before you leave. But there is nothing else to be said between us." I breathed deep.

"I have come to see Maria madam, and I shall not leave until I have done so."

"Maria is not here."

"I believe that I heard her a moment ago." A guess, but she flushed and I knew that I was right.

"Mister Smythe nor I will allow you to see her again." I breathed even deeper.

"Then I shall be your guest for eternity."

"If you persist with this foolishness I shall have you removed."

"I do not doubt that your servants could throw me out, but I will make more noise than an army, and Maria will at least hear me."

She pulled a silken cord by the mantel and almost immediately a footman entered. "Send word to the constable in Twyford, that we are invaded," she said with the same cool authority as on the hill above Prinknash, but then it had saved me, now it was consigning me. "Tell him to send two men, more will not be needed." She turned back to me, no anger on her face, just chill. "You can scream at will to the constable, Joseph. No one will attend." She followed the footman through the door, and before I could reach it I heard a key turn in the lock.

I hammered the door, calling for Maria, Mrs Smythe, the footman, pleading with them, then threatening, then as rage began to boil, abusing them. Nothing. No sound from the hall, no steps on the stairs. I kicked the door, black boot marks scarring the spotless white. I yelled until my throat hurt. I took a vase from the mantel and hurled it at the wall, smashing it to a thousand pieces. I was sobbing now, blind unreasoning anger, and the next ornament that came to hand was a water colour of Maria. I aimed that too at the wall, but missed. The window shattered into glittering shards as the picture soared through it.

Shouting in the hall, running footsteps, angry voices followed by the key turning in the lock. Edward Weld, urbane, in control, with two large servants to assist him. They pinned my arms and held me, struggling and kicking to no avail.

"I am sorry to meet you in these circumstances, Joseph. You have no right to cause such dismay to this house. Maria and I are betrothed and she has no wish to see you. You will now be evicted, and if you attempt to return, the servants are instructed to use violence against you."

They manhandled me to the front door, fighting, scratching, biting anything that came near my mouth. When one of the footmen reached for the handle, I wriggled free, sidestepped Edward Weld and ran down the hall. Three at a time I bounded the stairs, shouting for Maria. The three men in hot pursuit shouting too, but for my blood.

I reached the top only a moment before the others, but in that moment I saw Maria on the landing. I am now not certain what I saw in her face. I thought I saw love, anguish at my predicament, anger at my pursuers, but it was just a second, the tick of a clock. Then Edward Weld's fist hit me behind the ear and I struck out behind with my elbow.

His jaw snapped as I hit it. I felt the crunch, heard the cry as he fell back into the two servants, and the splintering of the bannister as they crashed through.

I looked down at the floor of the hall where they lay. The two servants groaning with pain, Edward Weld still, his head in a bloody pool. I turned to speak to Maria but she and her mother pushed past me and flew down the stairs. Maria cradled Edward's head on her lap, the stain of his blood spreading over her skirts. Mrs Smythe ordered the maids to bring water and cloths and ointment, still cool and in command. I have no love for Mrs Smythe but I should like her on my side in a battle.

Slowly I descended the stairs. As I neared, I heard Maria whispering. Words of love and comfort, but not for me, "There, there my love, lay still now, the surgeon is coming, trust in me, my darling," tears brimming in her eyes, her face deathly white. His face was grey and drained, and he had a terrible gash across his temple. I stood for a moment beside them, nothing to say, nothing to give, and then Mrs Smythe knelt by them, closing the circle, no place for me there.

I ran from the house, wild in my despair, down the avenue of limes, along the Twyford road. Not caring that the rain was slashing my face, soaking the few clothes I wore, running and running and running until I came down a hill into the village. The lane was rutted with a dozen little streams rushing down to the Itchen, and I tripped and fell headlong in the mud. Such was my obvious distress, that a parson riding past on his way to evensong, helped me on to his horse and took me to his house. He must have been a charitable man, for my appearance was singularly disconcerting – blubbering like a baby, muddy as a pig, and sporting a stubble that would have frightened the Captain.

His wife fed me soup and toasted buns, and when I told the good parson that I knew the bishop of Winchester he sent word to the Cathedral. His messenger returned on the box of a carriage, with a note commanding me come at once to Cathedral Close. Thus, for the third time, I went soaked and filthy to an audience with his Grace.

But I was not to meet the ancient prelate that evening. It was Hester Chapone that awaited me in the Palace. She told me that his Grace was staying the night with the Dean, prior to leaving for Farnham in the morning. She showed me to a bedchamber the size of a throne room, in the centre of which stood a bed large enough for a game of cricket. Laid thereon was a change of clothing which prompted the first alarm bell to ring. The second followed almost immediately.

"I think you will find these comfortable, Joseph, I already know your size."

This was said beneath fluttering eyelids that seemed a foot long. There was a light shining in her eyes that I had seen before, the day I emerged from the barrel, naked save for a gallon of blood and guts.

After I had bathed and shaved, I am ashamed to say that I stole from the Church. I crept downstairs, purloined a bottle of claret from the cellars, then retreated to my room and locked the door. For I had known more than sufficient vintage passion in the fat white arms of La Galli, and the aftermath of that encounter was still painful. I lay on the bed and drank the contents of the bottle.

The next experience I am able to record is of sharp white daggers of light stabbing beneath the curtains, and being clubbed to death by a monstrous pain behind my eyes.

The circumstances of my return to London were a considerable improvement on those of my flight therefrom. I sank into a corner of the red leather seats in the draped opulence of his Grace's carriage. The old codger sat opposite, and I suspect from his demeanour that he had consumed more claret than I the previous night. His eyes were red and his pallor grey, and he suffered the brightness of Mrs Chapone's endless chatter with mournful resignation.

As on my journey down, we rested the night at Farnham. But not at the inn, and not in a flea ridden bed full of foul smelling travellers. For not only does his Grace own a palace at Winchester and an elegant London house, he commands the entire county of Surrey from a fortress high on a hill. Here he holds court, protected from the people by massive ramparts and ditches a chain across. I cannot conceive why he needs such an eyrie. Perhaps he feels closer to the Almighty, or perhaps his beatitude needs regular refuelling. For when he has climbed the steep street, where little cottages pay homage to his procession, and passed through a pair of formidable gates, the king of the castle is able to look out on a town full of dirty rascals.

The local bumsuckers turned up that evening, and we must have dined on a whole farmyard of fowl. Not that farmyards abound in this part of England, for every acre is planted with hops. We consumed a goodly portion of their produce too. I recalled Wesley and his threadbare joy. I concluded that the Church of England should practice a little more of the frugality that it preaches.

But I must not show ingratitude. The letter that my Lord Bishop gave me in the morning has become my most prized possession. It will open doors for me wherever life takes me, and it was the first of a number of munificent gifts that marked the conclusion of my eighteenth year.

> *Whereas Our Lord in all His wisdom has brought unto us the hand of our brother Joseph Paget to succour our life upon this earth, it is our bounden duty to commend his truth and courage to whomsoever it may concern.*

It was signed in a long flowing hand and bore the Great Seal of Winchester.

And so to Friday the nineteenth. Eighteen years to the day since my innings began. Or is it eighteen years less one day, for I was born on a Saturday? If I live for another hundred I shall not unlock the mysteries of the Gregorian calendar[132].

A morning of presents: two from Fanny – a box of silk handkerchiefs that must have cost a week's wages, all with my initials embroidered thereon, and a gentle second application of ointment, which went on too long and had the inevitable result. There was a book of dance instruction from the delicious duchess of Devonshire; a history book of London from Uncle Tom; a silver topped cane from Charles Fox and an invitation to join him for dinner to discuss 'a matter of mutual interest'; and a visit from Miss Tuthill, who brought a letter from Mr Selwyn and an exquisite bundle that still went by the name of Mie Mie.

She was nearly four now, with curly golden hair and blue eyes that laughed at all the world – until she could not have her way. Then she turned the colour of a mulberry and shrieked with Italian rage. Her temperament was undoubtedly maternal, but I suspected that her pigment had hibernian origins.

There were three letters for me. Mr Selwyn's note informed me that he had settled an annuity in my favour which would bring me a thousand a year. A thousand pounds every year. Twenty pounds every week. I sat at the kitchen table, mouth opening and closing like the carp at Matson. Trying to come to terms with the fact that I was rich.

As the shock abated, I opened the second letter. It was from Bailey Cove and Co., bankers of Bristol. It begged leave to welcome me as a customer now that Captain John Howell, a much favoured customer, had instructed them to open an account in my name, and deposit therein the sum of twenty thousand pounds.

The third letter doused my fire as surely as a bucket of water on a mounted dog. It was from Maria. It must have been smuggled out of Brambridge for it addressed me as *'My dearest Jo'*, and concluded *'with all my love and good wishes for your future life'*. Unfortunately the passage between was one of stark and pitiless rejection. It told of dear Edward's chronic state and his brave fight for life, his need for constant attention, the certainty of his demise if she left his side. Her duty was clear. She must become his wife and nurse him back to health. She must never see me again, and I must respect this final decision. Well, fuck her, I thought.

The most notable event of that notable day was the birth of this journal. I travelled with Jack and Harry to Strawberry Hill in the afternoon where Mr Walpole presented me with his father's diary. Not a word had been written therein despite it being already fifty years old.

On my return I wrote my name, most carefully on the first page, underlined it, then wrote JOURNAL OF MY LIFE in brave capitals. I spent a great deal of time composing the first sentence in my head, and had written 'I was born' when Tom and Jem called. I shall not tire you with the remainder of my birthday, simply direct you to chapter eight, where a perfectly adequate description is already in print.

It was to Devonshire House that I went to meet Charles Fox. Just a few hundred yards from Cleveland Court, but it could be a few hundred miles. For this is where the Whigs gather, men who, in Uncle Tom's view *"speak with their hearts and think with their backsides"*; men who, in my view, light a grey Tory world with colour and poetry. We have argued long into the night, Uncle Tom and I, but I cannot win, for he invariably concludes that *"all men should be Whigs until they grow up"*.

I had expected that, after a year of marriage, Georgiana would have blossomed into a flawless bloom of fashion, but she was as fresh as the day I danced with her – without paint or pomade, in a simple dress, and with fair hair that tumbled and curled around her shoulders as if she had walked in a high wind. It was tempting to think that she was a servant of the house. A lowly one at that, for the footman that ushered me up the wide marble stairs was adorned in livery that belonged to a palace.

She was pouring tea for Charles Fox, who looked as though he needed it. The dark jowls were flaccid, the thick brows knitted, and his eyes were those of a melancholic spaniel. In Georgiana I detected the same feminine trait that Fanny had betrayed when my loins were afire. She fussed over him and when I appeared, spoke with that same forbearance of a governess reporting an errant child to its parent.

"We must be kind to Charles today, for he is as low as his cards, and as lame as his horses. And his head is sore, for he has been attacked by a jug of port wine."

"I am sorry to find you unwell, sir."

"Unwell, Joseph, unwise and unpaid," he sighed, wobbling with remorse. "I've not one horse as good as Pyrrhus, and not one rider as good as you".

"Come now, Charles," the brisk Georgiana. "No man ever made you gamble, and no man ever made you drink."

"My father made me gamble," grumbled Charles. "He said it would benefit my education, and you shall drive me to drink if you prolong this satire."

"A very short drive, Charles," she murmured sweetly, handing him his cup of tea.

He shook his head, like a huge labrador, and sniffed loudly. "The business in hand," he said. "What are your plans Joseph?"

"Plans, sir? Do you mean for the rest of the day?"

"I mean for the rest of your life."

"I have no plans. Life has treated me rather well thus far, and I've never made a plan yet."

"Good, because I have a plan for you." His eyes were keen again, his expression alive. It was as if his malady had flown from him in an instant. I had heard tell of his powers of recovery, speaking in the House after a day at Newmarket and a night at Almacks. I recalled two lines of a ditty I had heard in a tavern: *"Never take a liberty, with Charlie James Fox, memry like a nellyphant, stomach like a nox."*

"The war in America is now inevitable. The King shall not back down, and nor shall they. The news that comes to us will be expurgated and it will never be possible for us to make considered judgements. We need reliable reports on the progress of the war. We need a correspondent we can trust, and one who is unknown to either side."

I recalled waiting for the mists of Uncle Tom's overture to clear, and of George Holyoake's strictures on male behaviour. I said nothing.

"We need an educated correspondent, but one without obligation, filial or bounden. He must be young and strong, for there may be privations to endure, and he must be a Whig, for there would be little point in sending a disciple of His Majesty."

"In short," said Georgiana, "we need Joseph Paget."

Bacon said *"a wise man will make more opportunities than he finds"*. I believe that wisdom is all very well, but too much of it will bury you. It is all too easy to wait for the next opportunity. Waiting becomes a habit, and habits become shrouds. It is but a short walk to the grave, and you might just as well follow the pretty route. I propose to pursue every opportunity that comes my way without thought of consequence. The art, of course, will be to distinguish between opportunity and delusion. This was no delusion.

"Then you have him," I said.

The arrangements were left to Georgiana, for it was to her that my reports were to be addressed. We assumed that no-one in authority would have the nerve to open intimate letters from a young buck to the Duchess of Devonshire. She gave me letters of introduction from Charles, from Edmund Burke[133], from her husband. And I already had my key to all persons of the cloth. She ferried me to banks, tailors, chemists and booksellers. She chose my clothes, my medicines, my reading. She was much more enthusiastic than I, and I gained the clear impression that she would rather go to war than be a duchess. I could not agree with her. I would give absolutely anything to be the Duke of Devonshire.

I sent a note to the Captain, to tell him of my plans and enquire as to the movements of the *Jamaica Sun*. His reply awoke in me such emotions as I have never known. She would leave Bristol at the end of the month. She had business in Dublin and would thereafter cross the Atlantic. John Darling was now her master and would be pleased to accommodate me. I recalled the night she slipped away from us into the black sea, when I could hardly breathe from the excitement. I remembered the warm dark depths of John Darling, his strange northern dialect; and above all I could see Pierce Creagh, and his gentle poetic confusion with the harshness of life.

There followed two golden weeks – of precious days spent with friends. Jack took me to see his father at Drury Lane, and Harry taught me the rudiments of fencing. Tom and Jem hired a chaise, and the three of us went on a sketching tour of the Kent orchards, heavy with the snow of blossom. Charlton drove Uncle Tom and I to Primrose Hill, where his view across the city was blurred by his tears. And Fanny crept into my bed in the dark of the night and kissed me to sleep. I left them all on the steps of Cleveland Court, waving and calling to me, as Mr Selwyn's coach took me down to Hyde Park Corner and away to Matson. I hope I shall never again feel so alone.

The few days at Matson were spent with Mie Mie, almost all of them leading her around the field, perched on the back of Bewitched. We had an identical conversation at the completion of each circuit. I would venture that it was time we went in, and she would yell, "Gen – Gen," until we set off once more. As Mie Mie grows up she will need a companion, and there cannot be a better one in all the world than Bewitched.

I hugged all the Holyoakes, then went to Prinknash and hugged all the Howells. I am well nigh a full grown man now, but when I put my arms around Jimmy's neck, he swung me aloft and carried me out to the garden, as if it were the first day I had seen him. I left a letter for Maria with Elizabeth Howell, for I knew it would be delivered. I told her that I understood, that her decision was sensible, that Edward would make a far more reliable husband than I. I also told her that I was due to embark for America on the morrow. I thought the tone of sporting acceptance, the whiff of new horizons, the romance of the unknown, would be sufficient to give her second thoughts – which was not very kind.

I could find no words at all for Mr Selwyn, yet I knew I owed him more than anyone. At dinner that night I was as voiceless as the snotty child in Hannah's bed, and in the morning I could do no more than shake his hand and mumble my thanks. He stood in the courtyard, Mie Mie tugging at his silk coat, playing with his silver buckles, for all the world a splendidly overdressed governess. He smiled, languid as ever.

"Do hurry, Joseph", he said. "I prefer the company of children and you are growing older by the minute".

And so to Bristol. and the salt smell of the sea, and the swarming docks, and the sleek black brigantines hungry for the tide, John Darling, somehow bigger, striding the decks, a hundred men, each at his service, each scampering to obey his commands. For now he was master of the *Jamaica Sun*. He feared no man, no ship, no storm.

We sailed on the evening tide, nosing down the Avon to the wide shallow waters of the Severn, then reaching down to Bridgwater Bay before setting a north west course to follow the Welsh coast. As England slipped away into the gathering night I wondered when I would see her again, but then the door closed and I could think only of the adventures that lay ahead.

Notes to Chapter One

(1) John Kemmett, a Tewkesbury ironmaster, formed a Canal Company in 1755 and was granted an Act of Parliament to construct a Navigation without locks from the Severn to the woollen mills of Stroud. The proposal was to straighten the River Frome and install cranes, designed for the purpose by his engineer Thomas Bridges, to transfer goods to each change of level. Construction had reached Stonehouse (about 10km) when the money ran out. John Kemmett and his backers were left in dire straits. Fosbrooke, the Gloucestershire historian commented "that the projectors and executors of such a scheme were great fools. I am only astonished that their wives, persons often more interested in their husbands affairs than themselves, and never unwilling to advise, did not torment them out of it, before they had almost ruined themselves".

(2) Old John Small was the greatest batsman of the Hambledon Club which met on Broadhalfpenny Down. For three decades the isolated Hampshire village was a mecca for the chief patrons and the best cricketers in the land; to say nothing of the vast crowds that turned up for big matches. Small was a bat maker and a sign on his house proclaimed, "Here lives John Small, makes bat and ball. Pitch a wicket, play at cricket, with any man at all." He once carried his bat for three whole days and when Lumpy Stevens bowled him at Bishopbourne Paddock in 1772, it was "the first time for several years". The deeds of the Hambledon Team are charmingly recorded in John Nyren's The Young Cricketers Tutor by Charles Cowden Clarke and first published in 1833.

(3) Journeymen were unemployed craftsmen, members of one of the early trade societies. An organised system to mitigate hardship had existed since medieval times. The member was sent off to tramp the country and given bed and board ('entertainment') at specified inns ('turn houses'). In depressed times, thousands of workers travelled the roads between provincial towns, carrying their possessions and often accompanied by their families. For detailed reading see Travelling Brothers by R.A.Leeson.

(4) The Oxford Wagon or Woodstock Wagon so called by Arthur Young, was described by Marshall in his Rural Economy of Gloucestershire as "the best farm wagon in the Kingdom". It was elegant, efficient and its basic design remained unchanged until well into the 20th Century. An invaluable aid to the study of cart and wagon design is John Vince's booklet Discovering Carts and Wagons.

(5) The Shire is the largest of all draught horses – seventeen to eighteen hands and weighing not less than a ton. Bred for military purposes, the desire for quicker and more thorough cultivation brought it to agriculture. Infamous hauling contests for large stakes were held in the 18th Century. The horses were set to pull wagons full of sand, wheels partly sunk in the ground, with wood blocks in front to increase the strain. These cruel tests ruptured many horses. My standard reference is the Book of the Horse, edited by Brian Vesey – Fitzgerald.

(6) In the summer of 1643 the Civil War seemed to be going the way of the Royalists. After the capture of Bristol, Prince Rupert took one part of the army to the west, while the King took the rest to Gloucester. Charles had the impression that the City would surrender only to him personally. He was wrong; there was solid support for the Parliamentarians. Confident of a bloodless victory, he laid siege to the City but Colonel Massey, the Governor, set fire to 241 houses outside the walls and dared the Royalists to attack. Charles commandeered Matson House, where he established his Court and resided with his sons Charles and James for five weeks. Lord Essex relieved the starving but unbowed City on 5th September. Charles 11 eventually avenged his Father and was crowned in 1660. After his death James reigned for three years during which time he recounted to Major General William Selwyn "My brother and I were generally shut up in a chamber on the second floor at Matson during the day, where you will find that we have left the marks of our confinement inscribed with our knives on the ledges of the windows." Of the countless books on Gloucester and its County, my favourite is the lyrical Companion into Gloucestershire by R.P.Beckinsale. There is a history of Matson House by Audrey Jennings.

(7) In the fifth year of Queen Elizabeth's reign, Parliament passed "An Act touching Divers Orders for Artificers, Labourers, Servants of Husbandry and Apprentices" – Queen Betty's Law. It aimed to sum up and draw together centuries of custom and legislation and thereby regulate the economic life of craftsmen. It controlled entry into trade "lest crafts should eat up and consume each other". Once again I refer the reader to R.A.Leeson's admirable book *Travelling Brothers*.

(8) George Pitt entered Parliament as member for Shaftesbury in 1742 when only twenty. A very handsome man, he was a great favourite with the fashionable ladies of Society. He was created Baron Rivers in 1776 and lord lieutenant of Dorset in 1793. He acquired the noble ruin of Sudeley Castle through his marriage to Penelope Atkins, but took no apparent interest in it. Horace Walpole, who

celebrated Penelope's charms in his writings, never tired of praising "his lovely wife, all loveliness within and without"; but he describes George Pitt as "her brutal, half mad husband".

(9) The English Grammar School movement was born in the 16th Century of the high ideal that classical education should be universally available. By 1700 it had become lethargic and narrow in its curriculum and parents began to seek a wider education for their children. Headmasters were frequently local parsons with no ability to motivate and John Chester was typical of his genre. Vicar of Brockhampton near Cheltenham and later of the Leigh parish as well, Chester appears to have been both ineffectual and inoffensive. Happily the Grammar School flourishes today. There is an entertaining History by Arthur Bell.

(10) The Roman road from Calleva (Silchester), crossing the Fosse Way at Corinium (Cirencester) to the colonia at Glevum (Gloucester).

(11) In 1768 Lieutenant James Cook was put in charge of an expedition, sponsored by the Admiralty and the Royal Society, to watch the transit of Venus in the South Pacific. He charted the New Zealand coast. He then sailed West and charted the eastern coast of New Holland. He landed and took possession for the Crown, naming the new colony New South Wales because of its resemblance to Glamorganshire.

(12) Known as the 'Father of Boxing', Jack Broughton was born in Cirencester in 1704. He introduced science to boxing and was unbeatable in the early days. He became English champion in 1740 by beating George Taylor at Tottenham Court Road and held the title for ten years. He was finally beaten when ten to one on to beat John Slack on 11th April 1750. He was blinded early in the fight and when the Duke of Cumberland, who lost £10,000 shouted, "What are you at, Broughton", he staggered around the ring shouting "I cannot see you, your royal highness". In one championship fight he killed George Stevenson and was so grieved, he wrote a set of rules to try and prevent such a tragedy recurring. Broughton's Rules were the basis of all Prize Fighting for almost a century. The Hamlyn Encyclopedia of Boxing by Gilbert Odd is a mine of information.

(13) So many books have been written about John Wesley that commentary is superfluous. He is the Father of a worldwide Parish and his teachings and his

example give comfort to millions.

(14) George Whitefield was Wesley's close friend and associate. The two travelled together to Georgia and although, in later years Wesley departed from Whitefield's narrow Calvinism, they remained close. Whitefield was the great orator of his time. His fire and majestic evangelism thrilled vast gatherings. It was said he could be heard by 30,000 sinners. Son of the Landlord of the Bell Inn at Gloucester he attended the Crypt Grammar School; one of the rare 18th Century successes of the system.

Notes to Chapter Two

(15) Cheese Rolling. There are records of this ceremony for over 1300 years and its origins are buried deep in a pagan past. In various forms, it was performed throughout Britain and was probably a celebration of fruitfulness. Cheeses used to be rolled from the feet of the Uffington White Horse, and the tip of the Cerne Giant's erection. Both of these prehistoric chalk carvings are on steep slopes that have, in common with Coopers Hill, a fresh water spring at the bottom. This was a potent symbol of the renewal of life.

(16) Great was the emnity between the British and French as they competed to expand their empires. During the Seven Years War the French planned an invasion. The fleets at Toulon and Brest were to unite and convoy troops across the Channel. The Toulon fleet left harbour but was spotted going through the Straits of Gibraltar. Admiral Boscawen started in pursuit in under three hours and destroyed the French off Lagos. The Brest fleet fared little better, being chased to Quiberon Bay where it was decimated by Hawke. The Treaty of Paris in 1763 ended the war. In America, Great Britain received Canada, all French territory east of the Mississippi, Cape Breton Island and all other islands in the river and gulf of St Lawrence. She received Florida from Spain, Dominica, Tobago and Grenada in the West Indies, Minorca in the Mediterranean and the African settlements on the River Senegal.

(17) There has been a house at Prinknash since the 14th Century. Owned by the Abbots of Gloucester until the Dissolution, Henry V111, a visitor to the house as a young man, gave the property to Sir Anthony Kingston in 1540. It then passed through a succession of private hands until being restored to the Benedictines in

1928. The bas relief on the ceiling that stared at Joseph, is a relic of the Civil War and the many battles that were fought along the Severn Valley. The monks built a new abbey across the valley and moved there in 1972. They gave the old house the name St Peter's Grange. It is open to the public only at certain times of the year.

(18) When a high spring tide races up the Bristol Channel and meets a strong current of the Severn, a wave or 'bore' begins to appear near the Guscar Rocks at Woolaston. As the river narrows the wall of resisting water can grow to five feet in height and reach a speed of a dozen miles an hour. The *Elver Express* was described by John Speed in 1607 as "a rage and fury of waters, raising up the sands from the bottom, winding and driving them upon heapes. Unhappy is the vessel which it taketh full upon the side".

(19) George Augustus Selwyn was Member of Parliament for Gloucester from 1754 to 1780. He found the duties tiresome, and when forced by a division to attend, he not only remained silent but was usually asleep. It is surprising therefore that he was a noted conversationalist and wit, well known throughout sporting and dissolute society and a friend of many literary luminaries. His kindness and affability were renowned and although never married, he loved children. His one disturbing tendency was a fascination with public executions and the products thereof.

(20) Famine in the sixties brought great hardship to the new industrial workers and their families, who were without the means to feed from the land. The textile workers of the Stroud valleys were hit particularly hard and there was much rioting in the area.

(21) Amboina, capital of Moluccas or Spice Islands, province of Indonesia between Celebes and New Guinea. Of volcanic origin, the Moluccas are mountainous, fertile and humid. They are the original home of nutmeg and cloves. Explored by Magellan (1511 – 12), the islands were taken by the Dutch who secured a monopoly on the clove trade.

(22) The Kingswood Forest once covered an area of two hundred square miles East and North of Bristol. Much was cleared by early farmers and with the discovery of coal and the growth of the City, the remainder was felled. The Kingswood Colliers were a fiercely independent band given to violent protest against all attempts to

govern them. Wesley and Whitehouse became the heroes of the Forest, addressing vast open air crowds with missionary fervour. Their legacy was an enduring tradition of Methodism. The Forest was also home to a number of self sufficient gangs of highwaymen and footpads, far less susceptible to Jesus.

(23) Bristol was the principal home port of the Privateers. These licensed pirates roamed the seas in search of foreign merchant shipping. Although their activities were aimed principally at Britain's enemies, no trader was safe when the Privateers smelled bounty. John Howell married Elizabeth in Jamaica and on the birth of their first son, retired from active duty to spend some of his immense profits. These journals make no further reference to Jacob and we can only assume the pair were competitors.

(24) The village of Framilode is the hub of elver fishing, Epney being the collecting station. Born in the Sargasso Sea, elvers, or young eels, take an average of two years to wriggle across the Atlantic and reach the Severn in Spring. They are caught in gauze nets on a timber frame, lightly fried in butter and devoured with almost indecent relish by gourmets the World over. The ones that elude the nets return to the Sargasso without spawning. It is Nature's most pointless migration. The Severn supports almost every kind of British freshwater fish and is also visited by whales, sharks, dolphins, sturgeons and lampreys. The City of Gloucester annually provides a lamprey pie to the Sovereign.

(25) Richard Clutterbuck, an idle country gentleman, beneficiary of industrious forebears, who lavished a fortune on the marshy village of Frampton on Severn. Like his friends, Walpole and Selwyn, he never married, devoting his life to effete pleasures. His mansion remains one of the finest of its kind in Gloucestershire, notable for the richness of its interior woodwork. He built an extraordinary garden house at about the same time as Selwyn was extending Matson. Both reflect admiration for Walpole's extravagances at Strawberry Hill.

Notes to Chapter Three

(26) Walpole lived at Strawberry Hill Twickenham, a house that he contrived to turn into a 'little Gothic castle'. He built a grand refrectory with a library above, a picture gallery and cloister, a round tower and tribune. A great north bedchamber followed and these were adorned with battlements and arches and painted glass.

When he died he left the house to his cousin for her life and thence to his great niece, the Countess of Waldegrave. His fantasies remain intact and unmolested, and are there to delight us to this day. The house is open once a year when a Strawberry Fair is held to raise money for charity; but it can be seen at any other reasonable time provided permission in writing is sought. It is one of the most original literary and architectural monuments in all England.

(27) Mary Farringdon, lady in waiting to Queen Caroline, married her cousin Colonel John Selwyn in 1707. John was an aide de camp to Marlborough and the couple were very much part of Court life during the reigns of George I and George II. They lived mostly in London, at Cleveland Court in St James. They had three children. John born in 1709 was delicate and lived with his parents until his death, within months of his father, in 1751. Albinia, who married and bore six children before her death at the age of 25, and George Augustus.

(28) Donna Constanza Brusati, daughter of the Marchese Brusati, had performed as a singer and dancer in Italian opera. She was famously beautiful and married Giacomo Fagnani, the feckless son and heir of a wealthy Milanese family. His parents objected to the marriage and the young couple left Italy to travel Europe, sometimes together, sometimes apart. In 1769 they came to London and soon entered (and were entered) into the spirit of prevailing society. She gave birth to Maria Emily in August 1771 to great speculation as to the father. One school of thought maintained that George Selwyn must have performed the uncharacteristic act, whilst others nominated Lord March (later Lord Queensbury – 'Old Q'). These journals suggest that Pierce Creagh was also in the frame.

(29) The Welsh Mountain breed has always had a high reputation among the ponies of the British Isles. They are founded on the prehistoric type of Celtic pony, but from earliest times have been crossed with Arabs, which were being imported in pre – Roman times. They are the most direct descendants of the little chariot ponies which created such a sensation among the Roman invaders. The racing pony Merlin (13 hands) of Arab descent, was a stallion on the Welsh Hills in the 18th Century.

(30) Gloucester Cathedral has presided over its city for nine hundred years. The foundation stone of the Abbey Church was laid in 1089 and the building that stands today was complete by the end of the 15th Century. Only a visit can do justice to its glories. In September 1327 King Edward II was murdered in Berkeley

Castle and three months later his body was interred at Gloucester. His son Edward III funded the transformation of the dark Norman choir into a magnificent royal mausoleum, lit by a new east window. This window, the largest in medieval Europe, stands like a gigantic triptych behind the high altar, still containing much of its original glass. Edward's tomb became one of the foremost places of pilgrimage in England.

(31) It would appear that JP met the famous William Warburton. A vigorous intellectual and defender of the established Church, he was a prolific, albeit intolerant, writer, who poured scorn on all dissenters. He once attacked free thinker William Webster, editor of the Weekly Miscellany, saying 'Webster and his fellows should be hung as they do vermin in a warren, and left to posterity, to stink and blacken in the wind'. It is impossible to exhaust the list of controversies in which he revelled. He steadily rose in the Church, but took his episcopal duties as easily as most of his brethren. He was made Bishop of Gloucester in 1759 but only took up residence ten years later. He was injured in a fall in 1770 and never fully recovered. He appears to have been in decline when JP saw him. He died on 7th June 1779 and was buried in the Cathedral. Walpole called him a bully and a sneak, Johnson said 'he had a mind full of reading and reflection'. Take your pick.

(32) Fanny Murray became London's most celebrated whore. At the age of 14 she was living in Bath with Beau Nash, who, despite his 63 years, was passionately enamoured with her. After a jealous row she took to the streets of London, starting with poor apprentices and working her way up the social scale until she was invited to join Jack Harris's Whores Club. Jack Harris moved in high society and his customers were young rakes and landed gentry. The fair Fanny was soon Queen of the Courtesans. She married the actor David Ross with whom she lived peaceably until her death in 1778. Wits Wenches and Wantons by E.J.Burford is an enthusiastic romp through the bawdy houses of Covent Garden.

(33) Privately owned and driven four wheel vehicles were known after Phaeton, son of Helios, coachman to the Sun God. A dashing youth, he drove the sun one day, but lost control and nearly set the world on fire in the ensuing crash. Drivers of these carriages were thought to have the same devil may care attitude. The crane necked phaeton was a sporting vehicle with a turn of speed. It had a high seat for two, front wheels of five feet in diameter and rear wheels sometimes as much as eight feet high. They were called High Flyers, as were the young blades who usually drove them.

(34) The hamlet of Over was the lowest crossing point of the Severn until recent times. Here the river splits around Alney Island and the two channels are easy to bridge. The haunted ruins to which JP refers must be those of the deserted Bishops Palace which stood in its own vineyards on rising ground close to the mouth of the Leadon. It was a fine building and I can trace no good reason for its abandonment. The Talbot Inn still stands and is now known as The Dog. The bridge was demolished around 1820 being replaced with a splendid new design by Telford. This in turn became redundant in the 1970's but has been preserved and is well worth an inspection.

(35) Thomas Lyttleton was born in Hagley in 1744. He was the nonpareil of rakes and libertines. His excesses were legendary and his nickname of Bad Lord Lyttleton was well earned. He was known to George Selwyn which may explain his presence in Gloucester. He married Apphia Witts of Chipping Norton at Halesowen Church in June 1772 and deserted her for a barmaid the following April. His death was a most extraordinary affair, dealt with at some length later in these journals.

(36) The Oxford Dictionary describes hwyl as an emotional quality which inspires and sustains impassioned eloquence. It is the fervour of emotion chracteristic of gatherings of Welsh people. It was once described as 'the intangible and untranslatable hwyl of the Eisteddfod'.

(37) This is a reference to an old horse dealer's trick. When a prospective buyer came to view, the usual practice was for the horse to be led from his stable and paraded in the yard. If the horse was not as eager or alert as the dealer had inferred, a stick of ginger inserted under his tail would bring him out of the stable like a dressage champion. The practice was known by the coloquial term of 'figging'.

(38) The ancient borough of Newnham commands one of the ferry crossings of the Severn. The town grew as a small shipbuilding and glass making port and at the time of JP's visit was flourishing. It is very likely the site of the battle in the 1st Century AD, between the armies of Roman general Ostorius and Caratacus, the young leader of the Silures (Welsh). Although the Britons, with their formidable warriors, had the high ground west of the Severn, the disciplined and well armed Roman soldiers forded the river and won a crushing victory. It was the crucial battle in the colonisation of South Wales and the establishment of Venta Silurum (Caerwent) and the great fortress of Caerleon.

(39) Henry Frederick, Duke of Cumberland, wild and profligate brother of George III. Short and bumptious, Walpole dismisses him as 'a pert, chattering, dissipated and frivolous youth, proud of his exalted rank almost to vulgarity, yet at the same time preferring low society'. He was notorious for his excesses and exerted a Machiavellian influence on his nephew George, Prince of Wales, which the long suffering King failed to counter. A love of sailing was his only redeeming feature. In 1775 he put up a twenty guinea silver cup for a race on the Thames, which led to the formation of the Cumberland Sailing Society, forerunner of the Royal Thames Yacht Club.

(40) There are a number of nautical terms in this passage which I summarise as follows:

- Gunwhales — The upper edges of a boat's side.
- Bow, stern — Foremost and hindmost parts of the hull.
- Bowsprit — A spar projecting forwards from the bow.
- Port, starboard — Left, right.
- Halliard — A running line for hoisting the sail.
- Shroud — A fixed line to laterally support the mast.
- Gybe — To change tack with a following wind.

(41) The Noose is the point at which the Severn changes her nature from rural to maritime. As if finally released from the stays of the Nabs and Knolls and Cliffs and Rocks that chart her course down the Vale, she spreads into a great lake of shallows and rivulets washed twice daily by the Channel tides. Today a railway winds down the Welsh shore but before it came, Gatcombe was a busy little harbour sharing much of the Dean trade with Newnham. Many boats were built here and the Gatcombe Stop Boat, which JP describes, was famous from Bristol to Gloucester.

(42) From a stop boat, anchored in mid stream with a line to shore, two counterbalanced poles, crossed at the gunwhales, would be extended upstream. The wide mouth of the lavenet would be held open by the poles leaving the long tapering trap to flow back under the boat. Thus the salmon entering the net could be seen by the fisherman who was able to close the mouth with draw strings and haul his prize aboard.

Notes to Chapter Four

(43) The pirate John Gow, a native of the Orkney Islands, was mate on the George Galley bound for Santa Cruz. He led a mutiny, killing the officers and took command, renaming the ship Revenge. They roamed the Atlantic coasts of Spain and Portugal where they took a few prizes, but none carrying the riches they sought. They sailed north to hide in the Orkneys when the Navy began to hunt them. Caught and tried in London, Gow and seven of his crew were hanged at Execution Dock on 11th August 1729. At the first attempt Gow's rope broke and although it was customary to reprieve survivors, he was hastily resuspended to rot in chains on the banks of the Thames.

(44) Jo was unable to see Jack Broughton's house because by 1771 he had moved to Walcot Place, Lambeth, where he died in 1789.

(45) Edward I, elder son of Henry III was king of England for thirty five years until his death in 1307. 'Longshanks', majestic and affable, was truly one of England's greatest monarchs. His wife, the incomparable Eleanor of Castile, perhaps the most beloved of all English queens, died in 1290. Edward bought her body from Harby in Nottinghamshire, to Westminster and at each of the twelve places the procession rested for the night, he erected a memorial, an Eleanor Cross. One remains at Geddington in Northamptonshire, another at Hardingstone Northamptonshire, and a third at Waltham Cross in Hertfordshire. The best known, in the forecourt of Charing Cross station, is a Victorian version of a much older cross that stood in the hamlet of Charing, and possibly has nothing to do with Eleanor. Edward's tomb, of black Purbeck Marble slabs, and the magnificent gilt bronze effigy of Eleanor, are in Westminster Abbey.

(46) On the site now occupied by St James's Palace, originally stood a hospital for lepers, founded in the 12th Century. The building became the property of Henry VIII, who erected a royal palace in its place. It remained the residence of the Sovereign until George IV acquired the adjoining Buckingham House and built the Palace that stands today.

(47) This is a reference to Doctor Samuel Johnson, a contemporary but not a friend of Selwyn and his circle. The autocratic man of letters was courted by all distinguished society, an oracle of the salon, the common room, the parlour, and of

a circle of friends, Burke, Goldsmith, Gibbon, Garrick, Reynolds and Burney who between them, were the heart of the great 18th Century renaissance of English Literature. Samuel Johnson has a unique place in English history, for although much of his work is dead, he lives on in the pages of Boswell who, in the eyes of some, was the greater genius. *Life of Johnson* by James Boswell, Oxford University Press.

(48) The Adam brothers, James, John, Robert and William were the foremost architects of the age. They not only designed buildings, inside and out, but fireplaces and staircases and ceilings and furniture, so that an Adam room could be distinguished by its harmony. They also controlled a major building contractor and thus the massive Adelphi development was truly all their own work. It was completed in 1772 when David Garrick moved into the centre house of the Royal Terrace. The brothers were all commemorated in the street names, and Thomas Rowlandson, about whom we shall hear much, died in Osbornes Hotel, John Street in 1827.

(49) Blackfriars Bridge was originally called Pitt Bridge. It was designed by Robert Mylne, a young Scotsman. The first pile was driven on 7th June 1761 and it was opened on 11th November 1769. Foot passengers at first paid a toll of one halfpenny, and on Sundays, one penny. This led to rioting and the Government bought the toll, thus freeing the bridge, in June 1785. There were nine eliptical arches and from wharf to wharf it measured 955 ft. It was demolished in 1860 to make way for the present structure. Robert Mylne became the Surveyor of St Pauls where he is buried.

(50) Few English schoolchildren are unaware of the rhyme *'In 1665, not a soul was left alive, In 1666, London burned like two sticks'*. The Black Death was an epidemic of bubonic plague which swept through Europe in the 17th Century. As much as three quarters of the population of some countries perished. The disease is caused by the bacterium Pasteurella pestis (now known as Yersinia pestis) which is transmitted to humans by fleas from infected rats. The Fire of London, although it destroyed most of the old city, was a blessing in disguise; for it also destroyed the rats. The Monument near London Bridge, was designed by Sir Christopher Wren and erected to mark the spot where the fire began. It formerly bore an inscription stating that the fire was started by Roman Catholics; hence Pope's lines, *'Where London's column, pointing to the skies, Like a tall bully, lifts the head and lies'.*

(51) In Roman times, a wooden bridge crossed the river, a little to the east of the present site. This was replaced by a stone one, built by Peter of Colechurch, in 1176 and finished in 1209. It is this ancient structure that Jo and Uncle Tom squeezed under. The buildings that it carried were removed in 1757.

(52) A yard of ale is a curious bell shaped glass, narrowing to a tube at the bottom, but then widening again to a bulb. When filled with ale it must be held almost vertical to drain the contents and this invariably results in a sudden rush which overwhelms the drinker. Some country pubs offer the contents free to newcomers able to drain the yard, in one draught, without spilling a drop.

(53) Two fighters on the bill that day deserve mention. Benjamin Brain, Big Ben as he was known, was born in Bristol in 1753. After some success around the local venues, he went to London in 1774. He was a coal porter at a wharf in the Strand and made little impression on the fight game until nearly losing a contest in the Long Fields in Bloomsbury in 1786. His eyes were so badly swollen that he was unable to see his opponent. The fight was paused while Ben's eyes were lanced, and a few rounds later he knocked his man out. His career was a catalogue of highs and lows, caused principally by the bottle, but his crowning victory was over the champion, Tom Johnson, at Wrotham in Kent on 17 January 1791.

(54) Tom Faulkner won the championship in 1758 and retired undefeated after a questionable defence against Joe James. Many said that Joe laid down "when the book was full". Tom then took to cricket but made the occasional comeback when his purse was empty. In 1789, when he was 53 yrs old, he took up full time fighting again, and was still at it in 1791, when he beat Sam Thornhill, the Warwickshire bruiser, at Studley. See *Pugilistica*, Volume 1, by H.D.Miles.

Notes to Chapter Five

(55) The Cotswold Games, or Olympick Games as they became known, were first held at the start of the 17th Century on the hills above Chipping Campden. They were a celebration of English country sports and pastimes, held with the support of James I and sponsored by Robert Dover. They were a unique event in the long history of British sport, immensely popular and much publicized by the literary lions of the day. They lapsed with Robert Dover's death in 1652 but were re-established after the Civil War. They continued until the middle of the 19th

Century by which time they had degenerated to an annual riot, unacceptable to Victorian morality. They were relaunched in 1951 and continue today. Whether or not you are lucky enough to visit Campden during the Games, their site is an essential part of any Cotswold tour. *The Book of Campden* by Geoffrey Powell is a beautifully illustrated guide to the town, and there is a pamphlet devoted to the Games entitled *Heigh for Cotswold* by Francis Burns.

(56) In Griffith's *History of Cheltenham and its Vicinity*, published in 1826, Southam is described as one of the most ancient mansions in Gloucestershire, or perhaps the kingdom. It is a magnificent house, retaining much of its original architecture. At the time of JP's journal it was the seat of Thomas Baghot de la Bere, and later the home of the retired Viceroy of India, Lord Ellenborough. It became a school in the 20th Century and is now a renowned Country Club and Hotel.

(57) A goodly slice of English history lies within the embattled walls of Sudeley Castle, and only a whole book and a visit can do it justice. A Saxon manor, a Norman castle, a Queen's palace, a pawn in two civil wars; finally laid waste by Massey, and left to become the ruin that JP saw. Ownership passed through a number of hands, including George Pitt, who was created Baron Rivers of Sudeley Castle in 1802. The Dent family, Winchcombe's greatest benefactors, acquired the Estate in 1837. The Castle lives today, due entirely to their efforts, and Emma Dent wrote a massive and valuable history in *The Annals of Winchcombe and Sudeley*.

(58) The reference to Sam Lucas is interesting, for eleven years after JP's visit, one John Lucas, then residing at Sudeley, broke open the lead coffin of Katherine Parr, which was discovered in the ruins. Her body was in a state of complete preservation, but not for long. Locks of her hair and other relics were soon on sale in the market, and when her remains were finally laid to rest by the Dents, there was little but a few bones. Whether John was son of Sam, and a former shin kicking champion, we shall never know.

(59) This is a reference to Jean Georges Noverre (1727 – 1810) who was the first great dancer of modern ballet. It was he who suceeded in finally banishing the dresses, masks, set order of dances and conventional rules of the ballet. Garrick called him 'The Shakespeare of the Dance'.

(60) *'By God's precious heart and Passion, by God's nails*

And by the Blood of Christ that is in Hailes.'

Chaucer, *The Pardoner's Tale.*

A relic of Our Lord, in the form of a few drops of his blood sealed in a silver chalice, were brought to the great monastery of Hailes by Prince Edmund in 1270. The authenticity of the relic was not questioned until the Dissolution of the Monasteries in the 16th Century. For three hundred years pilgrims made their way to Winchcombe to confess, and be absolved before the Shrine.

(61) The climate and soil of the Cotswolds produced some of the finest long wools in England; soft strong and pure. From early times it was one of the county's chief exports, much of it going to the prosperous weaving towns of Flanders and Brabant. The sheep had long faces, square bodies and the whitest wool. *'The noble dame, the goddess of merchants, the beautiful, white, delightful Cotswold lion'*. Not my words, I hasten to add, but those of the poet John Gower.

(62) All thoroughbred horses are directly descended from three stallions, The Godolphin Arabian, The Byerley Turk and The Darley Arabian. Eclipse, grandson of the last named, first ran on 3rd May 1769, to begin a matchless career during which he was never whipped, spurred or headed. He went to stud in 1771 and is still considered the supreme stallion of all time. He can still be seen, for his skeleton stands in the Museum of Horseracing at the Jockey Club headquarters in Newmarket.

(63) I quote from *General Orders and Rules for Cocking* published in 1723. *"The battle done, search and suck your cock's wounds, and wash them well with hot urine, then give him a roll of your best scouring, and stove him for that night. If he be swelled, the next morning suck and bathe his wounds again, and pounce them with the herb Robert through a fine bag; give him a handful of bread in warm urine, and stove him till the swelling be down. If he be hurt in the eye, chew a little ground ivy and spit the juice on it, which is good for films, hards, warts etc. When you visit your wounded cocks a month or so after you have put them to their walks, if you find about their head any swollen bunches, hard and blackish at one end, then there are unsound cores undoubtedly in them: therefore, open them, and with your thumb, crush them out, suck out the corruption, and fill the holes with fresh butter, and that will infallibly cure them"*.

(64) The Jacobite rising of 1745 was the most formidable of several attempts by Pretenders to the British throne, to dislodge the unpopular George II. Its hero was Prince Charles Edward, a man of daring and attractive personality. He raised a Highland army and marched south, taking Manchester and reaching Derby. Had he known that London was in panic and George was about to retire to Hanover, he might have proceeded; but he paused, and then returned to Scotland. It can be fairly said that he snatched defeat from the jaws of victory. Once in retreat he could not stop, and the English, under Cumberland, finally caught up with him at Culloden, near Inverness, in April 1746. It was a rout, and Cumberland earned the nickname Butcher, from the cruelty he showed after the battle. Many Scotsmen were executed, although Prince Charles, through the heroism of Flora Macdonald, escaped to France.

Notes to Chapter Six

(65) One of the great legacies left by the Roman conquerors of Britain was an unparalleled road network, connecting every major city town and settlement via straight, well engineered highways. It is a mystery why most of these fell into disuse, to be replaced by meandering tracks, little better than river beds, that sufficed until the twentieth century. Of the Roman towns mentioned by JP, Venta Belgarum is Winchester and Sorviodvnvm is Old Sarum (Salisbury). Calleva is Silchester, Corinium is Cirencester, Noviomagvs is Chichester and Glevum is Gloucester.

(66) In the vacuum of the Roman withdrawal, the kingdom of Wessex was formed by the Saxons, Cerdic and Cynric. They conquered the area around Southampton Water and the Isle of Wight and then moved inland, using the vacated Venta Belgarum as their base. They defeated British forces at Charford, Old Sarum and Barbury Castle near Swindon. Cynric's son Ceawlin extended the kingdom, first into Surrey, then north to the decaying Roman towns of Glevum, Corinium and Aqvae Svlis (Bath). When his Empire, as empires inevitably do, came to the attention of covetous neighbours, Ceawlin built the Wansdyke to protect his northern flank. It is an earthwork with a ditch and bank some ninety feet across, that runs twelve miles east from the Vale of Pewsey. Just south of Marlborough it reaches Savernake which was to become one of the favourite hunting forests of William the Conqueror.

(67) JP dismisses Edward Weld as a joyless man, dark and severe, but he lacks his

usual perception. Edward was 31 at the time of the Brambridge meeting and had only just lost his first wife Juliana. It was a happy, albeit childless marriage, and he would have still been in mourning. The master of Lulworth Castle was a modest man, not given to extravagance. He was unemotional, some would say calculating. But it is not fair to call him joyless, for he was an accomplished singer, and good sailor. Any man that can combine these two virtues cannot possibly be all bad.

(68) The great and glorious game of cricket, played wherever the Union Jack once fluttered (except North America, where our presence was never comfortably tolerated) can truly said to have been born in Hambledon. The notes to Chapter One refer to John Small and to the extraordinary effect this small village has had upon the refined world. The history of Hambledon has been lovingly recorded in The Biography of a Hampshire Village by John Goldsmith.

(69) Like any sport, the rules of cricket have been modified. In the 18th Century two stumps, not three, were defended by the batter; bowling was usually underarm, but as JP records, not necessarily less hostile; and a notch was a run. Betting was rife, and even if inflation is ignored the sums were hair raising. The odds to which JP refers mean that a bettor is being asked to lay out two units to win one and seven units to win four, respectively. The confusing use of four and eight in betting odds (five to four, one hundred to eight, etc.) is a legacy of the times when four crowns made a pound sterling, and a half crown was a common coin.

(70) King George III was known throughout his kingdom as Farmer George. A benign character, slow but honest, he stood out from his profligate relatives like a tree on a prairie. Although customs dues have been levied since Carthage ruled the trade routes, they were a minor source of revenue until the 18th Century. The expansion of the British Empire, the interference in European politics, the "spirited foreign policy", pursued by the Georgians, had to be paid for and heavy duties were levied upon imported goods. When Farmer George was crowned in 1759, 800 items were dutiable. During his reign a further 1300 were added. In addition to wines and spirits, tobacco and spices, tea, coffee, chocolate, sugar and dried fruits; silk, lace, leather, brocade, scent, gold, silver, pearls and a host of artefacts were deemed fair game by the Treasury. In the way of the English, avoidance of these dues became an art form and smuggling a national sport.

(71) Richard Nyren, father of John (The Young Cricketer's Tutor) was the landlord of the Bat and Ball Inn on Broadhalfpenny Down (still open today and well worth a

visit). It was under his auspices that the Club flourished, for he presided over the meetings, captained the side, was principal bowler with Tom Brett and became the acknowledged consultant on any matters of precedent or law. By the time of JP's visit, he had moved to the George in the centre of the village.

(72) On 19 July 1545, Henry VIII's new flagship, the Mary Rose, was ordered to sea to intercept a fleet of hostile Frenchmen sighted off Portsmouth. The knight in charge had his gunports open and ready for battle, but as she felt the wind, Mary Rose heeled rather more than expected, due to the weight of armaments on her upper decks. She flooded through the lower ports and in full view of the King and his court, and the wife of the unfortunate knight, sank, drowning most of her crew. In 1967 a sonar scanning device located the wreck and in 1982 the vessel was raised from its grave. Her remains are on view in Portsmouth.

(73) In an age of lawless bands, the Hawkhust Gang was pre-eminent. Led by Arthur Gray, their smuggling activities and violent clashes with the Preventives, became folk lore in Kent and Sussex. They built a major distribution centre on Seacox Heath, a kind of illicit bonded warehouse, and woe betide anyone who tried to look inside. They captured Customs Officers and tried them in their own Courts, attacked Customs Houses and reclaimed seized goods; and on many occasion freed their comrades from gaol. Their leaders became wealthy men and boasted that they were able to raise "five hundred armed soldiers within the hour". This represented most of the male population of Hawkhurst. The flavour of those violent days is preserved for us all in The Smuggler's Song by Rudyard Kipling and for a fuller account I commend you to The Smugglers 1 and 2 by Shore and Harper.

(74) Until the formation of the Coastguard Service in 1822, the battle against smuggling was in the hands of the Customs Houses, who operated smacks, cutters and sloops patrolling British waters; and the Riding Officers who harried the carriers with troops of dragoons, on search and seize missions. The Speedwell, a 194 ton cutter with twenty guns and thirty one men, cruised between Weymouth and Cowes.

(75) Before water closets, most privys were sensibly placed at some distance from the living accommodation. In the dark and inclement weather the journey thereto could be arduous and frightening for children, particularly young girls. The mother and daughter seat, with a smaller hole alongside the regular one, was developed to facilitate togetherness whilst undertaking this intimate activity.

(76) At the time of JP's glimpse and waspish observation, Broadlands was undergoing an architectural transformation to the elegant Palladian mansion we see today. The 2nd Viscount Palmerstone employed Capability Brown to embellish the Jacobean manor house and landscape the grounds that slope down to the River Test. The result is generally regarded as one of Brown's greatest masterpieces. Henry John, 3rd Viscount, became the owner of Broadlands at seventeen. He was one of the political giants of Victorian Britain, holding the three great offices of state, Foreign Secretary, Home Secretary and Prime Minister. Broadlands became even more famous in the 20th Century as the home of Lord Louis Mountbatten. The Queen and Prince Philip began their honeymoon here in 1947, as did the Prince and Princess of Wales in 1981. The House is now open to the public.

(77) Elizabeth Brownrigg was executed at Tyburn on 14th September 1767. Mother of sixteen children, she was a midwife who took care of poor women in labour in the workhouse. She took young girls as apprentices and treated them cruelly, beating, whipping and scalding as punishment for minor offences. They were frequently chained naked all night in the yard with the pigs, and expected to work for twelve hours the following day. Mary Clifford escaped and upon recapture, was stripped, hung from a hook and horsewhipped senseless by Lizzie and her son. She told a neighbour and Lizzie cut her tongue with scissors. When the Parish Officer, alerted to the girl's plight, demanded a sight of her, Mary was found, horribly injured, in a cupboard. She died two days later.

(78) Hugh and Ralph are approximations of the sound made by the sick, as they hang from the gunwhales. Further sailing terms used in this Chapter and not already described in the Note (40) are as follows:

- Sheets — Lines for controlling sails.
- Bowline — A knotted loop, much used by sailors.
- Jib — The foremost sail.
- Monkey Fist — A balled knot at the end of a line.
- Gaff — A spar along the top edge of the mainsail.
- Cleat — A double hook for securing a line.
- Main Peak — The high point of the mainsail.
- Main Tack — The bottom edge, fixed to the boom.
- Howsed Down — Tightened.
- Taffrail — The rail around the stern.

Notes to Chapter Seven

(79) If asked to nominate the worst Prime Minister Britain has ever had, a majority of historians would plump for Lord Frederick North. Yet he was a distiguished Parliamentarian, a witty and magnetic speaker and an efficient administrator. He became Chancellor of the Exchequer in 1767 and then, as leader of the King's friends, Prime Minister in 1770. He was regarded as simply a mouthpiece for George III and his tenure, a period of personal government by the Sovereign. He spent twelve years at the helm, during which time the American War of Independence bequeathed a profound lesson to future generations – that a nation state, intent upon its own salvation, is deuced difficult to subdue. This lesson has since been universally ignored.

(80) Eyre Coote, Robert Clive and James Wolfe were three of Britain's greatest military heroes. They were at the forefront of a period of untarnished glory in which the French were finally defeated, Canada secured and the Indian Empire established. Clive blazed the trail for the East India Company, as they fought like dogs with French and Dutch commercial interests, over the carcase of India. He held a garrison at Arcot with 500 men whilst besieged by an army of 10,000. He led 1,000 troops and 2,000 sepoys into battle at Plassey, against an army of 50,000 raised by the Nawab of Bengal, and won an overwhelming victory. Coote too was at Plessey and then in 1760 had sole command at Wandewash, where the defeat of General Lally ended all French influence in India. He became Commander in Chief in India in 1779. Wolfe's theatre of war was Europe and America. Distinguished at the siege of Louisburg he was made Major General in 1759 and given command of the force sent up the St Lawrence against Quebec. He was killed in the battle of the Heights of Abraham, leading the scaling of the cliffs, in one of the most brilliant victories in military history. His body was brought back to England and buried at Greenwich. Many Lives of all three men have been published.

(81) Thomas Newcomen, born at Dartmouth in 1663. In 1705 he constructed an improved form of Thomas Savery's engine, first made in 1698. It was an atmospheric (steam condensing) pumping engine which was used for raising water from mines and remained the standard model until superseded by James Watt's seperate condenser engine in 1769.

(82) The Purbeck Hills form a ridge that crosses the peninsular from Swanage to Lulworth. It bears the marks of many ancient peoples. Barrows and tumuli and

earthworks and forts are scattered along its fourteen miles. There is one break, at Corfe, where a mournful castle stands gaunt and deserted on a lofty tor. The hills run down to the beach at Arish Mell and it is tempting to imagine that this was where the tribes came, to begin a tradition that still entwines men of Dorset with the sea.

(83) Guelph and Ghibelline are Italianised forms of the German "Welf" and "Waiblingen", the names of two rival princely families whose conflicts made much of the history of Germany and Italy during the Middle Ages. The feuds between these two factions continued in Italy during the campaigns of Emperor Frederick I, and later developed into the fierce struggles of the 13th Century, between emperor and pope. The present Royal Family of England is descended from the Guelphs through the House of Brunswick.

(84) Doctor James Graham, part fanatic, part quack, opened his Temple of Health in Panton St to promote earth bathing. His patients were seated on a magnetic throne and buried up to their neck in mud. He claimed to know the secret of *'the whole art of enjoying health and vigour and exalting personal honour and loveliness'*. Flanked by near naked nymphs (one was the future Emma Hamilton) he unveiled a Celestial Bed in his Temple of Venus at the Adelphi, which he hired out to reinvigorate the impotent. He titillated society with erotic lectures. He used to prophesy that masturbation, or the Heinous Sin of Self Pollution, would cause *'debility of body and mind, infecundity, epilepsy, loss of memory, sight and hearing; distortion of the eyes, mouth and face; feeble, harsh and squeaking voice; pale, sallow and blueish black complexion; wasting and tottering of the limbs; idiotism, horrors, extreme wretchedness and even death itself'*. He died insane and was buried in Greyfriars' Churchyard.

(85) JP records that he counted thirty-two gun ports and presumably there were a similar number on the far side. Technically, sixty four guns made her a fourth rate war ship, one below the minimum to stand in line. However, Agamemnon was a similar size and she was Nelson's favourite.

Notes to Chapter Eight

(86) Betsy Coxe. There was a well trodden route by which a poor girl could ascend to the sunlit uplands, and few started lower, or climbed higher than Elizabeth

Green. She was a destitute child when Bad Lord Lyttleton helped himself to her, and for some years she was misused by him and his friends. At seventeen she was the toast of many brothels, and at twenty she adopted the name of her most regular client, Captain John Coxe. Her next protector was Lord Falkirk, who became the Earl of Alford, and under his patronage she became known as the 'Rage of London'. Her first stage appearance was at Drury Lane, and curiously she achieved widespread fame as a male impersonator. For the imprudent, the well trodden route also descends the other side of the mountain. As her beauty deserted her, so did her admirers. She died in poverty.

(87) Luminaries always seem to come in pairs, and one light is lost in the glare of the other. Thus Boswell laboured in Johnson's shadow, Attlee in Churchill's, and Mill House in Arkle's. Ben Jonson's place in history has suffered from being contemporaneous with Shakespeare. But he was as famous a man in his day, and his works have endured, though not in the abundance of the Bard. His wit was universal and timeless. There are many anthologies of his sayings, and a browse through one never fails to remind me of the transience of modern life. The truths of 1600 are just as true today:

- *Apes are apes, though clothed in scarlet.* (The Poetasters)
- *Drink to me only with thine eyes.* (To Celia)
- *Money never made any man rich, but in his mind.* (Timber)
- *A fool may talk but a wise man speaks.* (Timber)
- *If he were to be made honest by an Act of Parliament, I should not alter in my faith of him.* (The Devil is an Ass)
- *Sweet swan of Avon, he was not of an age, but for all time.* (To the Memory of Shakespeare).

(88) The gateway of Temple Bar marked the western limits of the City of London. Although the old gate survived the Great Fire, it was replaced by Wren around 1670. On the west of it were placed figures of Charles I and Charles II and on the east those of James I and Anne of Denmark. It was also used to display the remains of traitors. It was removed in 1877 to accommodate traffic flow and lay in pieces for a decade before the brewing magnate Sir Henry Mieux had it erected on his estate at Theobalds Park, Cheshunt. It is now in a very dilapidated state and many feel that it should be restored and moved back to a suitable site in the City.

(89) The play that JP attended was *She Stoops to Conquer* by Oliver Goldsmith. In an all too short career, this elegant Irish playwright enjoyed brilliant success. He was born, probably at Pallas, County Westmeath in 1730 and died on 4 April 1774. A complete edition of his poems and plays, with meticulous chronology and text is edited and introduced by Tom Davis.

(90) Signora Caterina Galli was a formidable Italian opera singer of legendary volume and capacity. She blasted her way through London society around the middle of the century leaving a trail of used inamorata in her wake. By the time JP heard her she was in reduced circumstances, singing at inns for her supper and selling her prodigious favours to the highest bidder.

(91) Packington Tomkyns took over the Shakespeare's Head from his Father in 1754. Under his guidance it became the most notorious, and the most popular, tavern in London. It had two invaluable assets; for the head cook was the renowned John Twigg, famous for his turtle soup; and the head waiter was Jack Harris, who ran the Whore's Club and annually published the best selling directory in town, the *List of Covent Garden Cyprians*.

(92) As a young man in York, George Stubbs, an artist with a growing reputation, was commissioned to illustrate a book by Dr John Burton *An Essay towards a Complete New System of Midwifery*. He employed body snatchers to secure the corpse of a young woman who had died in childbirth. This was dissected to enable him to produce the plates, which are his earliest known works. His first love was the horse and a few years later he rented an isolated farmhouse near Horkstow in Lincolnshire where he worked for two years, with no other companion than his assistant Mary Spencer. They bled a horse to death, skinned and disembowelled it, and then suspended it on hooks from the ceiling. He dissected it, muscle by muscle, organ by organ, until he reached the skeleton. He produced a series of concise drawings published in 1766 in *The Anatomy of the Horse*, which even today remains the standard work. The publication was a landmark, for it not only made Stubbs famous, it changed the manner in which the horse was portrayed in art.

(93) Colen Campbell followed Wren as the most influential architect of the day. The first Earl of Tylney commissioned him to produce a Palladian mansion to rival any in the land. The result was a magnificent palace at Wanstead, that served as the model for many other country houses of the eighteenth century. Campbell died in 1729 and his creation outlived him for only a hundred years. Profligacy and debt

resulted in Wanstead House being sold for building stone in 1824. All that remains are the stables, now a sports clubhouse, and a summer house called the Temple.

(94) Boudicca, wife of Prasutagus, king of the Iceni. On his death his territory was siezed by the Romans, his widow scourged and his daughters ravished. In revenge, Boudicca, at the head of a formidable host, burned Camalodunum (Colchester) and inflicted heavy defeats upon the Romans. The Governor General, Suctonius Paulinus, reinforced his army and overthrew Boudicca in a bloody battle. It is said to have been fought around the hill fort of Ambersbury Banks. The Queen, seeing that her men were losing, committed suicide with her daughters, by eating poisonous berries.

(95) Harold II, King of the English. Edward the Confessor ruled the English for twenty four years, but as he grew old, the factions intent upon succeeding him made their plans. Harold, his brother in law, was best placed to inherit, and by astute political manoeuvering, became the most powerful man in the kingdom. But he tried to be too clever. He swore to aid the claims of Duke William of Normandy, whilst forming an alliance against William, with Torstig and Harold Hardrada of Norway. When Edward died he proclaimed himself King. Trouble from Normandy was inevitable and Harold kept his forces in the south. Tostig and Harold Hardrada, aggrieved at Harold's perfidy, attacked and occupied York. Harold raced north and met them at Stamford Bridge. The Norsemen were slain but in his hour of triumph, Harold heard that William had landed at Pevensey. By a series of amazing forced marches, Harold returned south, and on the way stopped to pray at the new abbey he had built at Waltham. The two armies met at Senlac near Hastings. Harold was killed and William won the day. The dead King was taken back to his abbey for burial.

(96) After the death of Boudicca, the Iceni were allowed to keep their kingdom under a system of tribute to Rome. They were, in common with most of their brethren on this belligerent isle, warlike. They were probably forerunners of the British cavalry, for they were famous for their horsemanship and their wicked scythed chariots, in which they would charge into the enemy ranks and literally mow them down.

(97) The Jockey Club has its origins in the Star and Garter Tavern in Pall Mall. Their are no records of early meetings, which were probably simply groups of like minded individuals, planning some sport. In 1752 they acquired land in

Newmarket and built coffee rooms thereon. Their influence grew and questions and disputes began to be referred to them. By 1762 they had a membership that included a royal duke, five other dukes, a marquess, five earls, a viscount and a baron. Not surprisingly there was a queue to join such distinguished company. They became the governing body of racing simply because they were racing. Woe betide anyone that questioned their authority. Even the Prince of Wales was drummed out after the dubious running of his horse Escape in 1791.

(98) Before the all seeing eyes of the media had crept into every niche of our life, touts were the eyes and ears of the gambling fraternity. They observed all training gallops, usually through a spyglass, for they were hated by trainers, who would use dogs to clear the Heath before stable stars were given their head. Their job was to report on the fitness and form of the horses and in particular, to time their runs.

(99) From the village of Reach, on the edge of the Fens, to the cover of the woods at Ditton, the open door of Newmarket Heath invited wild tribes of the north, and marauding Danes, into the kingdom of the Iceni. So they built the Devil's Dyke. For six miles or so, this remarkably accurate fortification crosses the plain at an average height of eighteen feet. With a ditch at the foot, it rises in places sixty two feet from the bottom of the dyke. It later served the Saxons, as part of their boundary between Mercia and East Anglia, and later still the racing public, as shelter from the wind.

(100) This intriguing reference by JP adds fuel to the rumours about Harry Angelo's parentage, that were in circulation even before he was born. Domenico Angelo Malevolti Tremamondo, a romantic and flamboyant Italian, came to London in 1755 as ecuyer to the Earl of Pembroke. He was famed as a rider and swordsman. Such was his success that he decided to stay and settled at Wilton where he simplified his name to Angelo. He was said to be enamoured with the actress Peg Woffington, whilst his wife preferred the charms of Charles Douglas, Lord March, later to become the third Duke of Queensbury. Henry (Harry) Angelo was born in 1760.

(101) The Iceni finally retreated to the island of Ely, in the swamps, driven by centuries of Roman, Dane, Saxon and Norman hordes. They built their monastery which became the Queen of the Fens. I can only urge you to visit it, and savour it.

(102) In the Middle Ages, horses were trained to perform a wide variety of movements, to fit them for battle at close quarters. The lighter and better bred horse could outflank the big clumsy war horses that had been used. By the 14th Century equestrianism had become an art, calling for a high degree of training and skill from horse and rider. Haute Ecole establishments were in vogue all over Europe. The coming of firearms changed the needs of a cavalry officer, speed and strength being the essentials. The only institution in the World where the traditions of the Haute Ecole are unimpaired, is the Spanish Court Riding School in Vienna. Here the Piaffe (marking time) the Spanish Step, the Levade (rearing and standing) and the controlled hops and jumps of the Capriole, are taught to magnificent white Lipizzaners, proud and muscular horses of Arab and Spanish descent.

(103) The Rowley Mile at Newmarket commemorates Old Rowley, the favourite hack of King Charles II.

Notes to Chapter Nine

(104) In an age not known for its care of the hungry, the life of Thomas Coram is a beacon of kindness. A master mariner, born at Lyme Regis in 1668, he had strong links with America and was one of the first trustees of the new state of Georgia. His great love was for the abandoned children of London, of whom there were thousands. The grand old sailor and his flock of foundlings were a common sight around the streets and eventually he pricked enough consciences to persuade a group of noblemen and ladies to petition the King. Fifty six acres in Lamb's Conduit Fields were purchased, and work on the Foundling Hospital was begun in 1742. With separate wings for boys and girls, a countrywide system for the fostering of babes, and education and training for them after five, the Hospital soon became a Mecca for deserted mothers. Rules were made: only the first child of 'a previously untarnished mother' would be admitted, and it had to be under twelve months old. Hogarth was a Governor and great admirer of Coram, of whom he painted a fine portrait, Handel was a tireless benefactor, and later, Dickens spent much time in its support. Thomas Coram, having seen the completion of his dream, died penniless in 1751. He was buried in the Hospital, and his tomb removed to St Andrew's Holborn in 1926. His statue stands in Brunswick square.

(105) The citizens of Massachusetts, and particularly Boston, had been hostile to the Crown since the passing of the Stamp Act in 1765. This involved a tax on the Colonies, seen by Parliament to be necessary to mitigate against the cost of the

Seven Years War. *"No taxation without representation"* became a cry difficult for many Englishmen to resist, for their own democracy was founded on just such a premise. Neverthless, by a process of ill considered legislation, Parliament inflamed the Colonists to such effect that open rebellion was in full swing by 1770. The taxation laws were repealed but with magnificent folly the duty on tea retained. Ships of the East India Company were boarded by a party disguised as Mohawks and three hundred and forty chests of tea thrown into Boston Harbour. The War of Independence that followed, which France Spain and Holland all joined, seeking to settle old scores, ended with the recognition of the United States at the Peace of Versailles in 1783. The United Empire Loyalists, of whom there were a great many, were driven north to Canada.

(106) Samuel Foote, born at Truro in 1720, was one of the most brilliant mimics of all time. Comic dramatist, producer, impresario, his place in the history of the stage has been usurped by Garrick, but he was as influential, and probably more innovative. He was no horseman, but after boasting of his skill one night in the Shakespeare, he was invited by Lord Mexborough to join him for a day's hunting. The purpose was to provide a diversion for his principal guest, the Duke of York. They laughed at Foote's clothing, chortled at his lack of knowledge, then put him on a dangerous animal from which he was thrown. He broke a leg, which had to be amputated.

(107) The duke of York with commendable, albeit unusual compassion, granted Foote a life patent of the Little Theatre in Haymarket, upon which stage he had presented his most famous satires and farces. Foote not only resumed his profession, but turned his disability to effect by appearing as Old Faulkner, a man with a wooden leg from Dublin (I say, where did the other leg come from ?) and Sir Luke Limp. He wrote The Lame Lover, and The Devil on Two Sticks, and played the lead with an endless stream of jokes and double entendres about his missing member. The Theatre was built in 1720 on a site adjoining the present Theatre Royal. It received no licence due to powerful opposition from Drury Lane and Covent Garden, and was soon in financial trouble. Henry Fielding produced his satires there in 1735, as a result of which the theatre was closed and censorship introduced. Samuel Foote reopened it in 1747 and flouted the licensing laws by advertising free admission, but charging for chocolate and coffee served during the performance.

(108) Thomas Weston drank himself to an early grave just three years after JP saw

The Bankrupt. Although he acted and looked the part of the elderly thespian, he was only thirty nine when he died. When still a boy he was sent to sea as a midshipman, but escaped and joined a travelling theatre company. He found his way to Bartholomew Fair in the fifties and was introduced to Samuel Foote. He made his first appearance at the Haymarket in 1759 and began an association between the two men that only ended when they died within months of each other. Despite his heavy drinking, he never forgot his lines, never missed a performance. He won high praise for his acting, not least from Garrick, who considered Weston's playing of Abel Drugger superior to his own, although it became one of his most famous comic parts.

(109) Mohocks were gangs of aristocratic ruffians who roamed London streets early in the century, bent on mischief. They were often violent and at times killed their victims for fun. Anyone not of their own class was fair game; they raped servant girls, tortured the elderly, and such was the concern at their activities, a royal edict *"Regarding Unusual Riots and Barbarities"* was issued, including £100 reward and immunity. They had disappeared by 1750 but about twenty years later another set of wild young men, styling themselves with the same title, made their presence felt. They were accorded a great deal of attention by the Press, but they revelled in the notoriety and for a few years terrorised the Capital with impunity. Their leader, Rhoan Hamilton was arrested in 1774, but jumped bail and settled in Paris. Of the others, Ossie Osborne was an American law student and Charles Hayter son of a wealthy property speculator. Theodore Anthony Frederick was not an Italian as JP thought, but an impoverished descendant of the king of Corsica. He styled himself Captain Frederick, but when killed in the battle of Germantown, Philadelphia, on 4th November 1777, he was an ensign.

(110) Bedlam was the popular name for Bethlehem Royal Hospital in Moorfields. Built around 1670, it was a palace to compare with the finest buildings in the City. But behind its glorious facades, beyond the two great statues by Cibber, Madness and Melancholy, its sad patients were chained in galleries of cages. Visitors were welcomed and the asylum became a profitable entertainment, attracting huge crowds to just stand and stare, much as we do today at the zoo. By 1770 entrance was by ticket only, but it seems that James Gillray was a regular visitor.

(111) Slaughterhouses abounded in the Smithfield area, where the streets often ran red on market days. It would have been a simple matter for Rhoan Hamilton to obtain a few buckets of blood and entrails.

(112) I assume this reference is to the Hunting Lodge at Hanworth, although at fifteen miles it is surprising that JP could discern it. Henry VIII greatly enlarged and enriched the building then gave it to Anne Boleyn, while she waited five years for the King to divorce Catherine of Aragon. Anne is the tragic heroine of Tudor England. The divorce she caused was opposed by Rome and brought about the Reformation and establishment of the Church of England, Mother Church to the Anglican movement. She was Queen for just three years. She gave birth to one child, a daughter, and then in January 1536 a prince was stillborn. During this second pregnancy Henry dallied with Jane Seymour and concluded that she would be more likely to bear him a son. Anne was tried for treason, which included both adultery and incest, found guilty, and sentenced to death by her uncle the duke of Norfolk. She was beheaded on 19 May 1536, and Henry married Jane Seymour the following day. Anne's five alleged lovers, including her brother Viscount Rochford, had all been executed two days before. The charges were probably fabricated, her only crimes being failure to produce a son and inability to contain Henry's lust. But she had the last word, for despite a succession of wives he fathered only one son to survive infancy. — Edward VI was nine when he succeeded Henry and sixteen when he died of consumption. His sister Lady Jane Grey lasted but nine days and was followed by Mary, who plunged the country into a bloodbath by marrying Philip, heir to the Spanish throne. It was Anne Boleyn's daughter Elizabeth, who reigned for forty four years and steered England from poverty and distress to a golden age of adventure and learning. The house at Hanworth was destroyed by fire in 1797 and is survived only by part of its moat. An airport was opened in 1929 and the Graf Zeppelin landed there in 1932. It was closed after the War, because of its proximity to Heathrow.

(113) Kano Motonobu (1477 – 1559) is esteemed as one of the greatest Japanese painters. He revived the Chinese school of delicate, simple landscapes, with much use of mists and lakes and far mountains.

(114) William Almack opened his Club in Pall Mall in 1762. He was already a successful tavern owner and knew what his customers wanted. Members were offered dinner, newspapers, gambling and freedom from ladies,. The Club was split in 1764 to Boodles, and Brooks; but as this reference by Horace Walpole demonstrates, older members stuck to the original name.

(115) A village on the banks of the Thames that became a fashionable retreat for persons of artistic and genteel leanings. Alexander Pope came here in 1719. He

converted a cottage into a Palladian Villa and devoted the rest of his life to poetry, which survives, and gardening, which unfortunately does not. We have only contemporary accounts of the enchanted gardens and grottos that he created on the banks of the river. Twickenham may now be more famous as the home of Rugby Union but its artistic pedigree can never be diminished. Not only Pope and Walpole, but J.M.W.Turner, Vincent van Gogh, Tennyson, Walter de la Mare, William Hickey, Thomas Hudson and Kitty Clive all lived here; and Henry Fielding wrote Tom Jones in lodgings just down the road from where Charles Dickens wrote Oliver Twist.

Notes to Chapter Ten

(116) Elizabeth Chudleigh was once the rage of the Court of George II. After a perfectly respectable upbringing (her father Thomas Chudleigh was lieutenant governor of Chelsea Hospital) she appeared one night at a masquerade given by the Venetian Ambassador. Her dress was fashioned from gauze, entirely transparent, and she wore nothing but a small garland of flowers underneath. Thereafter, the lechers of the day beat a path to her door. She wed Augustus Hervey, the future Earl of Bristol, who was the first aristocrat to fall. He was quite a catch but later the Duke of Kingston began to call, and Elizabeth saw her chance of becoming a duchess. Without bothering to divorce Hervey, she married the duke, and by all accounts, kept him very happy in his decline. When he died he left her his entire fortune which did not please his other heirs. They discovered her bigamous marriage and she was brought to trial before the House of Lords, found guilty and demoted to Countess. It seemed to matter little to her, for she then blazed a trail through Europe, and died in her own royal palace in France, at the age of 68.

(117) The masque was a ceremonial social entertainment of the aristocracy. It consisted of a combination of poetry, vocal and instrumental music, dancing and pageantry. Modern ballet, opera and pantomime owe a great deal to the masque. This particular one was commissioned from Thomas Arne, conducted by his son Michael, and performed, badly it would seem, by 'young nobility of both sexes'. Wagner said that the whole English character is expressed in the first eight notes of *Rule Britannia*. In addition to this most famous of all tunes, Arne is remembered for the incidental music he wrote for his theatrical productions, especially Shakespearean ones such as 'Where the bee sucks', 'Under the greenwood tree' and 'Blow blow thou winter wind'.

(118) This reference to the Duke of Cumberland is probably wrong. The King's

brothers were the bane of his life. Their profligacy and scandals, mostly conducted in the pleasure gardens and brothels, were the gossip of London. *"Every place"*, wrote Horace Walpole, *"is like one of Shakespeare's plays: 'Flourish. Enter the Dukes of Gloucester, York, and attendants"*. Lady Towshend complained *"This is the cheapest family to see, and the dearest to keep, that ever there was"*. But by 1774, Henry was shunned by all of society and it is unlikely that he would have been invited to the wedding of the year. After countless scandals he married Anne Horton in 1771. *"The new Princess of the Blood"*, wrote Horace, *"is a young widow of twenty four, extremely pretty, not handsome, very well made, with the most amorous eyes in the world, and eyelashes a yard long"*. This caused the King such distress that he banished his brother and encouraged everyone else to do the same.— It is more likely that William, Duke of Gloucester was the prince that JP saw. Not that he was much better. He was the least intelligent of the brothers and he too was snared by an ambitious widow, when just out of boyhood. This one however was Lady Waldegrave, a captivating beauty with a queue of suitors, and Horace's niece. These clandestine weddings led to the passing of the Royal Marriage Bill precluding any English descendant of George II from marrying before the age of twenty six without the consent of the Sovereign.

(119) Tyburn Tree was the name given to the gallows that stood at the modern junction of Edgeware Road and Bayswater Road. It was the principal place of execution for four hundred years. The triangular gallows could accommodate twenty one victims. They were surrounded by grandstands and hanging days, which were public holidays, attracted crowds that would turn Spurs green with envy.

(120) *"Deerhurst in Gloucestershire was where he went, and there he found the first great surprise of his life. He had expected to be surrounded by self denying monks, ever so much better than himself. But instead he found a careless, selfish set of men, who had forgotten the vows they had made and thought only of being comfortable"*. Life of St Alphege, Archbishop of Canterbury 1012. The cloisters have long since disappeared, but fortunately the monastic church remains for posterity. If you have never visited the simple, dignified Church of St Mary, with its high tower amidst the chestnuts, then I urge you to do so.

(121) The magnificent Abbey Church at Tewkesbury has the largest Norman tower in the world. It has watched over the old town for nearly nine hundred years and witnessed some of the bloodiest and most significant episodes of English history.

(122) I have not heard of this term before, but assume it to refer to Jethro Tull. After training as a barrister, he acquired Prosperous Farm near Hungerford, where he stayed until his death in 1741. He invented the seed drill and wrote *Horse hoeing Husbandry* which became a standard work. He is best remembered for the ridge and furrow method of sowing that he extolled. Where pasture rises and falls in uniform waves, it was once arable land and the farmer was a disciple of Jethro Tull.

(123) Like Ely Cathedral, I simply do not have the words to do justice to Tintern. Visit it in the winter, on a cold grey day, or in the early morning before the sun has cleared Offa's Dyke.

(124) There have been many bones of contention between the English and Welsh, not least the annual blood letting at Arms Park or Twickenham. Over the centuries, the bridge at Chepstow has often been the butt of this rivalry. The river at this point is subject to fierce tides, and the only way to cross it with regularity is via a high bridge. The Romans recognised this, as did the Normans. But when the English and the Welsh were finally left to control it themselves, they found it deuced difficult to agree. At any time there was either a lot of Englishmen trying to get into Wales, or a lot of Welshmen trying to get into England. Thus when one side were keen to spend money on it, the other side were not. For centuries the old bridge was in a permanent state of imminent collapse. Sometimes the Gloucestershire side would be repaired, so that travellers could at least reach midstream in safety. At other times they had a hair raising struggle over rotting timbers to the stone central pier, to find the Monmouthshire side safe and sound. In 1812 a ship tied up to one of the piers and a tourist boat from Tintern fouled its cable. Six ladies and a boatman were drowned and the bridge was badly damaged. Thus finally a new bridge was commissioned, and the graceful iron structure that is still in use today, was opened on 24 July 1816.

(125) There is only one other dedication to St Arilda, at Oldbury on the Hill, fifteen miles to the east. She is a Celtic saint, beheaded by local tyrant Muncius for refusing to break her vow of chastity. St Arilda's Well, a mile away at Kington is said to run with her blood. She was buried here, but then removed to Gloucester Cathedral where many miracles were ascribed to her.

(126) *'Bounteous Buckingham, the mirror of all courtesy'*, as Shakespeare would have him. Favourite of the King, he made the mistake of many a politician since.

He became too popular, and Henry came to see him as a threat. He was arrested at Thornbury, taken to London and found guilty of treason, although it is difficult to discern any crime that he committed. His sentence by the duke of Norfolk is a chilling reminder that we are not far removed from the Dark Ages. He was to be *'led to the King's prison and there laid on a hurdle and so drawn to the place of execution; and there to be hanged, cut down alive, his members cut off and cast into the fire, his bowels burnt before him, his head smitten off and his body quartered and divided at the King's will'*. His reply was dignified and brave, so much so that the King relented and reduced the sentence to mere beheading.—Emperor Charles II commented: *'A butcher's dog has killed the finest buck in England.'* — Shakespeare gives him these last lines: *'All good people, Pray for me! I must now forsake ye: the last hour Of my long weary life is come upon me. Farewell: And when you would say something is sad, Speak how I fell.'*

Notes to Chapter Eleven

(127) The Chelsea Waterworks were incorporated in 1723 and consisted of low lying canals which filled at high tide. The water was then retained by sluice gates and pumped to the reservoirs and houses of Westminster. The cuts and canals extended to some ninety acres in what is now Pimlico. The works themselves were on a site now covered by the Churchill Gardens estate.

(128) The Beef Steak Society was a club of twenty four nobles or gentlemen who met for a beef dinner every Saturday evening from November to June. Garrick and Sheridan, Wilkes and Hogarth were all members. They wore uniforms of blue coats and buff waistcoats.

(129) John Wilkes was born in Clerkenwell in 1727, the son of a malt distiller. He was as profligate as any in his twenties but by 1760 had become a radical and virulant member of Parliament. He started The North Briton in which he launched a series of barbed and witty attacks on the Premier, Lord Bute, which led to the downfall of the latter. He then published a violent attack on the King's speech, for which he was imprisoned in the Tower. He was by now a popular hero, and his fame was widened by his highly obscene parody of Pope's *Essay on Man*, entitled *Essay on Woman*. This has been called the most scandalous poem of the 18th Century, and even today would raise more than a few eyebrows. It contains the immortal lines, *'Life can little more supply, than a few good fucks and then we die'*. Wilkes was outlawed and fled to the Continent, where he remained for four years. On his return he was again imprisoned. He continued his turbulent career after

release. He was expelled from the House on three occasions, but was worshipped by the common man who's rights he endlessly defended. He was an active champion of the American colonists and was accused of inciting them to rebellion. Cynical, malicious, debauched, it has been said of Wilkes that he never did a good thing without a bad reason. Yet he was scrupulously honest and an unrivalled wit. He was without doubt the most popular Lord Mayor London has known, and his importance to English history is immense. If you can find a copy, read *That Devil Wilkes* by Raymond Postgate.

(130) Wat Tyler led an insurrection by the peasant's of Kent in 1381. Their main grievance was the imposition of the Poll Tax. Jack Cade led a similar rebellion in 1450.

(131) In 1774 Parliament passed a number of Acts that made war inevitable. The Boston Act shut up the town of Boston against all commerce until the 'stolen tea' had been paid for. The Massachusetts Act changed the charter of the colony and appointed Thomas Gage governor and commander in chief. The Quebec Act extended the boundaries of Canada over the whole territory north of the Ohio and east of the Mississippi. On September 5th the First Continental Congress was convened in Philadelphia. This was the first truly national body in American history and it challenged the authority of Parliament and the Crown. Thus was spawned the United States.

(132) The civil calendar has been borrowed from that of the Romans. Romulus is said to have divided the year into ten months only, a total of 304 days. It is not well known how he disposed of the other days. The Ancient Roman year commenced in March, hence the names September, October, November and December. January and February were added later. Julius Caesar reformed the calendar and the first Julian year commenced in 46BC. His calendar is the most convenient but it supposes the year is too long by 11 minutes 14 seconds. It could not maintain without correction, the purpose for which it was devised, that of preserving always the same interval of time between the commencement of the year and the equinox. Thus Pope Gregory XIII directed that ten days be suppressed. As the error in the Julian calendar was found to be three days in four hundred years, he decreed that every year divisible by four shall be a leap year, excepting the centurial years, which are only leap years if divisible by four when the two noughts are omitted. Thus 1600 was a leap year, 1700, 1800 and 1900 are common years, 2000 will be a leap year. England adopted the Gregorian calendar in 1752.

(133) Edmund Burke was the moving spirit of the Whigs. Born in Dublin, son of a Protestant father and Catholic mother, he passed through Trinity College and came to London in 1750. As a political writer he reigns supreme. He applied his doctrine of political relativity to all the problems he confronted, English, Irish, American, Indian and French. *'He tells the English they are treating America as if it were England; it is not, and no law will make it so. So he tells them about Ireland and India; you are ignoring their genius, their religion, their past history. And he tells the same thing to the French. You cannot cut yourself off from your past; to build on mere theory is to build upon the sand'.* Robert H. Murray.